V 92
67

N:

KT-221-014

Anne Perry lives in Portmahomack, Scotland, and her well-loved series featuring Thomas and Charlotte Pitt has recently been adapted for television.

THE ONE THING MORE

It is January 1793. Revolutionary France is at war with Belgium, Prussia and Austria, and its new leaders have just sentenced Louis XVI to death. The public believes justice will be done, but, in Paris, a small group of people fears for the future. Célie's life has changed beyond recognition since the Revolution began. Reduced to working as a laundress for the secretive Monsieur Bernave, she finds aspiration in his determination to rescue the King from the scaffold. But just four days before the execution, Bernave is murdered. Célie — and the fugitive she is protecting — must risk everything to piece together Bernave's plan . . .

Books by Anne Perry
Published by The House of Ulverscroft:

THE INSPECTOR PITT SERIES:
CALLANDER SQUARE
SILENCE IN HANOVER CLOSE
CARDINGTON CRESCENT
BETHLEHEM ROAD
HIGHGATE RISE
BELGRAVE SQUARE
BEDFORD SQUARE
HALF MOON STREET

THE WILLIAM MONK SERIES:
A SUDDEN AND FEARFUL DEATH
THE FACE OF A STRANGER
SINS OF THE WOLF
WHITED SEPULCHRES
THE TWISTED ROOT

ANNE PERRY

THE ONE THING MORE

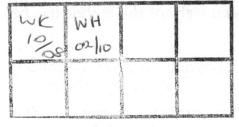

Complete and Unabridged

CHARNWOOD
Leicester

First published in Great Britain in 2000 by
Headline Book Publishing
London

First Charnwood Edition
published 2002
by arrangement with
Headline Book Publishing
a division of Hodder Headline
London

The moral right of the author has been asserted

British Library CIP Data

Perry, Anne
 The one thing more.—Large print ed.—
Charnwood library series
 1. France—History—Revolution, *1789 – 1799*
—Fiction
 2. Suspense fiction
 3. Large type books
 I. Title
 823.9′14 [F]

 ISBN 0–7089–9308–7

Published by
F. A. Thorpe (Publishing)
Anstey, Leicestershire

Set by Words & Graphics Ltd.
Anstey, Leicestershire
Printed and bound in Great Britain by
T. J. International Ltd., Padstow, Cornwall

This book is printed on acid-free paper

To June Wyndham Davies
With thanks for turning dreams into reality

But if you knew the one thing more . . .

1

Célie Laurent stood in the crowded darkness of the public gallery of the Convention. The deputies had been debating the sentence on the King since 14 January — three days now. Tonight they were returning their verdict, each emerging from the shadows to climb the rostrum for his moment in history.

She watched the man who stood up there now, the candlelight shining on his face as he stared out at the packed room, exhausted after hours of argument. He said only the one word, 'Death', then scuttled down the steps, feet clattering on the wood, and disappeared.

His place was taken by another. It may have been midwinter outside, but in here the press of bodies and the excitement made the air close and heavy. This next man's skin was pallid and sheened with sweat. He hesitated a few moments, disregarding the faint rustle of impatience from the men sitting squashed in the front rows.

'Death!' he said huskily, then stepped down. His feet slipped and he snatched at the rail to steady himself, before reaching the bottom and being swallowed by the shadows again.

Célie cared intensely what happened. She was not a royalist. All her life she had heard of the idleness and profligacy of the court at Versailles. Her father had spoken of it with anger and disgust, her mother with the passion she had devoted to causes all her life. Célie remembered her mother's pale-skinned, beautiful face always alight with zeal, gazing at her father, seeing only him, listening to his every word. She remembered her own loneliness, and how she had been shut out, even from the disillusion that had followed.

But that was in the past. They were both dead now. She was twenty-nine and it was all too late to repair.

There was much in the revolution that Célie believed in. She had not been born to poverty, but since her father's collapse she had certainly become acquainted with it. She had worked to survive, like any of the labourers and artisans who had suffered generations of oppression, out of which finally had been brought forth this night.

The next deputy who stood in the pool of light had the bloodless face of an albinoid: his eyes were pink-tinged, his lashes and brows invisible: Joseph Fouché, the deputy from Nantes in Brittany. Yesterday he had promised to fight for the King's life. Now he said the single, dry word — 'Death'.

Célie shivered. They had been voting for hours. Hardly anyone had spoken for life, or even incarceration of all the royal family until the last of them should die of old age.

Maybe she did not really need to stay any longer. The outcome was already certain. One violence had followed another since the storming of the Bastille three and a half years ago in 1789.

Now they almost expected it. The streets were full of frightened people, most of them cold and hungry. The fury of centuries had exploded, destroying everything in its path. Wasn't that what Marat had said — 'I am the rage of the people'?

The thought of him was cold inside her. Célie had only seen him once but, like everyone else, she knew his power. He ruled the Commune, and more importantly, the copper-faced, hollow-eyed mobs from the tanneries and slaughterhouses of the Faubourg St-Antoine, and out into the suburbs beyond and on every side.

There was a buzz of excitement around her, a shifting of position, a craning forward as the giant figure of Georges-Jacques Danton climbed the rostrum to cast his vote. He had returned from the war in Belgium only yesterday. There were rumours that he would plead mercy for the King. Could that be true?

Célie watched as he moved into the light. His head and shoulders were bull-like, his face scarred by pox. His vitality filled the room. She could feel it like the charge of electricity before a storm. The surreptitious coughing and shuffling stopped. Everyone's eyes were on Danton.

The candles flickered, yellow light making a gargoyle of his head.

'Death,' he said simply.

A sigh of relief rippled through the room. Someone let out a little cry. Several people shifted as if a tension had been broken at last. They had passed some invisible point of no return. If Danton said 'Death', it must be right.

He stepped down into the shadows and was lost in the press of bodies. Another took his place in the light and said the same word, but with a greater confidence. Now there could be only one judgement.

But each of the seven hundred and twenty-one deputies must have his say. The charade would drag on until the small hours of the morning. People were fidgeting, restless for the end. This was merely ritual now. The candles on the rostrum were burning low. The drag and shuffling of feet up the steps and down again seemed endless.

Then suddenly there was a different sound, the sharp click of high heels. Célie's attention snapped back. The man who stood in the candlelight was immaculately dressed in shades of green: a nankeen jacket with perfectly cut lapels, a high waistcoat and neatly tied cravat. His hair was curled and powdered in the old style of the *ancien régime*. His small face was neat-nosed, feline, his skin an unhealthy white. He peered myopically into the gloom of the chamber.

'Everyone here knows how I dislike making long speeches,' he began. He was renowned for making interminable speeches, his sibilant, pedantic tones so low that listeners had to lean forward to catch what he said. Every so often he would hesitate, so people thought he was finished. Then he would start again.

But no one laughed. No one ever laughed at Maximilien Marie Isidore de Robespierre. He

4

would have considered it blasphemy.

As always he spoke at length about purity, the evils of the aristocracy, the necessity of justice and a new way, of a rebirth of virtue, but mostly he spoke about himself. In the end it all amounted to the same thing: another vote to send the King to the guillotine.

There was no need for Célie to remain. Nothing could turn the tide now. She had learned all she had come for. She turned and began to push her way through the crowd behind her. The people were nervous and excited, thronging together in the passages and half blocking the doors out into the street, but they took little notice of her. With her strong features and slim body, her straight, flaxen hair half hidden under her cap, in the half-dark she could have been taken for a boy.

'Excuse me,' she muttered, elbowing her way. 'Pardon, Citizen!'

Outside at last the cold air hit her from the January night, and she pulled her jacket tighter across her chest, holding the collar high up to her chin. She went down the steps, bending her head against the wind.

A thin man with straggling hair was standing just within the pool of the lights. His shoulders were hunched, his hands knotted against the chill.

'Leaving, Citizeness?' he asked, looking at her curiously. 'Are they finished already?'

'No,' she answered, avoiding his eyes. 'But no one will change it now, so it makes no difference.'

'Thank — ' he began, then stopped.

She knew he had been about to say 'Thank God', then remembered just in time that there was no God, no power to resurrect the dead, no one to comfort the tearing grief for a lost baby, to promise a heaven somewhere. Religion was anti-revolutionary, and therefore a crime. Nobody could even estimate how many priests had been murdered in the massacres last September when the Marseillais had gone mad, slaughtering the men, women and children in the prisons.

Of course religion had been contradictory, absurd, and the Church greedy and corrupt. Célie knew that, but she still ached for its loss, cried alone in the night from the emptiness without it.

'Thank you, Citizeness,' the man finished self-consciously.

She forced a smile at him, sickly and false, then hurried along the pavement. The lights from shops and cafés glistened across the wet stones. It was easy to see where she was going. It would be a lot harder when she was at the other side of the river, into the Cordeliers District.

She walked quickly. The night air was fiercely cold, and movement at least kept her blood pumping. She stepped over a puddle and her foot slipped on the wet cobbles. She was off the Rue St-Honoré now and into a narrower, darker street. She could smell the dampness and the sting of ice in the air. At least there would be torches along the quayside, reflecting off the black surface of the water, and it would be easier to see.

Of course she cared about the vote. She was a Frenchwoman; this was her city and her country. But she had come specifically because Bernave had sent her. He wanted to know the moment the verdict was irrevocable. Tomorrow morning was not soon enough. She did not know why it mattered so much to him. He had sent her on a lot of strange, urgent errands lately, trusting her far more than most men trusted any servant, let alone one they had known only a few months.

She was closer to the river now. Ahead of her the street opened out and she could see the light of a rush torch swaying in the darkness, trailing jagged streamers of fire. A man shouted to somebody out of sight.

'Heard the news, Citizen?'

The answer came from the gulf beyond him. 'Yes! Convention has voted to execute the King! Equality at last!'

'Liberty!' the other replied, and laughed, his voice sharp in the frosty air, slithering away in a wild note.

Célie crossed the street on to the bridge. Beneath her the water was oily black, torchlight glittering in long ribbons of gold.

She reached the Quai de Conti on the far side and hurried into the shadow of the streets towards the Boulevard St-Germain. She had to slow her pace now, feel her way with more care. She was nearly home, but there were no torches here and hardly any chinks of light from windows.

She turned in under the archway, crossing the familiar courtyard, passing the pump. The kitchen door had been left unlocked for her and she opened it easily, closing it again when she was inside and hearing the slight click as the latch fell home. She felt for the candle on the table, fumbling for a moment, then lit it. The soft pool of light showed the wooden surfaces, worn with use, the polished pans hanging on their hooks, and the dark outline of the stove. There was a lingering warmth and a faint smell of dried herbs in the air.

Célie took off her wet jacket and cap, and hung them on the drying rail, then picked up the candle and tiptoed across the floor to the next room and the door to Bernave's study. She knocked softly, barely touching the wood with her knuckles.

There was a moment's silence, then the sound of someone on the other side, and the latch lifted. The door swung open.

'Come in,' Bernave ordered.

She obeyed, closing the door behind her. The room was warm from the stove, and four candles were burning. A book was open on his desk. He searched her face, and must have seen the answer in her eyes, because he nodded almost imperceptibly, his lips tightening. Perhaps he had known to expect it. He should have, the signs had been plain enough.

'They voted for death,' she said aloud. 'I didn't stay to the end because there was no point. After Danton there wouldn't be any change.'

Bernave stood motionless. He was not a large

man, but his energy seemed to fill the room, his intelligence to command everything.

'So did the Girondins,' she added, just in case a shred of doubt still lingered in him.

They had all hoped for so much from the Girondins when they had first come to power in the Convention. They had seemed to embody the noblest republican ideals. They had talked prodigiously. She remembered their voices in her parents' home before she had married Charles, before Jean-Pierre was born. Charles had died, but it was Jean-Pierre's death that had drowned her world in pain.

The Girondins' endless posturing, chatter, her father's agony of disillusion and her mother's refusal to believe it, all belonged to another part of life. When it came to the passing of laws and taking control of a chaotic situation, the Girondins had proved indecisive, quarrelsome, self-regarding, and finally ineffectual.

'I long since ceased to expect anything from them.' Bernave's voice cut across her memories, a bitter weariness in it, and as he returned to his seat she saw a droop in his shoulders she had not noticed before. 'Not that they will last much longer,' he added. 'If they don't develop a little courage and a lot more brains, their days are numbered.'

She did not ask what would happen to them; she already knew. Some of those, the bravest, would cling to the dream to the end, regardless of the truth . . . like her mother. Others, like her father, would retreat into despair and eventually oblivion.

'When will the execution be?' Bernave asked, interrupting her thoughts.

'The twenty-first,' she replied. 'Four days' time.'

He took a long, deep breath and let it out slowly. 'I want you to take a message to Georges Coigny. Go and tell him that the verdict is in and will not change. He is to assure the first and second safe houses. St Felix will do the third. Do you understand?'

'Yes,' she said firmly. 'I am to tell Georges Coigny that he is to assure the first and second safe houses, and St Felix will do the third. I'll go tomorrow.' She thought of the dark streets, overflowing gutters and the bitter wind that hurt the skin.

'Now, Célie,' Bernave said quietly. 'Tonight.'

'It's after midnight!' she protested. 'It's perishing out there!' St Felix might be prepared to creep around the streets at all hours. She was not!

'Now,' Bernave repeated, and there was steel in his voice. 'There is no time to sleep. Go and tell Coigny what happened in the Convention, and what I said.' He looked at her steadily. He had a powerful face with lean, hard bones — a face of hunger and tragedy. But one expected dark eyes and his were blue-grey, very clear, as if his mind were visible through them, both the light and the darkness of it.

These were the days of equality. She wanted to understand why he sent St Felix, who was apparently his friend, out on all sorts of errands in the cold and the dark. Often he came home

10

exhausted, sometimes even injured, and it seemed he went willingly enough. Certainly he never argued. But why did Bernave not sometimes go on these dangerous missions himself?

Bernard was staring at her. He smiled with a twist to his lips.

'Are you cold and tired, Célie?'

'Of course I am!' she said vehemently. Her legs ached and her feet were soaking wet and numb.

He leaned back a little in his chair, his eyes meeting hers unwaveringly. 'Is Amandine in bed?'

It was the last thing she had expected him to ask. It was utterly irrelevant.

'Pardon?'

His eyes widened. 'Is Amandine in bed?' he repeated. 'Is that not plain enough? I am hungry. Like most of France, I can work on an empty stomach but I cannot think on one! Perhaps also, like most of France!' A flash of humour lit his face as he watched her, but it was full of the knowledge of pain.

'I'll fetch you some bread and cheese,' she offered. 'And an onion, if you like?'

'The only woman in Paris who cannot cook!' he said with a sigh, but there was no unkindness in his voice. 'You have done well, Célie. You have intelligence and courage. And at the moment — since there is hardly any decent food to be had, but a great deal of work to do, and most of it dangerous — those virtues may be of more use to us. What a comment on our times!' He looked at her steadily for a moment, to be sure she understood that he meant what he said, then turned back to his book. It was dismissal.

She went out through the hallway to the kitchen again, taking the candle with her, his praise still sweet in her ears. A corner of the room had been set aside for the flat iron and a basket of sewing needles, scissors, threads, and pins so she could care for the household linens and occasionally make a garment or two. But the cooking area was Amandine's.

She set the candle down and found the bread — a scarce commodity in Paris these days — and cut a large portion from one of the two cheeses, and half an onion. She set them on one of the red, white and blue revolutionary plates with its pictures of republican symbols. She thought they were vulgar, but everyone had them these days. It was politically advisable, whatever your actual beliefs. She put it on a tray with a knife, a glass, and half a bottle of wine, then, with the candle on it as well, she carried it back to the study and tapped on the door with her foot.

Bernave opened it and she carried the tray in and set it on the desk.

His eyes flickered over it and he smiled very slightly. 'Thank you. You should have brought two glasses.'

She was not sure if it were an invitation to stay, or an order to wait for further instructions.

'Well, don't stand there!' He looked at her with a bleak smile. 'Go and fetch another one! I have something more to tell you.'

She obeyed silently, and returned to find him with a quill in his hand, but the papers in

12

front of him still blank.

'Pour it,' he ordered without looking up.

She did so, and sipped the wine with pleasure, feeling its clean taste on her tongue and its warmth slide down her throat. She remained standing. It would be an impertinence to forget he was the master and this was his house, and his room.

He looked up at her at last. 'I have decided to tell you why you are going out tonight.'

She swallowed.

'Sit down.' He pointed to the chair opposite him.

She obeyed. Suddenly she was frightened. Her throat was tight, her heart jumping. What was he going to say? Was Georges going to have to flee again, leave Paris, maybe even leave France? Who were the safe houses for? Was Bernave himself going? That thought should not have hurt her; she had known him only a short time. But he had shown a kindness to her, a clean, hard honesty she admired.

'Do you know what is going to happen when we kill the King, Célie?' he asked, studying her face.

She wanted to give an intelligent answer, one he would respect. But why was he asking? Testing her loyalty? To what, or whom?

'We shall be a republic,' she replied, a tiny thread of pride in her voice, barely detectable. 'No more aristos, no Church, no more privilege of birth.' It surprised her that she should feel it. She had thought all such emotions dead in her. And yet somehow she despised it, hated it for what it had taken from her, she felt a touch of her mother's passion for a new order, for reform, justice at last.

'And is privilege of birth so much worse than privilege of strength, or money, or cunning?' Bernave asked curiously. 'How about privilege of conquest?'

She was confused. 'I don't know what you mean!'

'No, I can see you don't,' he agreed wryly. 'We are at war with Belgium and Prussia in the north, with the Austrian Empire in the east, and our soldiers have little food and even less ammunition.' His voice was tight in his throat and she knew it was anger. 'We are unhappy and frightened even here in Paris. How long do you queue for bread these days, Célie?' He waved his hand in dismissal. 'No, don't bother to answer. I already know. And when we have killed the King it will get worse, because we will descend into civil war. We will have no government in control at the heart, so there will be risings in the provinces.'

She wanted to argue, but she knew too little. And she thought Bernave must be right because she had heard people say things like that when standing outside the bakery and there was no bread left, or at the other shops when there was no soap, or no candles.

'But surely once . . . ' She tailed off, seeing his face and silenced by the emotion in it, even though she did not understand it.

He leaned forward a little, his voice more urgent. 'Célie, all those countries around us are ruled by kings: not only Austria and Prussia but England as well, and Spain! All the royal houses of Europe are allied, by blood and by common interest. If we cut the throat of our King like a criminal's, and set in his place the rabble of Marat's Commune who run around like blood-crazed animals, if we can't feed our own people or impose any law except that of the tumbrel and the knife, then they'll see us as a nation of madmen, a blight to be cut out at any cost, before the contagion spreads and all Europe is stricken with it!'

His words sank on her like a lead weight, immovable because she could see they were true.

'We are walking a razor's edge, Célie,' he continued, his voice dropping, 'with corruption on one side, and anarchy on the other. England will use the death of the King as an excuse. It will give them easy cause.' His eyes were clear and sad in the candlelight. It flickered faintly in the draught, and wavered on the shelves of leather-bound books.

'You really have very little idea what we have done to ourselves tonight, have you?' he said bitterly, searching her face. 'You just see a people risen up against centuries of oppression and injustice, against an effete aristocracy playing games in palaces and gardens, preoccupied with fripperies of dress while the poor starve. You think the rage of people like Marat and his followers is justified, and that when it is answered with equality, this will all be over.'

'It is justified,' she whispered. She had never doubted it. Her heritage was her mother's passion for the poor, the voiceless labourers who made the land rich, and reaped little from it.

He smiled, as if her answer gave him a moment of humour. 'Of course it is justified,' he agreed. 'That is hardly the point.'

'What is the point then?' she demanded, angry because he had threatened a certainty inside her, and that frightened her.

'The point, my dear,' he said steadily, 'is that no equality will satisfy them now, except the final equality of the grave. Danton was the last sane man who had wants and needs like any of the rest of us: land, money, women, possessions, admiration!' He picked up his wine glass and turned it slowly in his fingers, watching the light shine through it like rubies. His voice was low, echoing a faraway pain. 'They are things you can get, and even hold on to, if you're lucky. They are understandable. Stop any man in the street and ask him. If he were honest, he'd admit to liking them, even needing them.' He tipped his glass and drank the rest of the wine. One of the candles guttered and went out.

'Danton's political ideals are simple: a roof over every man's head and a chicken in every pot,' he went on. 'Equality before the law. Do away with the privilege of the Church, but probably not destroy the Church itself. His wife is religious, like most of the ordinary women of France.' His eyes widened for a moment. 'Did you know that? Above all I think he wants stability.' His hand curled on the desk top. 'Space for people to get back to a decent life. These are real things.'

16

'Maybe he will take power in the Convention?' she said, trying to make herself believe it.

'He loves too many things too much,' Bernave replied, his eyes distant, as if he spoke from his own heart. 'He wants to drink deep of the wine of life, to enjoy all the beautiful artefacts he's looted from Belgium, the fine linens by the wagonload that are pouring into Paris, the gold and silver chalices and reliquaries, and other such necessities of civilised living.' There was laughter in his eyes but his voice was heavy with sarcasm. 'At least he's a patriot. That is our one hope of him, even if he's also a fool!'

'Isn't Marat a patriot?' The words were out before she thought better of them.

Bernave gave a snort of derision. 'Marat is half Swiss and half Sardinian. Why should he love France? Who do you think 'redirected' the boots, the coats and the munitions meant for the army on the Austrian front, and had them brought to the Commune here in Paris?'

'Redirected?'

He shrugged sharply. 'Stole, if you prefer.' For a moment his anger was naked, raw-edged with pain. 'And that idiot Pache hasn't the power or the wit to prevent it. Our soldiers on the battlefields fighting to save us from invasion are freezing cold and defending themselves with few guns and less shot because their supplies have been taken by Marat's 'peoples' army' — so we can fight each other here in Paris!'

She said nothing. The cold and the darkness of the night outside seemed to press in on the room and the candlelight be too frail to stand against

17

it. Only Bernave's will was strong enough to make her believe in the possibility of any kind of hope.

But what did he want? Not the King back at Versailles with a crown on his head! France had already tried every kind of monarchy, and each time the King had failed them, gone back on his word, bent with every wind of fortune, lied and lied again.

'Marat wants glory,' Bernave went on, as much to himself as to her. 'Revenge for all the years the Académie Française slighted him and refused him membership; and more glory — endless, boundless glory.' He edged the word with a unique bitterness. 'He wants his name to be immortal, as the man who released all Europe from the chains of slavery.' He twisted the stem of his glass in his fingers. 'And, of course, revenge in general,' he added. 'Plenty of blood. Rivers of it.'

She stared at him. She had not realised until this moment how profoundly her own beliefs were affected by his. There was a core of belief inside him, a wholeness untouched by the fevers outside. He was the rock around which all else ebbed and surged. 'Isn't there anyone else?' she asked desperately.

'Robespierre?' His voice startled her with its bitterness. 'Him least of all. The 'Virtue of the People'! What is that, for God's sake? Do you suppose even Robespierre himself knows what he means, let alone the rest of us?'

'It probably means whatever he wants it to mean,' she answered, meeting his eyes.

A flash of appreciation crossed his face. 'You're right. Today one thing, tomorrow something else, and none of it real. You can't work with a man like that. You can't anticipate him, bribe him or make common cause with him for a purpose. There are no bargains.' He was silent for a moment. The fine lines in his face were all downward, as if he remembered too much grief and too many old battles. He sighed. 'And the King may have the soul of a grocer, but the Girondins couldn't run a shop if their lives depended on it. Odd how anyone can be so provincial and yet at the same time so incompetent!'

'Madame Roland writes wonderful letters,' she said instinctively, speaking her mother's words, her passionate admiration, and perhaps also because she wanted to defend the one woman she knew of who had been close to power.

He gave her a withering look, his grey eyes bright. 'As long as you have no sense of the absurd.' His voice was thick. ' 'Letters from a Roman Matron'! We used to be the wittiest nation on earth . . . and now look at us!' His lip curled. 'It's enough to make the angels weep. Perhaps that is our greatest punishment? We've lost our sense of humour. What do you think, Célie?'

She watched his shoulders, hunched a little, his arms stiff on the desk in front of him, and saw that his hands were clenched, the knuckles pale, the thick scars showing white. He had never said where the scars came from.

'They were all too busy posing for history to

19

see what they were doing,' he went on, his voice heavy with disgust now. 'God help us, there is no other answer. We must save the King, not for the throne, but from martyrdom. Get him away quietly to live out his life in some peaceful little town in England, or Italy, where he will be merely one more fat, middle-aged man who likes to tend his garden and play with his grandchildren.'

Célie gazed at Bernave with incredulity, but even as words of disbelief formed on her lips, she saw the whole possibility with all its desperate logic and its insane danger. She knew the rumbling anger in the streets. She had seen it more than Bernave himself had. She was the one who went out for the few bits of shopping that were still available; she was the one who stood in queues for hours at a time. She had heard the rumours of war and felt the fear of it brush them all. She could remember the panic as the frontier cities had fallen.

'What are we going to do?' she whispered, as if even in this silent room she might be overheard.

He looked at her steadily. 'We are going to rescue the King on the way to the scaffold,' he answered, 'and get him out of France, to somewhere where we can see that he is safe.'

It was staggering — preposterous.

'It's impossible!'

'Not impossible,' he replied calmly, 'if someone else is prepared to take his place. They only have to think he is the King for a few moments. It will be enough.'

She was appalled.

'When they find he isn't, they'll kill him!' she protested. 'They'll tear him to pieces!' Her imagination was hideous with the vision of it.

'I know. And he knows.' His eyes did not leave hers for an instant. 'But he loves France. He understands what will happen to us if we kill the King — civil war, hunger, violence on the streets, fear everywhere, and eventually foreign soldiers in our fields and villages, in our homes. All the gains we have fought for, the liberty and the justice destroyed under another monarchy, not even our own. He will do it, Célie. I know him.' He leaned forward across the desk, his cheek and wide brow golden in the candle flame. 'Now go and tell Georges Coigny to check the first and second safe houses! If you get wet or cold, what is that in the balance? I have letters to write. We have only three whole days!'

★ ★ ★

The cold outside hit Célie like a stinging slap across the face, making her squint against the wind. She was shaking inside with fear and excitement. Suddenly all the errands she and St Felix had run for Bernave made sense. They were part of a hare-brained conspiracy to rescue the King and prevent chaos from consuming all France, everything that was left of hope and humanity and the dream of a new age of freedom.

She could not hurry because as soon as she was off the Boulevard St-Germain it was too dark to see. She moved along alleys which had

21

become familiar only lately, and it would be easy to miss her way, easier still to slip and fall. The wind funnelled between the walls with a knife-edge, finding every gap between the cloak around her shoulders and the cap over her head.

This was the Cordeliers District, where Danton lived with his wife and sons. Perhaps it was stupid ever to have pinned their hopes on him, but so many had — maybe once even Bernave himself. The people loved Danton. He was a natural leader, a man of gargantuan appetite for food, for money, for laughter, wine and life; but also a man passionate for justice for the poor, the ordinary people of both town and country, those who laboured for their bread.

Now it was too late. If Danton had ever really tried to stem the tide of destruction, he had failed.

Célie turned the corner carefully, feeling along the wall. It was more sheltered here.

Marat was the real power behind everything. He lived near here too, on the Rue de l'École-de-Médecine, working every day on his newspaper with its headlines screaming for bloodshed and revenge for the centuries of oppression. The mobs followed him, listening to his every word, feeding on them, believing him.

He had spent years in obscurity around Europe, consumed by his desire for glory in the academic world, and denied at every attempt. Bernave had told her that, late one evening when she had returned with messages for him. They had sat together in the book-lined room, everyone else gone to bed, the house silent

22

except for the wind in the eaves. He had recounted with a wry, bitter amusement, and she thought a grudging respect, how Marat had espoused the cause of the dispossessed, written his book *The Chains of Slavery*, and found his true vocation. Now his rage, and the smell of victory, kept him alive in spite of the disease which was rotting his body.

She crossed the Boulevard St-Michel, for a few moments seeing torch flares and hearing men's voices, then she slipped between the buildings into the alleys again. She stopped until her eyes readjusted to the darkness. This was the perfect place to hide. It was here, Bernave had said, that Marat had lived in attics and cellars, sometimes crouched in a cupboard for days, surviving on drops of water, when he had been hunted by the authorities in the past. Lafayette had sent in three thousand soldiers to flush him out and kill him — and failed. The thought of that gave her acute satisfaction, not for any love of Marat, but for the farcical aspect of it, and the fool it made of the self-important Lafayette.

She hesitated, uncertain of her way now she was almost there. The buildings were very old; they sagged and creaked in the darkness. Water dripped from the eaves, even though it was no longer raining. The damp made the cold eat into everything.

Left. She must go left, into the courtyard, then up the tiny stair outside the wall and in through the top door, then up again to the attic.

There was movement all around her, as if countless people were awake and listening. That

23

was ridiculous! She must control her thoughts. She moved forward determinedly. Her teeth were chattering. Fear? No — of course not! Only cold. She had been here many times before, bringing food, candles, fuel, or news. Georges had no money now he was hiding from the National Guard. She tried to ignore the guilt that stabbed at her for that, and as always, it hurt just as much.

With food scarce for everyone, every little neighbourhood was jealous of its meagre stores. No one welcomed a stranger — there was too little to share. Also someone might recognise his face from a poster. Turning in a wanted man was worth money. And apart from that, if one should get into trouble, to have gained a good name with the Commune might make the difference between release or the guillotine.

She crept up the first flight, and then the second, hearing every board shift under her weight. She started up the third. The steps were slippery with rain on top of the mould that covered them. At the top the door was unlocked. It was difficult to open but she was used to the eccentricities of the latch, and after a twist and jerk it pushed wide enough for her to squeeze through into the passage.

It was completely lightless, but she knew her way: ten steps forward, then to the right, and there was another door. This time she lifted her hand and tapped very gently on the wood.

It was opened and she stepped into a room not much bigger than a large pantry, lit by a solitary candle — tallow, of course, not expensive wax. There was no glow from the stove, and no warmth. It must be out. Georges Coigny was standing in the middle of the floor, his eyes wary, the blackness of his hair lost in the shadows. Then as he recognised her, he relaxed. As always, his smile was quick, warm. He smiled like that at everyone; it was a habit, a part of his nature.

'Come in.' He moved to close the door behind her. There was no furniture in the room except a table, one chair, a small cupboard and a straw-filled mattress on the floor by the wall. There were two or three blankets on it, and he passed her one of these now, holding it while she took off her wet cloak and cap, and then wrapped herself inside the blanket and sat down on the chair.

He stood, waiting for her to speak.

She shook her head fractionally. 'Death,' she told him, her voice a little hoarse. She saw in his face that he had known it would be, perhaps even known that Bernave would send her tonight, but also that he could not help having hoped.

He blinked, and turned away for an instant. He breathed in and out slowly, then met her eyes again, looking for the last confirmation. 'Even Danton?'

She wished she could have said otherwise. She had a sudden urge to protect him from the truth, which was ridiculous — Georges of all people! He was not vulnerable, not afraid as she was. He was always certain of everything, most of all of himself. He had that kind of shining inner belief that even the present chaos could not shake.

She squashed the feeling in herself. 'I'm sorry . . . he voted for death like everyone else.'

Georges looked at the uncurtained window, the candlelight reflected sharp and yellow on the planes of his face. When he spoke it was quietly, as much to himself as to her. 'He said he'd not sacrifice his own life in a lost cause.' Then he turned back to the room and she saw the defeat and the anger in him. 'And the Girondins couldn't organise an evening soiree,' he went on, 'never mind an effective resistance to Marat and the Commune, and all the others who believe that executing the King will be the beginning of a new birth of liberty.'

She shivered, even with the blanket around her. She must deliver Bernave's message. She watched him as he sat down on the mattress opposite her, awkwardly, because it was too low. He pulled one of the other blankets over his shoulders. He looked tired, strained, but there was no surprise in him now. He had been expecting this.

'When?' he asked. 'Did they say?'

'The twenty-first.'

His head jerked up, eyes wide. 'In four days!'

She nodded.

His shoulders slumped. He put his hands up over his face, pushing his hair back, and there was immeasurable defeat in the gesture.

'We're still going to rescue him,' Célie said in the silence. 'Bernave has it all planned. We just have to be . . . quicker . . . ' It sounded absurd, crazier than anything even the Girondins would think of.

He stared at her, incredulity slowly fading to amazement, and then a dawning hope. And he realised for the first time how far Bernave had trusted her.

'Bernave says you must check the first and second safe houses,' she said slowly. 'He's sending St Felix to the third.' She waited for a response from him.

He breathed in and out slowly, still absorbing the thought. 'We'd never get him out of the prison of the Temple,' he answered. 'The only place will be from the carriage on the way to the Place de la Révolution.'

'I know,' she agreed. 'Bernave told me that much. Put someone else in his place, just long enough to take their attention.' She shivered as she remembered Bernave's face in the candle-light, and the knowledge of what it would cost: not just death, but what kind of death. What sort of man was prepared to do such a thing? She wished she knew him! And yet it would break her heart if she did. 'But how?' she said aloud. 'And what after that?'

He took a deep breath. 'The streets will be lined with soldiers, and they'll be expecting trouble. All Paris will turn out to see it. After all, how often do you see a king ride to his execution?'

She had no idea what to say. What was he feeling? What was there in him she could touch or understand? What had he lost in this terrifying change . . . or found? Was the past sweet or bitter; lonely, or full of those he had loved and could never find again?

'Do you know him?' she asked. 'The King?'

He looked at her. His eyes were black in the faint light. 'Not very well,' he replied, and there was a trace of amusement that she should ask.

'What is he like?' she pressed.

'Shy, very ordinary, like an actor playing a part for which he hasn't been given all the lines.'

It was not what she had expected. It did not sound like a king, still less like a tyrant. Against her will it drew from her a kind of pity.

'Four days!' His voice cut into her thoughts. 'We'll need a lot of people, simply to cover what we're doing, but only say a dozen or so we can really trust. At least in Paris . . . '

'Can we do it in time?' she asked, feeling it pressing in on her, all the complication of what must be arranged, uncertain what Bernave had already planned, what would need to be changed now time was so short. 'Who can we trust?' she went on. 'Royalists? People who believe the King rules by God's decree?' She felt faintly ridiculous as she said it, but she knew such faith existed, or had done.

Georges bit his lip in a derisory humour. 'The royalists are a shambles. We've got rid of the Church and whatever priests there are still alive are in hiding . . . like a lot of us.'

She was painfully aware of his situation, and that she herself had brought it about, but there was no time for indulgence of guilt now, however deep. Time was urgently, desperately short. And yet Bernave had seemed so certain there was a chance!

'Bernave has the drivers.' Georges returned to

the practical, his face concentrated in thought. 'The safe houses can be taken care of. It's really the crowd to find to seize in on the King's carriage as it goes from the prison of the Temple to the guillotine, and then others to block the side streets with carts so they can't be followed by the National Guard.'

'Do you know enough for that?' she asked, trying to imagine the trust it would take to ask someone to do such a thing, to tell them how and where, and, above all, why! Georges would be placing not only the King's life in their hands, but his own, and those of everyone else who helped. And they would have to be men and women of great resource, ice-cool nerve even under the greatest pressure, incapable of panic, and willing to risk their lives.

'I think so,' he answered softly. 'I . . . think so.'

'And after that?' She watched his eyes, his face. 'We'll have to get him out of France altogether. Maybe to Austria? Or perhaps England? A lot of aristocrats have gone to England — at least that's what I've heard. It's quicker to Calais than to any other border.'

'And also more obvious,' Georges pointed out. 'It'll be the first place they'll look.'

'Spain?' Célie suggested. 'Or Italy?'

He hesitated. There was no sound in the room but the dripping of water off the eaves, and every now and then the faint flicker of the candle flame in the draught. She did not interrupt.

'Perhaps it would be best if we didn't know,' he said at last. 'Leave it to them at the time.' A very slight smile touched his lips. 'Bernave has connections. He'll have planned it. His business stretches all over France, and he imports silk from Italy, and sells it out again to Spain, and wool and leather to England. At least he will until we are at war with them too!'

He stood up, hitching the blanket around himself and shivering. 'I'd offer you chocolate if I had any, and the stove were going. But since I haven't, and it isn't, how about a glass of wine?'

'Thank you,' she accepted, watching him as he went to the cupboard and took out a bottle and two glasses. He set them on the table, uncorked the bottle and poured, measuring carefully to see she had slightly more than he, then passed her the glass.

'Thank you.' She took it and sipped. It was rough, but at least the warmth of it sliding down her throat eased out a little of the cold knotted inside her. 'Aren't there any royalists we could trust?' She had not meant her disbelief to be there in her voice, but she could hear it herself. He must also.

His smile flickered back again as he sat down awkwardly, holding his glass in both hands.

'No,' he said simply. 'They want him back on the throne, or the Comte d'Artois in his place. Either way they want a monarch. They haven't learned a thing. They watch history and it's like a parade to them, with all the commentary in another language. They understand nothing.' There was contempt in his face and impatience as well, and she was not sure if she saw pity or not.

She was sharply aware of knowing so little

30

about him, except that he was Amandine's cousin, and therefore like her, minor gentry from a once-noble family, in which the endless subdivision of lands had left them with hereditary rights, but little money.

She looked at him sitting hunched on the mattress opposite her. What had he believed before the revolution had swept away all the old values, and the old safeties? She had no measure of his courage, or his essential humanity. She had seen only his superficial kindness and his loyalty to Amandine, and that reminded her too much of what she had done, and why he was crouched here now, and afraid to go out in daylight. The lines around his mouth were deep in the yellow light, accentuating the weariness in him. He drank slowly from his glass and pulled his lips tight at the tartness of the wine.

'The irony of it is,' he went on with his train of thought, 'I don't think the King cares that much about the Crown himself. He'd have been far happier as a small farmer, or a grocer in some provincial town. That's what he is at heart: a village shopkeeper; good-natured, small-minded, rather humourless, domestic, eager to please whoever he is with.'

He was staring at the floor, his face turned half away from her, but she heard the sadness in his voice.

'He'd have made an excellent grocer,' he continued. 'All his customers would have liked him. He would have swapped local gossip with them and given apples to their children, and grown old, well-loved and quietly prosperous.'

His tone changed. 'Unfortunately he inherited the throne of France and never had that choice. So now in four days he'll go to his death, unless we can save him — and ourselves.'

She did not argue or question his judgement. The momentousness of what they were proposing filled her mind.

He turned towards her. 'Tell Bernave I'll check the safe houses. I have at least ten people here in Paris we can trust to mob the carriage. We'll find the coaches and drivers from the safe houses onwards out of Paris, and to their assigned border. But he'll have to find the passes out of the city.'

'I'll tell him.' She stood up, letting the blanket fall and drinking the last of the wine.

He rose also. 'Be careful,' he said softly, picking up her cloak and cap and going to the door ahead of her. 'I wish I could see you at least as far as the Boulevard St-Germain.'

'Well you can't,' she answered, while he helped her put the cloak on. It was her fault he could not, and she hated being reminded of it.

'Go carefully,' he repeated, his voice urgent with anxiety.

She turned away, not wanting to face him. 'I will.'

His hand was on the door latch. 'Tell Bernave we'll succeed,' he said. 'We've got to. If we don't, only a miracle will stop civil war.'

'Do you believe in God?' As soon as she had said it she knew she should not have. It was not a question one asked in France these days. But it was too late now, the words were out.

He raised his eyebrows. 'God? I don't think I've much idea who He is.' Humour lit his expression for a moment. 'Would you settle for not believing in the Church? I can say that with a whole heart.'

She wanted to laugh and cry at the same time. 'Then it's a good thing it's gone!' she retorted. She did not want him even to sense the confusion in her, far less see it. She hated the Church, its hypocrisy, its oppression and its greed. And at the same time, more than anything on earth, she needed its promises of a God who loved, who would have allowed her baby to have been baptised and taken to Himself, not buried in the cold ground where she could not even mourn him properly. She kept her face turned away.

Georges pushed his hands through his hair, scraping it back off his brow. 'It's a hell of a thing!' he answered. 'At least it stood for some kind of order . . . some recognition of . . . '

'Corruption,' she finished for him bitterly. 'Do you know how much land the Church owned, before we took it back?' She remembered her mother working it out precisely.

'Yes,' he said. 'And how much twisted morality, and how much unearned privilege and unnecessary guilt. But it still represented some kind of belief in a power greater than ourselves. It offered hope to those who had no other, and faith in a justice beyond anything there is here . . . which is too often a farce, or worse. If we are all there is,' he shrugged, 'we haven't got much, have we?'

She was crushed by the emptiness of it. 'If the best of us is the best there is, it's not enough . . . ' Unintentionally she turned towards him.

He grinned suddenly, a flash of teeth in the flickering light. 'But if the worst of us is the worst there is, it'll do nicely, eh? Hell doesn't need to be more than last September.'

'And since we've done away with God, miracles aren't very likely,' she said drily. Then before he could add anything else, she slipped out of the door and down the narrow stairs into the darkness. She did not look back at his silhouette against the light of the fading candle.

2

Célie woke with a start, her head throbbing, her body hunched under the blankets. It was still dark outside, but that only meant that it was not yet seven. Amandine was leaning over her, a candle in her hand, her face pale with anxiety and lack of sleep, her soft hair a dark cloud around her head.

'Célie, wake up! You've got to come and help me!' Her voice was shaking with anger. 'Bernave had St Felix out again all night! He's just come in and he's been beaten again, worse this time! Drunkards — Marat's men — Marseillais, I don't know. Get up and help me — please! He's bleeding and he looks terrible. Sometimes I could kill Bernave!'

'They're going to execute the King,' Célie mumbled, fighting off the remnants of sleep. She was so tired she felt drugged. Her throat was dry and the edges of her vision blurred.

Amandine's voice dropped. 'Yes, I know. St Felix told me. In three days.'

Célie sat up slowly. It was bitterly cold. There was no heating whatever in the room, and the air was like ice on her skin. At this hour probably no stoves had been lit anywhere in the house, except the kitchen. Amandine would have the stove going down there. Bernave's household was one of the few that could afford to be warm, at least some of the time.

35

She pushed her hair out of her eyes, and reached for her clothes. She put them on with clumsy fingers fumbling over buttons.

Amandine looked dreadful. She was smaller and more rounded than Célie, her face more delicately boned. There were dark smudges under her eyes. She stood with her arms folded tight and her shoulders hunched.

Célie tied a brown woollen shawl over her blouse and rough, full skirt. It was a sort of peasant garb, and she hated it, but that was what everyone wore in these days of ostentatious equality. The shawl was for warmth, not decoration. She would have liked a pink one, or bright yellow, something daring and individual, not a revolutionary colour. But that would be foolhardy, even if she could have found one.

Amandine moved from one foot to the other impatiently. 'Hurry, please! His clothes are torn and filthy, and there's blood on them, and he can hardly speak. You know more about medicine than I do!'

That was true. When Célie's father had died, and then her husband, leaving her with a two-month-old baby, she had had no choice but to seek the best employment she could find. It had been a stroke of good fortune that someone as extraordinary and talented as Madame de Staël had accepted her as lady's maid. She had several children herself, and had taken compassion on a young mother alone. In Madame's service Célie had naturally improved her skills in sewing, laundering, millinery, writing a neat and graceful letter, reading aloud, and seeing that a table was properly laid. She had on several occasions overheard some of the leading philosophers of the age talking into the night in Madame's salon, before that sort of civilised conversation had become impossible.

And of course a little minor nursing and medicine was necessary. No one called a doctor unless there was absolutely no alternative, and surgery was needed. Certainly one went to hospital only if carried there unable to resist.

Amandine was at the door, impatient, and Célie followed her downstairs and into the kitchen where half a dozen candles were blazing and the warmth of the stove engulfed her the moment she entered.

St Felix was sitting slumped on one of the wooden chairs, his legs out in front of him, soft boots stained with mud and effluent from the gutters that ran down the centre of most of the smaller streets. His coat was torn at the top of the right sleeve, as if someone had tried to pull it off him by force, and there were dark stains of blood on it, as well as smears on his cheek. His fine-drawn, dreamer's face was ashen pale and his eyes were closed, but from the rigidity of his body Célie could tell that he was obviously conscious.

Célie closed the door behind her to keep out any inquisitive Lacoste children who might be awake and think they could cadge some hot chocolate from Amandine, or any other titbit offered them. She went over to St Felix and regarded him closely.

He opened his eyes, which were wide,

37

grey-green and clear as the sea.

He looked at her, keeping his arms folded across his chest, but she could not tell whether it was to hide a wound, or simply because he was cold.

'Where are you hurt?' she asked him firmly, as she would have a child. She was aware of Amandine behind her, watching and waiting. 'Put the pan on,' she ordered without looking round. 'Make some hot chocolate.'

'I've got wine — '

'Chocolate's better,' Célie replied. 'And get a little bread.' She heard Amandine move to obey. She herself remained looking at St Felix. 'Is that blood yours, or someone else's?' she asked.

He blinked and looked down at his sleeve with slight surprise. 'Oh. Mostly someone else's, I think. I'm all right, Célie.' His voice was beautiful, perfectly modulated, even now when he was frightened and hurt. 'Just a knife scar on that arm, not deep, and a few bruises.'

'What happened?' She knew he had been across the river all the way to the slums and tanneries of the Faubourg St-Antoine, where Bernave had sent him, but Amandine would not know, and that was better so.

He made a tiny, dismissive gesture with one hand, but when he answered his voice shook. 'I ran into one of Marat's mobs. They were celebrating the verdict on the King and were a bit drunk. No harm intended.' His eyes betrayed the lie by omission. There was a fierce and terrible loneliness in him, as if he could tell no one the pain inside him.

38

'You'd better take your coat off and let me see.' Célie could not let the matter drop. He was beginning to shudder as the shock settled in him and she was not sure how much he may have bled or how deep the wound was. He might even have broken bones under the bruising.

'It's not . . . serious . . . ' he said between chattering teeth.

'Oh good,' she said sarcastically. 'If I can't be your doctor, then as laundress I'll ask you please at least get those filthy clothes off before you get into bed, or it'll take me a week to get the mud out of the sheets.'

The ghost of a smile lit his face for a moment, and slowly he obeyed, unfolding his arms and allowing her to unbutton and gently remove his coat. He winced and drew in his breath sharply as she tried to ease it off his shoulder and down over the bloody arm.

'Sorry,' she apologised without looking at him.

He allowed her to remove the coat, concentrating on getting it to slide down without turning his shoulder again. When it was off his shirt was exposed, soaked with blood from the forearm down to the hand, but the single wound was drying over. As far as she could see it was clean-edged, as if made by a butcher's or tanner's knife.

Amandine came over with a steaming mug of chocolate. It was thick and creamy. She had used the best ingredients, as Célie had known she would. Bernave himself would not get as much. In fact with Amandine's feelings the way they were, he would be lucky to get anything that did not give him severe stomach-ache.

'Put it on the table,' Célie told her. 'And get me hot water and a clean cloth.'

'You can't do this any more!' Amandine turned to St Felix, her voice trembling. 'He's wicked to send you! You could have been killed! And for what? Another deal? A few more sous?'

'He didn't know this would happen,' St Felix argued.

'Rubbish!' she snapped, her face crumpled with fury and distress, the shadows around her eyes dark as her hair. 'Anyone with two wits to rub together would know there were going to be mobs around last night. Where did he send you, anyway? What was there that couldn't wait until daylight?'

'Get me the water!' Célie ordered briskly. 'You can argue about it later.'

'Errands that are safer at night,' St Felix replied, evading the issue.

'Oh, yes!' Amandine said witheringly, turning away to obey, although she already had water on to heat. 'I've only to look at you to see how safe they are!'

'It wasn't a personal attack,' he told her, ignoring Célie, who was now opening his shirt and looking carefully at the purpling bruises on his body to try to judge whether any ribs were broken. 'Just exuberance and clumsiness,' he went on. It was perfectly apparent that he had been struck hard several times, almost certainly knocked over and kicked and rolled.

Amandine's disbelief was clear in her face as she returned with a bowl of water and set it on

40

the table. Clear also was her pain for him as if it were her own body that had been injured.

'It wasn't meant that way,' he insisted, his face softening as he looked at her distress. 'I was just in the wrong place and they mistook my intention. They were drunk. Poor devils! They dreamed of so much for so long, and the realities are thin . . . and bitter. They don't understand, and it frightens them.' His voice was tired but there was a sudden vibrancy of emotion in it, of pity and total belief. 'It's so easy to make mistakes when you're frightened.'

Amandine's eyes reflected her admiration for him, and her impatience for a gentleness that would defend even its own attackers.

'Celebrating the King's coming execution, no doubt,' she said. 'And wanting to beat anyone who looked like an aristocrat, however plainly dressed. Does it never occur to them that you can't help your ancestors any more than they can help theirs?'

'I very much doubt it,' he answered, wincing again as Célie touched a red weal across his chest where a boot had landed. 'Hate doesn't rest on reason, Amandine.' He spoke her name softly, as if the sound of it pleased him, breaking some tiny part of his loneliness. Célie did not need to turn and look to imagine the pleasure in her eyes as she heard it.

Célie left them and went back into the front room and up the stairs to fetch ointment and salve from her bedroom, and a mixture of restorative herbs she had kept with her from her days with Madame de Staël. She must clean the knife wound without making it bleed again. Somehow she must keep it closed, though she had no way of stitching or plastering it. She would have to bind it with linen. Fortunately the wound was in his arm and not in his chest. All the things she needed were locked in her cupboard, safe from the inquisitive eyes or fingers of the rest of the household.

It took her several minutes to go up and down two flights of stairs, creeping in the near dark, knowing every loose board. When she returned Amandine and St Felix were sitting opposite each other, leaning over the wooden table talking earnestly. He had his hands cupped around his mug — another hideous piece of revolutionary pottery — every now and then taking a sip. Amandine watched him, her face filled with a gentleness which transfigured her, giving a strength to her delicate features and lighting the beauty that was already there.

'It was only dangerous by accident,' he assured her again, looking down at the chocolate. 'Mischance. If I had gone round the other way I wouldn't have passed them, and then it wouldn't have happened.' He raised his eyes to hers. 'You mustn't blame Bernave.' Now there was urgency in his voice and in the angle of his body, resting on one elbow, shoulders tight. It seemed to matter to him very much that she understood.

'That doesn't excuse him,' she insisted, her face in the light filled with concern and fear.

Standing in the doorway Célie wondered if St Felix recognised it, or if his mind was so full of ideals he imagined she shared, and that her passion was impersonal, revolutionary visions for some perfect society. Dreamers such as he was could be blind to the ordinary, everyday feelings of others.

She came in and went to the stove, taking down a heavy iron pan from the rack to brew an infusion that would help restore his strength. Then she returned to him and carefully, painstakingly, cleaned as much as she could of the dried blood from the wound, put balm on it, and bound it up.

'You must refuse to do, this any more,' Amandine said suddenly, her voice thick with emotion. 'You don't have to! Let Bernave carry his own messages.'

St Felix did not reply. Célie knew he did not dare trust Amandine with the knowledge that his actions were part of saving the King's life. He would want to safeguard her. Or perhaps he had simply given his word to Bernave. Had he any idea how much Célie knew? Probably not. What would he think of Bernave trusting a laundress?

But why not? Weren't these supposed to be the days of equality?

That was a new and enormous idea. To talk about it was one thing, to practise it quite another. Anyway, equality between all men, between aristocrat and labourer, academician and illiterate, was still quite a different thing from equality between a man and his wife, let alone his maid. There had been a few white-hot arguments about that already. Célie had seen pamphlets and posters on the subject in the streets. There was one woman called Claire

Lacombe, who had caused a great stir demanding rights, and some Dutch woman, Etta something, had as well. One day when there was time she would learn more about that! Madame de Staël would have approved.

The water was boiling. She took it off the stove and poured it over the mixed leaves, waiting while it steeped.

Amandine was still smouldering on about Bernave as she left the table and began to prepare breakfast for everyone, cutting bread and cheese and banging the chocolate tin to try to get out every last bit of the powder. Sometimes the whole household ate together; it was more economic, particularly with fuel.

St Felix looked at Amandine, his face sombre. 'I am doing what I have to, what I believe to be right,' he said grimly, his voice soft, closed off within himself.

The discussion was over. He had withdrawn into that inaccessible region where his dreams lay, and his pain.

Célie understood that he believed the same as Bernave, that he saw beyond Paris to Europe and the world, and knew the danger of war, invasion, even the possibility of defeat. He also knew he could not explain that to Amandine or anyone else who believed in the revolution, who wanted and needed to. And perhaps he was afraid of the power of her feelings. He would try to protect her from herself, and her anger against Bernave.

But Célie did not understand why he accepted the worst tasks so meekly, or why Bernave gave them all to him, instead of doing some himself.

There was a cruelty in it that confused her. It was so unlike everything she knew of either man. Bernave was full of intelligence and power, smooth-boned, his grey hair lean to his head. He read voraciously, and there was always humour just behind his words, as if he knew some cosmic joke that he could share with no one else.

St Felix was a little taller, slighter of build. His face had an elusive beauty to it, as if he had seen a great vision and was on an eternal quest to find its reality. He would be incomplete until he did, and open to pain. She imagined him in the dark alleys of the Faubourg St-Antoine where the abattoirs of the tanneries were, coming round a corner and without warning running into the mob, drunken, hysterical with the taste of blood — a king's blood. They would have no thought for what they were doing, only hatred, and the thrilling, surging knowledge of their own power. They held Paris in their hands, and they could do anything they wanted. No law could touch them. God was gone, the Church was gone . . . who was there to deny them anything at all?

She strained the brew off the leaves into a cup and handed it to St Felix.

'That will make you feel better,' she promised. 'You should sleep for an hour or two at least.'

'Until noon,' Amandine corrected her, stirring the chocolate powder into a paste with the last of the milk.

St Felix drank down Célie's brew steadily, only flaring his nostrils very slightly at the smell, and then replaced the empty cup on the table. 'There'll be things to do before then,' he answered, standing up slowly, and wincing as the movement caused the fabric of his shirt to touch his wounds. He looked at Célie. 'Thank you. You are very kind.' He smiled at her, then at Amandine, and walked stiffly out of the kitchen towards his room, his footsteps uneven on the stone floor.

Célie turned to clear away the ointment and dishes she had been using.

Amandine's soft mouth thinned with loathing. 'Bernave does it because it amuses him,' she said between her teeth. 'He likes the taste of power, to see if St Felix will obey him! Give him a little strength over someone, and he uses it to satisfy his cruelty. He's like the worst of the revolutionaries, and just as tyrannical as any king!'

'Be quiet!' Célie snapped, afraid for Amandine above any concern for St Felix. 'Haven't you the wits you were born with?'

It needed no explanation. Amandine stared at her, eyes wide, lips tight. 'It's true,' she repeated fiercely, but this time in a whisper.

Célie put her hand on Amandine's arm. 'So are a lot of things that are better not said.'

As if to emphasise her words, the door was pushed open and Marie-Jeanne Lacoste stood in the entrance, a candle in one hand, and holding her baby, wrapped in a cot quilt against her shoulder with the other. She was Bernave's daughter, but she had little of his suffering in her face, and none of his sharp, probing nature. She looked tired and confused now, and more than her twenty-three years. Her brown hair straggled

46

across her brow and her eyes were full of fear. She was used to broken nights. She had three small children. It was a constant battle to keep them fed, clothed and as safe as possible in these violent and uncertain times. No one could plan for a future with any idea of what it would be, except more cold and more shortages.

'Has anyone heard if they are going to kill the King?' she asked, looking from Célie to Amandine and back again. She had no idea Célie had been to the Convention; she was merely asking for news anyone up early might have heard on the doorstep.

'Yes,' Célie answered quietly. 'They are. In three days.'

'Fernand said they would.' Marie-Jeanne was referring to her husband. She held the sleeping baby a little closer to her as she came over to the table. 'He'll be pleased. He was afraid they would lose their nerve.'

'Marat wouldn't let them,' Célie said cuttingly, putting the last of the dishes over on the bench. They would be washed together with those from breakfast, when there was more water heated.

The meaning was lost on Marie-Jeanne. 'Fernand is sure he'll be the saviour of Europe yet,' she answered, folding the quilt into a place for the baby on the floor near the hearth. 'I wish he wouldn't keep saying it in front of my father.' She spoke the word with almost no emotion, as if it were a mere title, not a relationship. 'Of course Papa Lacoste agrees,' she went on, a strange mixture of respect and dislike filling her expression.

47

'You should warn him to be careful,' Amandine responded, returning her attention to the chocolate. 'Citizen Bernave may have different feelings. These days it's best to be discreet.'

'That's what I keep saying,' Marie-Jeanne nodded, putting the baby down gently, smiling at her and tickling her very gently until she gurgled. Then she rose to her feet and began to set the table with new revolutionary crockery, with its painted political symbols: ancient Roman faces; red, white and blue cockles; a cannon with a crowing cockerel on top. If she thought they were ugly or absurd she was too tactful to say so.

She saw the extra candle Célie had lit to see St Felix's arm more clearly and, realising it was unnecessary, pinched it out. She was a frugal housewife. Perhaps Fernand did not realise what a blessing he had in her. She was good-natured, energetic, and she could make acceptable meals for the whole family out of vegetables and herbs, and each time they would be a little different.

She had no interest whatever in politics, but in the kitchen she had style, flair and ingenuity, even a kind of inventiveness which could be called wit. Like many ordinary women all over France, her family was what mattered to her. What they did in the Palace of Versailles, in the hall of the Convention, or in the Place de la Révolution where the guillotine stood stark, were of importance to her only as it reflected upon her home here in the Boulevard St-Germain.

Célie had often wondered if she were also like most women in having a religious belief. It went hand in hand with the ordinary decencies of so much of family life. She would not dare to mention it in front of her husband or father-in-law, but Bernave would not have objected. But then perhaps Marie-Jeanne did not know that. Maybe only Célie had seen the old, well-fingered breviary inside his desk, and noticed that he never took the name of the deity lightly or in vain.

'It will all be over in a few days.' Amandine smiled bleakly at Marie-Jeanne. 'Then we can begin to get back to normal.'

'We can't go 'back' to anything,' Célie contradicted her. 'We can only go forward to whatever happens when we've no Church and no king.'

Amandine shot her a look of warning.

Marie-Jeanne turned to Célie, her china-blue eyes widening a little with surprise. 'Don't you think it'll be better?'

Célie realised how easily her tongue had run away with her. She must be more careful. Without meaning any harm, Marie-Jeanne could repeat her words.

There was a heavy tread on the floor outside in the next room, and a moment later Monsieur Lacoste opened the door. He was a man of few words, his emotion contained within himself. He was in his early fifties and the scars of life were deeply imprinted on his bony face. Self-pity was unknown to him, but anger lay close beneath the thin surface of his patience. What pain or injustices he had seen were hidden in his memory and he shared them with no one. He was dressed in dark brown breeches, a faded shirt and leather jerkin, ready for work.

'What are you all doing up so early?' he demanded. 'Has something happened? Is there news?'

'Only what was expected, Papa,' Marie-Jeanne replied, shaking her head a little. 'They are going to send the King to the guillotine.'

'Of course they are!' he retorted, shrugging sharply. 'Did anyone imagine differently? Anyway, how do you know? Who said so?'

'Célie,' she answered.

He swung around and his glance fell on the sleeping baby. The anger disappeared from him. 'And how do you know?' he asked.

'I was out,' Célie explained. She could not tell him the truth. 'I heard them talking in the street.'

His eyes narrowed, fear returning. 'What were you out for at this time of the morning? It's too early for bread!'

'An errand for Citizen Bernave last night,' she replied, keeping her voice natural. She must not seem to resent the question.

'I don't know why he can't do his business during the daytime, like anyone else!' he said tartly, turning away from her towards the table. 'You shouldn't be sent out at all hours. It isn't right. Anything could happen to you.' He wanted to say something more but he did not know what.

'Nobody should!' Amandine said with ill-concealed anger.

Monsieur Lacoste forgot the subject and directed his attention back to the news. 'So

Marat won at last.' There was a faint curl to his lips, but in the candlelight it was impossible to tell if it was satisfaction or not.

No one answered him. Célie recalled the change in fortunes of one leader after another, and how they had pinned their hopes on each in turn. First had been Necker and Mirabeau, who had had such great dreams of order and financial stability, and failed; then Lafayette, whose words were filled with glory and liberty, and who last August had defected to the Austrians. Now Brissot and the Girondins were in power, once her father's idols, but it was only nominally. They were full of great words, oratory to rival that of Cicero and the ancient Romans — or at least they imagined it did — and internecine quarrels to match. They had been so preoccupied with jostling for position among themselves, they had allowed Marat to overtake them all.

Madame Lacoste came in silently. She was a slender woman, of no more than average height. Her features were striking; straight nose, level brows and deep-set eyes almost black. It was a face of passion and strength, and in a few sudden and startling moments, also of vulnerability. Célie knew very little about her; she seldom talked of herself, or where she had grown up, far more often it was of beliefs. But unlike her husband or son, these were not political but moral matters of right and wrong, questions of human love, honour and dishonour. She had no patience with the concepts of virtue by dictate of law in society as preached by Robespierre. Célie hoped she would have the sense of self-preservation not to say so. She had at least been careful enough not to mention the name of God!

'I suppose the verdict is in?' Madame asked, looking from one of them to another, then at the set table. Her lips tightened. 'I don't know what else you expected? They could hardly retreat now, could they? The very most would be to prevaricate, and then do it a week or a month later — as if that made any difference! It would not be a mercy, just the usual inability to make a decision. Is that chocolate ready yet, Amandine?'

'They could have lost their nerve,' Lacoste argued. 'Settled for keeping him in prison.'

Her face, dark-shadowed in the uncertain light, was full of scorn. 'It would take far more nerve to tell the people they couldn't go through with killing the King than it would to make the final gesture and condemn him,' she said tersely. 'They've gone much too far to turn back now.'

'You don't understand politics.' He moved away. 'It has a force of its own.'

'It's people,' she replied, as Amandine poured the chocolate into a jug and brought it to the table. 'They don't change on the inside just because they stand up in a pulpit or on a rostrum.'

He swivelled back towards her. 'Don't talk of politics as if it were the Church! These men aren't risking their lives to free the people in order to get themselves a safe living for the rest of their days, and then a soft seat in heaven!'

'Even they aren't daft enough for that,' she said witheringly, picking up the jug and filling

52

the cups. 'When they've just murdered half the priests in France!'

'Suzanne! Keep a still tongue in your head!' he warned moving a little closer to her, and raising his arm in an odd little gesture that was half angry, half protective. It hovered over her shoulder for a minute as if he would touch her, then moved away. 'Whatever you think, the revolution is a fact! Don't talk about what you don't understand.'

'Are you afraid I'm going to praise the Church?' she said with disgust. 'Don't worry, I thought they were just as corrupt as you did — maybe more.'

He looked a trifle surprised, but relieved also. 'You never said . . . '

'It's not political,' she answered with a smile, but inward, as if only she knew the joke. 'Sit down and eat.'

'It's over!' Lacoste pronounced with a sudden change to enthusiasm. His eyes lingered on the baby again for a moment. 'This is the beginning of a new age,' he said softly. 'In a few days France will be a republic! The people will rule!' He smiled across at Marie-Jeanne, his whole countenance startlingly different. 'No more need to be afraid! Your children will grow up free, able to do whatever they want, be anything.' He gestured expansively with his hands, still standing up. 'No more closed professions that only the aristocracy can join, no more refusal of promotions in the army because your family hasn't a coat of arms! As if that had anything to do with courage or the skill to fight!' His eyes were bright and gentle. 'Education for everyone! Justice in the courts! Freedom to say or believe anything you want! No more Church bleeding us dry. This is a great day!'

He glanced at Amandine. 'Fetch a bottle of the best wine we've got left, and we'll have a drink to the future. Call Fernand. We'll drink to the rule of the people.'

Amandine moved to obey and they waited in silence around the table until she returned. Fernand came in close behind her.

'Perhaps we should get my father?' Marie-Jeanne suggested half reluctantly. 'And Citizen St Felix?'

'He's gone to bed,' Amandine replied, tight-lipped. 'He was out all night, and came back hurt again — this time badly.'

'Bernave!' Lacoste said with disgust, sitting down at last, followed by the others. He glanced across at the window to the street. 'It rained most of the night. Where on earth could he have gone that couldn't have waited?'

'Ask Bernave.' Amandine spat the name. 'I don't know what for.'

'Is he going to be all right?' Madame asked, passing the bread round and cutting the cheese carefully.

'It'll heal,' Célie answered, 'if it gets the chance.'

Lacoste took the bottle from her, and Madame opened the cupboard and placed six glasses on the table for him. He poured the wine and passed the glasses round. The hot chocolate could wait. 'To the rule of the people . . . at last!'

he said with a smile.

'To the rule of the people,' they all echoed, each one with a different inflexion, and assuredly with different thoughts. Madame's face was unreadable. Monsieur held his glass high.

★　★　★

Late in the morning Bernave sent for Célie again. As usual he was sitting at his desk. The polished wooden surface was littered with papers, wax, sand and two jars of ink. Three different quills lay about. The penknife was open and nib shavings were scattered on a sheet now marked with splatters of ink.

In the grey daylight Bernave looked haggard. There was a pallor to his skin. The lines from his nose to mouth were deeply etched and there was grey stubble on his jaw. But in spite of exhaustion his eyes were clear and hard when they met hers, and there was no weakness in him, no indecision.

'I have messages for you to take,' he said, studying her carefully, weighing his judgement of her. 'I can put little on paper, in case you are caught and searched. You must memorise most of it. Can you do that?'

'Yes,' she answered immediately, but it was out of defiance rather than any inner certainty. There was nowhere to go but forward, and she would not let Bernave see any doubt in her.

He was regarding her now with wry humour, as if he were conscious of the incongruity of the situation: the wealthy middle-aged merchant sharing a desperate secret with his laundress, which could save France, or get them both killed. Here in this room with its shelves of books containing the thoughts and dreams of men down the ages, success did not seem impossible. There was something within Bernave, a power of faith he seemed able to call on, which when she was with him, she could grasp as well. She thought of the books on religion in amongst the other philosophies. Were they so precious he could not part with them? Or had he simply forgotten they were there?

'Find Citizen Bressard,' he said so quietly she had to concentrate to hear him. 'He is the manager of my office on the Quai Voltaire. Ask him to let you speak to Citizen Bombec, Citizen Chimay, and Citizen Virieu.'

She started to protest, then the words died on her lips. She could not let him see she was afraid.

'Are you listening to me, Célie?' he said sharply. 'Repeat the names!'

'Citizen Bombec, Citizen Chimay and Citizen Virieu,' she obeyed.

Bernave nodded almost imperceptibly. 'Tell each of them that we will act as planned — no more than that. Trust no one, not Bressard. A word in the wrong place . . . ' He did not bother to complete the sentence.

'Are they coach drivers?' she asked. 'What about getting out of the city? They will need passes . . . more than ever that day.'

He looked at her curiously, aware of her intelligence and perhaps even more of her feelings. She had caught the vision of the disaster

56

which threatened them all, and she cared. An appreciation of that flickered in his eyes. There was something which might even have been respect, and it mattered to her more than she wanted to admit. It was uncomfortable to care what he thought of her. It restricted the anger she wanted to let free.

'Yes, they will need passes,' he replied coolly. 'St Felix will attend to them. It's not your concern.'

She accepted the paper but stood her ground. 'Is it dangerous again . . . getting the passes?' she asked him. 'He was hurt last night. He could have been killed!'

Bernave's expression was impossible to read. 'Life is dangerous, Célie. We all take risks for what we want. Go and deliver my messages.'

It was dismissal, and she dared not press him any further, but she was perfectly sure he was sending St Felix into another situation in which he might well be injured again, or worse. She did not understand why St Felix accepted the situation. Bernave could perfectly well have carried many of the messages himself, and yet St Felix never seemed to rebel, or even to question. Such meekness was beyond her understanding. She could not decide whether it was nobility or cowardice.

'What is it?' Bernave asked as she remained standing.

'The man who will take the King's place?' she said quietly, thinking of someone prepared to be murdered by an enraged crowd when they discovered him. What passion of loyalty drove a

57

man to sacrifice his life in such a way? Was it love of the King, the idea of monarchy, or a terrible vision of France as it could become? She had no idea. Bernave had told her nothing of him, except that he existed.

The shadow of a smile touched Bernave's mouth. He laced his fingers together in front of him. His hands were beautiful, in spite of the scars.

'I told you, Célie, sometimes one has to pay a great price for what one wants. Sometimes what he will pay is a better measure of a man that what it is he is paying for.'

'A royalist?' She tried to imagine him, a man who could love a myth, a figurehead so intensely, even above life.

Bernave's eyes were gentle. There was a kind of love in him she had not seen before. It made him almost beautiful. 'Yes . . . but more than that, a Frenchman,' he said softly.

There was no answer she could give. It was complete and final. She had no right to intrude.

'What else?' he asked as still she did not move.

She took a deep breath. 'I need some money,' she replied.

His eyes narrowed, the fight dying from them. 'What for?'

'Food.'

Understanding flooded his face, and a swift amusement which made her blush. 'Ah . . . for Coigny. Of course.' He opened a drawer without the slightest disguise of what he was doing, and she noticed with surprise that it had not been locked. He took out a handful of coins and gave

58

them to her, then closed the drawer again. He had never bothered with the paper assignats of the early revolution, which had proved worthless within a short space of time.

'Thank you.' She pocketed the money and turned to leave.

'Be careful, Célie!' he said again, but this time sharply. 'Say nothing, however you may be provoked! Ask no questions and give no opinions. You are a laundress. You have no thoughts! Do you hear me?'

'Yes, Citizen,' she answered sarcastically. 'Liberty, Brotherhood and Equality!' And she went out of the door and closed it without waiting for his response.

★   ★   ★

Célie hurried through the grey, wind-scoured streets. It was not far — less than a mile — but time enough to get thoroughly cold, and to see other women with their heads down, carrying half-empty baskets after the morning's struggle for food.

A wagon trundled past with firewood, covered over, to keep it from getting wet. She passed a group of National Guards, their uniforms ragged, but the red, white and blue cockades in their hats still brave. Most of them had muskets, a few only swords or pikes. Her hand went automatically to her shoulder, to make sure her own cockade was safely pinned. It was illegal to be without it.

'Run, Citizeness!' one of the men yelled

cheerfully after her. 'Home to your fire!'

The others laughed.

She would like to have pointed out to them how few people had fires these days, but it was a stupid thing to draw attention, especially by arguing.

'Thank you, Citizen,' she called back. 'Keep the streets safe for us!' Hypocrite, she thought to herself afterwards.

A copy of last week's *Père Duchesne* blew across the pavement into the gutter. There was a crude drawing on the front, and the usual masthead silhouette of the comfortable old man with his big nose, and the pipe in his mouth.

Further up the street there was a loud argument, two women in browns and greys fighting over a loaf of bread. Half a dozen others stood by, faces sullen and frightened. Célie knew why. She had felt the same frisson of panic run through her when she had arrived at the end of the baker's queue too late and had had to return home empty-handed and hungry. It was happening more often. It was a long time till harvest. Where was all the grain?

'You got bread!' someone shouted, voice sharp and accusing.

'Liar!' came back the answer. 'I got nothing . . . jus' like you! Jus' like all of us!'

'Not like all of us . . . some got bread, an' onions, an' cheese!' another said, her face twisted with hatred.

'Yeah? Who? Tell the Commune! Hoarding's a crime.'

The woman gave her a filthy look. 'If I knew

who, I'd kill 'er meself! They're murderers o' the rest of us . . . that's what they are!'

The woman with a loaf of bread was enraged. 'Who are you calling murderer, yer ol' bag? I got me loaf, same as you, an' six kids ter feed! An' my man's up fighting the Austrians, God help him!' She spat on the cobbles, completely unaware of having called on a deity who officially no longer existed. 'Go an' look at some o' them rich bastards up St-Germain! They got plenty, I 'eard!'

A few yards along the street a National Guardsman swung a musket round threateningly and loosed a shot off into the air.

The women grumbled and started to move away.

Célie turned towards the Quai Voltaire and increased her pace.

3

Joseph Briard stood by the window staring out at the rain. It blew in gusts against the glass, but here in his room it was warm. The candlelight glowed on polished wood. Most of the floor was covered by a red rug, worn and mellow with time and the passage of feet. Two of the walls were lined with shelves of books and mementos of his life.

He had only three more days' fuel left, but it was enough. He would burn it all. After that he would not need it, nor the wine in the glass he was holding, watching the light in its ruby depths, letting its flavour fill his head. It was a burgundy — one of the best years.

He smiled as he thought of the past. In his mind he could see sunlight on rolling hills, smell the sweet grasses and the herbs of the south. Unconsciously he narrowed his eyes as if the reflection off blue water dazzled him, but it was only memory, the days of youth sharper and more real than this grey winter of the soul in Paris.

Would it all be futile anyway, a grand gesture, but no more? Or was it possible they could succeed? He had done everything, precisely as Bernave had instructed. Still there was so much room for error, circumstance unseen, unprepared for.

And if it worked . . . that was something he

would not think of. He had faced it once, imagined it, even the last few moments. Now it was best put from his mind. Sometimes your body could let you down, even when your heart had no doubt at all.

He sipped the wine again. There was also enough meat left for two more days, and vegetables and a whole loaf of bread. There was a good claret, but he would leave that . . . for Bernave, perhaps?

There came a rap on the door, twice, sharply, and then silence. It would be Bernave. He had come to tell him what Briard already knew.

He refused to hesitate. He went to the door and opened it.

Bernave stepped in, shaking the water off his hat and shoulders. His boots left wet marks on the floor. There was no need for him to speak; all that lay between them was in his eyes and the set of his lips — the hope, the fear, and above all the pity.

Briard swallowed. This was the moment.

Bernave closed the door.

'Have a glass of burgundy,' Briard offered, keeping his voice light. 'It's the best year I've tasted.' He turned and led the way back to the chairs beside the fire. Without waiting for the answer he poured a second glassful, a beautiful crystal glass engraved with lilies.

Bernave took it. For a moment the candlelight flickered through its burning heart.

'Long live the King!' he said softly.

Briard found his throat too tight to drink. 'Long live the King!' he answered, then filled his mouth with the clean, full taste of the wine.

Bernave was looking at him. Was he still uncertain, weighing him in his mind, or did he know now that he would do it? Which was worse, the decision committed and irrevocable, or not yet made?

'The die is cast,' Bernave said steadily. 'All is in hand. Have you met with the drivers?'

'Yes.' Briard recalled it vividly, playing the part of the nervous trader so concerned with his goods he was determined to travel with the most important cargoes, regardless of the personal danger or inconvenience. It had caused some amusement, and a little contempt, but he had not been disbelieved. 'Yes, I did,' he repeated. 'And I have the clothes.' He swallowed a little more wine to moisten his dry lips. 'Over there.'

In three neat parcels were the three different jackets he had worn; a dark green woollen coat of excellent cut, high collared with brass buttons in which to meet the driver west to Calais and the sea; a blue coat with lighter facings to speak to the driver south towards the Pyrenees and Spain; a brown jacket with buff-coloured collar, cuffs and lapels to introduce himself to the driver south and east towards Italy. They were all expensive and memorable. When another man with similar white hair and long nose turned up in the same clothes, it would be assumed it was he, still determined to ride with his cargo. Each parcel was labelled with the direction for which it was intended. Each one would be left at a different safe house, according to which route of escape the King was going to take. That would be decided upon at the moment, according to which seemed best.

Bernave glanced at them, and was satisfied. He said nothing else about it, no words of praise or debt, no questioning of his resolve, simply, 'I'm sorry', and then silence.

The rain splattered on the window, and in the hearth the logs settled lower. Briard leaned forward and put on another. Someone could inherit the claret, but he was damned if he was going to be cold.

'I never thought there would be any other outcome,' he said truthfully. 'As soon as they put him on trial there was never any other end possible. I can remember that farce as if it were yesterday. The ever-virtuous little Robespierre with his clicking heels and his green spectacles. He claims to be France's best hope for a pure future, you know — devoid of greed, corruption or immorality. And perhaps he is! Why do I hate him so much?'

'God! I hope not!' Bernave said passionately, his voice raw. 'You hate him for his lies of the soul! Because he takes the dreams of decent men and twists them into the shapes of his own starved nightmares. Because he finds filthy the human loves and needs of ordinary men, and makes of them something to be despised.' He sat absolutely still, but his voice was shaking, and there was a passionate misery in his face. 'He's read too much Rousseau. Lovers of the mind who never touch each other, but are in a perpetual anticipation, and never consummate anything, as if the reality would soil them.' He tried to smile, and it was a grimace. 'They are philosophers of the unfulfilled, and unfulfillable.'

Briard stared into his glass as the fire crackled and burned up. It was already beginning to seem far away, the pedantic little figure who was obsessed with purity, who never forgot an insult, or forgave a favour.

'Never do him a service, Bernave,' he said aloud. 'If you place him in your debt for anything he will never pardon you for it.'

Bernave's lips twisted back off his teeth. 'I will never do him a favour, believe me! I would rather deal with Danton any day, or even Marat.'

Briard was surprised. Marat's savage face came too easily to his inner eye. 'Would you? Would you really?'

'I think Robespierre's hatred for Marat will tear the Convention apart,' Bernave replied quietly. 'I pray I am wrong.'

'Does Danton hate him?' Briard was puzzled. 'I didn't see that. Danton does not seem to me like a man who hates.'

'Not yet.' Bernave sipped the burgundy, rolling it on his tongue. 'But he will. Robespierre will give him cause.'

'Any man who listens to Saint-Just — '

Bernave jerked his scarred hand dismissively. 'The man is mad! Madder even, than Hébert or Couthon. That we listen to him is surely the most terrible measure of what we have become. What more could anyone say to condemn us?'

Suddenly Briard saw the tiredness naked in Bernave's face, the weariness with struggle.

'And the royalists have no sense of political

reality,' Bernave went on. 'They either can't or won't see that the world has changed. They are still playing yesterday's game — and by yesterday's rules. The old bargains they could have made last year are gone. They always give too little — and too late.' His voice was flat, contemptuous. 'They don't listen. They have seen the convulsions of the last three and a half years, and they've learned nothing. Even in the shadow of the guillotine, with Marat controlling the streets and the Convention, in all but name, they can't see that we can never go back. The past is dead. The best we can do — all we can do — is save something for the future.'

Briard felt a shiver of apprehension. He knew the answer, but he still had to ask. 'You didn't tell them . . . anything?'

'No I didn't.' There was no impatience in Bernave's eyes, or his voice, no criticism for the question, even the bitterness was almost gone. 'I have been around far too long to trust any courtier from Versailles to keep his word on anything. I've watched them as the storm gathered around them on every side, the mobs marched to the palace gates, and still they understood nothing. I had a dog with more sense!' The regret and the loneliness in his face were as profound as another man's tears would have been. 'And more charity,' he added softly. 'And come to think of it, more perception of the absurd. It was a good dog.'

Briard smiled, but he did not reply. There was no need. They sat in silence while the fire burned hot, and drank the rest of the burgundy. Then

Bernave put on his coat again and went out into the rain. Everything had been said; to add anything more now would have been clumsy.

★ ★ ★

Célie let herself in by the back door. Amandine was in the kitchen and there was fresh bread on the table. Steam from the soup pot smelled sharp and fragrant, probably because there was too little meat in it and too many herbs.

Amandine swung round as soon as she heard the latch, the ladle in her hand, her eyes expectant. She tried not to look disappointed as she saw it was Célie and not St Felix. The colour warmed up her cheeks with guilt. They had shared many thoughts and feelings over the two years of their friendship, and ungraciousness was alien to her nature.

'You must be frozen,' she said sympathetically. 'Take that wet cloak off and warm your feet. Would you like some soup? It's hot.'

'Yes, please,' Célie accepted, doing as she was bidden. Her boots were so soaked it was hard to undo the laces and the sodden hem of her skirt flapped around her ankles, cold as ice. Her fingers were numb and it was hard to hold anything. St Felix must be out again. She knew it was he whom Amandine had hoped for with such urgency.

'Have you seen Georges?' Amandine asked instead. She cared about him too, in a different way, but no less deeply. They were not only cousins but had been friends and allies since childhood. How often she lay awake and worried about him Célie could only guess. Amandine had twice offered to take him food herself, but Célie had pointed out the additional risk to Georges if more people were seen going up the narrow alley to the steps, carrying baskets. And above all, they could not afford to awaken the suspicion of Monsieur Lacoste, or of Fernand, both of whom were ardent supporters of the revolution, and would certainly see it as their duty to the state, and even more the safety of their own family, to turn in any wanted person.

'In good spirits,' Célie answered quietly, easing off her other boot. She could not say when she had seen him, nor why. It would worry Amandine unnecessarily, and there was nothing she could do to help. Her fear for St Felix was more than enough.

Amandine looked at her doubtfully. She passed her the dish of hot soup, making sure she had hold of it in case her frozen fingers let it slip.

'He is,' Célie assured her, feeling the heat on her hands. She could say it with the ring of conviction because it was true. How Georges kept his courage, alone in that cold attic, she did not know. It was part of his nature, the unreachable confidence in him that nothing seemed to shake, as if he knew a secret no one else did. It was what both attracted her to him, and frightened her because it made him different, invulnerable. He needed her to bring him food, and news, but he would never need anyone, except perhaps Amandine, in an emotional way, and even that was because she

69

was family. Theirs was one of those old ties of land and birth that no outsider could break into.

Célie took a first mouthful of soup. It was very hot and she could taste the onion in it.

The kitchen door opened and Madame Lacoste came in. She glanced at both of them. She must have known that Célie had been out because of her wet skirts and the boots on the floor, but whatever she thought, whether she knew it was some errand of Bernave's or not, she refrained from commenting. She was a quiet woman, possessed of a quality of stillness which was an indication of a kind of peace of heart, a certainty about what she believed, and yet it was a thin covering for intense emotion. Célie had seen it in her face in repose sometimes, an overwhelming hunger so great it made her for an instant both frightening and beautiful. Célie had not been able to fathom her feelings for Bernave. She was always polite to him, but there was a tension in her as if that courtesy cost her some effort, and she did not often meet his eyes. Perhaps whatever he would have seen in them was too private, too dangerous to share. Her son was married to his daughter, and his family needed this home.

Célie wondered what Madame had been like as a young woman, what her life had held, above all what had drawn her to a dour man like Monsieur Lacoste. There was little wit or joy of life in him, but he had endless patience with the children, and Célie had seen a tenderness in him surprisingly often when he spoke to them. Fernand respected him, and Marie-Jeanne liked

70

him better than she liked her own father.

Madame flashed her a quick smile, then went across the kitchen to fetch clean linen from the press, and thanked Célie for it. She was almost to the hall when there was a noise outside the back door, it opened and Bernave came in. He slammed it behind him and stood on the stone floor, dripping water from his coat. He was obviously exhausted, his face gaunt in the candlelight, streaked with rain and almost colourless.

He stamped his feet, shaking the water off himself.

Amandine loathed him for what he was doing to St Felix, but her deepest instinct was to nurture, and before she had time for memory and emotion to curb her, she took a clean towel from the airing rack and went towards him.

'You are perished, Citizen. Let me take your coat,' she offered. 'Dry yourself.' She held out the towel. 'I'll get you some hot soup. Have you eaten today?'

'No . . . no time.' He took the towel and let her remove the coat and hang it near the door where it could drip without shedding puddles over the whole kitchen.

Célie glanced at Madame, and saw with surprise a look of alarm in her face. Was it concern, or fear? For whom? For Bernave or her own family?

Bernave looked across and his eyes met Madame's. They stared at each other for a matter of seconds, and then she broke the silence, speaking quite casually, her voice low.

71

'You must be cold, Citizen. It is a pity your business requires you to be out on such a day.'

'Lots of things are a pity, Citizeness,' he replied, his eyes still unwavering on hers. 'It does no good to think of them. We can only deal with what is.'

'I know that!' There was pain in her voice, raw as if some terrible wound still bled. Then an instant later she concealed it again. All emotion was gone, wiped away. 'We are fortunate to have a roof over our heads, our food to eat,' she observed. 'It is more than many poor devils in Paris can say.'

'Indeed,' he nodded, still facing her.

The seconds ticked by. She turned her head away and walked towards the door. 'Good evening, Citizen,' she said quietly. 'I hope you are able to rest now,' and she went out without glancing back.

He stood motionless for several moments, his expression unreadable in the candlelight. It could have been profound emotion in him, or simply a bitter amusement because he knew what he was attempting to do, knew how desperately it mattered, not only for him but far more for all France. He knew how short time was, and she guessed nothing. For all she understood, he could have been about some money-making affair.

Then he sighed and looked at Amandine.

She smoothed the expression from her face also, erasing the anger.

'Bring the soup to my study,' he told her. 'Célie, come with me.' He walked out the way

Madame had gone, and Célie drank another few mouthfuls from her bowl before following after him. She hated to leave it behind.

In the study there were five candles burning, making the room soft and bright. Amandine had lit the stove over an hour ago, and it was warm. Bernave stood in front of it, the steam rising from his wet jacket and breeches.

'Did you deliver my message?'

'Yes, I saw them all,' she answered.

'Good.' He stood wringing his frozen hands. They were white where the circulation had stopped, the heavy scars standing out livid. 'How was Coigny last night?'

She had told Amandine what she wanted to hear. She should tell Bernave the truth.

'Cold and hungry,' she answered. 'But still determined.'

He smiled, laughter in his clear eyes. 'You admire him, don't you, Célie?' It was hardly a question.

She resented the thought of admiring Georges. An instant denial came to her lips; then she realised Bernave would know it was a lie, and worse than that, he would know why. He seemed almost to look inside her.

'I admire his conviction,' she said defiantly. 'And his intelligence.'

Bernave's eyebrows rose. 'Oh? What did he say?'

Her answer was interrupted by Amandine knocking on the door, and at Bernave's command, bringing in his meal. She set it on the desk. He thanked her. Discreetly she placed

Célie's soup bowl, refilled, nearer the corner. Then she took her leave, closing the door behind her with a snap.

'Well?' Bernave asked, going over to the desk and sitting down. He gestured towards the cup. 'Don't stand there! Finish your soup. Then go and do whatever it is you do in the house. And, Célie!'

'Yes?'

'Thank you.' For a moment there was affection in his face, as if she might have been a friend.

She stared back at him for a long minute, then finished the soup and left.

She spent a little time working on the laundry, Marie-Jeanne helping her, taking the dry linen and clothes off the airing rack and folding them while Célie hung the fresh laundry in its place. It was wet and heavy and made her arms ache.

'Sugar's gone up again,' Marie-Jeanne remarked, flicking a pillow cover to get the corners straight. 'Three years ago it was twenty-four sous — today Citizeness Benoit told me they were asking fifty-eight! Can you believe that? She left it — of course.' She winced in a grimace of pity, and reached for a sheet, matching corner to corner. 'Her husband was injured in the storming of the Tuileries,' she went on. 'Shot in the shoulder, I think. He'd hardly recovered from that when he was called up to go and fight the Prussians. She heard just two weeks ago that he's been killed. And her eldest child is sickly. Poor soul doesn't know where to turn.' She pulled out the sleeves of a jacket and

74

straightened it on the rail. 'I gave her a cupful, but I can't go on doing that.'

'We've got more than most people,' Célie agreed. 'Citizen Bernave sees to that.'

Marie-Jeanne's face was deliberately expressionless. 'Yes. We're fortunate.' She shook a small shirt hard to take out the creases. Her fingers moved swiftly, gently over it, as if she were thinking of the child to whom it belonged.

Célie turned away. She could not think of anything so small without a return of the pain. She could remember Jean-Pierre so sharply, the weight of him in her arms, the milky smell. There were times when it was unbearable. She forced herself to turn back to the laundry. Some of the sheets were wearing thin. She would have to start cutting them down for pillowcases, or if things were hard enough, for shirts and drawers.

Marie-Jeanne was frowning, as though she felt the need to explain herself, but could find no words. She was unaware of the turmoil in Célie. She knew nothing of Jean-Pierre's death, or Amandine and Georges, or the terrible thing Célie had done in her agony.

She was examining a jerkin of Fernand's when St Felix returned. He came in through the back door again, soaked to the skin, his face and arms covered with mud, his hat missing, his hair plastered to his head.

'Oh, my heavens!' Marie-Jeanne dropped the jerkin and rushed forward. 'Whatever happened to you? You look awful! Where did he send you this time? No — don't bother! Sit down before you fall!'

Célie thought of the wound in his arm, but Bernave's haunted face was too sharp in her mind for anger.

Célie was profoundly grateful that Amandine was not in the kitchen. At least she might not see St Felix until they had got him warm and dry. The first thing was to see what damage there was beneath the dirt and sodden clothes. She went to get water and warm it, then a little vinegar to wash any cuts and abrasions, and wine for St Felix to drink. Marie-Jeanne disappeared to fetch him some clean clothes of Fernand's from upstairs.

Célie had the water warmed by the time Marie-Jeanne returned, followed by Madame Lacoste. Madame's face was dark and fierce, her brows drawn together, but she expressed no opinion. She could not know the urgency of the errand which had taken St Felix out. Whatever she thought of Bernave, she was too wise, or too careful to speak it aloud.

'Here!' she offered, taking the clothes from Marie-Jeanne and holding them out. Without looking at his face, she gestured to the blue jerkin and breeches St Felix had on. 'Put that lot out of the door. Let the rain clean it!'

He was too exhausted to argue, neither did he hesitate or look at her, but began to strip off. There were clean towels left where she had folded them only moments since.

He stood in the middle of the floor, shuddering, his fair skin raised in goose bumps, his face haggard, cuts and bruises dark, blood seeping red through the linen bound around his arm. He looked beaten and frightened.

Amandine came in. Her eyes went instantly to St Felix; she drew in her breath sharply, her hands clenching as if to stop herself from speaking.

Very gently Célie unwound the bandage and looked at yesterday's injury. It was angry and red, as if it had been caught by a new blow, but the bleeding was slight, and the edges of skin were still close together. The shock was that of revulsion and possibly terror more than physical damage. She could picture what must have happened. St Felix, for all the simple clothes he affected, might have seemed to someone like a gentleman. A joke would have got out of hand, became rough, and ended in a brawl. Ill feeling rose very quickly where there was drunkenness, and that strange turmoil of emotions that was in crowds these days. At last they had the power they had longed for, fought for, and yet they were still cold and hungry and just as helpless as before. The confusion turned to rage, but they did not know who or what to blame.

But far more urgent in Célie's mind than consideration of St Felix's state was whether he had succeeded in whatever Bernave had sent him to do. With less than three days left, it had to concern the King's escape, and that affected them all.

'Did you see the man Citizen Bernave wanted?' she asked him quietly as she rebandaged his arm with clean linen.

Madame Lacoste was waiting with the fresh shirt. Her black eyes shot Célie a warning look.

'Yes,' St Felix answered quietly. 'His business is agreed.'

Amandine ran her fingers through her cloud of dark hair, dragging it back off her face.

'Business!' she said with stinging contempt. 'The King is to be executed in three days, the city is on the brink of chaos, and Bernave sends you out with an injury like that — to God knows where — to conduct business!'

Madame looked at her. 'The King will be executed in two and a half days,' she corrected. 'They do these things first light in the morning. Not very long.' It was impossible to tell from her face whether she thought that a good thing or bad. There was a tension in her body so powerful Célie could only think she laboured under some fierce emotion, but it was beyond her to know what it was.

'That is all I can do.' She turned back to St Felix, tying the last knot in the bandage and moving away. She had stopped the bleeding and the bruises would mend themselves.

Madame gave him the shirt and he rose to his feet and put it on, drawing his breath in sharply as it touched his arm. Then he added the jerkin. He thanked her gravely, his eyes far away. Perhaps the horror he had seen, the violence and dirt and stupidity, still haunted him so he could see and hear it even in this quiet, candlelit kitchen with its scrubbed stone floor, the light gleaming on the pots, and the sweet, aromatic smells.

Amandine handed him a mug of hot broth from the pan, her hands shaking a little.

He met her eyes, smiling, and took it from her. All three women stood watching as he sipped it delicately, trying not to burn himself.

The door opened and Monsieur Lacoste came in, his feet wet and his hair plastered to his head and dripping.

'I couldn't find it,' he said with irritation, looking from one to another of them, his eyes lingering for a moment on St Felix, though he asked for no explanation. 'I'll try again tomorrow. I can't see a thing up there now.'

'What?' Madame asked with a frown. 'What are you looking for?'

'The leak! The leak in the roof!' he explained loudly. 'There must be a slate split.'

Madame glanced at Marie-Jeanne, then back to her husband. 'Where? It's not coming through.'

'It's not bad, but it'll get worse in this,' he replied, raising his eyes upwards.

Madame smiled at him and nodded, handing him a towel for his head. He rubbed himself briskly and gave it back to her. A moment later he went out again.

St Felix finished his soup and put down the empty cup, thanked them again, then walked awkwardly out of the kitchen. They heard his slightly limping step along the wooden boards to Bernave's study.

'Why does he allow it?' Amandine exploded savagely. She glared at Célie, then at Madame Lacoste. 'If Bernave thinks he has to do business today, then let him do it himself!'

Célie did not bother to point out that Bernave

had been out too. She could not explain where to, or why.

'These are strange times,' Madame said quietly, her face shadowed, the muscles in her neck tight as if it hurt her. 'We none of us know what another is doing, or why.'

It was an odd remark. Célie and Amandine glanced at each other. Neither was certain what to make of it. They were prevented from pursuing it by Fernand coming in, still wearing his leather carpenter's apron. He looked tired. There were heavy lines in his face. He made a quick acknowledgement of his mother, then looked around the room. 'Where is Marie-Jeanne?'

'Virginie was upset,' Madame replied. 'She was quarrelling with Antoine over something.'

'What about?' Fernand said angrily. 'What's the matter with him?'

'He doesn't know what,' she answered. 'He's frightened because everyone else is frightened.'

His face softened. 'Don't worry, Mama.' He put his arm around her in a quick, assuring gesture. 'It's all going to be all right, if we just keep quiet, keep out of sight. In a month or two it will be better. There'll be order again, and then food. They'll get rid of the speculators, and when the grain is released to the people, it'll settle down. Don't worry.' He shook his head a little and forced himself to smile. 'We've got a good house here. Bernave may be a pig to St Felix, but he's good enough to us. We're warmer than most, and we've got food.' His voice gained certainty. 'The decision has been taken. The

King will be executed, and that'll be the end of counter-revolutionaries. Marat will control the Convention and start to get things done. By spring we'll all have food, and there'll be peace again.'

She patted his hand in recognition of his intended kindness, but she said nothing, her eyes far away. There was fear and regret in her he could not reach.

* * *

The two households ate separately, as they frequently did, but after the children had gone to bed early, to keep warm, the adults went to the room at the front of the house with windows looking on to the street. The large wood-burning stove kept the air pleasant enough to be able to sit comfortably. They did not need to see, so one candle was sufficient. Even with Bernave's means, it was important to save where they could. If he chose to burn four candles in his study, that was another matter. He sat now in the shadows, his expression sombre, withdrawn into his own thoughts.

St Felix sat in one of the large chairs. He looked awkward, a little hunched to one side, protecting his arm. His expression was remote. He had a dreamer's face, fine-boned, etched with delicate lines. Célie thought that anyone seeing him had to be aware that his mind was turned inward, far from this quiet room with its worn rugs, the glimmer of polished wood and the candlelight flickering in the draughts from

81

the imperfectly fitting doors. The silence was punctuated by occasional shouts from the street beyond the dark windows, but they did not catch his attention, nor did the flaring torches as a group of men passed by along the footpath, and then returned.

Fernand, half sitting on the chest near the wall, also seemed sunk in thought, staring into space. His eyes were deep set, like his mother's, but he was fairer, gentler. Perhaps time would refine him to her strength.

Marie-Jeanne was knitting, her fingers guiding the needles by touch. It was only a simple piece of clothing, and obviously something for a child. She seemed at ease; the lines of her face were soft, in repose, close to a smile. She was not a pretty woman, but her features were such that the passing years would probably sit well on her, and with age she might even be handsome.

Madame Lacoste was sewing. She sat nearest to the candle and the light was sufficient to sew a hem to the pillowcase she was making from a worn-out sheet. She too seemed to work at least half by touch. The silver flash of the moving needle was rhythmic.

Monsieur Lacoste looked at her every now and again and the sight of her seemed to please him. The tight angles of his expression eased, but he did not speak. For once his hands were idle. Célie noticed a triangular cut where one of his chisels must have slipped. He was proud of his craft. The wood he turned was beautiful, the grain in it like satin.

Célie and Amandine sat closer to the door.

There was no sound inside the room but the occasional flicker of the candle flame, the click of Marie-Jeanne's knitting and the sharper, finer tick as Madame's needle caught against her thimble.

'They say the price of bread is going up again,' Marie-Jeanne remarked. 'Do you think when the King is dead they'll release the grain and it'll get better?'

'I don't think there is any grain,' Monsieur Lacoste replied. 'If there were, they would have released it already. Why not? The King couldn't stop them.'

'Maybe they'll do it for a celebration?' Marie-Jeanne's voice rose hopefully. 'They could be keeping it for that!'

Monsieur Lacoste growled under his breath.

Madame looked up at him questioningly.

He said nothing. His face was dark, hurt with disillusion.

A smile flickered over Bernave's face and vanished.

'It takes a while,' Madame said gently.

Lacoste stared at her, his eyes intense, black in the shadows. 'You're too patient,' he accused her, his voice raw with hurt. 'You forgive too easily. They've had three and a half years, and still there's no justice and precious little food. We expected as much of the prancing idiots at Versailles, but the revolution was to end all that!'

'It will!' Fernand turned to his father. 'Marat will see to it. First they have to get rid of the King. One thing at a time.'

'All I want is safe streets and food in the

83

shops,' Marie-Jeanne said with a sigh, turning her knitting round and beginning the next row. 'I don't care whether it's the King, or Marat or the Commune, or who it is. And I think most of the women in France feel the same. What's a revolution for if we're all still cold and hungry, and scared stiff of our neighbours in case they take a dislike to us and make a false report to some Section Leader, and the next thing you know, we're charged with something?'

Fernand started to speak, but Monsieur Lacoste cut across him. 'What we need is Robespierre in power,' he stated. 'He doesn't want anything for himself, not glory nor revenge, like Marat, nor money and the high life like Danton, nor to fritter his time away playing games at Versailles as the King used to. He doesn't even want power for himself, just the virtue of the people.' He was looking at his wife as he spoke. He was not standing particularly close to her, and yet the angle and gesture of his body seemed to suggest a unity with her, a protectiveness.

'Robespierre understands purity,' he went on urgently, his voice rising. 'There's nothing filthy in him, nothing perverted and obscene, like some of the others. You'd never think Hébert used to be a priest, or his wife a nun.' His face was heavy with disgust. 'There's the hypocrisy of the Church for you! That's one good thing the revolution's accomplished.'

Bernave looked up and spoke for the first time. 'Only a fool does away with the sacraments of God because men abuse them. Men will always need to forgive, and to be forgiven. Our sanity of soul depends on it. Otherwise there is nothing but madness and self-destruction in the end.' There was a passion in his voice for all its gentleness, although apparently Lacoste did not hear, or if he did, he did not recognise it.

'Rubbish!' he said roughly, jerking his head up. 'The whole Church was an abuse! A device created by greedy men to get power over others, and then milk them for their money and frighten them into obedience!' He glared at Bernave, daring him to contradict.

Before that could happen there was noise outside in the street, a group of people shouting. Instinctively everyone in the room looked out towards them beyond the rain-streaked window.

'They're hungry, poor devils,' Monsieur Lacoste said bitterly. 'They think we're hoarding food.'

Marie-Jeanne looked at him, frowning. 'Why should they think that? We haven't got any more than anyone else — just enough for today and tomorrow.'

'I don't know,' he replied roughly. 'Rumours. Fear. People say stupid things when they're desperate.'

More people were gathering in the street. Their voices were raised and angry. Madame looked towards the window, her hands tightening on the linen. The noise was growing louder and she turned to her husband.

There were a dozen or so torches visible beyond the glass and at least a score of people. They seemed to be in groups facing each other,

85

some waving either sticks or cutlasses.

Marie-Jeanne stopped knitting, even though she was in the middle of a row. She spiked the needle ends into the wool and put it down.

Monsieur Lacoste walked forward, peering through the dark windows at the scene beyond.

'It's nothing to worry about,' Bernave observed, remaining where he was. 'Just the usual scuffles.'

As if to mock his words a musket shot rang out about twenty yards away.

St Felix stirred, but he did not move from his place. He was the only one who seemed impassive, as if the threat had not yet broken through the shell of whatever inner grief it was that lay never far beneath the surface of his mind.

Fernand stood up and began to pace restlessly. The noise was now considerably greater, even though the shouting was indistinct, no words audible, just wild, chaotic anger, moment by moment becoming more shrill.

A National Guardsman ran across in front of the window, his uniform showing clearly in the torchlight, even to the red, white and blue cockade in his hat.

Fernand threw open the door to the outer room, letting in the cold air. 'The children'll be frightened,' he said to Marie-Jeanne. 'Go up and see they're all right.'

Monsieur Lacoste looked at him sharply, confused.

'They aren't coming in here,' Bernave said to Marie-Jeanne. 'They're just upset because of the shortages. It's the Convention they are angry with, not us. They'll get worse. You'll grow used to it.'

'Don't say that!' Fernand swung round on him, his shoes scraping on the wooden floor. 'You'll only frighten everyone, and it isn't true. It's the speculators who've caused this. Marat will get food back for the people. That's all he wants, freedom! That doesn't come for nothing! We have to fight for it, be prepared to suffer a little.'

'To hell with Marat,' Monsieur Lacoste said bitterly, gesturing towards the window. 'Those people are hungry and they're desperate. They think we've got food!'

Further argument was prevented by a volley of shots outside.

Marie-Jeanne gave a little shriek of fear, and swung round, then was uncertain what to do.

Upstairs a child's voice cried out, 'Mama! What's happening? It's wet up here! There's water coming in through the ceiling!'

Marie-Jeanne started towards the door to the stairs.

The shouting in the street seemed to be immediately outside now, and the household could see at least two score people pushing and shoving each other. Several of them seemed to be National Guardsmen, but most were ordinary citizens.

There were more shots. One whined sharply as it richocheted from the stone wall of the building not more than a dozen yards away.

Everyone in the room was on his or her feet,

even Bernave and St Felix. Célie was near the centre, facing the window; Amandine was somewhere to her left.

Torches flared scarlet and orange in the darkness outside, streaming smoke as they were waved back and forth in the surging of the quarrel.

More shots rang out in the distance, then two almost on top of the inhabitants.

They all swung round to face the street.

There was a crack and splintering of glass as the window was broken. The candle went out. Still more shots. Figures moving around. Célie saw somebody go forward, as if to the window to see, and the whole pane of glass disintegrated. He backed away, hands up, shielding his face.

Upstairs a child was screaming.

It was impossible to see anything but figures blundering about and hear the noise from the street. The cold air rushed in and the smoke from the torches stung Célie's eyes and throat. She heard coughing. Then there was a crash in the outer room as the street door flew open and hit the wall, then the thud of feet.

Someone charged over to the doorway just as it swung wide and half a dozen people jammed themselves into the space, their faces dark and their heads lit red and yellow by the flare of the torch held up behind them.

'You hoarding food?' one of them challenged.

Bernave moved forward into the glare. 'No, we're not,' he said firmly. 'Look for yourselves. The kitchen's that way,' he pointed. 'We have enough for tomorrow, that's all. We queue for it like everyone else.'

'Liar!' a woman shouted from the hallway. 'We've 'eard about you!'

'Who are you calling a liar?' Monsieur Lacoste demanded furiously. It was he who had opened the door and was now standing nearest to the woman. 'You watch your tongue!'

He took a step towards her. The light was swaying wildly. One moment everything was lit, the next it was dark.

Célie was petrified. She had no idea where everyone was, except Bernave, facing the intruders in the doorway, and she knew that only because she could hear his voice. She could not see Monsieur Lacoste any more.

More shots. Through the broken window they sounded sharp and terrifyingly close.

Someone swore under his breath as he tripped. It was impossible to be certain who, but Célie thought it was Fernand's voice.

Outside the shouting seemed to have lessened. People had moved twenty yards further down the street, towards the church of St-Germain-des-Prés.

The group in the doorway lurched forward again, angry and confused. She could not hear Bernave any more. It was almost dark. The torch had disappeared and there was no light except from the street. There was a confusion of voices.

'We have no more food than you have!' Madame said loudly, sounding to Célie as if she were almost where Bernave must have been. 'Is this what it has come to? You break into the houses of your neighbours to steal, and terrify the children? Is that what all the blood and pain has been for? We get rid of God and king so we can behave like animals, because there's no one left to stop us?'

The fury in her voice halted them, then the scalding contempt sent them backwards, into the outer room again, the torchlight flaring steady for a moment.

St Felix turned and stood beside her. Monsieur Lacoste was already moving forward to drive the invaders out, Fernand to his left.

Her hands shaking, Célie felt her way over to the table where Madame had been sewing, bumping into chairs as she went. She fumbled for the candle and tinder and struck a light, guarding it with her hand. The flame shivered up and she could see most of the room.

Marie-Jeanne was gone. There was glass over the floor, and the smoke from the torches outside was clearing. Amandine stood near the window, white-faced. St Felix was in the middle of the room, Monsieur Lacoste against the inner wall to the right of the door.

Fernand was coming back from the front door where he had seen the last of the intruders leave.

Madame stood about two yards from the doorway, motionless, her black eyes staring into nothingness. Close to her feet, almost touching her skirts, Bernave lay face down, the back of his shirt crimson with blood welling up from a wound in his heart.

4

Célie stared at Bernave, hardly able to believe what she saw. Her stomach was knotted, horror and dismay creeping over her skin like a kind of paralysis. She heard Madame Lacoste gasp. It was a strangled cry, as if someone had cut off her breath. Her face was white to the lips, her eyes black holes in her head. It might have been her own death she saw there on the floor.

St Felix looked amazed. His jaw was slack, his eyes wide and clear, highlighting the clean line of his brow.

'Is he — ' His voice broke a little. 'Is he dead?'

Célie bent to her knees and touched Bernave's neck and then his lips. They were warm, but there was no breath. She nodded, not trusting herself to speak. She looked at Amandine who was closest to her.

Amandine held her hand over her mouth, as if to prevent herself from saying anything. She forced her eyes from the still figure on the floor to St Felix, and then to the shattered window and the street beyond, now with no more than a handful of people in it. They had stopped shouting, and one or two of them were looking towards the house.

'What happened?' Fernand asked hoarsely. He followed Amandine's gaze. 'One of those bloody idiots out there shot wild, and it hit him?'

'Must have . . . ' Monsieur Lacoste spoke at

last, coming closer and taking the candle from Célie's trembling hand, and holding it in front of him to guard it from the cold air which threatened to quench it.

'I'll go and tell them what they have done,' Fernand said slowly, shaking his head a little. 'Otherwise we'll get the blame for it!' And without waiting for approval or otherwise, he went out of the door, and a moment later they saw him in the street and heard him shouting at the men still there.

Marie-Jeanne appeared in the doorway from upstairs. She saw the smashed window and felt the cold, smoky air. She was about to speak, anger darkening her face, when she realised there was something seriously wrong. She looked at her mother-in-law, then at Célie, still on her knees beside Bernave.

'Oh! Mother of God!' she breathed out, putting her hands up to her face. 'What happened? Is that my father?' Her voice caught in her throat and she lurched forward.

'Don't look!' Monsieur Lacoste said harshly, reaching out to prevent her, catching her by one arm. 'It was all over in a moment.'

Marie-Jeanne slumped into an awkward crouch beside Célie, hands stretched forward.

Célie held her, restraining her from touching the body. 'There's nothing you can do,' she told her gently. 'The rioters broke in. They thought we had food. Fernand has gone to tell them out there what they did. He'll fetch the National Guard.'

Marie-Jeanne snatched her hand away. 'Why?'

she demanded angrily. 'They can't help! Get a doctor! Dr Martineaux lives only three doors down . . . fetch him!' She looked up at Monsieur Lacoste.

Célie shook her head. 'There is no point.' She held Marie-Jeanne's arm, trying not to hurt her, but strongly enough to keep her from touching Bernave. 'He's dead.'

'What do you want the National Guard for?' Marie-Jeanne was still numb, confused. 'We don't want them in here!'

'Because he's dead.' Monsieur Lacoste bent down beside her, very grave, as became those suffering a death in the family, now that his initial shock had worn off. He touched Marie-Jeanne gently, putting one arm round her and his other hand under her elbow, helping her to her feet, lifting her weight. 'We have to show them what happened, just as it is, or else they may afterwards question it. Some busybody may blame us. After all, this is his house.'

'What?' She stared at him, uncomprehending.

He made a small, bleak gesture of irony. 'Well, I suppose as his only relative, it's yours now,' he corrected.

She gave a choked gasp. 'They couldn't think — '

'No, of course not!' he said quickly. 'We must just do it the right way, that's all. Things must be right.'

She relaxed her resistance against him, but she said nothing. Her face was filled with emotion, conflicting loss, and anger. She kept glancing back at the motionless figure on the floor, and then away again, as if she did not understand her own feelings.

Célie looked at Amandine, but she was staring at St Felix, still motionless in the middle of the room. He looked bemused, almost as if he could not fully comprehend what had happened. He did not seem able to take his eyes from Bernave. She might have wanted to go to him, but everything in his expression, the angle of his body, isolated him. He seemed to be alone with some overwhelming emotion which excluded everyone else. Even if she had touched him, it was easy to believe he would not have felt her.

Madame Lacoste was still paralysed, her face a mask.

Torches were passing in the street outside and Célie smelled the smoke of them, sharply astringent from the tar. There was a bang as the front door swung wide against the wall again, and a moment later there were three National Guardsmen in the room, followed by Fernand. Two of them stopped by the door; the third, a slender man, neat and straight, came forward to where Bernave lay. He had fairish hair, falling a little forward over his brow and his wide eyes were pale, but it was impossible to see of what colour in the wavering light.

He stared down at Bernave, then at the window, then very slowly he looked at each of their faces.

'They broke in,' Fernand said, pointing to the street, then to the hallway. 'They thought we had food. But I suppose you know that . . . ' He stopped.

'Menou,' the man introduced himself. 'Yes, I was there. They're half starved, poor devils. Willing to steal from anyone they think is hoarding.' His face darkened as he looked down at Bernave again. 'Bad business.' He turned to the window, squinting a little against the sting of smoke from the torches as it drifted in on a gust of icy air.

Everyone in the room watched him. No one offered anything else to say.

Menou walked slowly over to the body and squatted down beside it, regarding the wound with a frown, then very gently he turned Bernave over.

Célie did not want to look at Bernave's face. He had been so vividly alive, it seemed an intrusion now to stare at him when he was no longer there, the flesh so vulnerable without him.

Menou raised his head and looked at them each in turn.

St Felix was the first to speak.

'It must have been one of the men who broke in,' he said huskily. His voice sounded odd, lacking in timbre. Célie guessed how shocked he was, yet it could hardly be grief. He must have hated Bernave for the way he treated him.

Marie-Jeanne sat down heavily in one of the chairs. She was obviously close to tears. Her face was flushed and her lips trembling.

Fernand went to her and put his arm around her shoulders.

'He won't have felt anything,' he said quietly. 'He won't have known.'

She buried her head in his shoulder, clinging

on to him. Her body shook with sobs, but curiously she made no sound.

Menou hesitated. For a moment ordinary human grief such as touched people in Paris, or anywhere else, was more real than issues of belief, loyalties to revolution or aristocracy, questions of blame for riots, hoarding or carelessness.

'One of the men who broke in,' Menou repeated thoughtfully. 'Did they have guns? Who saw a shot inside here?' He searched their faces.

Monsieur Lacoste drew in his breath, then apparently changed his mind and let it out again without speaking.

Menou waited.

There had been no shots inside, Célie knew that. And worse, Bernave had been facing the crowd in the doorway, not with his back to them. They were intruders, angry and desperate men who had broken into his house. He would never have turned away from them, leaving himself so exposed.

'Citizeness?' Menou prompted. 'A flash? A report?' he looked at Madame.

'No . . . ' she said slowly, her voice a dry whisper. 'Not in here . . . '

Menou looked at St Felix.

'I didn't see . . . ' he admitted. 'There was confusion — shouting . . . '

'Threatening?' Menou asked, his eyes wide.

'Yes,' St Felix agreed. 'They thought we were hoarding food.'

'We aren't,' Fernand put in. 'We have no more than anybody else.'

'Did they have weapons?' Menou would not let go.

'Of course they had weapons!' Monsieur Lacoste said exasperatedly. 'They killed Citizen Bernave, didn't they?'

Menou stood still in the middle of the room, frowning. 'Men, armed with weapons, broke into the house determined to find the food they thought you had, threatening you in this room . . . '

'Yes,' St Felix and Monsieur Lacoste agreed together.

'Citizen Bernave went towards them and told them — what?' Menou asked, his eyebrows raised.

'That we had no extra food, and that they should leave, or something like that,' Fernand answered.

'And did they?'

'You know they didn't!' Monsieur Lacoste snapped.

Menou stared at him. 'But he turned his back on them?' he said slowly, his eyes still wide.

Célie was shivering. The room had lost all the heat through the gaping window, but it was not that which chilled her, it was the knowledge inside her hardening like stone. She knew which way he had faced, and what it meant.

'I think not,' Menou said slowly. 'I think Citizen Bernave would never have turned his back on armed intruders in his house. No man would!'

Amandine was rigid. She too had understood what Célie had known. It was written in the fierce angles of her body and the pallor of her skin in the candlelight. She was staring at St Felix.

Madame seemed past caring. Her face was gaunt, her cheeks hollow, eyes black, her brows too straight, her whole bearing too dark, too fierce, for loveliness. Only her mouth was beautiful, Célie thought, all the pain in the world etched in its lines.

'You see my logic, Citizeness,' Menou said calmly, dragging her attention back. 'I am afraid it is inescapable. Bernave was killed by someone standing behind him — someone at his back, where he expected no danger . . . '

'None of us has a gun!' Fernand protested. 'That's ridiculous!'

'I can see that,' Menou nodded, his lips tight.

They stared at him in disbelief.

'We assumed it was a shot, because we heard them fired,' Menou went on in the silence. 'But it could as easily have been a knife . . . a thick-bladed, narrow knife, plunged in from the back.'

Amandine jerked her hands up to her mouth, stifling a gasp.

Fernand held Marie-Jeanne closer.

St Felix sank very slowly on to the edge of one of the chairs. It was an awkward position, neither sitting nor standing. Célie could see only his profile. His expression was curious: passionate but unreadable. It seemed a strange mixture of relief — and utter and final loss. Except that that made no sense. It must be exhaustion, and the light.

Madame Lacoste spoke. Now her voice was surprisingly steady, except for the thickness in it, as though her throat were so tight it nearly choked her. 'You are saying that one of us murdered him!'

Menou looked at her unblinkingly. 'Yes, Citizeness, that is exactly what I am saying. And I intend to find out who, because Citizen Bernave was a loyal friend of the revolution, a man who worked tirelessly and secretly for justice, without seeking any reward for himself. His murderer must be punished.'

No one answered him. Célie stared round at their faces. Who could believe such a thing? It was the complete opposite of the truth! But of course no one else knew that. No one knew he was planning to rescue the King, and that the mission would all crumble to the ground without his knowledge and skill, and courage. He had been exquisitely careful, even to the minutest detail precisely because he knew the price of exposure.

Fernand's surprise was obvious, but it was almost immediately followed by relief, a sort of dawning amazement as if he were seeing Bernave for the first time.

Célie turned to Monsieur Lacoste, but he was further from the torches so his expression was thrown into shadow and half-profile, his features blurred.

'Was he?' he said, not a question but a comment on an irrelevance.

St Felix started to speak, and then changed his mind.

Menou saw it and looked at him sharply. 'You were going to say something, Citizen?'

'Only that we did not know that,' St Felix replied levelly. 'He was very discreet. We had no idea.'

'I hope not.' Menou made the words portentous and he turned his clear, bright eyes on each of them. 'Because, of course, if you did, it might give us cause to doubt your loyalty.'

'We are all ardent supporters of the revolution in this house!' Monsieur Lacoste said vehemently, and there was far more anger in his voice than fear. 'You insult us, Citizen Menou. Is it not enough that your men cannot control the crowds in the street, and they break into our house and — ' He stopped abruptly. It was impossible to read his face.

'Yes, Citizen?' Menou prompted. 'You were going to say 'and kill our benefactor'. Then you remembered that it was one of you in here, one of your loyal revolutionaries, who did that.'

'I . . . ' Lacoste was lost for an answer.

It was Marie-Jeanne who replied. 'He was not our benefactor,' she contradicted Menou. 'He was my father, and in return for living here we looked after him and kept the house. You speak as if he were a stranger, and that's not true.'

Menou glanced around, eyes appreciative. 'A large house. Sufficient for many people,' he remarked. He looked back at Marie-Jeanne. 'Who inherits it now, Citizeness? Are there any other relatives — you have brothers?'

Suddenly she realised her own predicament and her voice wavered. 'No.'

'None at all?'

'No. I was the only child, and my mother died when I was born.'

'A nice inheritance, Citizeness. Your father must have been a very wealthy man.'

They all caught the edge of criticism in his voice, perhaps of envy also. Property of any sort was a contentious matter these days.

Marie-Jeanne stiffened, but it was Madame Lacoste who answered, her head high, eyes burning.

'He worked hard and he saved to buy a house that many people could live in. That was his wish. Is it not what you would expect from a good revolutionary, Citizen Menou? To shelter the homeless, in return for work, and dignity?' She looked at him without a shred of fear.

Menou was taken aback. It showed naked for a moment in his eyes, then it was gone, deliberately masked, as if it were something he was ashamed of.

'Yes, Citizeness,' he agreed. 'He was a fine man. I will see that justice is done for him, don't doubt it. His murderer will go to the guillotine, along with all other traitors to the people.'

Célie stared at him. Did he really think it was political? It could be, but for the very opposite of the reasons he believed. Fernand and Monsieur Lacoste were ardent enough in their support of the new way to have betrayed Bernave, if they had known he was fighting to save the King's life. They would not have understood his reasons. Marie-Jeanne did not care one way or the other, but she would have killed to save her children. Placid as she seemed, Célie knew her well enough to understand that. She had seen the animal fury and courage in her when a soldier had tried to be vulgarly intimate with her small daughter. She had reacted instantly and without the slightest thought of consequence to herself. The soldier had been taken totally by surprise, and backed off as if his pet dog had suddenly sunk its teeth into his hand.

St Felix cleared his throat and looked enquiringly at Menou. 'What did Citizen Bernave do for the revolution? We should be proud of it.'

'Yes, you should,' Menou agreed fervently. 'He risked his life spying among royalists for the Commune. There are those, even at this late day, who would attempt to restore the King and undo everything that had been achieved. Never underestimate the enemy! The sooner the King is dead the better.'

Everyone murmured some kind of assent. It was not a comment one could allow to pass unanswered. Only Madame merely nodded.

St Felix was staring into the distance. He looked exhausted of all emotion, even of thought. Amandine was watching him. She was trying to seem impassive, hide her feelings from Menou, but Célie knew her well enough to see the fear under her paper-thin veneer of calm. It was in the angle of her shoulders, the tightly held fists only half concealed by the folds of her skirt, and in the muscles of her neck where her hair was swept back. It was St Felix she was afraid for, not herself.

Célie was impelled to break the silence. She stepped forward a fraction.

'Thank you for telling us, Citizen Menou. We had no idea that he was so brave. We shall honour his memory the more, and do all we can to help you secure justice . . . at least, I suppose all except one . . . if you are sure that it has to be someone in this house who killed him?'

He stood still in the lantern light, his face tired, his pale uniform breeches scuffed with dirt.

'I am sure, Citizeness. There is no other answer possible.' He looked round at all of them. 'I can do no more tonight.' He drew in his breath. 'Except of course search the house for the weapon that killed him.'

If he had hoped for a reaction, he was disappointed. No one moved.

'Naturally,' Madame Lacoste said very quickly. 'After that, may we board up the window? It is extremely cold.'

'And mend the leak in the roof?' Monsieur Lacoste added. 'The rain is coming through the ceiling into the children's room.'

'Of course,' Menou agreed. He turned to his men and signalled them to begin the search. 'Be thorough!' he warned. He held up his hands. 'A knife about so long, and narrow enough to make a wound that looks like that of a sword bayonet. It is here somewhere — no one has been out.'

They waited all together in the room, now freezing, except Fernand, who was permitted to go and fetch boards and nails from the workshop in the courtyard and make a rudimentary covering for the window. Menou went with him, and returned with him. Monsieur Lacoste lit a lantern and went up into the roof again to look for the broken slate and replace it. One of Menou's men went with him as far as the attic window, but not out on to the slippery ledge in the rain.

Half an hour after they had begun, the other National Guardsmen came back to report that they had not found any knife, except the one Amandine used in the kitchen, and that had far too broad a blade, and anyway, it was perfectly clean. They were obviously disappointed, and expecting criticism.

Menou gave it in his looks, but he abandoned the issue for the night, warning the household that he was leaving guards posted in the street, and they had better not attempt to dispose of the weapon, because they would be watched. Anyone caught doing so would be arrested immediately. He did not need to add that hardly anyone arrested escaped without some punishment, usually death. They all knew that.

When he was gone the household turned to stare at each other.

'Did you know he was spying for the Commune?' Monsieur Lacoste demanded from Fernand.

'No!' Fernand's voice rose. 'I thought he despised them!' He turned to St Felix, his face darkening. 'Did you? I suppose that was all those errands you ran for him, to Marat and the like. Who roughed you up, then? Or did they do that to hide what you were really doing?'

104

St Felix did not answer.

'Why should they?' Monsieur Lacoste argued. 'There's no sin in helping the Commune. It's any good person's duty. No one but a royalist, an enemy of the revolution, would condemn you for that.'

'It doesn't matter now,' Madame cut across them. 'He's dead. Citizen Menou won't rest until he knows who killed him, and he believes it was one of us.'

'He didn't find a knife,' Monsieur Lacoste pointed out. 'We couldn't have done it without one.'

She looked at him with contempt. 'That won't stop him. He'll be back tomorrow, and the next day, and the day after that, until he has someone.'

Célie knew it was true. If Menou believed Bernave had been a loyal revolutionary, then he would not rest until he had caught whoever was responsible. And she had an idea from his face and his manner that he was not a man to let a puzzle go unsolved. His pride would rest on achieving this kind of victory, the more so since he had now laid his reputation on it in front of his own men.

'Well, was it one of us?' Marie-Jeanne asked, sniffing and blinking several times. 'It couldn't be. Why would we?'

No one answered, each absorbed in his or her own thoughts.

'That is a question better not asked,' Madame Lacoste answered her. 'You should go upstairs and see that the children are all right. Change the bedding, now the roof is mended. You'll have to tell them in the morning what has happened. Célie will help me.'

'Help you . . . '

'Well, I'm not going to leave . . . Citizen Bernave . . . lying on the floor!' For the first time her voice cracked and she took a moment to regain control of herself.

'I'm sorry . . . ' Marie-Jeanne stood undecided.

'Go on!' Madame shooed her, waving her hands sharply. 'We don't need your help.' She turned to her husband and St Felix. 'We can manage. We only need you to carry him. Then you can go.' Obediently the others went out, feet dragging a little, weariness and shock making them clumsy. Fernand glanced a last time at his mother, then closed the door behind him.

Célie felt numb, as if the cold had eaten into her bones. Now in the silence the reality of death surged back, enormous, engulfing her. A chasm had opened up where Bernave's will and vitality had been, his passion, above all his belief.

Madame looked as if she too were dead. Something had gone from inside her. She bent and slid her hands under Bernave's shoulders. Monsieur Lacoste stepped forward and took most of his weight, St Felix the rest. Célie followed behind them.

It was an awkward job to carry the limp body through to the back room, which was out of the way of ordinary domestic use, and certainly the coldest. They laid him on his back on the bench that ran along the wall, and stood away quickly.

Monsieur Lacoste's hands were smeared with blood and he wiped them hard on his thighs, almost scraping them. Fernand shuddered. They were both uncomfortable, not knowing what else to say or do.

Madame dismissed them abruptly, barely thanking them, and as she closed the door after them, turned to Célie.

'Help me wash him and lay him out,' she commanded. 'He must have a proper burial. He was a man of position.' Her mouth twisted with an anguished irony, pain so close under the surface it seemed any moment her self-mastery must snap. 'Anyway, if he was a hero of the revolution, it would be unwise of us to do less for him.' Her voice cracked and Célie thought she was going to laugh or to weep, but she made a painfully visible effort, and the moment after her face was immobile again.

'I'll get clean linen,' Célie offered quietly. 'We can spare a good sheet. After all, they are his!'

They worked together for some time, neither speaking. It was a strange task. The spirit, the mind and reality of Bernave was no longer in any way present in the dead flesh, but it still felt intrusive to touch him so intimately. An hour ago this had been a man full of passion, intelligence and will to succeed, loved or hated, certainly feared. They would never have presumed to touch him then. Had they but known it, the fate of all of them rested on his courage and the quickness of his mind. Now his hands lay limp and the warmth was already leaving his flesh. There was nothing of life left.

Looking at Madame Lacoste's face, the gentleness of her fingers, Célie wondered whether her reverence was for Bernave himself, or for the fact of death. Perhaps it was some suppressed respect for religious faith. Célie had never known her before it had become illegal to believe in God. Maybe she had been devout then, like so many women.

They washed the blood away. Bernave's body was powerful, the muscles lean, no spare flesh. Célie was startled to see the white ridges of more scars on his back and across his chest. She looked up at Madame, and saw no surprise, but a tight, hard rage that made her hands shake so badly for a moment she had to stop and regain control of herself.

Menou was right, the mark of the knife was clear — not round like a shot.

'Could it be one of us?' The question was out of Célie's lips before she could think better of it.

Madame looked at her, her black eyes so deep as to be unreadable.

'St Felix had no love for him,' she said quietly. 'Nor Amandine either, because of St Felix. And it depends if Bernave was really a friend of the Commune, and if he was, who knew of it. Perhaps you? You ran enough errands for him.'

'I . . . ' Célie stopped. She had no idea how much Madame Lacoste knew, or where her loyalties lay . . . presumably to her husband. Now, suddenly everyone was suspect. It would be foolish to trust, even suicidal. She changed what she had been going to say. 'I see what you mean,' she answered instead.

Madame Lacoste almost smiled, and in the candlelight Célie saw her eyes were brimming with tears, but she did not know for whom.

5

As soon as the house was quiet, although there was no way of knowing whether everyone was asleep or not, Célie got up out of bed and dressed in a blouse, petticoat, her heaviest skirt and two shawls. She opened her bedroom door and then closing it silently behind her, crept to the stairs. She must tell Georges of Bernave's death. It changed everything. He was the only one who knew all of the plan, the places and details, the people. He had not only been the force behind it, but also the intelligence. And he had been the only one with money, if it were needed.

Georges would be frantic, imprisoned as he was, and unable to help. Could they salvage anything now? Or was this defeat?

She was at the bottom of the first flight and about to go down the next when she caught a glimpse of movement on the edge of her vision, and turned quickly.

Amandine was standing in the doorway, her hair loose and tangled, her eyes dark-smudged with exhaustion.

Célie went over to her and half pushed her back into the room, closing the door again.

'I must see Georges,' she whispered. 'I must tell him what's happened.'

'You can't get out,' Amandine replied fiercely, holding on to Célie's arm as if she would prevent her by force. 'Menou left guards outside.'

'I know,' Célie told her. 'I've thought of a way. Don't worry.'

'What?' The fear was sharp in Amandine's voice, even though she did not move. 'Be careful! Do you have to go? Can't you leave it until all this is over?'

Célie hesitated. She knew Amandine's anxiety for her, and her love for Georges. The truth was bitter, but she did not deserve lies, at least not about this.

'When do you think that will be?' she said quietly. 'It could be days — or longer — before Menou finds out what happened. And he won't go until he does. We can't wait for that!'

'It must have been — ' Amandine stopped. There was only one small candle burning in the room, on the table over near the bed, casting shadows on the rumpled sheets, but even so it showed the fear in her eyes. 'It must have been Fernand who killed him . . . or Monsieur Lacoste . . . I suppose,' she finished. There was so much more to say and they both understood it: the tearing away of old beliefs and nothing to put in their place; people you thought you knew who were too frightened to be loyal, and too confused to be honest.

'I have to tell Georges,' Célie repeated. How could she explain that it was so much more than merely murder, enormous as that was? This was bigger than any one man's death. Everything of the future might rest on it, the execution of the King and all that would follow in its wake, the fall of the Girondins, more power for Marat and the Commune, even worse chaos in the streets and less food, further riots, and quite soon something as terrible as war.

'I'll be careful,' she whispered. 'Stay here — don't waken anyone else.' She turned to the door and without giving Amandine the chance to argue, she went out on to the landing and back up the stairs again, towards the attic. Amandine was right about getting out. Every way that led to the courtyard and the street would be watched by Menou's men, and she would inevitably be caught. She must leave from the door of another house. The only way to do that was to climb out of one of the windows on to the roof, and in through someone else's, perhaps even as far as one of those at the back which faced on to the Rue de Seine.

It was difficult and far more dangerous than she had foreseen. Getting out of the window was not too hard, but once outside the slates were slippery with ice. Her hands were so cold she could barely feel them. And skirts were definitely highly impractical garments in which to do almost anything, certainly crawl up over angled roofs, heave herself over the ridges and slither recklessly and too fast down the other side. At least the roofs had wide valleys between one pitch and the next. Only a blind, overwhelming necessity compelled her to keep trying one window after another, prying at them with numb fingers and cursing under her breath. In the end she was delighted to get in through the first one she could pull open from the outside, and find the room unoccupied.

112

The people in the house must have been sufficiently used to noises through the night, alarms in the street and perhaps family members up for their own reasons, that no one seemed disturbed by her tiptoeing feet down the stairs, feeling her way to the front door and at last outside into the Rue de Seine.

She went as quickly as she dared in the near dark, knowing the way so well now that she could almost have counted the paces.

When she got to Georges' door she knocked sharply and waited with her heart pounding. She felt as if light and warmth would be inside, but that was absurd. It would scarcely be any better than the street.

Nothing happened. Panic rose inside her in case he was not there. She banged again, more loudly, bruising her knuckles.

There was a sound inside.

Without realising it she had clenched her fists, her body rigid.

The door opened and Georges' voice came in a whisper.

'Who is it?'

'Me, Célie!' she said urgently.

His hand came out of the darkness, felt for a second, then gripped her arm, pulling her in. He closed the door.

'What the hell are you doing here at this time of the night?' he demanded.

She could feel the warmth of his body. He had been asleep and was wearing no more than a shirt and hastily pulled on breeches.

'Bernave is dead,' she answered, trying to see

113

his face in the solid blackness of the room.

'What?'

'Bernave is dead,' she repeated sharply. 'Someone stabbed him. At first we thought it was an accident, now we know it couldn't have been. That's the worst of it, or almost. It was one of us!'

He said nothing. He must have been too stunned to speak.

'Georges!'

'Yes . . . I hear you.' His voice was low, almost a growl.

He was still so close she could smell his skin and the warmth of him.

'Put something on,' she whispered. 'You'll freeze.'

He did not move. 'What happened?' he asked. She could hear the shock in him. He must feel, as she had, that same numb disbelief.

'Put something on! I'll tell you,' she responded.

He stepped away at last, fumbling to find the candle and light it. The flame sprang up, showing the horror in his face, the shadows around his eyes, the dark stubble on his cheeks. He looked bewildered as he put on a second shirt and then a doublet. It was the first time she had ever seen him at a loss. Even at the beginning of the September Massacres, when the screaming, drunken crowd had swept them along and at last torn them apart from each other, he did not seem to have lost his instinctive confidence. She had expected him always to be like that: suave, sure, believing in himself. It was part of what she

114

liked most about him, and at the same time it angered her because it made him different from everyone else she had known, and unreachable.

Now it was gone. He looked as frightened as she was. His hand holding the candle was shaking.

She took it from him. Her hand was steadier. She had had longer to get used to the news.

'What happened?' he asked again.

She sat down in the single chair.

He sat on the mattress opposite her, hugging his arms around himself as if he were chilled, or wounded, watching her face while she recounted to him bitterly and with defensive sarcasm, exactly what she could remember, up to the point when the National Guard had come.

'National Guard?' he said quickly.

'Yes. The leader's name is Menou. He's investigating what happened, and he won't go away until he has the answer.'

'You mean until he finds which one of the intruders fired the shot?'

'No.' Her voice was flat, without life or timbre. She could hear the fear in it herself. 'Bernave was standing facing the men who broke in after the shots in the street. I saw him, and so did the others. Anyway, only an idiot would have turned his back to that crowd.'

He stared at her, frowning, at first not comprehending the meaning. Then it came to him.

'It was someone in the room?' His voice was hoarse. 'Someone behind him!' He looked bruised, as though he had been hit harder than he had ever expected or felt before, and he did not know how to accommodate the hurt.

She nodded, refusing to allow herself sympathy for him, or at least not so he could see. It made her too vulnerable herself, and she could not afford it. 'There isn't any other possibility,' she agreed more steadily. 'If the shooting hadn't stopped outside, or Bernave hadn't faced them down, if they'd been braver, or angrier and surged around him, we would never have known. Whoever murdered him would have got away with it.'

He looked at her earnestly, his face crumpled. 'Do you know who it was, Célie?'

She hesitated. If only there were any way to protect him from the blow, but there wasn't.

'What?' he asked urgently, his voice sharp. Her face with its clearly defined bones and wide mouth had always been too easily readable. 'Who was it?' he demanded.

She shook her head a little. 'It isn't that. I don't know who killed him. But Menou said he was determined to find out who it was because Bernave was a loyal supporter of the revolution.' She swallowed and licked her dry lips. 'He said Bernave had been a spy for the Commune, against the royalists still planning to restore the King.'

He stared at her, slowly comprehending the full meaning of what she had said.

She longed to see his confidence return. She waited for him to deny that Menou could find evidence that would betray them. Then like ice in the pit of her stomach, for the first time the

116

realisation came that Menou could be right. Of course he would never find proof that Bernave had actually been working to save the King, to prevent invasion and civil war, because there was no proof! Not for Menou . . . and not for them either!

How could Georges' confidence return — now, or ever? To be sure after this would be incomprehensible . . . insane. Who knew what the truth was, except that Bernave was dead and one of them had killed him?

Instinctively Célie reached forward and touched Georges' hand with her cold fingers. She had no idea what to say or do. One lunge with a knife . . . and everything was changed. The whole struggle had become hopeless. She tightened her fingers a little, holding on to him.

Then suddenly she realised what she was doing and withdrew quickly.

There was so much that needed to be spoken of, sitting hunched up in this icy attic. Climbing over the roofs and creeping through someone else's house she had been too frightened to think of physical discomfort, but now she was aware of how cold she was. It seemed to fill her body and she was starting to shake.

Georges was still too stunned to be aware of anything but the horror in his own mind. For the first time since she had met him at Amandine's house, nearly a year ago, there was no guard in his eyes, no mask, of laughter or bravado. Suddenly the real man was there, and she was sharply conscious of it.

'Could Bernave have been working for the

117

Commune?' He searched her face. 'Is it possible? Why haven't we all been arrested?'

'Not very dramatic.' She defended herself behind a black humour. 'I'd wait until the last moment, if it were me. Watch us until we try to rescue the King, and then take us all, when it's too late for anyone else to step in. If you're going to make a great gesture, do it when everyone's looking. No glory, otherwise, and Marat would never sacrifice a chance of that!'

He said nothing, but she could see he understood.

'We can't warn the others, Bernave's men,' she went on. She had to talk, tell him everything. 'We don't even know who they are. Only he knew that.'

The humour flashed in his eyes as well. 'I suppose we don't really know that they haven't been arrested already!'

She drew breath to tell him not to say such a thing, then let it out in a sigh. Was she glad the laughter was back in him again? Was it hope — or a mask, like hers?

'I don't know how we can succeed now,' she answered instead. 'I don't even know how far he got . . . '

Georges smiled, but faintly, a ghost of the way it used to be. 'What is this man Menou like?'

'Revolutionary,' she replied. 'He won't give up until he arrests someone.' Menou's calm, keen face came back to her mind, and the strength in it. 'He can't,' she added. 'He's already committed himself to saying it matters. His men heard him. And if Bernave really was working for

118

the Commune, then they will certainly want revenge. I expect Marat himself will demand it.' The thought was sickening. She pushed it away. 'But I can't believe that!' she said firmly. 'Not Bernave! He wasn't . . . ' she tailed off.

What did she really know of him? She had never even heard of him until four months ago. She had only ever seen him in the house in the Boulevard St-Germain. Apart from Georges, she knew no one he knew, except St Felix, and the Lacostes, and of course Amandine. She knew nothing of Bernave beyond what he had wished her to know, perhaps what he had deliberately shown her. And how much of that was true!

Without thinking about it consciously, or remembering why, she had formed the belief that there was some unspoken pain in his past, an old grief which had called on all his reserves of courage and hope to sustain him through it. Perhaps that was why he still kept the Thomas à Kempis, and other books like it, remembrances of an older faith.

Or maybe she had only imagined it, reading something into his face which was not there, into the scars on his hands and body, because of her own hunger for the certainties that would have comforted her. Maybe there was no corresponding reality, and never had been.

'Bernave wasn't what?' Georges' voice interrupted her thoughts, demanding she return to the present.

'I don't know,' she admitted. 'I was going to say 'anything like Marat or the Communards'. But I don't think I know very much at all.'

119

'Except that Menou won't let go until he finds out who killed him,' he answered for her.

'Then that means I've got to get him a solution.' The realisation was appalling, but inescapable. 'He's going to watch the house. He posted a guard in the street this evening.'

Georges stiffened. It was the first sign of physical fear she had seen in him. He must feel trapped here. Every sound, every footstep on the stair had to set his nerves jangling.

'He didn't see me!' she said quickly.

'How do you know?' He was only half looking at her, his head turned to catch any movement in the darkness beyond the door.

'Because I didn't go out on to the Boulevard St-Germain,' she explained. 'I didn't go anywhere near it until past the church.'

He was confused. 'You have to! There's no other way out.'

'Yes there is.'

'What?'

'Out of the attic window and in through one that was open, down their stairs and out into the Rue de Seine, then along the Rue Jacob.'

His eyes widened with incredulity. 'You went over the roofs! You're crazy!' Now there was fear in him — for her. 'Célie, you could have slipped and been killed! If you'd been hurt, no one would have found you! You'd have frozen to death up there. Never again, do you hear me?'

'Yes, of course I hear you,' she said with a sharp shiver of satisfaction. 'And I shall do as I please.' She leaned forward, cutting off argument. 'Georges, one of us in that house killed

Bernave. I don't know for what reason, but it could be anything. I thought I knew more or less what we all believed, but perhaps I don't! Maybe one of them is secretly a royalist?' She ignored the disbelief in his face. 'Or they can see what we can of the dangers if they execute the King, and if they knew Bernave was really working for the Commune . . . ' She left the rest unsaid. The conclusion was obvious.

A gust over the rooftops rattled the window, sending an icy draft through the cracks.

'St Felix?' he said with surprise. 'Wasn't he the only one who knew anything about what Bernave was doing?'

'I think so,' she agreed. 'Anyway, neither Fernand nor Citizen Lacoste have any sympathy with aristos, let alone the King.'

'Neither have I,' Georges said quietly. There was a regret in him, a sadness he would not name or explore. 'I just think executing him is only going to make things worse.'

Célie remembered the lands he had spoken of with such haunting loss. It was part of all the old way which was gone for ever.

'Citizen Lacoste is for Robespierre,' she reasoned aloud, watching Georges' face and wishing she understood more, and yet also afraid to. 'But he wouldn't be against anyone spying on royalists. And Fernand is for the Commune and Marat. He thinks they are going to be the saviours of us all.'

'God help us!' he said bitterly. 'And don't tell me not to speak of God! I might as well be hanged for a sheep as a lamb.' But his brief

121

half-smile vanished as if it had never been. 'What about Madame Lacoste?'

Célie tried to think back to ever hearing Madame speak of any political belief, even to seeing a reaction in her face to news of victories or reverses in any cause, but no sharp image came to her mind, no emotion over any of it, except pity or exasperation. With Madame it was individuals who mattered, not causes. There had been moments of regret for something she must have lost in the past, but there was no anger or surprise left. Whatever it was, she had accepted it long ago. She cared intensely for her family, but the rest was private. Célie did not even know what she had felt for Bernave. Something powerful, deeply hidden. She had assumed it was resentment for her family's dependence upon him, and fear in case he failed them, intentionally or not.

Then Célie remembered the tenderness with which Madame had washed his dead body, and laid it in peace. But that could have been religious faith, or the pity of a good woman for any death.

'I don't believe it . . . ' she began slowly.

'What do you know about her?' he pressed.

'I suppose nothing. I just remember the way she looked when she saw Bernave dead. She and Marie-Jeanne were the only ones who were grieved. And . . . and me.' Honesty compelled that. 'I liked him, in spite of the way he treated St Felix.'

His face shadowed. 'St Felix?'

'Yes . . . he gave him all the worst errands, the

122

most unpleasant and dangerous. I don't think I would have gone, not at the times and to the places he sent him.'

'Such as?' Georges pressed.

'Going to give messages . . . ' only now did she realise the import of what she was saying, ' . . . to men in the Sections . . . and the Commune. To do with getting the King out of the city. Marat's men . . . ' She looked at his face, trying to read it. She saw the quick leap of fear and it made her feel sick. 'Two or three times he's come back beaten.' She dropped her voice to little more than a whisper. 'Last time one of the mobs drifting around got hold of him. He really was hurt.'

'When?'

'Yesterday, the same day Bernave was killed. Do you think he found out that Bernave was spying for both sides . . . or the wrong side?'

'What else do you know about St Felix?' Georges persisted. 'Apart from the fact that Bernave seemed to trust him? Who is he? Where does he come from? How did Bernave know him?'

This time she thought for several moments before she answered, again trying to remember, disentangle facts from impressions. She was barely aware of how cold she was. She was clenched inside and her fingers were numb.

'He came a little after Amandine and I did, towards the end of October,' she answered slowly. 'He just turned up one day. Bernave obviously knew him already, but it seemed as if

123

they had not met for many years. Bernave was surprised, I'd swear to that. It was clear in his face. There was something about St Felix he did not expect, but he never said what, and I have no idea. St Felix's wife had died. Laura, I think her name was. He seemed very grieved about it, although I don't think it had just happened. Maybe a year ago. He still looked very distressed. I don't know if he had lost his home or the revolution had taken it, or why it was he didn't stay there.'

She struggled to visualise clearly the fleeting moments she had seen his face in repose, unguarded. She had felt an intense loneliness about him, as if the past returned to him and he could no longer keep at bay the loss and the regret which engulfed him. It had hurt her to see it, for him, and for Amandine, because it seemed no one could touch it.

'Where was it?' he asked. 'His home?'

'I don't know. He hardly ever speaks of it. Maybe the memory was too painful. I gathered the impression he simply wanted to leave the place where he and his wife had been so happy. I think I can understand that.' She tried to imagine loving someone so completely, knowing a time without blemish when everything that truly mattered could be shared, good and ill, laughter and beauty and pain. And then the unbearable loneliness when that person was gone . . . probably for ever, if there really were no God. Perhaps you could not endure to stay in that place. It should be left, a perfect memory, never without the one you had loved, never spoiled by anything that happened afterwards.

And it was easy to think of St Felix feeling like that. In her mind Célie could see his face with its sadness, and the elusive emotion in it that no one in the Boulevard St-Germain seemed able to touch. Perhaps Amandine came the closest, but the core of it escaped even her. There was a secret heart of St Felix, a memory or a dream, that he never shared. Its presence was in his eyes even when he laughed.

Georges was waiting for her to continue. He was watching her, sitting in an echo of the same hunched position she was, the blanket huddled around him as her cloak was around her.

'I don't know,' she said at last. 'It's a part of him he keeps locked away, perhaps so nothing will spoil it.'

'That doesn't tell us much,' he pointed out bleakly. 'When it comes to facts, it could be anything.'

She was afraid St Felix had killed Bernave, not for any political reason, but because he hated him for the danger and humiliation he put him through.

'What?' Georges demanded, reading her face. 'You thought of something.'

There was no point in not telling him. 'What if it was simply anger at the way Bernave used him?' she asked.

'Then why did he allow it?' he countered.

'I don't know! Anyone else would have refused ages ago, but he never did. It didn't matter what Bernave asked him to do, even if it was raining, or it was the middle of the night, he never refused. He never even complained. I don't know why.'

'Because he believed in the cause just as passionately as Bernave himself,' Georges answered for her.

She did not voice the other reason that occurred to her with swift and ugly clarity.

He did, precisely as if he had heard it in her mind. 'Or else Bernave had some power over him, a way of forcing him to do whatever he wanted, and that St Felix could not deny. Until last night.' He peered at her, searching her eyes to see what she thought of it.

The wind gusted against the glass again and spattered it with sleet.

'I suppose so,' she conceded. 'I . . . I can't think of St Felix like that. He seems . . . ' She lowered her eyes. 'Amandine is in love with him. If he killed anyone, it would be for a . . . a better cause than to escape coercion.' She looked up, confident again. 'If Bernave were forcing him to do something he felt was wrong, he'd have stood up to him and refused in the first place, not now after months.'

He put his head in his hands and rubbed his eyes slowly. In the silence she heard the faint rasp of his palms against his unshaven chin.

'God! What a mess!' he sighed. 'I believed Bernave completely. I never doubted him. It seems absurd, but there was so much else to care about.'

'There still is,' she assured him. 'And now Bernave is dead we've lost the only person who knew the whole plan, and all the people.'

He looked up at her. 'Are you prepared to go on alone . . . if we can?'

'Without Bernave?' Célie thought of all the things they would have to learn: who was prepared to take the King's place, how they could contact him. Who else knew the details and could betray them. What would have to be changed, for safety, how they would do it in time.

Georges was watching her, his dark eyes wide. 'If we don't the King dies, and we plunge into even worse chaos than this . . . and war,' he said. 'The risks will be higher. We'll have to change everything Bernave knew the details of, in case Menou was right and he told the Commune.'

The full enormity of it struck her, almost choking her breath. 'They'll be expecting some attempt! They'll double the guard, and wait for us!'

'Of course,' he agreed. 'We'll have to move earlier on the route than we planned before. I never told him where the safe houses were that I'd found. He didn't ask. But he knows the one in the Faubourg St-Antoine, because he sent St Felix there. We'll have to find a new one.'

'He knew the drivers!' she went on. 'He sent me with messages for them — Bombec, Chimay and Virieu.'

He was silent for a moment.

'What?' she asked.

'We can't change them,' he replied. 'They are the ones who knew the man who will take the King's place, who'll recognise the clothes when the King wears them, and assume it is him again.'

'Then that means they are not part of the plan! Not knowingly!' she pointed out. 'So Bernave will not have trusted them with anything — whichever side he was on! We can still use them! We just need to change the safe houses.'

There was the shadow of a smile, not on his lips but in his eyes. 'You'll go on, won't you?'

His certainty warmed her — and frightened her. 'We have to,' she replied, swallowing. 'Bernave is dead, but nothing else has changed. If we don't go on, all the other things will still happen: war, everything else.'

He nodded, with just a tiny movement of his head in the guttering candlelight. 'We need St Felix,' he agreed. 'He knows about the routes beyond the city, and he has the passes. You'll have to talk to him, see if he is still with us.'

'What . . . what if he was the one who killed Bernave?' She hated saying it; her voice betrayed her emotions.

Again the moment of humour came and vanished. 'If he did, then it was because Menou was right, and Bernave betrayed us to the Commune,' he said softly. 'St Felix will be with us. We just have to change everything Bernave knew about.'

She tried to keep her own voice level. 'And if it was Fernand, or Monsieur Lacoste, because they knew he was trying to save the King?' she asked. 'They wouldn't have turned him in to the Commune, even loyal as they are, because they'd know that if they did Bernave would go to the guillotine and the house would be confiscated, and the business. They'd all be out on the street, without a sou.'

'The same.' There was no hesitation in him. 'We change everything Bernave knew about, and keep going . . . if St Felix is with us.'

'I'll speak to him,' she promised, dreading doing it. She had no idea how he would respond, what arguments she would have to use. And yet he had endured all kinds of hardships, even misuse at Bernave's hands. He must be passionate in his loyalty to the cause. Perhaps he understood it even better than she did? 'Yes, of course I will,' she repeated more firmly. She made as if to stand up and begin already.

He reached across and caught her wrist. She felt the strength of his fingers.

'Something else you must do — tonight!' he said urgently.

She relaxed into the seat again, waiting.

'You must search through all Bernave's papers, before this Menou does,' he said. 'Destroy anything that could betray us — or that could look like it. He'll be sure to go through everything in the morning. He'll be looking for reasons for someone to kill Bernave. He's got to consider money and the business. I imagine Marie-Jeanne will inherit it. Even if no one else does, she'll go through all the papers herself. If she found anything she thought suspicious, or she didn't understand, she might show it to Menou. You must do it tonight.'

She nodded, her throat momentarily too tight

to speak. The thought made her stomach flutter with fear.

'Remember everything you can about the routes he uses to Spain, England or Italy,' he went on. 'Post houses where they change horses, properties he owns, anything that could be part of the plan, or of use to us. Don't destroy anything they'll expect to find, unless it betrays us completely. Don't take anything away with you. They might search you and you can't afford to be found with anything. Apart from the fact that it would draw greater attention to whatever it is, they'll have you for stealing.' He was still holding her wrist. His hand closed more tightly. 'Be careful, Célie!'

'I will.' The urgency in his voice was better than the fire of brandy, making the blood beat inside her. She stood up, feeling his fingers slip away, releasing her.

He stood also, as if they were in some polite salon, like the early days of the revolution and before. He was very close to her.

'I . . . I wish I could help!' All the rage and frustration of his imprisonment as a fugitive were in his voice, and in his face in the wavering shadows of the candlelight.

'I'll be careful,' she promised, to herself as well as to him. 'You couldn't come into the house anyway. And if it is one of us, the more discreet we are the better. I'll go now. I've got a lot to do before the others wake up.'

'How are you going to get back in?' he asked, taking her arm again.

'I don't know,' she admitted. She had not

thought that far. She could not break into anyone's house to return the way she had come, over the roof. 'I . . . I'll think of something.' But she did not move, because no idea came to her and she could imagine only too clearly being outside in the street all night.

'I'll come with you.' It was a statement, and his grip was too strong to shake off.

'Why?' she argued. 'You can't get in either, and you might be seen!'

'I'll help you climb up on to the roof from the Rue de Seine. I know a way. Walk beside me and say nothing. And don't ever do this again.' He blew out the candle and pinched the wick, then he opened the door and, taking her hand, led the way down the narrow, pitch-black staircase, through the door to the outside, then down the last stair into the icy street.

They walked together carefully, uncertain of the cobbles beneath their feet. The stones were erratic and uneven, the puddles deep. They kept their heads down against the wind and the gusts of sleet. They crossed the Boulevard St-Germain well before the church and went into the quieter Rue de Seine. There was hardly anyone about, only a distant flare of torches as half a dozen soldiers came up towards the Rue Dauphine.

When they reached the house before the corner, roughly level with Bernave's, and backing on to it, Georges stopped, holding out his hand to stop her also.

'There's a place to climb up here,' he whispered. 'I'll go first, then take my hand. From the second storey I can lift you up to the valley

131

between the roofs. From there you'll have to find your own way to your window. Be careful! Can you tell the right one?'

She was not sure if she could, but there was no point in admitting that now. She should have left a candle burning, but she had not thought of it.

'Yes,' she lied with confidence. He would think she was a fool if she told him the truth, and that thought was worse than the icy rooftops. 'Thank you.'

He started to climb, reaching down for her, and gripping as tightly as he could.

Hands almost numb, cursing her skirts, she made her way up the slippery ledges until he lifted her the last few feet and she felt the roof slates beneath her knees.

'Thank you,' she repeated, gritting her teeth. 'Go back before you're seen!'

'Be careful,' he said again, then the next moment he was gone, swallowed up by the dense shadow and she was alone amid the roofs. The ridges were black against the sky, the finials sharp and strangely beautiful.

6

Célie found the right window, even though it seemed to take ages. The catch was still off and she climbed inside and slid to the floor with intense relief, because for several moments her legs were shaking so badly. At least it was warm in here, far warmer than Georges' icy attic. Would it remain so, now that Bernave was dead?

That was a miserably selfish thought, but far too real to dismiss.

She stood up again, went to the door and listened. There was no sound in the house. She crept back to her own room, overwhelmed with relief, and took off her sodden boots and cloak, then realised how wet her skirt was as well, so she changed into a dry one. She looked at herself in the glass. Her skin was flushed with the cold, her pale hair shining. She brushed it to hide the damp ends, and went down the stairs to the door of St Felix's room. Should she knock, and risk anyone else hearing her, or simply go in, regardless of the intrusion? Propriety hardly mattered now, not in comparison with everything else that was at stake.

She lifted the latch and went in. It was totally dark. No light came through the windows which faced over the rooftops and there was silence except for the wind and rain.

'Citizen St Felix,' she said softly.

Silence. She could not even hear him

133

breathing. Surely he was here!

'Citizen St Felix!' In spite of herself, her voice trembled. She could hear the fear in it.

'What is it?' His answer came out of the darkness, sharp-edged with alarm. 'Célie?'

She remained where she was, leaning against the closed door. She did not want to move and trip over anything. She had not been in his room before. Amandine always returned his clean linen.

'Yes,' she replied, steadying herself, breathing deeply. Her heart was pounding. 'I must speak with you. Bernave's death changes a lot of things. We need to . . . to reconsider.'

There was a sound of movement in the dark. She was shivering. He must be frozen. Was he searching for his clothes? A moment later there was the scrape of tinder and a flame sprang up. She saw his hands, strong and fine-boned. He lit the candle and the flame burned up, showing his face, his grey-green eyes and the halo of brown hair. In this yellow glow he was gaunt rather than handsome — she would even have said he was beautiful.

'What is it you want to say?' he asked. He was not angry, but there was a remoteness about him and she knew she had unquestionably intruded.

It irritated her, because she found herself embarrassed. This was even more difficult than she had foreseen.

'I went to see Georges Coigny — '

'When?' he interrupted. Then he looked away. 'It doesn't matter now anyway. Bernave is dead. I wish we could tell Coigny, but Menou wouldn't let us leave the house until he finds who killed him, and arrests them.' His voice was tight with strain. 'I expect he'll hear . . . from someone.'

'I saw him just now!' She said it more sharply than she had intended. 'He heard it from me.'

His head jerked up, staring at her. 'What do you mean 'just now'? You couldn't have — '

'I went over the roof,' she said flatly. It sounded preposterous, and yet it was the simple truth. 'If I'd gone in the street they'd have stopped me. I had to tell him.'

He looked at her more closely, his eyes narrowed. She could see in his face that he was beginning to understand that there was something intensely important to her, beyond anything she had said so far.

It made her feel in some way naked. Remembered shame, never far from her mind, returned with dull, consuming pain. But that was all irrelevant now. She must tell him what Georges had said, persuade him to go on, to fill in the missing pieces, change the ones that must be changed.

'I'm not sure it was worth the risk,' he said with a sigh. There was no lift in his voice, no hope. He sat down on the bed and indicated the single chair for her. She tried to read his face. The candlelight made it more dramatic, etched deeper the lines from nose to mouth, the subtle curve of cheekbone and delicacy of brow, the sweep of his eyelid. It was a face of tragedy, too vulnerable to pain.

How different he was from Georges, who until tonight had always been so certain of everything.

135

It was that wall of confidence around him that both drew her, and angered her. Now she had seen it breached, everything was different — at least for a few days.

'He's willing to go on,' she said quietly.

'Didn't you tell him that Menou said Bernave was spying for the Commune?' St Felix asked with amazement.

'Of course I did!' she snapped back. 'That doesn't mean it's true. But if it is true, it doesn't alter what will happen if we allow the King to be executed. It just means we've got to plan everything again, use different people, different places . . . '

He leaned forward. 'If it is true, Célie, it means he's almost certainly betrayed us to Marat and the Commune! Didn't you hear Menou say he was a loyal son of the revolution?'

'Then why aren't we all arrested?' she challenged. 'Maybe Marat is the one who's duped! Of course we'll have to change what we know — just in case. But we can, if we try hard enough. He never knew the safe houses, except in St-Antoine. He never knew the crowd Georges got for storming the carriage, so he couldn't have given them any — '

'But he knew there was a plan!' he cut across her, bitterness in his voice. 'Marat will be watching, waiting to catch us. He'll be prepared.'

'He'd be prepared anyway,' she continued. 'He'll be expecting an attempt at the time of the execution, even if it was only the royalists. Isn't it worth trying?' She heard her voice rise, the intensity of her emotions pouring through the

136

simple words — her rage and confusion over Bernave, and the compulsion to justify George's faith in her that she could persuade St Felix, when he himself could not reach him. It was for the sake of everyone, all France, whether they understood a fraction of it or not. But it was passionately for herself as well, to claw back something from the guilt that swallowed hope inside her. It was not God she needed to find, it was the light inside herself, the beginning of the person she wanted to be, not the woman who had judged too soon, without knowledge, and let her grief turn to a rage which almost destroyed another person.

'What else should we do?' she demanded to St Felix. 'Just let it all go? Then whoever murdered Bernave has beaten us all, just in that one act?'

He stood motionless. The flame wavered, lighting his eyes, but she could not read his thoughts in them and he was looking beyond her.

'I don't believe he betrayed us,' he said at last. 'I knew him a long time. There was much in him I never understood. I could be mistaken that he's no traitor, but I'll take the chance. As you say, the only alternative is to give in without trying.' He shook his head fractionally. 'But I don't know anything about Georges Coigny, except that he is Amandine's cousin. That's not enough to trust him with all our lives.'

Célie tried to think what she could tell him of Georges so he would believe in his courage and dedication to the cause, and even more in his ability to accomplish what he said he would. But

137

what did she know herself? She was lost for words, impressions filling her mind, memories of the heat and blood of September, of her own emotions, and Madame de Staël's words in the coach as they left Paris.

St Felix was waiting, a spark of curiosity lit his eyes.

'Bernave trusted him, and he has not betrayed us in anything,' she said aloud. 'That's all you need to know. If I could tell you his life story it wouldn't mean anything.' She shrugged, perhaps exaggeratedly. 'He could be a Lafayette, couldn't he? Change sides at the last moment! Or he could die for his beliefs, like God knows how many priests.' She grimaced. 'Except I suppose they had rather put themselves into a corner, hadn't they? If you make your career telling everyone that the goods of this life are nothing and heaven is all, when you are asked to make the leap yourself, if you decline, then you brand yourself a hypocrite of the first order.' She gave a little grunt of disgust. 'Not that that seems to have bothered Danton, or Hébert.'

'What?' he said sharply.

'They both trained as priests,' she reminded him.

St Felix swallowed. She saw his throat jerk. There was a spasm of pain in him, but she could not even guess what it was for. Everyone had lost something precious these days, someone they had loved. Célie did not ask.

He looked at her, searching her face for the first time.

'Why do you care so much that you will climb

138

over roofs at night to tell Coigny that Bernave is dead?' he said gently. 'And why are you trying so hard now to persuade me? Is it for Coigny's sake? Do you love him?'

That angered her monstrously. It was patronising and grossly untrue. It brought memories of Thérèse, Amandine, and embarrassment. Her temper flared up, sending the blood burning in her face.

'No, I do not!' she retorted stingingly. 'Do you go to the Faubourg St-Antoine and get hurt and stabbed, and carry messages at all times of the night no matter how frozen or exhausted you are because you are in love with somebody?' She made it sound contemptible. 'Or because you believe in the cause of the people of France, and are trying to stop us descending into chaos and hunger and war?'

'Keep your voice down,' he said calmly. 'Do you want to have Citizen Lacoste in here asking what the devil we are doing?'

She burst into laughter, rough and painful. 'In your bedroom, at this time of night? He wouldn't be so tactless!'

Now it was his turn for the blood to flare up his cheeks.

'You didn't answer my question!' she went on, speaking quietly again, and between her teeth. 'Are you so arrogant you imagine only you can think beyond your own loves and hates to something greater? I can see what the countries around us will do if we execute the King. They are all monarchies. All related to one another, in interest if nothing else. They'll descend on us as

139

if we were a diseased thing to be got rid of, to save themselves. You don't have to be an aristo not to want that.'

'Where did you learn all this?' He raised his eyebrows slightly, his composure regained. 'You sound like Bernave. I can hear him saying exactly the same things.'

'But you believed them from him?' That was a challenge. 'Why not me?'

He hesitated. She could see the indecision in his eyes, his mouth. He did not wish to be cruel. How many times had she seen in him that forbearance with others, with the wilfulness of the children, the prejudices of Monsieur Lacoste or Fernand, the ignorance of Marie-Jeanne, the cruelty of Bernave? She had admired it then, seen the beauty of a greater understanding. Now, because it cut across what she needed him to believe, it felt like condescension. She was aware of her own double standards, and it made her the angrier.

'This is no time for politeness!' she hissed. 'Anything but the truth could send not only the King to the guillotine, but the rest of us as well!'

He shrugged very slightly. It was a graceful gesture, a gentleman's resignation to the inevitable. 'You are a laundress, certainly with some courage and imagination, and a great loyalty to Bernave, but a natural creature of the revolution,' he said reasonably. 'It is your people's battle against the oppression of centuries. It is the justice you have starved for and died for, now at last within your reach. Do

140

you ask me to believe that your loyalty to Bernave is so great that you will go against all that your nature and your life has taught you to trust, and throw in your lot with a cause that has so little chance, and at such great risk? Why should you? For love of what, if not a man?'

What could she answer except the truth? If she continued to protect herself, cover the wound, he would not believe her. It would mean opening it up again, but then it was only a pretence that it had ever healed.

There was no point in telling him about her parents. They had not been labourers, or oppressed, but they were ardent revolutionaries of the mind, of lunatic idealism, not reality. But instinctively she still concealed their weakness, their dreams and their failures which had cost so much. It was all irrelevant to anything St Felix needed to know, or would care about.

'I was lady's maid to Madame de Staël, from before the revolution,' she began. He had to understand that much, or it made no sense.

His eyes widened a little. She was not surprised. Madame was the sort of woman St Felix would have admired intensely, as did so many others. Had there been time, she could have closed her eyes now and seen the wonderful months when night after night Madame's salon had been filled with the greatest names in France. They had talked endlessly — wonderful, brilliant conversations of a vision to set Europe on fire with a new social order of justice and freedom. They had drawn from the learning of every subject to interest the mind of man, and

141

with such wit, such laughter. She had to try harder to remember that ringing through the house.

Then the dreams of civilised and peaceful change had been broken one by one. Successive ministers had failed to control the economy, break the stranglehold of the Church on lands and wealth, or to reform the corrupt and chaotic taxation system. Necker, Mirabeau, Lafayette had all made promises they could not keep.

The King had listened to whoever was the last to speak with him, swearing to act, then hesitating till the moment was lost, and harsher and more radical demands were made, and he refused them, bewildered and stubborn.

Finally individual greeds and ambitions had divided them and, pointless quarrels had paralysed the men who might once have accomplished the beautiful, noble revolution the philosophers had spoken of with such high hopes, so short a time ago.

Charles had died of fever, leaving Célie alone with Jean-Pierre. The thought of him clenched her stomach till it ached almost beyond bearing. She hated St Felix for making her live it yet again.

'My husband died.' She dismissed that in a sentence. The surprise and the brief sense of dismay had long since gone. It was actually little more than a year ago, but it seemed another life. But then the brief illusion of love had burned out some time before that, and for Charles and herself it was over. She was sorry for the distress of his illness, for the waste of his life, but she did not grieve for herself that he was no longer with her.

She looked up and caught an expression of such desolation in St Felix's face that if she had ever doubted that the darkness he carried within himself was for his dead wife, that moment would have dispelled it.

She looked away. That kind of pain could not be shared, and should not be witnessed by another. It was like seeing the soul of a man stripped naked of all its protection.

'It wasn't that which hurt.' She had to explain, whatever he thought of her. 'It was my son's death . . . my baby.' This was even harder than she had expected. The words were torn out of her like pulling off skin, but she must go on with it now. 'Usually I could care for him myself. Madame was very good to me in that. But sometimes it was impossible. That occasion I left him with Amandine. The reason doesn't matter now.' She must tell him this part quickly, without detail, and get past it.

He did not interrupt her, but she could feel his luminous eyes steady on her face. It was discomfiting, as if he could see the shame to come.

The words were still almost impossibly difficult to say. 'While he was with Amandine . . . he died. We don't know why. Don't ask.' Why should he? But she wanted to prevent him anyway. 'I wished I could die too.' She must go on, reach the point which mattered, which would explain to him why she cared about the King, and would do anything necessary to help

Georges Coigny, even risking her own life in this scheme.

He was still watching her, waiting.

'At first I accepted it.' She swallowed. Her mouth was dry, her throat tight. 'Then Thérèse, Madame's laundress, told me that Jean-Pierre died because Amandine neglected him while she lay with her lover. If he had cried, then she had ignored him, left him to . . . ' She still could not say the words — choke — suffocate. 'I could not forgive her for that,' she hurried on. 'The thought was . . . beyond bearing.'

'Of course,' he said softly. His whole manner had changed. There was a gentleness in him she had never seen before. He understood bereavement, that tearing loss which is like a pulling apart of the body. But could he understand her guilt, her hatred of Amandine? What would he think when she told him the rest? Contempt? It could hardly be anything like the contempt she felt for herself.

But half the story made no sense.

'Thérèse told me the lover was Georges Coigny.'

'Amandine's cousin?' He was amazed, incredulity in his voice.

'I didn't know that then.' What a weak excuse! She hastened past it. 'I believed Thérèse. I hated them both. All I could think of was Jean-Pierre.' Funny how sweet it was to say his name, and how it hurt. No one else spoke it, as if he had never existed. Amandine was afraid to, and the other did not know. 'I thought of his death over and over,' she continued. 'It filled my mind,

144

awake and asleep. I dreamed of holding him again . . . ' The tears spilled down her cheeks and choked her into silence.

She felt his hand close on hers. His grasp was gentle, but so strong she could not have pulled away even had she wanted to. The power of grief in him was as great as her own, binding them together. It was almost possible to believe he understood her guilt as well.

Except that she had treated grief differently. She could not look at him, even in the shifting candle flame, as she went on.

'I planned my revenge for it,' she whispered. 'To teach both of them.' She gulped. 'I waited until I knew when they would be together, then I repeated things Georges had said against the revolution. I told the National Guard, and I told them where to find him . . . in Amandine's house, so they would both be taken.'

She heard the sharp intake of his breath, but he said nothing. His hand tightened over hers. It was surprising how warm his grip was, and still how gentle.

'Then it was the beginning of September,' she said the words softly. There was no need to explain. Everyone knew of the September Massacres. 'People were trying to escape Paris. All kinds of people were hunted. We were terrified the Austrians were marching on the city. One of Madame's lovers was wanted by the National Guard. She hid him in her own house.' She could recall this oddly without pain, in spite of what had followed. There was a kind of freedom in thinking of Madame standing there talking to the Guardsmen, charming them out of searching.

'What happened?' St Felix prompted, his voice cutting across the pictures in her mind.

'The Guard came,' she replied. 'They were rough and angry, wanting to arrest someone, full of resentment for Madame's wealth and her bearing. She spoke to them as if they had been equals, as if they had the same wit and culture that she did.' Her voice lifted with warmth. 'She had been admired by all the finest men in Europe — philosophers and artists of an entire generation — and she looked the Guard straight in the face and smiled, flattered them so subtly they were not even aware of it. They simply believed she thought well of them, even liked them. And they did not search the house — not really.'

'They didn't find him?' In spite of himself St Felix was drawn into caring.

'No. He escaped.' She still remembered the sense of victory.

'And you?'

The tears were warm on her cheeks. 'I suddenly realised how beautiful it was to be brave, to save someone rather than destroy them. I wanted to be like her, with courage, charm, intelligence and honour, more than anything else in the world. And I hated what I had done.' The fierceness of her honesty blazed through the bare words, her voice shaking. 'I couldn't take back what I'd told them about Georges. No one would have believed me. All I could do was warn them — both.'

146

'And you did!' His voice was husky, filled with some passion of his own.

'Yes . . . but of course I had to tell them why Georges was wanted — that it was because I had betrayed him.' The word was terrible, but once it was said it did not need to be said again. Honesty was satisfied. She had been true to that self of the past which would never go away.

St Felix was silent, waiting for her to go on.

'I found Georges.' It all came back so clearly. 'It was the beginning of the September Massacres. We were parted in the crowds. Madame escaped, taking me with her. She went back to Switzerland, but perhaps you know that? It was in the carriage ride out of Paris that she told me Georges and Amandine were cousins and lifelong friends, not lovers. Thérèse invented that story out of jealousy. Georges . . . Georges is very handsome, very charming.' Why was that so difficult to say, even now? She knew it was not the shallow, easy thing she had thought it then.

'And Thérèse wanted him destroyed because he rejected her?' St Felix concluded softly.

'Yes. And I accomplished it for her.' She was choked with self-disgust. 'So now Georges is running and hiding in an attic, cold and hungry, and he dare not come out except at night, because every National Guardsman knows his face and there is a price on his head for being anti-revolutionary . . . and I put it there.'

St Felix smiled with a flash of bitter irony. 'He wants to save the King's life, Célie. That is about as anti-revolutionary as one can be!'

'He doesn't want him back on the throne!' she

protested, jerking her head up and staring at him. 'Any more than I do! He just sees that if we execute him all Europe will be against us, and all the good we have fought for, and so many have died for. It will be swept away by invading armies of foreigners, who are all royalist and will govern us in exactly the way we have just got rid of — only worse, because they won't even be French!'

'And you want to pay back your debt to Georges Coigny?' he added.

That stabbed with the sharpness of truth.

'Yes.' It needed no more than that one word. That was it all: to pay Georges for what she had done; to be like Madame de Staël, brave and compassionate and honest, not like Célie Laurent, who sought revenge for something which had not happened, and let her grief destroy her humanity, even her knowledge of what was right.

'Now I understand,' St Felix said quietly, and there was a passionate grief in his eyes that made her feel for a moment as if he truly did. They were not comfortable words he was saying, but a gulf had been bridged between them which she had thought could never be.

'And I shall trust you from now on,' he added. Then his tone changed. 'Nevertheless, if we are to continue to any purpose we shall need more than simply you and I can do in hardly more than two days.'

'There is no one else!' she pointed out.

'There is Amandine,' he answered.

'You shouldn't risk — ' she began.

148

'There is risk to all of us,' he cut across her, 'but I had nothing of great danger in mind. Only you and Amandine will be allowed out of the house, if anyone is. Menou will probably let you queue for bread. Had you forgotten that? You cannot do it all.'

She had forgotten, for a moment.

'If Coigny attends to the two safe houses nearest here, which he can reach, and the men to mob the carriage,' he went on, 'that still leaves us to find a new house in the Faubourg St-Antoine. And we must check on the drivers of all three coaches from the safe houses onwards, and all the way either to the sea, or to the borders with Italy and Spain. And the captain of Bernave's ship in Calais.' He frowned. 'I like that least.'

'He did not trust the drivers,' she explained. 'They don't know enough to betray us. It all rests on getting as far as the safe houses, and changing clothes. Do you have the passes for getting out of the city?'

'Yes.' He grimaced, moving his shoulders a little in memory of the bruising he had earned in the venture. Then his eyes widened suddenly. 'No! I gave them to Bernave!' His voice was sharp. 'They'll be among his papers!'

'I'm going to search them now,' she answered. 'I'll get them. But what about the man who is going to take the King's place? Do you know who he is?'

He looked blank. 'No. Only Bernave knew that.'

She said nothing. Her mind was racing to think of anything Bernave had said which would

149

tell them who the man was or how they could find him. They had so little time. Where could they even look for anyone else? Who dare they trust?

St Felix straightened up. 'Tell me what you find,' he said quietly. 'Otherwise we shall have to . . . to look for someone else.' But he said it without hope.

There was no more to add. Célie stood up. She was so tired her head throbbed and she was dizzy with it, but before Menou returned she must search Bernave's desk and all his papers.

She went out of the room without speaking again. After the candlelight in his room the darkness was total. She felt her way to the bottom of the stairs. Outside the rain was sporadic and the wind gusted roughly.

She had no idea if anyone else was awake. She would make no noise going through Bernave's papers, but she would have to have a light. What if someone else had the same idea, and found her here? She had no explanation. They would think she was looking for something to steal, or even worse, that she might have killed him for some reason, a clue to which was hidden in his room, and now she was searching for it. That was so far from the truth it was funny. And yet if she were caught, at best she would be thrown out, at worst handed over to Menou, for trial and execution.

Who else would look in Bernave's study in the middle of the night? Monsieur Lacoste, or Fernand, if they were afraid Bernave had royalist papers that would compromise his reputation, and thus his property, which of course would now come to Marie-Jeanne, little interested as she seemed. But they would be!

Célie dared not risk being caught there. The cost would be too high. But who could she ask? Who would come at this hour?

Madame Lacoste! She would see the necessity for searching through Bernave's possessions before Menou did, even removing anything which was personal or intimate — private letters, references to anyone in the family — that could be exposed to the National Guard and the prurient eyes of the Commune.

And there was always the simple matter of money. Who could say that the National Guard would leave every sou they found?

Célie began to tiptoe up the stairs again, still in the dark.

What if she knocked on the Lacostes' bedroom door and Monsieur answered, not Madame? What would she tell him? Would he insist on coming with her?

She stopped. Perhaps she should waken Marie-Jeanne instead? After all, Bernave had been her father, and it was her inheritance.

But all her instincts drew her to Madame's door. She could see in her mind's eye Madame's thin, gentle hands as she had touched Bernave's body, the shadows on her face. She would protect Bernave's reputation, some memory of dignity for him, as well as protect the house for all of them. And she had the mastery of herself not to betray them unwittingly when she faced Menou.

Célie was shaking with cold. She began to climb again.

She remembered also the emotion in Marie-Jeanne as she had spoken of her father. There was resentment there, no tenderness, no thought of past moments of love or the innocence of other times. She would have no respect to keep his secrets or guard his possessions from intrusion.

Célie was at the top of the stairs, the bedroom doors ahead of her.

There was no sound of breathing or movement, only the rain outside.

She raised her hand to knock, her heart pounding.

Before she touched it the door opened and Madame stood there, a candle in her hand. Her face was bruised with emotion, her long, black hair loose about her head and shoulders. She came out into the corridor and closed the door behind her before she spoke.

'What is it?' she whispered.

'In the morning Menou and his men will come back,' Célie replied under her breath. 'They will search Citizen Bernave's room, the papers in his desk. We should do it first, to make sure there is nothing there we would prefer they did not find.' Was that enough of an explanation? Would Madame suspect something more? The whole household knew Célie ran errands for Bernave. Would she guess his business was illegal, sufficient to get them all executed?

What would Madame do?

Nothing! Keep the house. If Bernave were

prosecuted then the house was forfeit and they would all be penniless and on the street.

'There might be business interests that are . . . private,' she added, her voice shaky.

'You are right,' Madame agreed. 'I should have thought of it myself. Come, quickly, before we waken anyone else.' She started down the stairs, holding the candle high, leaving Célie to follow. 'Although I don't know if anyone is really asleep tonight.'

Soft-footed, they crept one behind the other down the last flight of stairs and along the hall, boards creaking, to Bernave's door.

'Wait,' Madame ordered, giving the candle to Célie, then going in and closing the door behind her. She returned a moment later, ushering Célie inside. After a moment Célie realised that the curtains had been pulled across. It was a good thought. It should have occurred to her also that the light would have been seen outside. It would be as well if Menou's men out in the street were given no cause to wonder what they were doing down here in the small hours of the morning. It would be very awkward to find an acceptable explanation. Anything they tried to say would only draw more suspicion.

Instinctively Célie put the candle on the floor, so that the bulk of the desk hid the flame from the window. It would be awkward to look at papers bending or squatting down, but far safer. There would be no more than a glimmer to be seen from outside, and no shadows outlined or moving against the windows.

Madame nodded briefly, understanding. She

153

opened the first drawer in the desk and pulled it right out, laying it on the floor beside Célie. She lifted the contents out upside down, putting the sheets back in one by one as they had been read. From what Célie could see, looking at them from an angle, they appeared to be mostly accounts, receipts for wool, leather and silk, and bills of shipping.

She hesitated. Was this information of any value to her? Were these the names or addresses she had to know, the routes of escape?

Madame's dark face was bent in concentration, scanning only the addresses and amounts, then placing the papers aside, reaching for the next one.

Should Célie begin on a pile herself, or watch what Madame was doing? What did Madame Lacoste know of Bernave? Where did her loyalties lie? Had they changed now Bernave was dead and could not be hurt?

But his money was now Marie-Jeanne's, his continued business was the income for her family, and surely that would include Fernand's parents, and such servants as they chose to keep?

Madame's face was fierce in concentration, her thoughts unreadable.

Célie stood up, made her way to the desk and pulled out the next drawer. She returned to the light with it and started to go through the papers in the same way. They too were records of money, but far less interesting, mainly household accounts. The bottom bundle was carefully in order, money matched with receipts. The next ones were less neatly kept and there was no cross-referencing. The top ones were without any order at all. It was a clear indication that Bernave had learned to trust both Célie and Amandine, and no longer bothered to keep track of their expenditure. Célie found herself caught unaware by a wave of sorrow so sharp the tears prickled in her eyes. That was ridiculous! She had known Bernave trusted her. Why should it suddenly hurt to see this very pedestrian evidence of it?

Madame was staring at her.

She blinked and turned away, looking down at the papers again and flicking them over, conscious of tears spilling and running down her cheeks.

'It doesn't look like much more than bills and receipts here,' Célie whispered, sniffing and looking for a handkerchief. 'What have you got?' She would almost certainly not have another chance to see Bernave's papers. It was a judgement between the necessity of knowing and the fear of Madame perceiving the reason behind it.

'Just the routes in and out of Paris for cloth,' Madame replied. 'I can't see anything in this that could cause trouble.'

Célie held out her hand. 'May I see?' She was shaking very slightly, but she could not control it. Madame passed over a handful of papers.

Célie took them and started to read as quickly as she could, her heart pounding. Which were the routes he would use? She knew the names of the three drivers: she should look for them. Presumably they would travel the same routes each time? Would there be bills for post houses, hostelries, changes of horses? But if there were, wouldn't Menou see them and know just as much as she did?

Should they change them?

No. Chimay, Bombec and Virieu were the drivers who knew the man who was changing places with the King, and whose clothes they had seen before and would recognise.

They were caught, trapped in their own foresight and efficiency.

Madame was watching her. In this strange, upward lighting from the candle on the floor her expression was impossible to read.

'Just bills for transport, routes and so on,' Célie said, trying to keep her voice at exactly the right level of concern. 'Perhaps . . . ' she swallowed, 'perhaps it would be a good idea to destroy some of them, just so they don't know it all. It is a . . . a very prosperous business . . . '

Madame considered for a moment. 'Can you remember them, if we need to know them again?'

'Oh yes,' Célie agreed quickly. 'I'll pick just some for each route.' And before Madame could think better of it she chose all the papers she could see where any of those names were mentioned. She tore them up and put them in the stove, seeing the brief flare-up of light as the last of the embers caught them.

Then instantly she wondered if she had merely made them conspicuous by taking them out of the records! What if they were fully documented in Bernave's papers in his place of business? The fact that they were omitted here would make them different from all the rest, marked out. And she had done it herself. How stupid!

She must make her brain clearer . . . concentrate. Think logically. What would Menou be looking for? What would he deduce from what he found here?

Madame was going through the next drawer. They appeared to be legal papers, to do with the purchase of the house. She took out half a dozen and tore them up sharply. Her strong fingers moved quickly, almost with anger. The papers were shredded into illegibility even before she put them into the flames.

'What were they?' The words were out before Célie thought.

'Things Menou does not need to know,' Madame replied without looking up at her. 'Be quick. You never know when someone else will waken up and might come here and see the light.' A flash of bitter amusement touched her lips. 'They might even have the same thought we have, although I doubt it. Marie-Jeanne is exhausted. She thinks she had no love for her father, but sometimes bereavement can show you things in yourself you had not known — or wanted to know.' There was pity in her voice, but Célie thought she heard anger as well.

Obediently she bent her attention to further papers. What she needed was the passes. Without them the plan would fail. And something to tell her where to find the man who was prepared to die for the King. Without each of its individual pieces the whole, fragile edifice would collapse.

There were letters from friends, some dating

back several years, with addresses from all over France. There was no time to read them. She glanced at each one, trying to judge the tone and flavour, looking at the dates and discarding them.

'What are they?' Madame demanded.

'Letters,' Célie replied. 'I'm just . . . seeing if there is anything . . . personal.'

Madame hesitated, gazing at her in the shifting light from the single candle. The draft under the door made it waver.

'Burn them,' she ordered. 'Menou will never know they existed. He won't miss them. Then we'll clean the fire out and relight it. We don't want paper ash found.'

That was something else Célie had not thought of, she realised with a start of guilt. She should not underestimate Menou — nor anyone else.

Where would Bernave have put the passes? Would they be well hidden where no one would look? Or in plain sight where they would be taken for granted as being no more than a usual part of business and travel? After all, his trade was the import and export of fabric. He would quite naturally have passes to come and go.

In the open. Bernave was clever; above all things he would be astute, careful.

'Where do you think he would keep his record of orders in the near future?' she asked. 'We need to have those. If Menou takes them away we'll lose business.'

Madame did not argue but opened the rest of the drawers and passed the first one across to

Célie. Piece by piece they looked at every paper. Madame kept those she considered relevant to possessions, proof of purchase and ownership. Those things belonged to Marie-Jeanne now.

Célie flicked through seemingly endless orders for wool, silk, leather, even enquiries about cotton from Egypt. There were notes of purchase and sale, expenses of storage, weaving, dyeing, transport. Interspersed among these she found notes for travel, preferred routes, comments on the responsibilities of different drivers.

Then there they were: passes for Citizen Louis Bombec to leave Paris on 21 January 1793, and one for Citizen Claude Virieu, one for Citizen Albert Chimay, and one for Citizen Joseph Briard. Another driver? Or the King?

Madame was looking at more letters, her eyes down on the page, but even a flicker of movement would be seen out of the corner of her eye. She would certainly notice if Célie were to slip four sheets of paper into her pocket.

She laid them down on the floor on the pile of others, but slightly crookedly so she could separate them in an instant. She started on the next pile. There were more letters of business, prices for wool from Scotland, silk from Milan, offers and counter-offers of trade.

'These are all harmless, I think,' she whispered. 'What about the letters? Could they get anyone into trouble, even investigated?'

Madame considered.

Célie must make her get up, leave the circle of light and take something to the stove and burn

159

it. Then she would have her back to Célie, at least for a moment or two, longer if Madame made sure the ash was crushed as well.

'Even if they are merely personal,' she went on, 'perhaps Citizen Bernave would prefer not to have the Guard reading them. I would.'

'You're right.' Madame made the decision immediately. 'We'll burn all of them. It's none of Menou's business, or any of those clodhopping men of his, to read what someone else intended only for Bernave's eyes. Here, give them to me.' She held out her hands.

That was not what Célie had intended. Think quickly.

'There's nothing private here,' she answered. 'At least I don't think so. This is all information Marie-Jeanne might need. And Menou will know if we don't leave a certain amount. He'll wonder what it was. Burn those, and I'll look through these again, to be certain.'

Madame rose to her feet and went to the stove.

Célie took out the passes and stuffed them into her skirt, then made a noise with the other papers to mask the sound. Half a dozen at a time she replaced them in the drawer, in as close to the order she had found them as possible, and neatly, not to look as if they had been disarranged.

Madame crushed the ashes and placed a small piece of wood on top, leaving it to smoulder as if the fire had naturally burned out by itself. Who would have tended Bernave's fire, in the circumstances?

She looked around the room. 'Is there anything else?'

'The religious books?' Célie suggested. It hurt to think of destroying them. They were beautiful. The old leather was smoothed by years of touch, the gold lettering gleaming in the light. Someone had poured out their hearts writing them, someone else had printed and bound them, created the physical thing. And Bernave had loved them, or he would not have risked keeping them in these destructive, atheist times. They were a lifeline to another age, an age of hope beyond the known, a part of him he could not let go.

'Leave them,' Madame said huskily. 'Let Menou make of them what he will. No one in the house murdered him because of his books.'

It was as if all the light and even the residual warmth of the stove had fled from the room.

Célie did not answer her, but watched as Madame blew out the flame and felt for the door latch. They would return to their beds in darkness. Neither felt the need to explain why they would account for this to no one. Who else would understand?

161

7

The rain passed and the morning was bright and cold. Everyone was gathered in the kitchen. It was the warmest room in the house, and it seemed that, for their different reasons, they wished to be together. Marie-Jeanne sat in the largest chair nursing the baby. In the corner Virginie and Antoine were quietly playing a game with a pile of sticks, dropping them in a heap, and then seeing who could remove them one by one without upsetting the pile.

The other adults sat around the kitchen table slowly eating the last of the bread from yesterday, and drinking hot chocolate. They were probably all thinking — at least in part — of the same things, but nobody liked to say so. Now that Bernave was dead, where would their income come from? How much had it depended upon Bernave's skill? Could anyone else manage the business now he was gone?

Monsieur Lacoste was a natural Communard. He was an ordinary man, a locksmith and worker in metal, a man with no natural privileges — and to whom revolution offered the first chance of a voice in his own future, and his family's, and a feeling of being in control. He had enough repressed anger in him to understand the urge to destroy. Yet even he found Marat extreme. He preferred the abstemious Robespierre, always talking about virtue.

Fernand believed in the Commune, but he actually knew very little about it. At least Célie thought he did! Perhaps that was a misjudgement too. He was a cabinet-maker, occasionally turning his hand to a little other carpentry when business was slow. He was a respectable artisan. He would like to have started his own business, in time to have employed others, but no one did things like that these days. He had ambitions for peace, and he was prepared to fight to achieve it. Like his father, he wanted more justice, more chance to learn, and to speak his thoughts. They understood one another, and beneath the superficial quarrels now and then, there was both affection and respect.

Célie was also concerned, not only for the others around the table, but for herself. Did she have an employer any more? Would the Lacostes want or need her? Did they even approve of employing people domestically, or — in these days of equality — would they think it wrong, even dangerous? Célie would far rather be unequal in a warm, dry house, than theoretically equal, starving in the winter streets. And she knew perfectly well that most people felt the same, but nobody offered them a choice.

Apart from that, would there be funds anyway?

And without money, how would she continue to feed Georges? If she had to find another job, where would she begin to look? Was it callous so soon to think of realistic things? It was better than thinking of Bernave lying on the floor, the spirit fled from him, the emptiness left behind.

Where had all that passion and energy gone, all that intelligence, the unflinching purpose? Could it really have become nothing, in a moment destroyed for ever — like Jean-Pierre? Was that the reality, and all the faith of centuries a fairy story to keep the people obedient, and oppressed, as men like Marat claimed? She refused to believe it. Think of the present! Concentrate!

Foremost in her mind were the two questions: whose side had Bernave been on; and who had killed him? Someone around this table had held that knife and lunged, someone she was sitting here sharing breakfast with, someone sipping chocolate to disguise the taste of stale bread. Why?

Menou came in through the back door from the courtyard. Everyone stopped moving and stared at him, mugs halfway to their lips, bread in the air.

'Good morning, Citizens,' he said, closing the door behind him. 'I'm sorry to disturb your meal, but certain matters will not wait.' He glanced around curiously, although he had been here before when searching for the knife. Now he looked towards the stove where the last of the chocolate was simmering in the pan.

Célie felt her whole body frighten with fear. Everything depended on how they conducted themselves now. She could feel Menou's presence as if it were generating some kind of force in the room.

'You . . . must be cold, Citizen,' she heard her own voice in the silence, a little hoarse. 'Would

164

you like some hot chocolate?'

She half saw Monsieur Lacoste stiffen. Who had food enough to share these days? She deliberately ignored him. Who had safety enough not to share with the National Guard? She could hardly point that out to him now. She might later on — except that she never felt very comfortable with Monsieur Lacoste. She disagreed with his views, especially on Robespierre, and she was afraid he would know it if they ever had a conversation of any length. On a deeply instinctive level, Robespierre's virtue frightened her far more than Marat's rage. It was less human.

'Thank you,' Menou accepted.

St Felix moved a little to allow him room at the table, and he accepted the seat.

Célie went to the stove, taking down a clean, revolutionary china mug from the rack on the dresser as she passed. She poured out the last of the chocolate and brought it back to the table.

Menou took it with a gesture of gratitude. 'I don't suppose anyone has found the knife which killed Citizen Bernave?' he said, raising his eyebrows and gazing round at them one by one.

'No,' Madame Lacoste answered him with very slight surprise — presumably that he should ask.

He sipped the chocolate. 'I had not thought so.' He nodded slowly, swallowing. 'Never mind, we shall keep looking. It can't be far, can it?'

Again no one replied.

'I think . . . ' Menou spoke almost as if to himself, 'that we better go over exactly what

165

happened as each of you remember it.' He took another sip. 'It's very good.' The shadow of a smile crossed his face. 'I appreciate a woman who can make even simple things well.'

Amandine swallowed. 'Thank you . . . '

He gazed at her. 'You look uncomfortable, Citizeness. Does it embarrass you to be complimented on your skill? Or are you suffering grief at the death of your employer? Was he good to you?'

Amandine was caught completely off guard. Célie could see the indecision in her face. She knew she was thinking of St Felix and what she could say to protect him, and yet still be close enough to the truth not to be caught out. After all, one of those listening had killed Bernave, and meant someone else to be blamed for it.

Menou was waiting, his clear, grey eyes intent. Célie noticed in the daylight that he had dark lashes. If he had been anyone else she might have thought him good-looking.

'He was . . . fair . . . yes,' Amandine said awkwardly. 'I did not see a great deal of him. He . . . left me to get on with my work. He was not mean. He . . . trusted me.' She stopped, aware she was answering far more than he had asked, talking too much. She coloured awkwardly, and put up a slender hand to push her hair back off her brow.

Menou turned to Célie. 'And was he fair to you too, Citizeness Laurent?'

Monsieur Lacoste was watching her, waiting to see what she would say. He knew how often she had been sent out on errands in the rain and cold, and at late hours. Certainly it had been to less dangerous or unpleasant places than St Felix, but did he know that? What would she tell Menou? Her answer must be close enough to the truth. If she were suspected it would ruin everything.

'Yes, I suppose so,' she replied, meeting Menou's probing eyes and feeling his intelligence discomfiting. She forced the ghost of a smile. 'He was generous sometimes. Other times he sent me out late and in the rain. I imagine it was necessary, or at least he thought so.'

Menou was interested.

'Oh? What sort of errands, Citizeness?'

There was total silence around the table. Everyone was watching her. St Felix allowed his chocolate to go cold. Amandine was unconsciously crumbling her bread in her fingers.

'Letters sometimes,' Célie answered, trying to keep her voice light, as if it were of no relevance, and she were not weighing every syllable. 'And of course to the Convention now and again, to keep him aware of exactly what was happening. He liked to know what was said in the debates.'

'Why did he not go himself?' Menou asked, cupping his cold hands around his mug. He had good hands, strong and slim, and his nails were clean. It suddenly brought to Célie's mind Robespierre's bitten fingers fluttering as he spoke, and she shivered involuntarily.

'I didn't ask him,' she replied.

A touch of amusement crossed Menou's face and disappeared. 'And you reported back to him what you had seen and heard, Citizeness?'

'The best I could.' She must not appear too clever, or too well informed on political matters. He might suspect her of motives of her own.

'How interesting.' He stared at her. 'Not many men in these turbulent days would send a laundress to the Convention, to keep them abreast of matters of state. He must have thought remarkably highly of you.' He regarded her closely, right from the top of her sleek, pale head to her hands resting on the table, which was all he could see of her. 'Had you known him for long?'

She dreaded to think what he might be imagining. She could feel the colour warm up her cheeks. She had nothing to feel guilty for, in the manner she feared he was supposing. She wanted to say something sarcastic and funny, but she suppressed the impulse. Most revolutionaries had no sense of humour.

'Only since the middle of September,' she replied as steadily as she could.

'Célie and Amandine came here then,' Madame Lacoste confirmed. She was still white-faced, her eyes ringed with shadow. Her cheeks were gaunt as if she had not slept, but her look was completely steady and there seemed to be no fear in her.

'You came together?' Menou asked, turning from Célie to Amandine, and back again.

'No,' Célie corrected him. 'Amandine came first. She was good enough to recommend me. I came a few days later.'

'I see.' Menou obviously did not. 'And you do the laundry and the mending . . . and political observation . . . ' He left it hanging in the air, an unexpected shred of humour behind it.

'I did whatever — ' Célie started, then realised the double meaning and then stopped. 'I did whatever needed doing in the house,' she corrected herself. 'And when I had time, I carried messages or errands also. Citizen Bernave fed us well, and kept a warm house. As far as I know he was a believer in the revolution and wanted liberty and justice for everyone.'

Menou turned to Monsieur Lacoste, whose expression of contempt was so profound as to demand a comment.

As if suddenly aware of the attention, he smoothed away the anger, but it obviously required an effort from him. He measured his words very carefully. 'That's what he said,' he agreed turning to Menou. 'Fine words cost nothing. Perhaps you are right and he was working for the Commune. He didn't always behave like it.'

'You didn't like him, Citizen?' Menou asked.

'He was family,' Lacoste replied, as if that answered everything. Célie thought of his closeness to his son, his patience with his grandchildren, the way he accepted Marie-Jeanne, and above all his awkward tenderness for Madame. Perhaps it did answer all that really mattered to him.

'Ah yes,' Menou nodded. 'Your son is married to Bernave's daughter.' He looked across at Marie-Jeanne. 'That's you, Citizeness . . . '

Marie-Jeanne nodded.

Menou looked at Fernand. 'And you, Citizen,

169

what did you think of Bernave?'

'I didn't know he was working for the Commune,' Fernand replied cautiously, 'but it doesn't surprise me. He was a man of deep conviction, and as Célie says, he wanted justice for everyone.'

Menou smiled. He must realise they all knew that if Bernave were thought to be a traitor to the revolution, then the house would be forfeited.

'Just so.' He remained looking at Fernand. 'Tell me about last night, Citizen. What happened — exactly — as you recall?'

Fernand was startled. He glanced at his mother, then back at Menou. 'I . . . I don't know anything more than I told you then.'

'Perhaps. Remind me . . . ' Menou fixed him with bright, intelligent eyes, waiting.

Fernand looked unhappy, but he obeyed.

'We were all sitting in the front room . . . '

'You heard noises in the street,' Menou prompted, when he hesitated. 'You perceived there was a crowd, and some quarrelling . . . '

'Of course. We could hardly fail to see it,' Fernand agreed tartly. 'There were at least twenty people pushing and yelling, and then shots.'

'Ah yes . . . shots.' Menou turned to Marie-Jeanne. 'Do you recall the shots, Citizeness?'

'Yes.'

Menou looked back at Fernand.

'Did anyone leave the room?'

'I didn't see.'

Menou turned to Célie, his eyebrows raised

questioningly. If anyone had left, they would have passed close to where she had been.

'I did,' Marie-Jeanne said quietly. 'I went up to my children, to comfort them.'

Menou glanced at Virginie, who was staring wide-eyed at him, the game forgotten, and then at Antoine.

'Very natural,' he agreed. 'Anyone else?'

This time Célie was happy to speak. 'No, the rest of us were here.' She was aware of Madame Lacoste's black eyes watching her. What was she afraid of? Did she know which one of them had killed Bernave? What could she do to protect them? How far would she go? Or did she believe it was St Felix? Perhaps she did, because it was the only answer that would be bearable for her.

'And the exact order of events?' Menou turned to Amandine. 'You, Citizeness. Please tell me again.'

Amandine froze. It was several moments before she answered him. He watched her, looking at her soft hands, unmarked by working as Célie's were by laundry. She had clear skin and fine features. There was a natural delicacy to her. It was easy to believe she was a woman of grace and breeding fallen on harder times, like so many others. Did he see that? Did he resent it? She had not Marie-Jeanne's earthy domesticity, or Célie's challenging intelligence in her demeanour. Until lately she had never needed it — now it was too hard to assume.

Who was Menou? Where had he come from? The constant shifts of power in the revolution had thrown together all manner of people.

171

Yesterday's ministers and governors were today's prisoners and tomorrow's corpses. Yesterday's servants were today's masters. Célie studied him. He wore the revolutionary uniform, but so did scores of people, for scores of reasons: passion, conviction, the lust for power, or simply the desire to survive. Menou could be anything. His speech was ordinary enough. He could have been a footman or a tailor or an artisan of any sort before the revolution. Or he could be the third or fourth son of an aristocrat, with enough of an ear to adopt a common speech, and enough political idealism, or opportunism, to seize on the new order.

Or he could have been a lawyer, a moneylender or a thief.

He was very tidy. His hair needed cutting, but his clothes fitted him, and his hands were clean. His boots were rather good. She had noticed that when he came in. Was that breeding, or merely opportunity and the love of nice things, even a little personal vanity?

'There was a shot which broke the window, and the light went out,' Amandine answered very carefully, facing Menou. 'Then we heard the noise at the front door, and the crowd broke in, demanding food. They thought we were hoarding — which we weren't. We aren't! Citizen Bernave went over to them.' She shivered at the memory. 'He told them that.'

'And did they believe him?' Menou asked, and when Amandine did not answer immediately he turned to Célie.

'No, of course not!' she retorted. 'But he

would hardly say we were, would he?'

He smiled. That simple gesture startled her. In her experience revolutionaries never saw the funny side of anything, most especially anything which might remotely reflect on them. It was the thing which frightened her the most. It made them inhuman, outside ordinary life. Robespierre never laughed.

'What happened then?' Menou asked quietly, looking at Amandine again. But he went on before she had time to answer. 'Citizen Bernave remained facing the intruders. What about the other men in the room — Citizen Lacoste, Citizen St Felix, for example? Did they move forward to help?'

Amandine was confused. 'I . . . I suppose so. I don't remember.' She stared straight ahead of her, as if there were no one else present except herself and Menou. Her pose was unnaturally stiff, her slender back straight as she had been taught to sit, in some far-off schoolroom. Célie knew she was trying to remember where in the panic, St Felix had been.

Célie could not remember either. She had been watching Bernave, and the crowd threatening in the doorway. She had been only dimly aware of the others.

Menou turned towards her.

'And you, who are such a keen observer, Citizeness Laurent — what can you tell me? Where was Citizen St Felix standing?'

He had been standing, that was true, but how did Menou know that? She could not underestimate him, just because he was a revolutionary. It did not mean he was stupid, or incapable of judging them by their own standards, seeing their weaknesses, and their loyalties.

'I don't know,' she answered. She could not copy Marie-Jeanne's ignorance. Menou had seen she observed sharply, and he would not believe she panicked, she had no children to protect — not now. Jean-Pierre was beyond her power to help and shield from anything. That cold thought was never too far away to return. 'He was sitting in the chair opposite when the shot came through the window . . . ' Her voice was a little hoarse, her throat tight.

'And then?' Menou insisted. 'When the intruders threatened you, did he not go forward to assist Bernave?' He watched her face. The question sounded innocent, and yet the implications were inescapable.

Should she lie, and brand St Felix a coward, or tell what she thought was the truth, and place him where he could have killed Bernave?

Menou was waiting.

Célie felt her flesh prickle. His eyes seemed to stare through her.

Madame Lacoste answered for her.

'There was a great deal of noise and confusion,' she said levelly. 'The smoke from the torches out in the street was blowing in and stinging our eyes. It was very difficult to see. I was looking at the men in the doorway: they were the threat, not we who were in the room. I imagine Citizeness Laurent was as well.'

'I see,' Menou nodded, frowning. He turned away from Célie and Madame Lacoste to St

174

Felix. 'Where were you when the rioting in the street disturbed you?'

St Felix was startled, as if he had not expected to be addressed.

'I . . . I was in the other chair, opposite Citizen Bernave. I think I stood up. I don't remember. We were all alarmed, it was so close.'

Menou nodded. 'Tell me exactly what you recall.'

Célie glanced around. Everyone was watching St Felix. Monsieur Lacoste was frowning. He looked worried. Fernand seemed more concerned for Marie-Jeanne. He moved closer to her, defensively. It was only a step or two, but the emotion which drove him was unmistakable. The children were silent, aware of the fear without understanding it.

Amandine was rigid, her hands on the table locked till her knuckles were white. Had Menou been looking at her, rather than St Felix, he could not have helped noticing. Célie ached to protect her, warn her that she was allowing her face, her body, to betray her. But there was nothing she could say without making it worse. She realised her nails were digging into her own palms.

Madame Lacoste was staring at St Felix also, her expression sombre, her dark eyes unreadable.

'Citizen . . . ?' Menou prompted.

'I'm trying to be exact,' St Felix excused his silence. Célie could hear the tension in his voice; it was higher than usual, sharper. But Menou would not know that. The difference was slight, and his diction was as perfect as always.

175

'It happened very quickly,' he answered. 'There was shouting, movement, shots. The window broke. The candle went out. There was smoke from the torches. It was difficult to see. People were breaking into the house from the street. They were very angry and threatening. They wanted food. Citizen Bernave went towards them and told them we had no more than our own rations for the day. They did not believe him. The mood became very ugly.'

'Did they come forward?' Menou asked.

There was silence. Everyone understood the importance of the answer.

Célie did not mean to, but she could not help glancing at Amandine. There was tension in her face, but not the fear there would have been had she believed St Felix could have been guilty, whatever the provocation.

Célie felt sick for her. Please God she was right!

'No,' St Felix said at last. 'Not that I saw.'

'And did you go forward to assist Citizen Bernave?' Menou asked. 'No one else seems quite certain if you did or not.'

Again the slight hesitation, the understanding of what either answer would mean. 'Yes.'

'Of course,' Menou agreed. 'One would. And did Citizen Lacoste? And Fernand Lacoste?'

'There was great confusion, and it was dark. I believe so.'

Menou looked at both of the other men.

They each nodded.

Menou considered for some time before he spoke again. They all watched him, wrapped in

176

their own fears — for themselves, and for each other.

'It seems it could have been any one of you who killed Citizen Bernave,' he said finally. 'I shall, of course, continue to look for the knife.' He put down his empty mug. 'It is possible all of you are aware of what happened, and are concealing the truth, for your own reasons.'

Amandine drew in her breath sharply, and then said nothing.

'Yes, Citizeness?' Menou prompted.

'I thought I was going to sneeze,' Amandine lied quickly.

There was no way to tell if Menou believed her or not. He rose to his feet and started to walk slowly round the kitchen, regarding each of them as he passed.

They grew gradually more and more uncomfortable. Finally Menou broke the silence again.

'Citizen Bernave asked you to go to the Convention and observe the debates,' he said to Célie.

'Yes,' she agreed.

'And then to report to him?'

'Yes.' She had an increasingly uncomfortable feeling that he was leading to some kind of ambush, but she could not see it. She had no idea which way to sidestep. She knew Amandine was watching her, and she could sense St Felix's tension.

Menou frowned. 'Then what did he send Citizen St Felix for? It must have been something very dangerous, must it not? Something that was too dangerous for you.'

'More likely something I wouldn't understand!' she said quickly.

Menou raised his eyebrows and turned to St Felix.

No one moved.

St Felix remained silent, avoiding Menou's gaze.

'I don't know what it was,' Lacoste interrupted. 'None of my business. But St Felix often enough came back filthy and covered in blood and bruises.' He said it with a touch of defiance, knowing the implications. 'So perhaps it was dangerous.'

Célie wanted to laugh at the 'perhaps'. It welled up inside her hysterically, and she stifled it with her hand over her mouth.

Menou looked round the rest of them, to see if they confirmed or denied it. He read the admission in their faces, willing in Fernand's case, reluctant in Marie-Jeanne's, and terrified in Amandine's. Madame Lacoste was guarded, but Célie caught an instant of intense dislike for St Felix, then it was gone again, masked so completely it might have been no more than an illusion of the light on her dark eyes and the shadows beneath them.

Menou swung right round to St Felix again. 'Why were you prepared to endure such treatment at the hands of a man who seemed to have so little consideration for you, Citizen? Did you not dislike him for it?'

Again Amandine was on the edge of speaking, but just in time realised she might only make matters worse. She stared pleadingly at St Felix,

178

as if willing him to defend himself. Célie ached to be with her, to give her any kind of support, but she dared not. Menou would see and understand.

'No, I did not dislike him, Citizen,' St Felix answered quietly. 'He did what he did, and asked as much of others, because he believed in his cause. One does not dislike a man for that, one admires him.'

'Ah! So you knew he was working for the Commune! You did not say that before!' Menou accused.

'I knew he was working for the revolution,' St Felix corrected. 'For the good of France.'

A very slight frown puckered Menou's forehead.

'If he believed in his cause so powerfully, why did he not go on these dangerous errands himself?' he asked ingenuously. 'It seems the belief was his, and the sacrifice was yours.'

'I presumed he went on equally dangerous errands himself,' St Felix argued. 'He went out often.'

Well answered, Célie thought, with a lift of surprise and relief inside her. Perhaps St Felix would defend himself after all. If Bernave trusted him as he had, then he must have some steel in his soul.

Menou looked at Marie-Jeanne, the question in his face.

'That's true,' she nodded.

Madame Lacoste added her agreement.

'And came back injured?' Menou pursued.

There was silence.

179

Amandine took a deep breath. She was very pale. 'Yes — '

'Not seriously!' Célie interrupted. For heaven's sake, they could look at the body and see! There was not a recent mark on him. Had Amandine not thought of that? 'Mostly dirty, cold and exhausted,' she added.

'You know something about it?' Menou turned to her.

'Of course,' she said, trying to sound convinced. 'I think he sent Citizen St Felix to the Commune, with what he had discovered of the royalist plans, but he did not tell me that, of course. And went to the royalists himself, which was far more dangerous. If they were to have discovered what he were really doing, then he would not have come back at all!'

'That's right,' St Felix put in, his voice suddenly certain, as if he realised Célie's line of thought might rescue him.

Menou's reply was instant, his eyes narrow and bright. 'How do you know? He confided in you? You believed what he told you?'

St Felix hesitated. To admit that might be dangerous, especially since Célie was almost certain it was not true. Bernave had trusted no one with information of that kind. Menou might know that. It all depended which side Bernave had really served. St Felix might be making things worse for himself.

But for the matter, which side did St Felix really serve? The King, of course — some kind of order from the ashes of the old tyranny and waste. Nothing about him was naturally

180

sympathetic to the violence and vulgarity of the Commune.

Menou smiled. 'You read the messages he entrusted to you?' he said, regarding St Felix curiously.

St Felix hesitated yet again.

Célie wondered if he had read them. Did he alone know what Bernave was really doing? And was that why he had killed him: not because of the personal abuse, but because he had discovered his betrayal of the plan of rescuing the King from execution, and France from drowning in blood?

Célie caught herself with horror. She was seriously considering his guilt! She hated the thought! It could not be true . . . not St Felix, the man who forgave so easily, bore fear and danger with such quiet fortitude. He had too much sensitivity to others, too much humility to be an aristocrat; too much gentleness and too little hate to be a revolutionary; too much compassion to be either.

And yet the suspicion would not go.

'You read them?' Menou repeated.

'No,' St Felix replied. 'Bernave told me, and I believed him.'

Menou smiled. 'I see.' His voice conveyed neither acceptance nor denial. 'I have men outside. We will look again for the knife. It must be in this house somewhere. You will all remain here while we search. I would not like to think it was moved ahead of us all the way. You understand?' It was not a request, it was an order. Something in him liked to retain a

181

semblance of the courtesy of a past age. He could not altogether hate the *ancien régime*. Willingly or unwillingly, he admired something in it, hungered for its elegance.

He went to the back door and gestured for half a dozen guardsmen to troop in.

'Did you search the shed and the workshops?' he asked.

'Yes, Citizen,' the sergeant answered, then shook his head. 'Nothing.'

'Are you sure?' Menou insisted.

'Certain. Went through all the metal out there, and the wood. No knife.'

'Then take the men and look through the house,' Menou directed him. 'Look through everything. You, Lavalle, stay here and see no one leaves the kitchen.' He followed the other men out.

Amandine asked permission to clear the table and continue with her duties, and it was granted.

Célie asked the same, and it was granted also.

'Then may I go for bread?' she asked. 'If I don't, it will be too late.'

The guard gestured refusal. 'Then tell us who killed Bernave, Citizeness, and you can.'

'I don't know,' she replied. 'If I did, I'd have told you already.'

A sneer twisted his face.

'Maybe! Maybe it was your lover? Or maybe you did, eh? Did he try to rape you? You didn't want an old man — '

'He wasn't old, and he didn't force himself on anyone!' Madame Lacoste snapped. 'Watch your tongue, fellow, or I'll report you to Citizen

182

Menou. It is a hero of the revolution you are talking about!'

The man coloured hotly, but he did not answer back. He glared at her, then turned away. 'Get on!' he said sharply to Célie. 'Get on with the cooking, or the laundry, or whatever it is you do!'

'I do the shopping!' she returned, meeting his eyes angrily.

'Not now you don't!' he said with satisfaction. 'You don't do anything unless I tell you to!'

She went to help Amandine with clearing the table. Amandine glanced at her; their eyes met for a moment. Célie saw the fear in her. There was nothing to say which would make it any better. Lies would not help. She smiled at her, and slipped her arm round her for an instant as she passed. She felt a moment's answering pressure, then moved on.

She then asked permission to draw water from the pump in the yard. The guardsman stood in the doorway watching her, and keeping an eye on everyone in the kitchen at the same time.

She returned and went over to pour half the water into the sink for Amandine. Everyone else remained around the table.

'Do you think they'll find the knife?' Amandine whispered. 'If they do, it won't prove anything!'

'Of course not,' Célie agreed under her breath. The same thoughts must have been racing through Amandine's mind too. She looked at her and could see the doubt in her face as she bent over the vegetables, trying to sort the good ones from the rotten, her mind not on it. Was she at least entertaining the unthinkable — that St Felix was guilty, because he knew Bernave had betrayed them — and she was preparing to defend him?

'It won't mean anything,' Célie repeated. 'Unless it's somewhere only one person could get to.'

Amandine did not look up. 'Like where?' she asked, cutting the bad out of a potato and throwing it into the rubbish.

'Like the Lacostes' rooms upstairs, the children's rooms,' Célie replied. 'Anyone outside the family would have been seen there.'

'If Madame is here while they search the kitchen, she may notice the food is low,' Amandine said anxiously. 'What did you take for Georges yesterday?'

'Chocolate. I bought the bread and onions. Oh . . . I took cheese as well, the day before.'

'Damn!' Amandine swore under her breath and threw away another potato.

The guard shifted his position, feet shuffling on the floor.

'She may not notice the chocolate,' Amandine went on. 'I don't suppose she knew how much was in the tin, but she remembered the cheese. Said we'd have it today. She wouldn't believe me if I said it went off and I threw it out.'

'Hardly,' Célie agreed, trying to make more work out of piling the dishes, to justify remaining there. 'When did you ever throw cheese away? Even if it were green, we'd have eaten it.'

'No talking!' the guard said loudly. 'Get on with your work!'

They obeyed, Amandine standing over the bowl, Célie washing the mugs and putting them away. There was no sound in the room but the chink of crockery and an occasional squeak as Célie rubbed the cloth too tightly on the smooth surface.

Menou returned. It was obvious from his expression that he had not yet found the knife. He started to search the kitchen, looking in every cupboard and flour bin, every bag, box and tin himself, running his hand through the few dried peas and lentils they had, tipping out the chocolate on to a plate, and the coffee, lifting the cheese cover, taking the lid off every pan.

He found nothing of interest, and no hidden food.

Next he looked through Célie's laundry supplies.

'You haven't much soap,' he commented. 'No starch? No blue?'

'I used the last of the starch the day before yesterday,' she answered. 'It's hard to get blue any more.' Actually she had swapped it for coffee for Georges.

Menou returned to the kitchen table, his face creased with irritation.

'One of you murdered Citizen Bernave.' He looked round them slowly. Marie-Jeanne was still holding the baby, who was now asleep. Madame Lacoste watched Menou, her face pensive, full of shadows. Fernand drummed his fingers silently. Monsieur Lacoste fidgeted, biting his lip. St

Felix was completely motionless, his shoulders slumped. He looked as if he were bowed down with a weight of grief so heavy it crushed him.

Fernand's fists were clenched and his shoulders were high and rigid.

Menou faced him squarely.

'You have no right to say that!' Madame Lacoste replied at last, her voice cold. She sat very straight, with a dignity that did not lie in status or power, but simply in her own belief in herself. She was the wife of a man who laboured for his living, but she could have been of the old nobility as she faced Menou in her kitchen.

A flicker of admiration showed in his eyes, unwilling perhaps, but quite real.

'We cared for Citizen Bernave,' she continued gravely. 'And we grieve for his death. He was one of our family, and a true fighter for the freedom and prosperity of all France, and for justice which will last.'

'All of you, Madame — ' He realised his mistake and corrected himself quickly. 'Citizeness?'

'I don't know about Citizen St Felix,' she answered, deliberately not looking at him. 'Bernave was hard on him.'

'So it seems,' Menou nodded. 'So, indeed, it seems.' He straightened his shoulders. 'Remember: you are being watched! The revolution owes Citizen Bernave justice . . . and he will have it!' With that he went to the back door, opened it and went out, closing it with a bang behind him.

Marie-Jeanne rose to her feet, stiff from having sat so long. The baby in her arms had not woken.

She walked past them and out into the room beyond.

Fernand looked at St Felix, who was white-faced, then he turned and followed his wife.

Amandine stared at Célie.

Madame Lacoste said nothing, but her eyes were brilliant with tears.

8

Now that Menou had gone it was imperative that both Célie and Amandine, to whom St Felix had spoken, should throw themselves into furthering the plan. It was the nineteenth already. By this time in the morning two days from now, the King would be dead, and those who had gone to see the execution would be back at home preparing a late breakfast.

It was on Célie's lips to tell Amandine to go and do some shopping, and then find her alone, even outside in the courtyard if necessary, in order to give her more detailed instructions as to what she should say, and what she must learn. But Amandine was the senior servant in the house, and Célie would appear to be giving her orders. It would instantly arouse everyone's irritation, and almost certainly suspicion as well. She must be more careful than that.

Fernand glanced at the back door where Menou had just left.

'And what are we supposed to do for business while he has guards posted all round the place to keep us locked up? How does he think we're going to earn a sou in here?' he demanded angrily.

'He doesn't think!' Monsieur Lacoste snapped. 'Why should he care? He's worried about his own job, not ours. Are there so few

188

beggars in Paris you think anyone will notice a couple more?'

Madame looked up at them. 'It is barely twelve hours since Citizen Bernave was killed here in this house. What do you expect the man to do? No one has found the knife yet. He isn't going to let anyone leave except Célie or Amandine to buy food, and only then when he has had them searched. I imagine he doesn't suspect them, not seriously.' She glanced at St Felix, then back at her husband and son. She rose to her feet, a little stiffly, as if fear and exhaustion had locked her muscles. 'The time will hang less heavily if you do something. Marie-Jeanne will care for the children. I am going to return to Bernave's papers. We can't let the business slip: it maintains the house.'

'Thank you,' Marie-Jeanne said quietly. 'I haven't time to do it, and I don't want to.' There was a certain chill in her voice, as if she felt obliged to Bernave for their wellbeing, and it hurt her, even angered her, only for her family's sake she would not reject it. She held the baby a little tighter and reached out her other hand to touch the head of the three-year-old standing at her knee.

Madame acknowledged the thanks, then looked across at her husband. 'There are all sorts of things you could be doing,' she pointed out. 'The latch on the children's room is broken, has been for a month or more. The pump handle catches every now and again. I've at least three drawers that stick . . .'

'All right! I know.' He cleared his throat. 'I was

too busy to get to them before. Earning money comes before your own chores.' He turned to Fernand. 'And you can finish that chest for Virginie. You've been putting that aside since last August. And Amandine says there are lids in here that don't fit properly, and a hole somewhere that lets mice in.'

'Doorways let mice in,' Fernand responded drily, 'especially when they're left wide open!' But there was no ill temper in his voice. He shrugged very slightly and went out of the back into the bright, cold courtyard towards his workshop.

Monsieur Lacoste looked for a moment at Madame, with the same gentleness Célie had noticed before. She saw it with a jolt of pleasure, and loneliness.

When he was gone she looked to Madame. 'We are far later shopping than usual, because of Menou being here. Amandine and I had better both go to queue, if that is all right? Otherwise we may find we have missed most of what we need. We may find that anyway.'

Madame did not even think about it. 'Of course,' she responded straight away. 'I shall be in Citizen Bernave's room. You had better get some money from me.'

'Thank you,' Célie accepted, following her out, Marie-Jeanne close behind her, leaving Amandine and St Felix alone in the kitchen.

When she returned with the money for shopping they were standing close to each other, and had obviously stopped speaking only the moment she appeared. St Felix was watching

190

Amandine, as if to judge her reaction. Amandine had swung round in apprehension to face the door. Célie guessed he had taken this opportunity to tell her briefly of the plan and their part in it.

Célie made no comment, but walked over, offered Amandine half the money Madame had given her.

Amandine slid it into the pocket in her grey skirt. 'I'll try for bread and cheese, and of course if there's any meat.'

Célie raised her eyebrows. 'At this time of day? If it's still sitting around now there's something wrong with it!' She lowered her voice to little above a whisper. 'Where else are you going?' She glanced questioningly at St Felix, who nodded almost imperceptibly.

Amandine looked at him also, then back to Célie. 'To find the captain of Bernave's ship. He's in rooms in the Île de la Cité. At this hour he should still be there. He won't even know Bernave's dead yet.' Her face was tight. 'I shall have to tell him.'

'Watch him,' Célie warned. 'Look at his face as he hears. Judge whether you tell him what Menou said or not. I wish I knew more!'

'We all wish that,' St Felix agreed with feeling. He moved his weight from foot to foot, his whole body expressing the frustration and sense of entrapment he felt. He could do nothing but give instructions and wait. He did not even have a craft to occupy his hands. 'Where are you going?' he went on sharply to Célie.

'To the Faubourg St-Antoine,' she replied. 'To

191

see if the safe house is still safe.'

'How are you going to do that?' he persisted.

'I don't know! Watch, listen, ask about it.' She was thinking as she spoke. 'Maybe I shall pretend I want to buy it! That would give me an excuse to ask all sorts of questions.'

'But . . . ' Amandine began, then stopped.

'I don't have to have any money,' Célie said with raised eyebrows. 'I'm not going to take it, for heaven's sake! I'll look at it carefully, then tell them it is too small for my needs — or my taste!'

'I was going to say that the Faubourg St-Antoine is so dangerous!' Amandine's voice was a little high, threaded through with fear. She knew what had happened to St Felix there. Now she was frightened for Célie.

'I know, but I'll be all right,' Célie said more gently, trying to make herself smile. She did not want to think about it, still less did she want to go there, but the only alternative was to abandon the plan. She could not send Amandine. With her manner and soft diction she would be in far greater danger. Even she must be aware of that, unselfconscious as she was. St Felix could not leave the house, and there was no one else. It was much too far for Georges to risk in daylight. She did not want to explain or discuss it. 'I'll look just like anyone else there,' she assured her.

'How are you going to explain having the money to think of buying a house?' Amandine was still full of doubts.

Célie thought quickly. 'My husband! I'll say he was a soldier on the Austrian front and got killed. God knows, enough of them have! Still are . . . '

'And more will be,' Amandine said bleakly. 'And on the Spanish front, and at sea if Spain and England attack us too.' Her face was very white, her eyes focused and motionless in the strange stillness of horror. In that moment Célie understood profoundly why Bernave had planned to rescue the King and why now she could not argue with anyone's risk, or try to protect them at the cost of jeopardising their chance of success. The alternative was over-whelmingly, consumingly awful.

She smiled with an assumed confidence for Amandine's sake. 'I'll be fine. I don't care if they think I'm a drunk and a fool, reaching after something I've no chance of affording. I can always ask the price last.' She put more bravado into her voice and straightened her shoulders. 'Anyway, we don't know what it's like. It could be awful! Maybe a soldier's widow could afford it?'

'It is one of the first social reforms the revolution wants to bring in — decent pensions for army injured and sick after battle . . . and the old,' Amandine said with a mixture of humour and hope.

'In theory,' Célie retorted bitterly. 'Nobody's seen much in practice yet! Ask some of the crippled soldiers about . . . there are enough of them. And if Pache keeps all the guns here in Paris instead of sending them up to the front, they'll be more!'

The anger in her voice caught them for a

moment. There was silence in the kitchen. She could hear the creak of boards as someone moved about upstairs, and the voice of one of the children calling out.

There were footsteps outside in the courtyard.

'I'm going,' Amandine said quickly, 'before anyone catches us talking! We must be careful.' She took her cloak off its peg and put it on, picking up a basket in which to carry whatever she was able to buy. She looked back at Célie and then St Felix, smiled hopefully and opened the back door just as Fernand came in with his hands full of tools.

'Me too,' Célie agreed, striding towards the hook where her own coat was, and pulling her cap more firmly round her ears.

Should she try walking all the way, and risk being asked why she had been so long? Or see if she could find a public diligence and spend a few sous, and risk having to account to Madame for the money?

Time was more easily explainable. Queues moved slowly. One got to the head of them and found the woman before you had bought the last of whatever it was you needed. It happened only too often. Anyone would believe that, whereas Madame Lacoste would know the exact price of everything to the sou. Every woman did.

Reluctantly Célie put her head down and strode out. It was bright sunshine, but the wind was hard and cold, its raw edge whipping her face as it came up off the river.

She hurried across the Pont Neuf and the few yards of the tip of the Île de la Cité. There were

194

several people about, mostly idling, watching passers-by, waiting for news. A woman sold hot coffee. A youth distributed copies of *L'Ami du Peuple*, Marat's newspaper.

Célie crossed over the river again. This was where the public laundresses washed, when they could buy soap, starch and blue to do so — crouched on the stones regardless of the weather. She looked down and saw there was no one there today — the shortages were biting everywhere.

Around her the trees along the bank were bare, branches thin and black against the sky. The Church of St-Germain-L'Auxerrois was to her left.

Beyond it was the gorgeous palace of the Louvre.

Would Georges have visited there, before the revolution? What had his life been then? While her father was dreaming of being a great orator who hired men to fight for reform, and her mother had sat with luminous eyes, praising and encouraging him, filling his mind with her ideals and her courage, had Georges been watching empty masques at Versailles? Had he danced the night away, as they had argued, sipping sugar water in the salons of the Girondins, wearing togas and calling each other by antique Roman names?

Now one world was shattered for ever, and the other fast failing in the remnants of dreams they had neither the wit nor the will to seize.

She and Georges had never discussed the days before the Bastille. It was another world, gone for ever. Did he never speak of it because he had not been part of it, or because it did not matter now? Or because he was ashamed? Not only had the world changed, but, like so many others, he had also.

Or had it mattered too much, and he could not bear to remember it, like a person who will not mention the name of someone dead whose loss they have never accepted?

Or was it simply too dangerous because he knew she had been no part of it, and could not possibly share his feeling?

Célie found she was walking faster. She told herself it was to keep warm. She knew it was because she was angry, and excluded, and the exclusion hurt.

★　★　★

Georges woke early. He lay still for a few moments, then memory of Bernave's death and possible treachery flooded back like an icy, drowning tide.

He was shivering under the blankets. The mattress was hard and the room was freezing. There would be a skin of ice on the inside of the window.

It was still dark, but he could hear wheels on the cobbles outside. It was time to get up, the longer before full daylight, the better. He must warn those whom Bernave might have betrayed, if they were not already arrested. He was no stranger to betrayal. He would not be here at all had not Célie thought him to blame for her baby's death, and in revenge told the National Guard that he was anti-revolutionary.

He had had no time to hate her for it, because he had known nothing until she had risked her own life to warn him. Then they had been parted by the hysterical crowds thronging the city just before the Massacres.

When Amandine had explained to him, afterwards, about Jean-Pierre's death, and Célie's grief, the emotions were too overwhelming. It seemed pointless to cherish one more hated among so many. Too much was lost already, and he knew she regretted it more than he ever would, no matter how cold or hungry or cramped he was now. And there was a certain ironic justice in it. Who could be more anti-revolutionary than a man who planned to save the King's life?

He had told Célie he would check on the safe houses closest to him in St-Sulpice and St-Honoré. He had left the one in St-Antoine, the furthest, and in the worst district, to her.

He threw the blankets off in one movement and felt the bitter air hit his body through his shirt. He hated lying in it, but he had no such luxury as a separate one for the night, and if he left it off he would be too cold to sleep at all.

He lit the candle. There was a little water from last night and he washed his face. He shaved, cutting himself slightly. He should have been accustomed to using cold water by now. He had been running and hiding for nearly five months. It didn't do to think back on servants with steaming jugs, fresh linen smelling of wind and sun, a clean, bright room overlooking the sweep of woods and fields — the home farm, a good horse to ride. Nothing from the past could be kept — not by him, not by anyone.

He dressed in a woollen jerkin and trousers and a high-collared coat, the warmest things he had, ate half of the bread he had left and drank a little wine. He would have preferred coffee, but he had nothing with which to heat it.

He would begin by going to see Maurice Doué. It was he who had found the men and women to surge forward out of the crowd and mob the King's carriage on the way to the execution so as to mask the change from the King to the man who would take his place. He must warn him even before he checked on the safe houses. Doué would have to judge for himself whether he needed to replace the people with new ones, in case any of them were compromised. They should not be. He had told Bernave nothing except that they had been engaged.

The question was, how much did St Felix know, and what might he have told Bernave? Perhaps new people would be safer, although safety was relative. No one could count on being free and alive next week, let alone next year.

He blew out the candle and pinched the wick, then opened the door. It must have rained in the night; the stairs were slippery from the leak in the roof. He closed the door behind him, pulling it sharply to force it shut over the place where the wood was swollen, then crept down carefully.

Outside there was a slight paling of coming

198

daylight over to the east, but he could see little more than the outlines of the buildings against the clear sky, and he had to continue to pick his way. It was numbingly cold and the night's ice was slick on the cobbles.

He thought longingly of the south, of home as it had been only a few years ago. It was an illusion, of course, but his memory always created sun there, the long sweep of the earth, a gold in the air, men working in the fields and over the vines, faces streaked with sweat and dust.

He had thought it an ideal life then, just as his father always had. He could see him in his mind's eye, straight-backed, eyes narrowed against the sun and wind, stopping to talk to a worker here or there. He had cared for them, known them by name, worried about nurturing the land for them, as Georges had meant to do after him.

Had it really been oppressive, too paternalistic, denying them a chance of equality? Had their polite smiles hidden hatred underneath, because the land was Coigny's while they worked it and owned nothing? Was what he imagined to be benevolence really a mark for another kind of tyranny? Not even honest in the end, because it clothed itself in virtue.

Georges had loved his father and admired him. Such a thought was itself a betrayal the old man would not have understood. It would have been better if he could have died before the mobs took the house and the land and destroyed so much, five generations of care. He could not

199

forget the old man's face when they had burned the barns and driven the horses out, terrified, plunging into the darkness, the flames roaring up behind them into the night sky. He would far rather have given them the whole thing, if only they would have cherished it as he had.

But that was all gone as if it had been decades ago, not a mere eighteen months. There were other things to fight for, something that might still be saved, and no doubts clouded his mind about that.

It took him nearly two hours of walking, standing, questioning and walking again before he discovered Doué across the river near the Place de la Bastille. By this time Georges was tired, cold and extremely hungry.

They met in a farrier's yard, in a small shed close to the forge, blessedly warm from the heat of the fires, but dim, and smelling of horse sweat and manure.

Doué was another fugitive like himself, moving from attic to cellar through one alley or another, always one step ahead of pursuit or betrayal. As it was, when Georges found him, Doué was standing with a knife in his hand, ready to fight for survival, if need be. He relaxed only when Georges took off his hat and let the thin winter light show his face, dark eyes wide, cheeks thinner than before. Only his smile was the same, charming and a little wry.

'Oh . . . it's you!' Doué was surprised. He lowered the knife and held out a half-empty bottle of wine. It was a generous gesture.

Georges took it, but drank only a couple of

mouthfuls, feeling the liquid hit his throat with a glorious heat. There was however no time to waste, so he handed the bottle back with thanks. 'Victor Bernave was killed last night.' He watched Doué's face tighten in the grey daylight that came in through the half-open doorway.

Doué took the bottle and put it down. Wine was too precious to be drunk casually. He was obviously startled.

'Accident?' he asked, pushing his brown hair out of his eyes.

'No.'

'Not the guillotine?' Doué made it more of a denial than a question. 'You said Victor Bernave?'

'Yes . . . why? Didn't you think he would be guillotined?' Georges asked.

'Don't know. Unlikely. What for?'

It was not the answer Georges was seeking. He did not bother to point out that little enough reason was needed these days. 'Why unlikely?' he pursued.

'Too careful,' Doué replied. His expression was impossible to read in the gloom. 'Clever bastard. Why are you telling me?'

There was no answer but the truth.

'Because he was the one behind the plan.'

Doué's eyes narrowed. 'Bernave? Victor Bernave behind the plan to rescue the King?'

The cold settled inside Georges' stomach. 'I told you so.'

'Not before, you damned well didn't!' Doué exploded. 'God in heaven! How much did he know of us — of our men?'

201

'Nothing from me, but from anyone else, I don't know. Warn everyone — '

'You're damned right I will!' Doué swore and clenched his fists in a gesture of helplessness. 'What a bloody mess!' he said furiously. 'The Austrians and the Prussians are pouring over our borders. The Convention's in chaos. The Commune is doing whatever Marat tells it to do, and the puritans are following Robespierre, God help them.' His voice was thick with emotion and he seemed to find it difficult to catch his breath. 'The few rational men in the middle are listening to Danton, for whatever that's worth,' he went on. 'And the Girondins are quarrelling among each other like a bagful of cats — and about as much use. They couldn't make a decision what to do about anything.' His face was twisted with scorn. 'A roomful of them couldn't even agree with each other what day it is. And if Marat came in and said 'Boo!' they'd all run away. Probably fall over each other and get wedged in the door on the way out.'

Georges laughed at the vision, but with bitterness for the truth of it. He moved closer to the forge. He was getting warmer, and aware of how cold he had been.

'I know,' he agreed. 'And we choose now to chop the King's head off and provoke what's left of Europe that isn't at war with us already.'

Doué stared at him, squinting a little. 'So are we going on with our plan?'

Georges had never doubted it. There was nowhere to go back to, for anyone. The past was broken with.

'Yes. Find new men,' he said aloud. 'Warn the old ones. Maybe they should get out of Paris, if they can . . . at least for a while.'

'God help them, if Bernave was working for the Commune!' Doué shook his head.

'Was he?' Georges asked.

'To tell you the truth, I'm not sure,' Doué answered, sounding surprised at himself. He moved a little closer to the wall that backed on to the forge fire. 'Vadier told me some other news about the Commune, to do with Pache and the guns, and he said something about the Comte d'Artois and some scheme to rescue the King.' He took a quick drink, upending the bottle. 'I didn't believe him. Told him it was nonsense. But he said he had it from an excellent source, spy among the royalists for the Commune. I asked him who. He told me he didn't know. It could have been Bernave — or any of fifty others.'

Georges said nothing. The fear was gripping tighter inside him, and he realised the feeling was hurt as well, which surprised him. He thought betrayal couldn't hurt any more. But he had trusted Bernave. He was repelled by what Célie had told him of his abuse of St Felix, but he had assumed there must be some reason. He had still trusted Bernave's honour, his sense of purpose. He had seemed to share Georges' own vision of events so clearly, so very rationally. If he were too careful of his own skin to risk it when he could risk St Felix's instead, or if some old enmity with the man had made him use this chance for revenge, then they were flaws in his character

203

Georges despised. But they had not destroyed his fundamental belief in his political honesty.

'Or he could be feeding the Commune a lot of rubbish,' Doué went on, looking at Georges with one eyebrow raised. He rubbed his hands together in the cold. 'After all, it wouldn't matter to Artois! The Commune would guillotine him if they could catch him, regardless!' He took another long pull at his bottle.

'Can you find out?' Georges asked.

'If it was Bernave?' Doué regarded him steadily. 'Possibly, but not without raising suspicion, and certainly not before tomorrow night, which is about the last chance we have to change anything. Who killed him anyway?'

'Don't know. Fellow called Menou, from the National Guard, is trying to find out.'

Doué jerked his head up, staring at Georges. 'Who told you Bernave was dead?'

'Better you don't know,' Georges replied softly, Célie's passionate, stubborn face coming too easily to his mind. 'Someone with enough courage and imagination to get out without being seen, and to help us go on with the plan. Can you get new people for the crowd?'

'If I need to,' Doué conceded. 'Maybe I'll replace one or two, as you say, or simply tell them they're in danger and to get out of Paris, or at least out of wherever they are now.' He pulled a face as if the previous mouthful of wine had been sour. 'Most of them have nothing to lose. Whatever they had once they've lost now . . . mostly home, family. You'll not be betrayed by any of them.'

Georges nodded. 'Just thought you'd a right to know.'

Doué lifted one shoulder in a slight shrug of acknowledgement. He held out the bottle.

Georges took it, drank another short swig, then passed it back. 'Thanks. I've got other errands. Goodbye.'

''Bye.' Doué watched him leave.

Georges hurried back westwards towards the Rue St-Honoré, passing almost within the shadow of the Louvre. He barely looked at its massive glory of stone now, with its ageless grace. A few years ago his family would have been welcome there, had they chosen to live in Paris rather than by the Loire. That was what he regretted, not the old life in Paris or Versailles. He had never cared for the balls and masques, the afternoons at the races or evenings of endless conversation. There had always been something alien about them. But the château overlooking the river, the evening light on the trees, the width of sky and the birdsong was home as nothing else could be. Its loss still hurt with a deep and abiding pain.

Had it simply passed to someone else who would have loved it as his father had, nurtured it and understood its needs, perhaps he could have borne it. But they had had to stand by helplessly as ignorant men, full of hatred for possessions and those who held them, had broken and destroyed centuries of beauty. It was senseless. Nobody gained. And yet it was the tide which engulfed all France, and if it was not stemmed soon, nothing would be left. In a generation's

205

time, who would there be left who even remembered it, knew what certainty was, and untarnished dreams?

He forced the ache from him. There was no time for grief. He turned right off along the Rue St-Honoré and up the Rue Cambon. The Place de la Révolution with its stark, jutting posts of the guillotine was behind him now, hidden by the buildings along the Rue de Rivoli, but he could never forget its presence. His mind's eye saw it, whichever way he faced. This was a fashionable area, far from the slums and alleys where the dispossessed and the hunted could find some sanctuary. The National Guard would have plenty of informers here, but no one could search every alley, and on the day of the King's execution the streets would be teeming with life, everyone packed together, craning forward, trying to see. Once the exchange was made they could flee down an alley, pursuit blocked by a quickly moved barrow. Their route was carefully planned, and as short as possible. Up here to the right was the stable yard where they could take the cart and hide it while the King slipped into the loft and changed into the merchant's clothes, then came down again on the other side and continued on his way.

It had been a long walk in the cold. Georges thought of Célie having to go all the way to the Faubourg St-Antoine. He could picture her in his mind, not her pale, beautiful hair, but her eyes — the anger, the courage and the guilt in them — and the soft generosity of her mouth. Her legs would ache far more than his by the time she got all the way to St-Antoine and back. And how would she explain her absence for such a time to Madame Lacoste?

But he could not go. It was too far to risk in daylight. Too many people could recognise him from the posters around, naming him as an enemy of the revolution, or from a sketch in one of the pamphlets, like *Père Duchesne* or *L'Ami du Peuple*. He had seen one or two of them. Even in the rough strokes of the pen, a few lines, they had caught his brow and the angles of his cheek and nose, the way his hair grew from his brow.

He had kept mainly to the busy streets where there was plenty of traffic, hoping to be unnoticed, but now he must go up the Rue Cambon.

All the usual shops were open, and there were queues of people for bread, coffee, candles, soap and sugar. Some stood silently, faces set hard in lines of despair, others were quarrelsome, ill-suppressed anger spilling over at the slightest provocation.

He started up the street, walking at what he hoped was a normal pace, avoiding meeting anyone's eyes. He intended looking for a man called Romeuf who owned the stable inherited from his brother who had been killed on the Austrian front. He had no love for the Girondins, despising their incompetence, their cowardice and the personal ambitions which tore them apart and rendered them totally ineffective in controlling the Convention. He had protested against Pache's diversion of boots

207

and guns from the army to the Commune, and incurred Marat's personal wrath for his temerity. A considerable number of very ordinary people had taken up his cry. He was no lover of royalty, but he had a larger vision of patriotism than the gratification of a local hunger for power, whatever the cost. He had been close to his brother, and proud of him. He saw his life sacrificed senselessly, not through a military defeat which was inevitable, but because he was sent to fight and then robbed of the means to do it by the Paris Commune.

Georges had never mentioned Romeuf to Bernave. He told no one anything they did not need to know. Still, could Bernave know Romeuf's name and his connections to the royalist cause from some other source? Had he betrayed him to the Commune? Georges must at least warn him.

He stepped off the kerb to avoid a group of women talking together, their voices raised, but he did not swing quite wide enough. He brushed past the basket of one of them, knocking it sideways.

She swore at him.

He turned to apologise. 'I'm sorry, Citizeness.'

She was a sharp-faced woman of almost fifty, her clothes drab, sagging over her thin body. Her eyes narrowed. 'I know you . . . I've seen yer somewhere!' It was almost an accusation.

It was ridiculous to be afraid. There were a hundred reasonable explanations. He swallowed.

'Probably. I come now and then. Good day, Citizeness.' He took a step to continue.

'Just a minute!' she challenged him, her voice shrill.

Should he stop, or keep on as if he had not heard? No, that would look like running away. And yet why should he stop for her? She was a stranger to whom he owed nothing.

'What is it, Citizeness?' Better to placate her if possible. A few yards would make no difference anyway. His heart was pounding and he could feel the sweat on his skin.

'Yer got a familiar look about yer.' The woman screwed up her eyes, peering forward. 'Summink about yer I seen on a poster.'

'I'll lay yer odds 'e's wanted,' the woman next to her said knowingly, glaring at Georges. 'Think 'cos we got nothing, yer can come 'ere, live in our 'ouses, an' eat our bread. Well, yer can't!' She stuck her chin out aggressively. 'We're just as loyal ter the revolution as anyone! Any o' them fancy poets an' lawyers in the Cordeliers! Your days is numbered, they is! Our day'll come, you see! Marat's for us. This is our revolution, an' don' yer forget it!'

They all moved a little closer to him, their attitude threatening, arms akimbo, faces set.

'I know it is,' he agreed, forcing himself to smile. He hoped it did not look as sickly as it felt. 'Citizen Marat gains more power all the time. One day we'll have a government truly of the people.' He did not add that he hardly expected Marat to live to see it.

There was a rumble of assent.

He smiled very slightly and turned away again.

'Coigny!' One of the women said loudly. 'I

knew I seed that face somewhere! 'E's wanted! Grab 'im!'

Georges took to his heels and ran, hearing them shouting after him, at least two of them yelling for the National Guard. He went wide round the corner of the Rue Cambon into a side alley. He shinned up a wall and over the top, dropping down the other side into a stonemason's yard. He could hear feet in the alley behind him.

There was no time to hesitate. He ran forward again, dodging round the stones, startling a man with a hammer and chisel in his hand. He passed him without a word, and went out of the gates into a side street. Left or right? He did not know this area. There was a threadwork of narrow passages towards the Rue des Capucines. He had gone down one once with Romeuf. He must be sure not to lose his sense of direction and come out again where he went in.

He swivelled on his heel and started running, feet clattering and sliding on the last of the ice. There were more footsteps behind him. He had no idea whether they were anything to do with him or not, and no time to find out. He ducked in a narrow doorway and scrambled up a flight of stone stairs. He put his shoulder against the door at the top and forced it open. There were half a dozen people in the room.

'Sorry!' he shouted, half jumping over them and lurching against the wall, regaining his balance and going up another flight of stairs, this time inside. If he could get up and out over the roof he could come down anywhere, the Rue des

Capucines, or the Place Vendôme. But he must be quick, or they would have the whole block surrounded and he would be trapped.

He stopped at the top; he could not hear anyone following, only his own breath rasping in his throat. That meant nothing.

He went up another flight and into the attic. Damn! It faced on to the Rue Cambon. He was not even certain he had not been seen. The street seemed to be full of people. Even in one short instant he saw half a dozen red, white and blue cockades.

He stepped back so quickly he almost fell. He burst open the door on the further side and ran to the window. Thank heaven! That looked out over crazily angled rooftops. There was no time to weigh a decision. He opened the casement and clambered out. The slates were wet and he slid several feet before finding his grip and beginning to move sideways along towards the east and the tanneries.

He was watching his handhold and looking towards the outline of dormers and gables beyond, when the first shot crashed on to a slate a couple of yards away. It richocheted with a sharp whine and ended rattling down into the valley between the roofs.

Georges scrambled forward, up to the ridge as if the devil were behind him. He found strength he never knew he possessed. His fingers reached the ridge tiles and he hauled himself up as the second shot struck a chimneypot and the third splintered a tile on the dormer to his left.

He rolled over the ridge, lost his balance and

211

glissaded down the other side, landing hard at the bottom of the valley, bruising his back and shoulders. But there was no time for thought of injury. He scrambled to his hands and knees, then up to a crouching position, and ran forward as fast as he could to the junction of the next two valleys, looked to see which was the larger, chose it and made his way along it as fast as he could.

He heard gunfire, but it seemed further away now. One more turn and he found a drainpipe. It gave him something to hold on to, to guide himself as far as another ledge, then a ten-foot drop down to the top of a stone stair and into a courtyard.

He landed with a jar which shook his bones, Which way now? His hands were skinned and bleeding. His trousers were soaked with rain. He had very little idea of where he was, or even how far he had come from the queue of women who had started the alarm. His heart was thumping so wildly he felt as if he must be shaking all over and he had to work hard to get enough breath. He was horrified to find his legs were weak.

He felt a sharp stab of guilt for having regarded Célie's trip over the rooftops so lightly. He had been concerned for her, but had not realised just what risks she ran on his account.

Except, of course, it was not really for him, it was for the cause she believed in, and more than that, underlying everything, the guilt for having betrayed herself by being so much less than she wanted to be. He was incidental; she would have felt the same for whoever it was. That hurt more than he would have expected. He wished it had been for himself, that it was he who mattered to her.

He had had long enough to get his composure back. He could not wait here. Someone would see him and wonder who he was.

He walked past the well in the centre of the yard and out of the arched gateway into the street ahead. Thank God! It was the Rue des Capucines. Opposite was a basket-maker's shop, then a harness-maker and saddlers, a cutlers, a button-maker on the near side, and a man standing selling copies of a political pamphlet.

The other way there was a currier, a grocer, and a little further along a pewterer. There was a queue outside the grocer. He should avoid that. He started the other way quickly.

He crossed over and headed back towards the Rue St-Honoré.

He kept to the alleys and passages parallel to the main street, fear tensing his body and making his gait stiff and tiring. Every time he heard a shout or saw a knot of people he felt a chill.

The women in the queue would move up as the goods were sold. They would not willingly lose their places. To the hungry, food is everything. In half an hour, or maybe an hour, they would be gone, replaced by others. He would return to the Rue Cambon, perhaps coming from the other direction.

It was nearly ten o'clock by the time he found Romeuf, working at the back of his small shop making candles. The smell of tallow was strong in the enclosed air, but it was at least warm over the vat. Everything seemed to be surrounded by

213

hanging candles, running and dripping pale gobbets.

Georges told Romeuf the news of Bernave's death. Romeuf was shaken, but it did not slacken his resolve to play his part in the plan, only to change it a little. He would still find a wagon, only a different one. His brother's stable yard was still the best place to change clothes.

'It shouldn't surprise me,' he said bitterly. 'I heard whispers. What the hell is one more disillusion?' His agreeably ugly face with its broken nose was ghostly yellow in the reflected light. 'Long ago I believed in the possibility of persuading the King to govern with a parliament, like the British King.' He was working with the tallow as he spoke. 'I thought we could institute reforms, get rid of the court at Versailles, the ridiculous privileges of the aristocracy and the financial stranglehold of the Church.' He kept stirring the liquid. 'I dreamed of a day free from corrupt taxation and the incessant delays of the law. France is an enlightened country, full of wit and imagination, art, science, literature, music and theatre. It should have a just government for the benefit of all the people.'

Georges made no reply. There was none to make. There had been so many promises, so many steps forward: the renunciation of feudal rights in the National Assembly back in August of '89, the Declaration of the Rights of Man, Church property nationalised. The next year religious orders had been suppressed, except those engaged in teaching or charitable works. The titles of the hereditary nobility had been abolished. A decree had imposed the civic oath on the clergy.

In '91 the King had fled to Varennes, and been brought back by force. In September he had accepted the Constitution.

Then it had started to go wrong. The King had gone back on his word, vetoing the decision against the emigrés, then against the non-juring priests.

It had been worse in 1792. In March the ministry had been replaced by the Girondins. In April war had been declared. In June the King had dismissed the new ministry.

In July the terrible Marseillais had marched into Paris. All the Paris sections but one had petitioned for the deposing of the King. An insurrectionary Commune had been formed. In August the mob had stormed the Tuileries and the King had been suspended from all functions. The ministers had all been reappointed.

That same month that Lafayette had defected to the Austrians, the Duke of Brunswick had led his armies across the frontier into France. Longwy had fallen to the Prussians. Verdun had surrendered.

Then had come September . . . blood-soaked, nightmare September, never to be forgotten and perhaps not even forgiven either.

On the twentieth, the same day as the battle of Valmy, the Convention had been constituted. The day after, it had abolished the monarchy.

And now in two days' time the King would go

to the guillotine, and France would enter a new age of chaos.

Nature and violence had taken everyone from Georges, almost everyone he loved. The gentle, beautiful world in which he had grown up was lost. Of the past, its ignorance and its beauty, its tarnished understanding, only Amandine was left.

He talked with Romeuf a little longer, then thanked him and took his leave, going out into the alley with his collar turned up as far as possible and his hat pulled down.

He was hungry, but he had only a few sous left. He realised with a jolt just how much he had relied on Célie since September. It was a frightening knowledge. Unconsciously he increased his pace, retracing his steps back towards the Île de la Cité, not sure where he was heading. Dare he go back to the attic in the Cordeliers? Or might the whole area be alerted to watch for him?

But he must. He must check on the safe house at St-Sulpice.

He laughed, and it risked going out of control, hysteria more than humour. What delusions of importance! He was being absurd! The Commune was supreme. In two days they would send the King of France to the scaffold like any common criminal. On the battlefield they were prepared to defy Europe — hopelessly, perhaps, but they did not seem to realise that. What did one minor dissenter matter to them? Fun of the chase, perhaps, but little more, forgotten the moment it was no longer succeeding.

He had eight sous left. If he could find bread, it was usually about three sous a pound, but he was far too late in the day now. To stand in a queue for it was out of the question. Memory of queues pinched his stomach more than hunger.

He went into a café and sat in the corner. He bought a bowl of stew and a slice of bread for four sous, and was glad of the warmth.

He ate alone, careful to catch no one's eye. Then outside in the cold night air again, he walked towards St-Sulpice. He made his way through alleys and up and down stone steps, through a deserted garden, to find Alphonse le Bon. A month ago, on what used to be Christmas when religion was legal, the two of them had shared half a chicken and a bottle of very good wine.

It began to rain. Was there any point in all their careful checking of details, the miles of walking, the finding of new people, a new wagon, searching Bernave's room for the passes? Without the man who was prepared to replace the King in the carriage, and die for him when the crowd realised the substitution, there was no plan. Only Bernave had known who he was — that is, if he really existed. They had two days in which to find another.

Georges came across le Bon in the yard behind a hairdresser's shop. He had a bundle of outdated newspapers and pamphlets in his arms, and looked surprisingly cheerful.

'Still got your head, I see,' he remarked with a smile. He was a thin, fair-haired man with a handsome nose. He was probably about thirty.

He surveyed Georges up and down as if assessing him for a new suit. 'You look wet. I might know where I can find a new pair of boots for you, if you like? Your feet are bigger than mine. Commune's full of boots that should have gone to the army, poor sods!' He sniffed. 'But I suppose you know that! I don't fancy their chances of fighting the Spanish barefoot!'

'Thank you,' Georges accepted, although he had no idea if either of them would survive, or meet again to give or take the gift.

Le Bon shrugged, almost dropping his papers. 'I don't know why I hang around Paris, except that I'm compulsive about hearing the news, and this is where everything is happening. Centre of the world — at the moment. God knows what it will be next year.' He cocked an eyebrow. 'Heap of ruins, I should think. 'City of blood, lust and lies', wasn't that what Madame Roland called it? Or something like that. I must be mad.' He smiled cheerfully, but Georges could see behind the mask of humour a deep despair.

He remembered how much he had liked le Bon, how they had laughed together over silly jokes, as if that were all that mattered. For a while they had pretended that the September Massacres and the war and the hunger and chaos did not exist. It had been a supreme act of will, because they both knew so much better.

Instinctively Georges put out his hands to take half the newspapers, and clasped le Bon's arm.

'I'll help you carry them,' he stated. 'Wherever you're going is good enough for me.'

'Thanks,' le Bon accepted, passing them over.

'What the hell have you done to your hands?' He surveyed the cuts from the slates.

'Nothing that matters,' Georges replied with a shrug.

Le Bon smiled, knowing not to pursue it. He gestured to the papers. 'Roll them up tight, they'll do a little while as fuel. More use than their original purpose. Did you know anybody talk or write as much drivel in your life?' He started to walk towards the gate to the alley and Georges went with him. 'The hot air put out by the Girondins could warm France, if it could only be directed!'

'If you could face all the Girondins one way at the same time, then you could probably part the Red Sea as well,' Georges said bitterly.

'If you could face all the Girondins in one direction it would be a bigger bloody miracle than parting the Atlantic!' le Bon responded.

Georges laughed; for a moment it rang of true humour.

'It's going badly,' le Bon said. 'Fellow I know, good man, not frightfully clever, just an ordinary chap, but decent, came back from the Austrian front the other day. Lost his arm. Nobody gives a damn. Said it's chaos out there.'

They crossed a small courtyard and went under an arch into another alley.

'No guns,' le Bon went on. 'Not much ammunition, short rations all the time. Coats that wouldn't keep a dog warm.' He glanced sideways. 'What's happened to us, Georges? We had such dreams ... but we haven't made anything any better. It's worse in some ways. I used to know who my enemies were. Now I don't even know that.'

'Marat!' Georges said helpfully.

'Robespierre!' le Bon answered. 'He doesn't believe in us any more — hadn't you heard? The Convention told him we didn't exist.' He sniffed. 'Or perhaps they told us he didn't? Either way, we don't know each other any more.'

'God help us!' Georges sighed.

He hitched up the papers a little higher. They were heavy and slipping. He had no idea where he was going. He liked le Bon, but time was too short for indulgence of mere conversation.

Georges followed him across a swirling gutter and into the shelter of a vacant, rambling shed.

Le Bon dropped the papers and invited Georges to sit down. An old stove in the corner gave off a little heat.

'Can't stay here long,' he said ruefully. 'Owner's away, so it'll do for a few days. Everything could change by then anyway.' He peered at Georges in the gloom, trying to read his expression. 'What's wrong? You look like hell!'

'Victor Bernave was murdered last night,' Georges answered. 'I need to know if the place in St-Sulpice is still all right?'

'Was he?' Le Bon's voice rose in surprise. 'By whom, do you know?'

'No, I don't . . . nor why. What about the house in St-Sulpice? Who else knows of it?'

'No one. Listen to everything. Say nothing.' Le Bon began rolling the damp papers up tightly and produced several lengths of string from his pockets to tie them into rough logs. 'Duplicitous devil, Bernave. I thought he was clever, but looks as if he wasn't so clever after all. Played them off against each other one time too many.'

'Off against each other . . . ' Georges repeated. 'Who? Royalists against Commune? Danton against Robespierre? Girondins against each other?'

Le Bon grinned, looking up from his papers. 'Probably all of that, but mostly royalists against the Commune. Right hand never knew what his left was doing. Pity . . . I mean pity he's dead. He was interesting. He had a sense of humour, of the absurd. Never trust a man who can't laugh — and cry. And that's most these days.'

'He was knifed in the back in his own house.' Georges watched le Bon, and continued rolling papers himself.

Le Bon was startled. He stiffened and looked up sideways at Georges. 'Then how can you not know who did it?' he asked. 'It wasn't domestic, surely? Not Bernave! I don't see him as a deceiving lover! Although I've been wrong before. In fact probably more often than I've been right — or I wouldn't be crouching here in somebody else's damn shed. If a toad like Marat can have a mistress, then anyone can.'

'I doubt it.' Georges finished a bundle and tied it as tightly as he could. He wished le Bon would put one on the stove now — he was frozen — but perhaps they were too precious to be used until the last already burning was almost gone. 'More likely political,' he went on. 'Someone

221

thought he was on the wrong side.'

'Interesting you should say that,' le Bon replied thoughtfully. 'You aren't the only one asking about him, you know.'

Georges stopped what he was doing, his fingers motionless. 'Someone else is? Who? Commune or royalist?'

Le Bon was curious. It showed in his eyes and the tilt of his head. 'You care a lot who killed him. Why? What was he to you?'

'The master behind the only plan which has even the ghost of a chance of working,' Georges answered. 'Perhaps 'ghost' is the right word now. And yes, you're right, I care who killed him. And I care even more which side he was on . . . or if he was playing both sides, or would come down for whoever wins . . . or whoever will pay him the most.'

Le Bon looked at him gravely. 'I think that warrants something on the fire,' he observed, opening the stove door and putting the last completed bundle in, then slamming it shut. He squatted on his heels, regarding Georges curiously. 'You think he could have betrayed the plan to the Commune?'

Did he really think that? No . . . but the fear of it would not go. It was possible. Perhaps his disbelief was only the slowness of his imagination to grasp what had really happened? He was still finding it hard to accept that Bernave was dead.

'I don't know any more,' he admitted, rubbing his hands together to keep the circulation going, then stretching them out to the fire. The warmth was making the cuts and scratches smart as circulation returned. 'I thought I was certain of him. Now I've learned a lot about him I didn't know . . . none of it good. Who else was asking about him, anyway?'

'I can't tell you because I don't know,' le Bon confessed. 'It was just a question here, a question there, all very discreet, but I got the impression, from the bit I overheard, that it was also pretty angry. Whoever it was, was no friend.'

George said nothing. His mind raced. Who else suspected Bernave? From which side? How much did any of them really know about St Felix? Could he have been a genuine royalist, and discovered Bernave was using him against his own cause? That would have been the ultimate betrayal, with the bitterest irony laced in.

How that would hurt Amandine! He could hardly bear to think of it. She had always wanted to believe so much of people. He could see her as a little girl, long ago on the banks of the Loire, listening to the stories of the old man in the long evenings, wide-eyed, taking in every word, slow to realise when she was being teased, and then laughing as hard as anyone.

But that had been meant in kindness.

As she had grown up she had been quick to give her friendship, but slow to give her heart. He could remember her first real love — sweet, hesitant, wildly unsuitable. It had ended in an innocent parting. She had told him about it, in whispers, one summer evening in the hay loft. He had ached for her sadness, and smiled in the dark that it had gone so cleanly, with nothing to regret.

Célie had said Amandine cared very deeply for St Felix, and admired him intensely. This would leave a bitterness behind, something that would not heal over. Amandine was not a fighter, like Célie.

But he could hardly blame any man for killing someone who used him in such a fashion. But to knife him in the dark, in his own house, was a little cold-blooded, and a little careless of other people's involvement.

'You don't know what this questioner discovered?' he said aloud.

Le Bon shook his head. 'Sorry. It was only snatches here and there, a word or two overheard.' He grimaced. 'I get to stand on street corners a lot these days, and hanging around alleys in a way I wouldn't normally choose. I'm a watcher and a listener, because I don't know what to do!'

'Who does?' Georges said with a wave of hopelessness. 'Every time I take a step, the ground moves from under me.'

'Something else about Bernave,' le Bon said quietly. 'I don't know if it's true, but I heard there was a royalist plan to rescue the King from the Temple prison.'

Georges looked up. It was a crazy idea. The Temple was an enormous, virtually impregnable building, guarded day and night.

'Surely even they have more sense than to try that!' He felt a flutter of sharp, sickening fear. 'Obviously it didn't succeed — but the very fact

224

that they tried will have warned Marat, the Commune, everyone!'

Le Bon put out his hand and grasped Georges' wet sleeve. 'Don't worry!They didn't do anything. The plot was foiled before it got that far. I didn't learn how — but I did hear by whom.'

Georges swallowed. 'Who?'

'Victor Bernave.' A wraith of humour lit le Bon's lopsided face. 'I don't know whether he was preventing the King from escaping, preventing the royalists trying to put him back on the throne, or preventing them all from setting out on a plan which couldn't possibly succeed, and would forewarn Marat and the Commune, and ruin our chances.'

Georges shook his head, overwhelmed. It seemed as if every certainty was shifting even as he reached for it.

'Have a piece of bread,' le Bon offered. 'At least that doesn't change. We still have to eat.'

Georges hesitated. It was not a time to eat another man's food.

'Go out in style!' le Bon urged. 'I've a bottle of pretty decent Bordeaux. Its owner won't need it any more, poor devil. You can feed me tomorrow — if there is a tomorrow.' And without waiting for Georges' reply, he straightened up and went over to a ledge in the wall, into the shadows, and took down a dusty bottle, and a loaf of bread wrapped around with a clean towel. There was also a fair size piece of cheese. He divided them scrupulously and offered Georges half.

225

'Are we still going on?' he asked after a few moments.

'Yes,' Georges replied with his mouth full. 'Just changing it a little. Different places, different people.' He grimaced. 'Can't change the time.'

Le Bon laughed abruptly. 'Still want my help?'

'Yes.' Georges watched le Bon's face. 'Discreet place for a gentleman to change his clothes before leaving Paris in a hurry, and privately.'

Le Bon smiled, turning the corner of his lips down.

'Not for Varennes, I trust?'

'No, not Varennes,' George agreed quietly, remembering the royal family's abortive attempt to escape. They had very nearly made it as far as the Austrian border before they were caught and brought back.

Le Bon looked at Georges steadily. 'We don't have much chance, you know. Quite apart from Bernave — '

'I know,' Georges cut across him, not wanting to hear it. 'But can you think of anything better?'

'No — not living in this madhouse, anyway. It'll only get worse.' He held up the bottle in a salute. 'What the hell! Here's to going down in glorious flames — last fire before the darkness. Who needs to live to see that?'

9

Célie tiptoed up the attic steps again. She did not like coming here in daylight; she was too likely to be seen and arouse curiosity. Someone would know she did not live here and wonder what she was doing.

She reached the top and rapped lightly on the door. There was no answer, and she felt a surge of disappointment. This was ridiculous. She had known Georges could not avoid going out in daylight, now that Bernave was dead. She should not stand here with her heart in her throat.

The door opened and she saw the familiar outline of his head against the thin daylight with a surge of relief.

'Oh! Y-you're here,' she stammered.

'Célie! Come in.' He stepped back to make way for her.

She went inside and closed the door. She should explain herself. He must have heard the emotion in her voice. 'I thought perhaps you were still out.'

He looked at her anxiously. 'Are you all right?'

'Yes. Of course I am,' she said decisively. She held out the food for him and he took it, thanking her. She launched straight away into what she had come to say. It was embarrassing to give and receive thanks every time she did a small service like bringing bread. He was dependent upon it, and she did not want the reminder any more than he must.

'I found the passes,' she told him. 'They are made out in four names, I suppose to cover all possibilities. I gave them to St Felix, in case I am searched again as I go in and out of the house.'

'Good.' Something in him relaxed; there was a slight easing of his shoulders. With his back to the light she could not see his face clearly except in outline. 'Did you destroy any of the other papers?' he asked. 'What was there?'

She breathed in deeply and hesitated a second. She was not sure if she had done the right thing or not. 'We destroyed quite a lot — '

'We?' he swung round, his body stiffening.

'Madame and I,' she explained. 'I was afraid that someone else might have the same ideas for different reasons, and if I were caught it would be the end of everything. They would think I was stealing.'

'Yes, I understand.' He was watching her intently, trying to read her face. She found it discomfiting, and yet his indifference would have been worse.

'If she were with me then no one else — '

'I understand,' he repeated. She heard the edge of the tension in his voice.

'We burned the papers we thought might arouse envy or too much curiosity, and kept only what was necessary to continue the business.' She met his eyes. 'That included keeping some of the trade routes and destroying the ones used by the drivers we knew, and records of the property in St-Antoine . . . which seems to be still safe, as far as I can judge.'

'You've been there this morning?'

'Yes.'

His voice dropped: 'You must be exhausted . . . after last night. Have you had any sleep? Anything to eat?'

'Probably as much as you have,' she replied truthfully, then looked away with a little shrug. 'And I was warmer. That's something to thank Bernave for! I wonder how long it will last without him. I don't think Marie-Jeanne knows or cares anything about the importing or exporting of cloth. So far it is Madame who is looking at the papers.'

'Did she know what you burned?' he asked. 'Sit down. Do you want some wine? It isn't good, but it's better than it might be.'

She did, but she should not drink the little he had. It was far easier for her to get more, and Amandine would have hot soup on the stove when she got back home.

'No thank you. I had some coffee in the street,' she lied. She had spent the money on bread for him, but she did not want him to know that. It would be embarrassing, and he would feel obliged. The last thing she wanted was a sense of debt.

He did not argue. She hoped he did not see through her.

'I met with St Felix last night,' she hurried on to fill the silence. 'We talked for a little while.' She felt hot now at the remembrance of what she had told him, but there had been no choice if she were to persuade him to trust her. 'He will do all he can, but of course he can't leave the house until Menou allows him, and that is hardly likely to be in time to be of any use to us.' She sat down on the chair, suddenly aware of how very tired she was. Perhaps it was quixotic to have refused the wine, but she would not go back on her refusal now.

He sat uncomfortably on the mattress opposite her, hunched up, his arms wrapped round his knees. He was cold and tired as well. The grey light on the side of his face towards the window showed the fine lines around his eyes and mouth. He looked older than before, perhaps closer to thirty-five. It woke a sudden sense of intimacy in her, and compassion. Under the handsome face, the ease of manner, he was as vulnerable as she was, as able to be tired and frightened and hurt.

She did not need the wine.

'He wanted to bring Amandine in as well,' she said quietly. 'It was his condition for continuing. I wish it weren't necessary.' She saw the quick lighting of his face. She knew he would hate endangering Amandine and although she hated it too, she felt a thin stab of loneliness that he did not care so quickly, so instinctively, that she should not be in danger. 'She went to find the ship's captain for the crossing,' she hurried on, covering the gap. 'That is, if they go to England. I think it would be better if they didn't. In a way it is the most obvious route. It's the shortest.'

'I know,' he answered, meeting her eyes. 'It's a last resort. What did he say?'

'I don't know. I haven't been back yet. What

about the other safe houses — St-Honoré and St-Sulpice?'

'They seem good.'

'And the crowd?'

He nodded very slightly. 'Working on it. It's all right, don't worry about that. We still need to speak with the other drivers. That will have to be you or Amandine.'

There was something else pressing on her mind with more urgency.

'Without the man to take the King's place, none of this is any good.' She watched him as he spoke, not because she wanted to judge or weigh what he said, but more because she needed to believe there was still hope, and that he had some kind of answer beyond the short distance she could see. He had always had a kind of inner belief, a confidence that they would succeed. It was like light, or warmth, and she hungered for it now.

He looked down at the floor. 'I know that. I don't know who Bernave had in mind or where to start looking for him, and I daren't ask. He could be anywhere.' He lifted his eyes to hers. 'And if any of us start searching for him, asking questions, we'll draw everyone's attention to him. Even if we could find him in time, we would have sabotaged our own cause.' He bit his lip. 'Don't worry, Célie, I'll find someone else.'

'In a day and a half?'

A sudden smile lit his face. 'It won't be much good after that!' Then it vanished. 'Célie . . . I heard something else.'

'What?' She knew from his voice it could not be good.

'There was a royalist plan to rescue the King from the Temple.'

'That's stupid!' she said in amazement. 'It would never succeed! There are guards everywhere. The rescuers would be more likely to end up inside with him.' The thought of the royalists in the Temple did not bother her in the slightest, but the warning they would give the guards, the Commune, the Convention, was a nightmare. 'Georges — '

'They didn't try it!' he assured her quickly. 'They were betrayed before they could ever begin.'

'Thank God!' she said, engulfed by relief.

'By Bernave,' he finished.

'Bernave?' She should have expected it from his voice, but she was stunned. 'Bernave betrayed them? Are you sure?'

'I think so.'

'But . . . that doesn't make any . . . ' She tailed off. It made only too hideous sense.

'You thanked God when you knew they hadn't tried,' he reminded her wryly.

'Yes, but . . . ' Then she understood. 'You mean he might have betrayed them because he knew they couldn't succeed, and would only make our job harder?'

His smile was twisted. 'He might have. We'll never know. There's no one to ask.'

She did not know what to say.

Georges looked up at her, frowning now. 'Bernave mentioned once that he had a partner in the business, someone who helped him get started. I don't know how long ago.'

She tried to think, but she could not remember Bernave ever speaking of him. 'Who? What was his name?'

'Henri Renoir,' he replied. 'I don't know if it would be any use finding him, but it might be.'

'At least he would know more of Bernave than we do,' Célie reasoned. 'He may be able to tell us where his loyalties really lay. Bernave may have trusted him with the truth. He might even help us!'

'I don't know,' he said dubiously. 'We still aren't sure which side Bernave was on, let alone Renoir.'

Suddenly Célie was aware of how cold she was. There was a dampness in the air, even inside the room, and it ate into the flesh till it seemed to reach the bones. For a moment she had allowed herself to forget that Bernave could have been the enemy. Perhaps she had made herself forget. She did not want to believe St Felix had killed him, not for any reason, not even because he had betrayed them all to the Commune. She could not dismiss her liking for Bernave — it had been too deep and too real. She wanted to think he was loyal to what he desired to be, and that Monsieur Lacoste or Fernand had discovered the plot and . . . what? Killed him to prevent it being carried out? Rather than tell the Commune, and risk losing the house, and the business?

In that case, who was next? St Felix? Amandine? Herself! Everyone in the house knew that she ran Bernave's errands. Did they think she was innocent because she was the laundress? Not clever enough, not trustworthy enough to be involved, except blindly?

Did they think the same of Amandine? They would not of St Felix. Or perhaps they thought that without Bernave the plotters would give up anyway. She could not afford to forget, not for an instant. One word could be enough to betray them all.

'I'll find Renoir,' she said with determination. 'Where do I look?'

'The Jacobin Club,' Georges replied. 'Apparently he's there most evenings. He certainly will be now, coming up to the execution.'

'Is he a revolutionary?' She would not let him hear in her voice that she was afraid. She wanted him to think she was as brave as he was, equal to anything he could ask. But she hated the Jacobin Club and the people in it. It had started out as a place for deputies from out of town to spend their evenings with other men of like mind — strangers and idealists all burning with the same dreams, longing to talk endlessly and plan the great new society. Now it was filled with the men whose names frightened her most: Robespierre, Hébert, Saint-Just, Couthon, and a dozen other allies who hung on their words and would obey anything and everything they said. 'Why would he be there?' she said aloud.

Georges laughed abruptly. 'Because it is the place to be in order to listen and learn what is most likely to happen. The Jacobin Club is the tail which wags the dog of the Convention. It's

234

the place to be if you are a spy, an idealist, a lunatic, or simply someone who wants to know what is politically safe, and which side you should be on if you want to survive.'

She caught the bitterness in his voice and did not argue.

'Look at Renoir and listen to him, Célie,' he said with sudden, fierce seriousness. 'Don't tell him anything at all, except that Bernave is dead — which he probably knows already. Be careful!'

'I will,' she promised, the cold inside her thawing a little.

He leaned forward and grasped her wrist, not painfully, but too firmly for her to pull away. 'I mean it! We don't know who killed Bernave, or why. All that is certain is that it was someone behind him in that room. Someone already carrying a knife! It wasn't a fight, it wasn't an accident and it wasn't in defence of themselves, or anyone else. Someone used the confusion of the crowd breaking in to move up behind Bernave and plunge that blade into his back.'

'I know,' she whispered, finding her mouth dry, her throat tight. She wanted to touch him, to feel the warmth and the strength of him, but that would be weak and stupid! And it would make him think all the wrong things about her. It was only fear and the power of her imagination picturing what had happened in that room, and what could still happen . . . again.

She was tired and cold, that was all. She would be better in a little while; then she would be glad she had not given in to such idiocy.

'I will.' She pulled her hands away from him

and stood up. Her legs ached, her feet were wet and sore and her skirt swung icily around her legs. 'I'll go home now and talk to Amandine and St Felix, then this evening I'll go to the Jacobin Club and find Renoir if I can.'

'I'm sorry,' he said softly, standing up also.

'What for? I believe in this as much as you do! I'm not doing it for you, I'm doing it because I want to.'

He stood still. 'I know that. I just meant that I should be doing it.'

'You can't!' She sounded cold, and hurt. 'It isn't safe for you, and we both know why that is.' The moment the words were out she wished she had not said them, but they were there and it was too late to take them back. What could she say to redeem the situation?

She was at the door. In a moment it would be too late. She looked at him. He was standing with his back to the window. She could see only the side of his cheek clearly. Outside it was raining again. The water ran down the glass of the window, wavering the lines of the roofs beyond.

'I'll be careful,' she promised, her voice gentler. It was wet and cold outside, but she was going back to Bernave's house, Marie-Jeanne's now, and it would be warm there. She would have hot food tonight. He would still be cold. She smiled at him, meeting his eyes and feeling her heart tighten. 'I'll find out what there is, and I'll tell you. Don't worry. It might still be all right.' And before he could tell her that was absurd, she opened the door and went out on to the small landing. She closed it behind her so he could not see her creep down the stairs and she would not be aware of him watching her.

When she got back to the Boulevard St-Germain, she spoke to the guard in the courtyard and then let herself in through the back door. She found Amandine alone in the kitchen, cleaning out the empty bins where dry food was stored. Presumably the other members of the family had eaten already. She gave Amandine the shopping she had collected for the house, her justification for having been out.

'Did you find the captain?' she asked under her breath.

Amandine stood up off her knees and straightened her skirt, the gesture something left from the days when her clothes had been pretty and worth caring for. Her eyes searched Célie's for news of Georges, but she answered the question. 'Yes. I think he's all right. I wish I knew better how to judge. He didn't seem to know anything about any special passages, or if he did, he couldn't say to me. I think he didn't know. Bernave simply told him to be ready to sail with cargo for a wool merchant on the twenty-first.'

'Bernave didn't trust him!' Célie concluded.

'I'm not sure he trusted anyone. It's the feeling I got in St-Antoine.'

Amandine looked at her closely, her face, not her wet clothes, or hair straggling over her brow. 'Do you really think it can work?' she asked softly. 'Have they got anyone to — '

'No . . . not yet.' Célie knew what she was going to say. 'But Georges is looking. He says he'll find someone.'

Amandine regarded her with quick sympathy.

'You look cold — and tired. Do you want something to eat? You should. And then go and get dry clothes. A skirt, at least. You're sodden.'

'Yes please.' She remembered the cold attic and the wine she had refused.

Amandine turned to the pot on the stove and stirred it briskly before reaching for a bowl from the cupboard and ladling out a generous portion with several pieces of meat and potato in it. 'How was he?'

There was no need to explain.

'Cold, but quite well.' Célie thanked her, took the bowl and went to the table where she sat down and began to eat.

Amandine did not speak for several minutes and Célie was halfway through when Menou came in through the back door.

'Ah . . . so you have returned, Citizeness.' He put a very slight edge of emphasis on the remark, as if there were a deeper meaning to it.

'Yes,' she replied expressionlessly. 'Mostly a waste of time, but one has to try. I got some candles and some onions, and a little soap. Have you eaten, Citizen?'

His face relaxed a trifle. He was apparently surprised that she should ask. 'No, not yet.'

'Then you'd better have some of ours,' she offered. 'Amandine is a good cook, even without much to use.'

'You're very gracious,' he accepted, sitting down.

With tight lips Amandine fetched him a bowl

and served him a less generous portion than Célie's, and one slice of bread.

He thanked her, but still looked at Célie as if waiting for an explanation.

'You are the soldiers of the revolution,' she said, looking back at him levelly. 'You keep the peace in the city, and you will guard us if we're invaded . . . ' She permitted no sarcasm whatever into her voice.

'Invaded!' His hand jerked up and he spilled a little of his stew.

She kept her own hand perfectly steady although her heart was pounding.

'Well, I expect we shall be, after tomorrow, when they see we've executed the King,' she explained elaborately. 'After all, every country around us is monarchist. They can't afford to have our ideas spread, can they?'

'Who told you that?' he demanded, his eyes wide, very clear grey-blue.

'Nobody,' she said innocently, taking another mouthful of stew while it was hot. 'It stands to reason. Don't you think so?'

He obviously had not thought of it.

She smiled at him. 'So of course we are honoured to feed you . . . who wouldn't be?'

Amandine's cooking was excellent, but he seemed to lose his pleasure in it.

Fernand had come in from the courtyard, his jacket hunched over his head against the rain. He stood in the centre of the floor, dripping.

'Rubbish!' he said crossly, pulling his jacket straight and stamping his wet feet. 'We won't be invaded. Of course we won't! That's just silly

239

talk. You've been listening to gossip in the queues. You should have more sense.' He walked across the room and went out into the hall, slamming the door behind him.

Menou looked at Célie very carefully. 'Did you hear that in a queue, Citizeness?'

'No.' She shook her head. 'It just seems common sense. Monarchies can't afford to let ideas like ours spread, or they'll be deposed too, and maybe finish up with their necks under the headman's axe, or whatever they use there. I wouldn't if I were a king — would you?'

He stared at her without answering.

'Or a cardinal,' she added for good measure, taking another mouthful.

'Oh, so now you'd have Rome against us too, would you?' he said sharply.

'Since we've abolished the Church and killed most of the priests, I'd be surprised if they weren't,' she retorted, eating her bread.

Suddenly his voice dropped and became almost silky. 'And you disapprove of that, Citizeness?'

She heard the warning with a chill. The bread seemed to catch in her throat. She swallowed. 'On the contrary. I think it was an excellent thing to get rid of the Church,' she answered quickly, only a slight tremor in her hand as she held the spoon, but she did not risk raising it to her lips. 'We should have taken its lands and property years ago and given them back to the people.' That much she could mean. It was the ritual she needed, the surety that the priests believed in God, a faith stronger than her own, whatever

240

other sins they were guilty of.

He relaxed, wiping his mouth carefully on the napkin Amandine had given him.

'Who killed Citizen Bernave, Citizeness?' he asked.

She should have expected the question, but it caught her by surprise. She froze for an instant before answering, her mind still for a moment on the Church.

'I've no idea, except it seems that it has to have been one of us.'

'Did you see the knife?' he went on.

'No.' That was totally honest.

'What was Citizen Lacoste wearing?'

'Wearing?'

'Didn't you hear me, Citizeness?'

'Breeches and a brown jacket, I think. The same as he usually wears.'

'With large pockets?'

'Just an ordinary jacket. Yes, I suppose it had largish pockets.'

'I've seen them. Large enough to hide a knife?'

'I suppose so.' She tried to think if she had noticed any strange shape that evening, any distortion. She frowned. 'I don't think he carried a knife around with him. Why should he? He couldn't know there was going to be a riot in the street that night.'

'Someone did,' he pointed out.

She was startled, for a moment not understanding. 'You mean someone began it on purpose?'

'Someone carried a long sharp blade into the room,' he said, watching her face. 'Ready to use

— when the opportunity was made.'

'Did they?' With a jolt of understanding she realised that almost certainly that was not true. Someone could too easily have noticed it, and St Felix had been wearing a coat with shallow pockets which would have been ripped by an unguarded blade. It was infinitely more likely the knife had been left in the drawer of the chest or in the small cupboard near the door.

Menou must have read her expression. He leaned forward, his eyes wide and bright.

'What have you thought of, Citizeness? What is it you remember?'

Could she lie?

Amandine was standing rigid, the soup ladle in her hand. Her fear filled the room like electricity before a storm.

What would happen if Célie gave an answer Menou did not believe? He would think she was protecting someone. He knew her affection for Amandine. He knew they had come here because they were friends. He could see Amandine's care for St Felix — a blind man could see it. He would assume it was St Felix she was protecting.

No, she could not lie.

'I just realised that the knife was probably already in the room,' she answered with very nearly perfect composure. She looked into his clear eyes. 'In one of the drawers of the chest, or in the cupboard by the door. It would be much safer to leave it there, against opportunity, rather than carrying it around where someone might see it, or it might cut through the cloth and be

242

obvious. Also there would be no chance of accidentally injuring yourself.'

Menou nodded slowly and let out his breath in a sigh. 'Oh, very well thought, Citizeness,' he said admiringly. 'I knew you were observant, but that is excellent. I begin to see why Citizen Bernave sent you to do his errands for him, and to report back what occurred in the Convention. You are wasted as a laundress. Tell me — how did the murderer of Citizen Bernave get the bloody knife out of the room afterwards, and where did he hide it?'

She must be very careful indeed — not too clever, not too foolish. He could trip her in even the slightest mistake. She could feel Amandine behind her, like a string about to snap.

'I don't know.' She tried to sound ingenuous. 'I suppose in the confusion in the dark, the surprise, they put it somewhere out of sight, maybe even back where they got it from. Then afterwards hid it . . . I've no idea where. I don't know the house all that well.'

'You're the laundress!'

'Exactly,' she agreed quickly. 'I work in the kitchen or the linen cupboard. I never go into the Lacostes' rooms. I have no occasion to.'

His eyebrows rose questioningly. 'Are you saying one of the Lacostes stabbed Citizen Bernave?'

'No,' she repeated patiently. 'I am saying I don't know the whole house. Anyone could have gone upstairs to their rooms later on, or to the attics or anywhere else. Into Citizen Bernave's rooms, for that matter.'

'Or Citizen St Felix's?' He looked at her closely.

'I imagine so. I don't know where the knife is.'

'And would you tell me if you did?'

'Of course,' she said blandly. She was lying, and she knew he knew it. She never imagined she would be believed.

'How long had Citizen Bernave known St Felix?' he asked, changing the subject suddenly.

'He never told me.' That was true, as far as it went. 'They both came from the same town, but they had lost touch a long time ago.'

He shifted position a little, leaning closer towards her. There was silence in the room except for their voices.

'I'm asking you what Citizen Bernave said!' he urged. 'Why did he take into his home and look after a man he had not seen for years? He had not a reputation for such casual philanthropy.'

'I don't know.' This time she could answer without having to think. 'He never spoke of it.'

Menou smiled. 'And you never noticed? You, the so-observant Citizeness that he trusted to watch and listen to the great political debates of the revolution and report their meaning to him!' His voice hardened and there was a tiny flicker at the corner of his mouth. 'I cannot help thinking your loyalty is misplaced. This man thought highly of you, he trusted you! He was murdered — stabbed to death, surrounded by his family, in his own house . . . where incidentally you still live.'

Célie was stung. She knew that was exactly what he intended, but she still could not help it.

244

'I don't know who killed him, Citizen Menou!' she retaliated. 'Of course I observed something of his feelings for St Felix, and St Felix's for him. It seemed to me they had known each other well long ago, but that a lot of time had passed since then and much had changed.'

'For example?' he demanded.

She must be careful. No lie must be suspected, let alone proved.

She tried to make her voice level again, iron the anger and the fear out of it. 'I don't know. If they spoke of it, it was not when I was there. All I ever heard was discussion of the present situation, of the revolution and what was likely to happen, the chances of war on all sides if we guillotine the King.' She saw Menou wince. 'I am only telling you what they said, Citizen.'

'Are you now trying to say that Bernave was against executing the King, Citizeness?' His eyebrows rose and he looked at her very steadily.

She saw the trap for St Felix. 'He spoke of the dangers,' she said meekly, keeping her eyes on his, but making them gentle. 'I am sure Citizen Marat himself is just as aware of them. After all, he has travelled a great deal, so I hear. He even lived in England for a while. He will know better than any of us.'

'Of course he will!' Menou agreed a shade too quickly. She saw the fear for an instant in his eyes also. He seemed to have forgotten Amandine over by the stove. 'What about St Felix? What did he say about it?'

'I was in and out. All I heard him say was that it was a danger.' The less she concerted herself to

245

this view the better. Above all she must not let Menou suspect Bernave of having used and betrayed St Felix, or any of them.

'No more than that?' Menou said incredulously.

She smiled back at him, very slightly. 'He was discreet,' she explained. 'Perhaps he did not trust me as much as Citizen Bernave did, or seemed to.'

'Or seemed to . . . ' he repeated. 'Yes, I see what you mean, Citizeness. As I observed before, you are very perceptive. I would sooner have you as a friend than an enemy.'

'As long as you are for the welfare of France, you will,' she answered a trifle sententiously. Then she added very quickly, 'And that means of the revolution, of course.'

His face lit with a sudden flash of amusement. 'Of course.' He stood up. 'Thank you for the food. Now show me the drawer where you think the knife was left, and the cupboard. What are they normally used for?'

Célie felt the chill run through her. For a moment her mouth was dry. 'Linen,' she answered. The truth was the only possible thing. If he asked anyone else they would tell him. 'And candles.'

'Remarkable,' he said with a little shake of his head. 'And no one noticed a knife! Not even you, returning the clean laundry.'

She thought of half a dozen excuses, then decided not to say anything. It was what he was expecting. It would only lead her into the possibility of more mistakes. Silently, and

246

without glancing at Amandine, she led him to the front room and pointed out the cupboard and the drawer.

He walked over and opened the cupboard. He moved the candles gently, licked his finger and ran it over the wood, then held it up. There was the brown stain of dried blood on it.

'Thank you,' he said thoughtfully. 'I think that may explain a great deal. No cut pockets, no having to disappear to find the blade. An opportunity perfectly seized — well, almost perfectly. It is just a matter of motive — ' he looked directly at her — 'isn't it?'

She swallowed, her lips dry. 'I suppose so.'

'And I will find that, Citizeness, I promise you. Citizen Bernave will not go unavenged. I am very close now, very close indeed.'

There was only one thing she could possibly say. 'Good.'

★ ★ ★

Célie remained in all afternoon. There was laundry to do, and she would have aroused suspicion if she had not attended to it. Monsieur Lacoste was still busying himself with chores around the house, small repairs that had been awaiting his attention for weeks, if not months. Fernand was occupied most of the time in his shed across the courtyard.

Madame sat in Bernave's study and read old invoices and accounts to try to familiarise herself with the daily nature of his business. Someone had to keep it up if the family were to continue to prosper from it, and it seemed to be what she wished to do.

Marie-Jeanne was comforting and instructing her children, as usual, upstairs in their own rooms.

Only St Felix prowled the house, unable to relax, hands idle, mind racing from one possibility to another, one moment seeming to hope, the next to despair.

It was nearly five o'clock, just after dark, when Amandine, Célie and St Felix found the opportunity to speak together alone. They were in St Felix's room where Célie had taken clean laundry as she usually did, and Amandine had managed to join them.

'We know that all three of the houses are safe,' St Felix said softly, indicating the chair for Célie to sit. Amandine sat on the bed, he stood. 'What about the captain?'

Amandine repeated what she had told Célie.

'Good,' he nodded. In the candlelight he looked less tired, his body less knotted with fears. The glow of it put a little colour in his skin, and caught the lighter streaks in his brown hair. 'We must check on all the drivers tomorrow.' He looked at Célie. 'What about the crowd? What did Coigny say?'

'He will find them, that is no trouble . . . '

'But?' he said quickly.

'But we still do not know who will take the King's place in the carriage,' she replied. 'He is the one person who will not come out of this alive, win or lose. And only Bernave knew who he is.'

'So he said,' Amandine spoke quietly, but there was a world of bitterness in her voice, of anger and disbelief. In that moment Célie realised with shock how deeply she had despised Bernave, and it hurt; it challenged memories of something that, in spite of herself, she had cherished.

St Felix looked at Amandine, gentleness softening his face. 'Bernave would not betray us,' he said to her. 'He was a strange man, often cold in ways I could not understand. He had more self-discipline than any other man I have ever known.' There was no hesitation in him, no uncertainty at all. 'But he was honest to his own cause. There was strength inside him that . . . that was frightening.' As he said it there was fear in his face, in his eyes, and pain he did not try to express. 'But you could trust him with your life, and never regret it.'

Amandine stared at him. She could not hide her confusion or her disbelief. She drew in breath to speak, then let it out again silently.

Célie felt a momentary relief. If St Felix, of all people, could say that, and so obviously and passionately mean it, then perhaps it was true. And if it were not, then Bernave had not betrayed them and they still had a hope of success. Also it meant St Felix had not discovered any betrayal and killed him.

But if St Felix had not, then either Fernand or Monsieur Lacoste had. And surely that would only be because they had somehow learned of the plan. Célie leaned forward urgently.

'If Bernave was truly with us, then one of the

249

Lacostes killed him.' She looked in the faint light from St Felix to Amandine. 'Could there be any other reason except that they knew of the plan? They wouldn't tell the Commune, or they'd lose the house, and maybe the business, but they'd kill him to prevent anyone saving the King. Either of them would! Maybe even Madame, or Marie-Jeanne, for all we know.'

'That's true,' St Felix said, so quietly she could barely hear him. 'We must be very careful indeed. It is not only Menou we should fear, but everyone else in the house. Never let your guard slip.' He looked first at Amandine. 'Watch everything you say. Maybe you don't need to go out again.' He turned to Célie. 'How much more is there we must do?'

'Georges told me that Bernave had a business partner,' she answered. 'Someone who helped him start up, a man called Renoir. I am going to see if I can find him. He might know more about Bernave and his loyalties. He might even be part of the plan.'

Amandine swung round to look at her. 'Where? Where can you even look for him? And why? What can he tell us that we have to know? You can't go out alone!' Her voice was sharp with anxiety, and there was fear for Célie in her eyes.

'At the Jacobin Club,' Célie replied. 'Georges said he spends a lot of time there, especially now so close to the King's execution.'

'Be careful!' Amandine warned. 'You don't know if you can trust him!'

St Felix nodded, his eyes searching Célie's.

250

'But he may have been part of the plan,' Célie argued, looking from one to the other of them. 'We still don't know who was going to take the King's place, but maybe Renoir does! It has to have been someone Bernave trusted absolutely. Perhaps it was even Renoir himself! He would be the right age, if they started together. Otherwise we will have to find a replacement, and that is the one person who cannot hope to survive, if we succeed.'

Amandine shuddered. 'Do you think he'll know, this partner?' There was fierce, almost choking pity in her voice, and her eyes were dark with the terrible understanding of it.

'I don't know, but we should try.' Célie did not add that she had promised Georges she would, because he did not trust Bernave as seemingly St Felix did. He knew about the royalist plan, and its betrayal. That was something she did not need to tell St Felix, or Amandine.

'It's a risk,' Amandine said unhappily, still staring at Célie.

'I know,' Célie agreed. 'But it's worth it. Maybe Bernave trusted him. He did for business, at least. Maybe he did for more.'

'How will you get out of the house?' St Felix pursed his lips. 'What will you tell Menou — and Madame Lacoste? She'll ask where you're going.'

'I don't know yet; I'll think of something.' Célie stood up. 'Now we must leave. We can't be caught here talking or they'll wonder what it's about. We can take only so long putting away laundry!'

Amandine stood up quickly, smoothing her

251

skirt. She went to the door and looked out, then beckoned Célie to follow her. They tiptoed down the stairs together, avoiding those that creaked, and leaving St Felix alone in his room. Amandine looked back once, but the door was closed.

* * *

Georges got out the food as soon as Célie had gone. While she was there he had barely realised how hungry or how cold he was; now it was inescapable again. He was far more worried than he had let her know. She counted on his optimism, his confidence that somehow all would be well. It was what she needed from him. And he found himself struggling to give it, hiding his own feelings, no matter how difficult. He was caught unawares by how much it mattered to him that he should be what she wished.

He ate the bread and onion cold, with almost a glass of wine. He drank it from the bottle, but he guessed it was that much. He was grateful she had not taken any; there was too little left. Had she wanted it? Probably. Thinking back, picturing her face so very clearly, with its strong features, generous and brave, she had looked terribly tired. Her eyes had been shadowed round, her skin unnaturally pale. He had wanted to be able to protect her from some of the truth, the fear, but she would have resented it. It made him feel closed out, as if they were not man and woman, and yet at the same time he admired her for it.

It was typical that she had refused the wine. He was not even sure whether it was true that she had had the coffee. But it was not for him she declined, it was the guilt again. It was peculiarly lonely to realise that, and it surprised him how he was hurt by it. He was merely the one who happened to be involved, no more. She would have felt exactly the same whoever it had been. He was the symbol of the way she regarded her own worth, and she could not live with it until she had proved herself better than that.

What would she do then? Not want to see him again, because he reminded her of a part of herself she had left behind?

He should not think of that; it was far ahead. Before then there was much to do, and far too little time. He must find someone else to take the King's place, and he dare not even go outside to begin looking until the daylight began to fade. He could not risk another episode like this morning's. He might not be so fortunate next time.

He stood up, then sat down again. He was shudderingly cold, and the room was too small even to pace back and forth. He stared out of the window blurred with rain, and watched the light on the grey jumble of roofs, willing it to fade so he could begin.

At what he guessed to be about quarter to four he could wait no longer. He put on his coat and went down the stairs, along the alley and into the street. The wind hit him with a knife-edge of ice in it, and he bent forward to protect himself from its bite. At least it gave him an excuse to

253

turn up his collar and hide the lower half of his face. Everyone else he saw was doing the same. After this morning even modesty did not delude him he was easily forgettable.

On the corner a woman was selling hot coffee. The aroma of it was exquisite, tempting him almost beyond bearing. He stopped, breathing it in. He had only a few sous left and without Bernave there would be no more.

A new and grim thought came to him. Since Bernave was gone, what would Célie do? Would she still be able to live in the house in the Boulevard St-Germain? How safe was she there now? Fear for her gripped him. One of them had killed Bernave, almost certainly because they knew what he was really doing. A bitter laughter engulfed him. Or they believed it, as he had — and were wrong! What a supreme irony if Bernave, a loyal supporter of the Commune, had been murdered by another loyal supporter, misled into thinking what Georges, Célie and St Felix thought — that he wanted to save the King! It would be someone who could not see beyond the blind idealism of the revolution, who was so bewitched by the dream that they saw too little of the reality. Fernand? Monsieur Lacoste? Even one of the women?

He should have warned Célie more urgently and made certain she understood exactly how real the danger was. In a way she was more at risk than he. Another irony.

He fished in his pocket and brought out a coin. He gave it to the woman and took the coffee gratefully. It was hot and strong, filling him with its delicious taste and the slow, sweet warmth down his throat to his stomach.

He drank it a sip at a time, his mind racing. There were at least two people he could ask who bore some resemblance to the King, sufficient to pass at a glance — the age, the height, roughly the colouring. One was too thin, but a little padding under his jacket would take care of that.

Georges glanced around him. There were quite a few people still about in the street, mostly women returning home after waiting in queues for vegetables, soap, salt or fuel. He wondered how many hours were wasted standing in huddles in the icy streets hoping for the necessities of daily life, instead of working, caring for children, or the sick, or doing any other useful thing. They were tired and angry. He could hear it in their voices as they passed him, and see it in their bodies as they hurried by, baskets half empty. Too many promises had been made and broken. Too much risk had paid for too little return. If the King were executed there would be worse ahead.

He finished the coffee, gave the cup back to the woman and went on his way. The first man to find was Lazare Carichon. He had been a minor Girondin, until disillusion had dashed his last hope of political competence. He understood the dangers of sweeping away all the established boundaries of a way of life. The whole nation would be hurled into the unknown, a life without rules or sanctions, where nothing was too outrageous to be tried. There would be no ultimate power any more. Man would become

255

his own god, and that thought was terrifying. Georges drove it out of his mind and hurried on.

At this hour Carichon would almost certainly be at his home on the Rue des Écoles. If Georges waited outside, with any luck he would catch him alone.

He walked briskly along the alleys doglegging to the south of St-Germain, then hastily crossed the Boulevard St-Michel, behind the Musée de Cluny. He walked over the Rue St-Jacques, head down, looking neither right nor left, and into the network of alleys between the Boulevard St-Germain and the Rue des Écoles. There were few people loitering — it was too cold — but he was aware of being watched. There was a pervasive atmosphere of tension, anxiety, the knowledge that something was about to happen which was irretrievable.

He thought of Célie going to the Jacobin Club this evening, looking for Renoir. She had the courage and the nerve all right, but had she the skill to ask questions without arousing suspicion? He should not have agreed to her going! She could give herself away too easily! All the craziest, most vindictive revolutionaries in France were there, men like Robespierre and his admirers: the crippled, hysterical Couthon; Saint-Just, disciple of the Marquis de Sade; the renegade monk, Hébert. The list was endless. She could have no idea what they were really like. She was too consumed in her admiration for Madame de Staël and her desire to be like her, instead of consumed by guilt for her all-too-human revenge for her baby's death.

He found himself smiling as he thought of that now, of her coming to warn him, of her desperation when they were parted in the crowd. She had cared so passionately to undo it his anger had vanished. Perhaps it had never really been there? There had been too little time. When he had realised fully what she had done, and why, it was all over.

The thought of himself and Amandine as lovers was absurd; they were too close for that, almost brother and sister. But he could understand how Célie could have thought it. He had charmed enough women. He had always been able to smile with that easy brilliance and win almost anyone. His wit, his air of confidence had smoothed the path for him all his life, until this last couple of years when his home had gone, his father died and all the old certainties — the assumptions of safety, the natural arrogance of a man who was handsome, well born, rich enough, who needed no one's favour or protection — were no longer hidden.

He had behaved as if he had courage because he wanted to be seen that way, and then found at the last that he had no alternative, and it had become real.

But he wished Célie saw him more as himself rather than the hero she needed him to be.

He was opposite Carichon's house now. He hurried across the street and knocked on the door.

It was a moment or two before Carichon answered. He was still dressed in the rather affected clothes chosen by the Girondins. His jacket was overlong and loose, and his cravat too big.

'Good evening, Citizen Carichon,' Georges said quietly.

Carichon started, then caught his breath. 'Coigny!' He swallowed hard. 'What are you doing out? Come in, before anyone sees you!' He stood back and barely refrained from actually putting a hand on Georges to pull him over the threshold. The instant he was inside he closed the door. 'What is it?' he demanded. 'Why are you here?'

He already knew a little of the plan, just the bare outlines. In any other circumstances Georges would not have trusted him with the heart of it because he told no one anything they did not need to know. But he was desperate, and Carichon held sufficient resemblance to the King to pass for him in a moment's haste and emotion, if dressed the same and with a little powder in his hair to lighten it. He was the right height and had a rather long nose and heavy jowls and neck.

There was no choice.

'Bernave is dead,' he said quietly.

They were in a narrow, warm room with heavily patterned wallpaper and sparse furniture.

Carichon stared at him, his eyes wide. 'What?'

'Bernave is dead,' Georges repeated. 'He was murdered yesterday evening.'

'Oh God!' Carichon went pasty white, even in the yellow candlelight. 'What about the plan?'

Georges did not answer immediately. Should he tell Carichon about Menou's statement that

258

Bernave was a spy for the Commune?

Carichon was staring at him. 'We've got to save the King — it is the only way to avoid war! And there will be war! All the rhetoric on earth won't help then!' His voice was rising with his anger. He gestured wildly, only just missing the edge of the wooden desk with his fingers. 'Tell the mothers of the dead, tell the wounded and the blind and the homeless that England shouldn't have taken offence, or Spain shouldn't have minded if we sent Louis XVI to the scaffold — because we were tired of kings!'

His voice was raw-edged, his body tight under its exaggerated clothes. He backed further into the room, which served him for study and dining room. There was a stove burning in the corner and it was that which made it so much warmer than outside.

'God knows I tried!' he went on, jerking agitatedly. 'I did all I could to move the Girondins, to make them forget their own quarrels and act for France, but the blind futility of their ambitions is bleeding away what little hope there was left.' He gestured wildly. 'All around us Paris is crumbling into civil chaos, and we seem incapable of addressing the issues that really matter.'

'I know,' Georges agreed, moving down to the stove.

'I tried to persuade them to face the Convention,' Carichon went on with a bitter laugh, as much to himself as to Georges. 'Stop following after them and lead, for a change! To hell with what Marat and the Commune want

. . . we're the government!' He moved closer to Georges. 'France isn't in any state to fight a war on all sides. If we didn't kill the King, we might even make peace with Austria.'

He shrugged angrily. 'But they parroted back at me: 'We can't abandon our principles, we have a far nobler vision than Marat and his followers.' ' He lowered his voice to little more than a whisper. His brows were drawn down, his eyes earnest and frightened. 'Marat's a lunatic, you know that, Coigny? You should have seen him when he burst in on the celebrations Talma gave General Dumouriez last year. It was a very civilised party.' A smile lit his face for an instant as he recalled, then it vanished. 'We were all listening to harp and piano music,' he continued. 'Drinking a little sugar water and indulging in conversation. Then all of a sudden there was a fearful clatter on the stairs outside, and the next moment Marat burst into the room with a bunch of his hooligans.' He drew in his breath sharply. 'He was filthy! The memory of the stench turns my stomach even now.' His lips curled. 'He was wearing one of those carmagnole jackets like the Marseillais, black trousers, no socks, and boots covered with nameless ordure which he left all over the carpet.'

Georges opened his mouth to speak. He knew the story.

But Carichon went on regardless. 'He was twitching like some wretched animal. The women were terrified. He stared at us and shook his fists, calling us whores and counter-revolutionaries. He even spat on the floor.' His nostrils flared. 'After he'd gone, we had to open all the windows and go around with a perfume bottle.'

The smell was a consequence of Marat's disease and therefore irrelevant, but Georges did not bother to argue that. He could see the revulsion in Carichon's face and the emotions behind it, the knowledge of violence, the unknown and the uncontrollable. Despair had overtaken him at the sheer ineffectuality of the Girondins, their lack of urgency and, when it came to the point, of courage.

'I know,' Georges said quietly. 'I already heard all about it.'

'What is there ahead?' Carichon's face filled with bitterness. 'Invasion, civil war and bloody chaos!' He was so angry his body shook. 'It's so idiotically futile, so blind to the flesh and passion and dirt of reality. They're as unrelated to living, breathing human beings as Rousseau. It's all words, scribbles on miles of paper that means nothing at all — '

Georges made his decision, not with certainty but as a desperate chance, the lesser of evils.

'We'll still try it,' he interrupted. 'Just change the arrangements, in case whoever killed Bernave knew something of it. Change everything you can — men, places. We can't change the time.' He watched Carichon's face intently, looking for the slightest flicker of deceit. He saw the spark of hope again, and the knowledge of fear.

Carichon hesitated barely a moment. 'Good,' he said softly. 'Good. It's our only chance.'

'There is only one thing we lack . . . because

261

of Bernave's murder.'

'Oh? What's that?' There was no shadow of denial in Carichon, no foreknowledge of what Georges was about to say.

This was the moment. He would test Carichon's commitment to its ultimate limit. 'Bernave was the only one who knew the man to take the King's place in the carriage,' he said. He did not add the rest; it was obvious after an instant's thought.

Carichon's jaw dropped. 'But without him it won't work! It can't! You'll have to find someone else!'

'I know that.'

'Then why are you here telling me?' Then the blood drained from his face as he realised what Georges was saying. He backed away, stumbling against the table and putting out his hand to save himself. 'Oh no! You can't ask me that! I'd be . . . ' he swallowed and almost choked, 'I'd be . . . torn apart! They'd . . . ' It was beyond him even to give words to it. He stood there shaking his head, gasping.

Georges did not argue. Looking at the man's terror was enough to know that even if he promised to come, his nerves might render him incapable at the last moment.

He nodded very slightly, touched Carichon on the arm, and turned and went out of the door again into the street. Perhaps he should not have expected the ultimate sacrifice from Carichon, but he still felt a suffocating disappointment. Carichon had seemed the best chance. There were not many Georges could ask, because to do so he had to trust them with so much of the truth.

It was dark now, but as he passed a woman buying coffee from one of the sellers, she turned and stared at him in the light from a café window. She was probably about thirty-five, but fear and hunger made her seem older. He must be more careful than he had that morning. He smiled at her, using all his charm.

'Good evening, Citizeness!'

She relaxed and smiled back. 'Evening, Citizen.'

He hurried on towards the river. He was glad to move quickly; at least it set the blood coursing in his veins. He must find someone tonight. He dare not be out tomorrow, and by dusk tomorrow evening it would be too late.

And what after that — after the King was saved, or dead? He could not expect Célie to feed him for ever. She might be fortunate even to feed herself. If he did not find some form of work he would starve, or die of the cold. People did. And if this sort of misery and chaos continued there would be more and more of them. He was young and strong — what about the ill, the weak, the old, the very people the revolution was supposed to protect? Was this what all the dreams and hopes had come to: suspicion, fear, and even more grinding poverty?

He was in the Rue St-Antoine now. The Place de la Bastille was just ahead. That had been a bitter joke — storming the one prison in Paris which held only a few indigents for whom it was more of an asylum than an incarceration! They had stumbled out into the daylight totally confused, suddenly frail — and now homeless.

He crossed the place, head down. Fortunately the wind made that a natural thing to do. No one took any notice of him.

He found what he was looking for, a cooper's yard. He turned the corner into the shelter of the wall. The man he had come to see was working with the barrels, a trifle awkwardly as if he had not been born to labour. Now at a glance he looked ordinary enough but under his dull, brown working clothes he had a certain dignity, and when he looked up he stood with his shoulders square. His hands were soft, although they were dirty. He had a long nose and heavy cheeks, and he was barely average height, but his eyes were clear and he looked at Georges squarely.

'Can I help you, Citizen?' he asked.

'Possibly,' Georges replied, keeping his voice low.

The man peered more closely. 'Coigny? You look like him!'

'I've seen better times,' Georges agreed with a smile.

'Haven't we all?' The man laughed abruptly. 'And it'll get worse.'

Georges raised his eyebrows. 'You think so?'

'You can't be that naïve,' the man said with anger in his voice. 'Of course it will! There'll be no stopping war on all sides. We'll have got rid of the King, poor sod, in the name of freedom; and imposed a tyranny greater than anything we had before. Certainly we were in a bad way then,

264

with corruption everywhere, but this cure is worse than the disease.'

'The operation was a success but the patient died,' Georges said succinctly.

'You've got it!' the man agreed. 'What can I do for you? It must be something important to bring you out here.'

'You have some royalist sympathy . . . '

'Sympathy, yes,' he agreed. 'But I don't want the King back on the throne. I just don't want the poor devil executed because it'll bring war down on us all, and leave these lunatics in charge. I nearly said 'in control', but nobody's in control of anything. The Girondins couldn't organise an evening salon, and the Commune doesn't want to. Chaos is their natural state.'

'Are you prepared to do anything about it?' Georges asked.

'Anything?' the man said slowly, watching Georges. 'You still have hope that something can be done?' There was incredulity and derision in his voice. 'I don't know whether to envy you, or pity your innocence. It's too late. I would do something if I thought it would work. I don't. I'm not giving my life pointlessly. Bad as it is, I'd still rather be alive than dead.' He shrugged with a bitter smile. 'That's the trouble with atheism: it breeds few martyrs. We can't imagine some glowing heaven where we are rewarded for sacrifices here.' He gestured with his hand. 'If this is all there is, we'd better hang on to it as long as it's bearable. Few of us can cope with the thought of extinction.' He shrugged. 'Funny that: no matter how little a man thinks of himself, he cannot imagine the world functioning just as well when he is no longer part of it.'

Again Georges did not argue. There would be no purpose, only risk. He bade him goodbye and went out into the street again. The wind was edged with sleet.

He could not blame either of them that they were not willing to be torn and bludgeoned to death in the King's place. The thought was enough to quail anyone, sicken them and turn their insides to water. He could not look at it himself.

His clothes were wet through and his muscles were locked with cold.

Did he believe in the King's rescue enough? How much of his commitment was really only words? How frightened was he of a few moments of agonising, unimaginable pain, his own body destroyed while he was still aware of it? Everybody died eventually, sometimes after long illness. Wasn't that worse?

Yes. But that was in some unforeseen future, not the day after tomorrow! And not of his own choosing.

But it would still come . . . one day. And who would he be then? A man who had not lived up to his beliefs. A man who was willing to ask others to sacrifice what he would not give up himself. A hypocrite, who in the moment of final decision was a failure.

But he was the wrong age, the wrong build, the wrong colouring to make anyone believe he was the King!

And there was so much he still wanted to do,

to say, people he could not part from yet. Amandine, Célie . . . especially Célie. There was so much to learn about her, and even more that she needed to know about him — weaknesses and strengths, little things, a time for laughter as well as courage. Above all they must have at least one time together when they were honest, without pretence, without the past and the future in the way. He could say what he meant, and touch her just once.

And yet if he did not take the King's place, perhaps the real parting was already accomplished. She might forgive him. She understood the failure to live up to your dreams. But he would not forgive himself. He understood, and that would be the judgement.

He must find the right clothes, the wig, the padding, whatever it required. He must take the King's place, without telling anyone else. There were no real difficulties, only excuses.

He put his head down and walked into the wind.

10

Célie invented an excuse for going out, for Madame Lacoste, should she ask, and for the guard in the courtyard. It cost her dearly because she felt self-conscious and foolish, but it was the only one she could think of which was ordinary and common to all.

'A lover!' Amandine said with a smile, looking up from peeling vegetables.

Célie's mind flew to Georges, for no reason at all, and she felt the heat burn up her face. 'The guard might let me go for that,' she said defensively. 'Please help! I've got to see if I can find Renoir.'

'Only one way to discover,' Amandine replied. 'Although the only other likely reason would be to buy something on the black market, which is illegal.'

'I haven't any money anyway,' Célie said ruefully, smiling herself, happy to change the subject. 'There was some in Bernave's desk, but I didn't take it.'

'Of course you didn't!' Amandine agreed. 'Anyway, if the soldiers didn't take it themselves, Menou will know how much there was. The last thing either of us needs is to be thrown out for thieving.' She put her hand in her pocket under her apron and brought out a gold Louis. 'I wish I had more to give you, but most of mine was spent ages ago. This is the best I can do for

Georges. You're the one running all the risks . . . ' There was admiration in her face, and a swift warmth of affection. 'I do appreciate it. He is the only family I have. But even if he were not, he'd still be one of my dearest friends. Thank you — and for heaven's sake be careful!'

Célie laughed a little to break the tension. 'I will! Now let me ask the guard if he will allow me to go and see my lover! I wish I were a better flirt!'

'So do I!' Amandine said ruefully. 'Don't try too hard. You'll make him suspicious.'

Célie wrinkled her nose at her. She pushed the coin down her blouse between her breasts and fastened the buttons again.

'Don't flirt now!' Amandine said with a flash of her old lightness. 'You could have a disaster!'

'Cat!' Célie retorted. 'I'll leave you to think of a good answer if Madame asks where I am.' And before Amandine could complain, she went to the back door, took her cloak off its peg, carrying a shawl, leaving her hair loose.

The guard stopped her as soon as she was in the courtyard.

'Where are you going?' he demanded. 'No bread at this hour, Citizeness.'

She smiled at him, looking straight into his eyes. 'I know,' she said quietly. 'I have an hour or two off, away from the Citizeness's eye. I . . . To tell you the truth, Citizen, I have a lover. I have not been able to see him since Citizen Bernave was killed. I am only human . . . so is he!' She shrugged very slightly. 'All I want is a little time with him . . . please?'

He considered her appreciatively for a moment, his eyes on her cheeks, her throat, the pale silk of her hair. 'I'll have to make sure you don't have anything hidden. Citizen Menou'll have me punished if I don't.'

'Of course.' Her fingers shaking a little, she opened her cloak and invited inspection.

He looked up and down lingeringly, his eyes bright. He smiled and lifted his hands.

Her heart sank. The shiver of revulsion she felt was secondary to her fear that somehow he would feel the coin and ask what it was for, or worse, take it from her. She forced herself to smile back at him. It felt sickly. He must see how artificial it was.

His hands touched her body.

She wanted to hit him as hard as she could. It took all her strength to control the impulse and look at him sweetly instead. She must think of something to distract his attention.

'You must be cold standing out here by yourself, Citizen,' she began. What a senseless thing to say!

'Perishing,' he agreed.

'And bored,' she added. Keep talking, his mind is on what you are saying, not the search. 'Have you always been a soldier?' That was it — make him talk about himself — most people liked to talk about themselves. 'It must be a hard and dangerous life. Perhaps we don't value you enough — until there's danger.'

He looked at her with a flash of a different kind of appreciation. 'That's certainly true, Citizeness. Hardly anyone sees that.' His hands

270

patted her skirts, not too closely. He was looking for a knife, not money.

'Where are you from?' she asked quickly.

'Faubourg St-Marcel,' he replied.

'Is that where you grew up?'

His face lightened a little, memory awakening. 'Oh no, I was born in Nemours.'

'Is it beautiful?'

'Better than Paris!' he said with feeling.

She took a deep breath and let it out in a sigh. 'Then we are in your debt that you stay here to serve the revolution. Tell me about Nemours. I've never been there.'

He did, haltingly at first, then with increasing ease as memory found the words for him.

She listened, and his search was thorough, but not so intimate as to find the coin. He was not looking for anything so small.

When he had finished she smiled at him again, meaning it this time.

'Thank you, Citizen.' Then she hurried out under the arch into the street. She had a considerable way to walk along the Boulevard St-Germain, across the river and along the Rue St-Honoré to where the Jacobin Club was. She went briskly for several reasons: time was short and it was far too cold to dawdle, but also she did not want to attract any attention to herself or seem to be without purpose.

She stopped at a small shop and bought a few dried lentils and a couple of small onions. Of course no one had bread at this hour of the day. This would have to do. It fitted quite easily into the pockets of her skirt.

She thanked the storekeeper and left.

The Jacobin Club, like many other buildings in Paris, had originally belonged to a religious order. It had begun its secular life as a social club for deputies from the provinces and other 'friends of the revolution' to spend time together. They enjoyed one another's society and spent endless hours in talk of ideals, and plans for a glorious and virtuous future. Robespierre, who had no appetite whatsoever for pleasures of the flesh, was to be found there on most evenings. The rooms were ideally suited to the building's present purpose, and the situation was excellent. Robespierre lodged close by in the house of the carpenter Duplay. The Place de la Révolution, where the guillotine did its bloody business, was only a few hundred yards away.

From such small beginnings the club now had three hundred members who were deputies in the Convention. Other members controlled the Commune and the Paris mob. Recently it had set up affiliates all over France. Its influence was enormous, and its power was growing week by week. During the debates that were held in its rooms the ideas were born which later became the rallying cry for the masses as far afield as the borders with Belgium and Germany in one direction, and the Mediterranean shores in the other.

Certain parts of the club were open to the public if they wished to listen, and in her browns and blues Célie appeared an ordinary enough young, working woman to cause no suspicion as she made her way quietly into the chamber. With a look of great respect in her manner and lowered eyes, she said a discreet 'Excuse me, Citizen' and 'Thank you, Citizen' as she passed.

She chose a mild-faced young man wearing a woollen jacket and a leather apron to speak to first.

'Pardon me, Citizen,' she said politely.

He turned to look at her. A flash of approval lit his face for her fair skin and generous mouth.

'Yes, Citizeness?'

'Do you know Deputy Renoir, from Compiègne?'

'Not to speak to, but I'd recognise him,' the young man replied. 'Are you looking for him?'

'I have a message for him.' Célie always told the truth if possible. Too many lies become difficult to remember.

'He's probably in the chamber,' he said with half a smile. 'Camille Desmoulins is speaking. He's usually worth listening to.' There was an ambiguous expression in his eyes, as if his opinion jarred with his words, but he had more sense than to say so. Most people thought twice about frankness these days.

She thanked him with an answering smile, and followed him in the direction he led.

There was already a buzz of excitement in the chamber when she squeezed her way in behind him. She found a place to stand, elbow to elbow in the crowd. The room was wood-panelled, which darkened it, and the grey January light from the windows made the candles look yellow. Only the press of bodies warmed it.

A young man with a passionate countenance

273

and the careless dress of an artist was speaking from the rostrum. His words flowed easily, full of grand ideals and hope for a marvellous tomorrow. He praised the virtues of others and seemed convinced of their general goodness. This was Camille Desmoulins, the writer and ardent friend and admirer of Danton.

Célie looked at the faces around her. Everything that Camille was saying she had heard before and could have predicted. Perhaps many of the other people here could as well, but these were the things they wished to hear, and they gave him unqualified approval. She could see him basking in it, his dark eyes glowing, his cheeks flushed.

She dared not ask for Renoir once a speaker had taken the floor. Any interruption would be resented, and she could not afford to incur dislike.

Camille was followed by another equally ardent young man, but he had not spoken for long before Célie realised he had about him a greater pomposity and even less humour. Discreetly she searched the faces around her one after another. Everyone seemed to be listening with total attention. Their expressions were deadly earnest. Perhaps what Bernave said was true: the revolution had taken away everyone's appreciation of wit.

Was it really necessary to be humourless in order to be good? Could one not possibly bring about social change for the better, and still keep the ability to see the absurd, and to laugh at it?

To judge from those around her, apparently not.

'Who is he?' she whispered to the man who had directed her here and who now stood barely a foot away.

'Fabre d'Eglantine,' he answered without turning. 'He is a great poet. He won the Eglantine Laurel a while ago.'

She had never heard of it, but it would obviously not be prudent to say so now. Presumably he had taken his name from the event.

'How wonderful,' she replied, knowing he would not understand she meant it was wonderful that anyone so mediocre should win anything.

A middle-aged woman in front told them to hush, and Célie obeyed reluctantly. Almost any conversation would have been more interesting than the tangled nonsense being spoken from the rostrum. If Danton was really this man's friend, then that fact said more for his loyalty than his political sense, or his literary judgement.

There was no time to waste. If Renoir was not here, where else could she look for him? It would be justifiable to ask further. After all, he was Bernave's business partner. He had a right to know of Bernave's death. No one could complain of that.

Fabre came to the end of his speech to enthusiastic applause and his place was taken by a young man with a smooth brow, classic nose and chiselled lips. He would have been beautiful had he shown the slightest warmth or animation.

As it was he stared out across the room with the impassivity of a statue, perfectly carved, so flawless as to lack humanity.

'The vessel of the revolution can arrive in port only on a sea reddened with torrents of blood!' he cried with ringing fervour, his voice vibrating but his face still curiously impassive. 'We must not only punish traitors, but all people who are not enthusiastic. There are only two kinds of citizen, the good and the bad. The republic owes the good its protections. To the bad it owes only death!'

Célie looked at the people next to her to see how this extraordinary statement was received. She saw one man wince and his eyes widen. Perhaps he felt the same chill in the stomach and involuntary tightening of muscles that she did. How could all these people stand passively and hear such hysterical words without protest? Did they not have the sense to be frightened? It was as if something in them had died, some laughter and humanity, a sense of proportion to know what was sane, or excessive and absurd.

Except the words were not hysterical in any usual sense. The man who had spoken them remained marble cold as the words poured out of his mouth. There was no ranting, no waving of arms, not even any rise in the pitch of his voice.

'We will build a new France,' he went on. 'Virtues will be paramount. We will sanctify ourselves by our battles, we will be washed clean of vice by our blood. Weakness shall be done away with and we shall rise from the dead in pure, clean power. We shall show the rest of mankind the way forward.'

'Virtue!' an old man beside Célie spat the word under his breath, his face creased, the skin rough as if with constant exposure to wind and rain.

She shuffled a trifle to stand closer beside him.

'Why do you say that, Citizen?' she whispered.

'Don't you know who that is?' he asked her bitterly.

'No. Who is it?'

'Louis Saint-Just,' he replied with a tiny shiver. 'He knows anything I would recognise as virtue about as well as I know the King of Spain. He robbed his mother of all her jewels, and ran away to become a worshipper of the Marquis de Sade. He wrote a long, pornographic poem which disgusted even me, and I'm no prude.'

'Perhaps he's changed?' she suggested, not because she believed it, but to see his response.

'He once wrote to Robespierre telling him 'I know you as I know God', whatever that means,' the man retaliated with deep sarcasm. She had the conviction that if he had been outside he would have spat on the stones.

'Not at all, by the sound of it,' she said, and then wished she had held her tongue, as he looked at her with sudden widening of his eyes, and a flash of warmth, almost hope. That was exactly what Bernave had told her not to do. She realised with a spasm of pain how much she missed his irony, and his courage. She must hurry and find Renoir.

Saint-Just was propounding his plans for the citizens of the future.

'All boys over five years of age will be taken and cared for by the state,' he said with humourless determination, gazing out at his silent listeners. 'They'll be raised in battalions as soldiers . . . or farmers.'

Obviously he had never had a child, never loved it, held it in his arms and felt that protecting it was the most important thing in his life, or he could not have imagined such a world except in nightmare. Célie wondered about girls, but he did not mention them. Perhaps in his world they were not worth it.

'We shall all wear simple clothes made of coarse cloth, every man alike, ruler and worker and soldier,' he continued, lost in his dream. 'We shall sleep on straw mats. He who does not conform must be driven from the gates of the city!'

Célie thought the idea appalling. If that was freedom, then slavery might well be better. At least it allowed for a little individuality, a little colour. She would like to have said that aloud, to see if anyone else felt the same way — claustrophobia closing in on them, the slow sick fear of something terrible and inescapable — but she dared not. No one around her moved or spoke. Disagreement, even questioning, would be seen as counter-revolutionary, and that was a crime.

Bernave had spoken of the danger of this kind of oppression: uniformity, colourlessness, loss of all warmth and passion and laughter. What was the point of life without them? She remembered his face as he had spoken, the power of emotion in him, as if in that moment he had relived some splendour of the soul which had illuminated and made precious all his life since.

She looked at the cold face of Saint-Just and was overwhelmed by the burning need to save the King's life. He might be stupid, fat, autocratic and totally ineffectual, but he was human. He loved his wife and his children. His weaknesses were those anyone might possess, however profoundly they deplored them. There was a fear in the unknown which was too vast to find the strength to face. Everything precious and familiar was being engulfed in a spiritual void.

Was she as alone here as she felt? Or did any of these people packed around her, with their overcoats steaming, boots sodden, feel as horrified as she did by Saint-Just's vision? Could it possibly be what they wanted? Or thought they wanted?

She remembered Madame de Staël, her wit and conversation, the endless vivid discussions that would go on all night, full of energy and great bursts of laughter. Perhaps they were unaware of the cold and the hungry thousands shivering only a few hundred yards away on the streets beyond their beautiful houses. But were Saint-Just and his like any more aware?

Célie looked back at the rostrum. Saint-Just was talking about blood again. He seemed obsessed with it. It was disgusting.

But part of her revulsion was because she understood the craving for revenge too hideously well. She would not be here now if she had not betrayed Georges to the National Guard for what she had imagined he had done to cause Jean-Pierre's death. She could remember the emotions she had felt very clearly, the white-hot hatred, the tireless energy even when her body ached and her mind was exhausted. Nothing had been too hard, if it had served the cause of Georges' destruction.

Now she was even more ashamed of it. It was not what she wanted to be: a destroyer, consumed with rage and hatred, who damaged everything she touched and spread misery all around her, like someone who carried the plague. Such people incurred hatred in return, or fear, or pity . . . never love. They created nothing, gave nothing.

Saint-Just seemed the embodiment of it all as he finally stepped down to tumultuous applause. He did not smile even now.

His place was taken by the huge figure of Danton, who was as unlike him as any man could be. There was nothing cold about him, from his expansive gestures, his volatile temper, his laughter, his appetite, to the plainness of his choice of words. He was as homely as a farmyard, and just as immediate in his impact.

Célie wanted to get out, go and search the other rooms for Renoir, but she could not move without treading on someone's foot. She would cause a stir if she forced her way. People would notice her and perhaps remember her afterwards. She could not afford that.

She might as well stay here and listen. She studied Danton and wondered what he was like as a person, a friend, even a husband. Bernave had said that he adored his wife, who was a gentle, pretty woman, an innkeeper's daughter, and a devout Catholic. She remembered the softness in his voice as he had said that, as if she reminded him of someone else. Danton had two sons. Remembering that made him seem more reachable, someone who could speak of realities, not the arid dreams of St-Just or the flowery rhetoric of Fabre d'Eglantine.

The people around her seemed to have relaxed also, as if this was a man they could understand. The room had grown more comfortable. People felt free to glance at each other and exchange a moment of understanding, even a smile. They were no longer afraid of their own thoughts.

Célie could not help wondering what Danton really felt about the King. Had he tried to save him? Would he still, if he could do it without risking his own head? He was not talking about torrents of blood, but rather about real, sensible things: food and boots, and guns for the army in Belgium.

Someone mentioned Marat's name, and there was a murmur of anger, but it was impossible to tell at whom it was directed. There was a restless energy again, and even the bold sanity of Danton's voice could not override it. Several people stood rigidly, shifting from one foot to the other as if impatient to move. It was growing hot and airless with the press of bodies. Célie was hemmed in. It was hard to breathe.

Danton was pouring scorn over the ineptitudes of the Girondin government, which had left the armies hungry, half clothed and weaponless. His anger was mounting; his great face twisted with outrage. His voice bellowed. He raised a fist like a ham, clenched as if to shake someone like a rat. If he had punched with it, he could have felled an ox.

All around Célie there were murmurs of uneasy anger. Did the crowd even begin to understand that he was talking about war against France, real violent war with soldiers dead and Belgians or Prussians or Austrians marching unhindered on to French soil, into French towns? Did they see the looting and the burning, the refugees, the dead? Danton had seen it. He had been in Belgium in the midst of war until only a day or two ago.

Didn't anybody realise that if they executed the King, they would have the English navy down on them as well, and possibly Spanish soldiers on the southern borders?

Without realising it, Célie was clenching her fists too.

Danton finished and she turned and tried to move towards the door, pushing her way without speaking. But before she reached it, the neat, meticulous figure of Robespierre was on the rostrum in Danton's place, and again she was trapped.

Instantly the shuffling and fidgeting ceased. Robespierre began softly. Around her people strained to hear him. His voice was hoarse, a little whispery, as if he were speaking not to a crowd, but to a few friends in his own salon. Yet his language was pompous and completely impersonal. Célie could not imagine using such

282

a manner towards anyone she knew.

She watched as he leaned forward a little over the rostrum, pushing his green-tinted spectacles up into his head and peering around the room.

'My friend Danton speaks of food and clothing for our armies in Belgium, and rightly is he concerned for them, as we all are,' he began. 'And I defy any man here to prove his interest is in the slightest way shallow, unworthy or dictated by selfish concerns, or the desire for personal gain, the love of indulgence of the fleshly appetites or of beautiful possessions. All who say so are liars, and worse, are blackguards desirous of bringing into disrepute one of the staunchest allies of the revolution, one of the architects of the great new republic we shall build upon the ashes . . . ' He hesitated, blinking.

Everyone let out their breath, presuming he had finished.

Then suddenly he went on, a continuation of the same prolonged sentence.

' . . . of all the sin of the past, washed clean in the baptism of blood.'

He drew in his breath, his little, nail-bitten hands fluttering. 'Those who say Danton is carousing with loose women, camp-followers and the like, do not know him as I do.' He poked the air. 'I challenge them to put forward their names, and repeat such villainous charges here, from this stand, where we can all judge the worth of them.' Again he stopped. He stared around the room. No one moved or looked away from his mesmeric gaze. 'You see!' he said triumphantly. 'No one dare repeat such a slander in front of me . . . in front of us!'

Silence. Not even a rustle disturbed the room. Beside Célie an old man breathed in raspingly.

'But we must not lose sight of the real goal, which is a pure, new society,' Robespierre suddenly went on again. 'Built upon the virtue of the people, those hard-working men and women who have placed their trust in us . . . ' He poured out endless, convoluted sentences, so abstruse and full of hesitations that it was impossible to follow his meaning, but again and again he used words like 'virtue', 'blood', 'purity' and 'hope'.

Célie had an increasingly uncomfortable feeling that for all his protestations of loyalty and admiration, he had planted more suspicion of Danton's motives than any he had allayed. Was that clumsiness, or intent?

At last he finished. Célie was free to leave. Before anyone else could reach the rostrum and begin she turned to the man who had brought her in.

'Have you seen Citizen Renoir?' she asked him.

'No.' He shook his head slightly. 'No, he does not seem to be in here.'

'Then I must go and look in the rest of the rooms. If you would be good enough to tell me where else I should try, I would be most grateful.' She must find him. He might have known Bernave long enough, and well enough, to be certain where his loyalties lay. They had trusted each other with money and judgement of business, perhaps Bernave had also trusted him with the plan. She could not help the surge of hope that Renoir would know who was to take the King's place. It might even be himself.

The man she'd asked was leading the way out and she followed him, elbowing her way through the throng and out into the corridor where it was cooler, and far less suffocating. Which way now? She looked at her guide.

'I need to see Citizen Barbaroux,' he excused himself. 'But you should try that way.' He indicated, and she thanked him and turned.

Ahead of her a little group of men were huddled close together, talking in voices so low she had to concentrate to hear.

'I've just come from the north,' one of them said urgently, his thin face pinched with worry, fair hair straggling over his brow and collar. He moved agitatedly from one foot to the other. 'The news from Austria is bad. I saw soldiers in a terrible state, ragged, boots worn to bits. They said it's chaos up in the battle lines. Mud everywhere.' His voice was sharp. 'Nobody knows what they're doing. They're desperate for news from Paris and can't understand why we don't help them.'

Another man gave a bitter laugh, but no one answered. It was the truth and there was nothing to say.

'What about Danton?' one of the group asked, looking at each of the others in turn. 'He's been up to the battle front in Belgium. He knows what it's like. None of the rest has any idea.' He sniffed hard. 'Couldn't we prevail on him to do something?'

'Battle front!' The first speaker almost spat the

285

words. 'He went to Brussels to loot the palaces and churches. There are bloody great wagon-loads of plate and tapestries and linen coming back to Paris! There's nothing to loot on the Austrian or Prussian battlefields. We're losing. It'll be the Emperor Francis's soldiers and ministers coming to take France's gold and silver back to Vienna soon.'

They fell into an abrupt silence as a couple of deputies appeared at the far end of the corridor.

Célie approached the group who had been talking.

'Excuse me, Citizens,' she said tentatively.

They all turned to look at her, their faces wiped clean from the anger of a few moments since.

'Are you lost, Citizeness?' one of them enquired.

'In a way.' She forced herself to smile, hoping she did not look as nervous as she felt. 'I am looking for Citizen Renoir, from Compiègne. I have a message to give him.'

'Don't you know him?'

'No. It is a message from someone else . . . who is ill and cannot come themselves. Do you know where I can find him?'

'What does he look like?' the fair man asked.

She had no idea. She made a guess, more prompted by hope than knowledge. If he were indeed the one Bernave intended to take the King's place, then that description would fit.'

'He is about fifty or so, not very tall, a little . . . heavy . . . '

'Yes, yes, I know who you mean.' The man

held his hand up. 'Obviously not Charles Renoir, he is very tall. You mean the other Renoir.'

'Yes, Henri Renoir,' Célie agreed. 'Do you know where he is, please?'

He directed her round the corner and up a steep flight of stairs. In the dark-panelled room at the top she found a group of men in close conversation.

'Excuse me, Citizen Renoir?' she asked.

One of them turned. 'Are you looking for me?'

'Citizen Henri Renoir?' Her heart plunged into disappointment. He looked very little like the pictures of the King she had seen. His heaviness was a breadth of shoulder and chest, not corpulence, and his features were blunt and powerful. No one would have mistaken him for the long-nosed, flabby Louis Capet.

'Yes.' He turned and came towards her. 'What can I do for you, Citizeness?'

'May I speak with you privately? It is a delicate matter I have been asked to tell you.' She saw the look of alarm in his face. 'It is not personal, Citizen!' she assured him. 'It is an issue of business, but I expect you would rather speak in private. I work in Citizen Bernave's house, on the Boulevard St-Germain.'

His anxiety cleared.

'Oh! Yes, I see. Of course. I am sure we can find a more discreet place.' He excused himself to the other men and led her out of the room and along the corridor to a stretch where there was no one else. 'Now, what is it, Citizeness?'

She searched his face as well as she could in the wavering light from the torches on the wall.

She saw no sign of grief, or of fear, but he was guarded. There was no trust in him. She did not imagine his patience was long. There was a scar down his left cheek which looked as if it had been made by a blade. A soldier or a street fighter?

'Citizen Bernave is dead,' she said simply.

His eyes widened in surprise. 'Bernave dead? I didn't know. The last I heard he was quite well. I'm sorry.'

It was not the reaction she had expected. Why was he not shocked, distressed, even alarmed?

'He was murdered,' she said abruptly.

Now he was startled. 'Poor Bernave,' he said, his voice dropping. He bit his lip. 'I should have seen that coming.'

'Why?' Then as soon as she had said it she realised it was too forward. She had told him she was Bernave's servant. That gave her no right to ask such questions. Perhaps he would assume that she spoke from shock or fear. She should try to look a little more distressed and vulnerable.

He shook his head. 'Dangerous times,' he replied.

That answer was of no help. She blinked, as if to control tears.

'Then we could all be murdered!' she exclaimed. 'Citizen Bernave was stabbed in his own house! By someone living there.' That should shake him out of his philosophical mood!

He raised his eyebrows. 'Was he?' But still he did not seem amazed. 'Poor Bernave,' he repeated.

She stared at him, trying to understand.

288

'I'm sorry to bring you such news, Citizen.' She must go on, give him the excuse she had worked out. 'Madame Lacoste has the business papers. I don't know what you may need, but until they have arrested someone, the National Guard are in the house and will not let any of us out, except Amandine, the cook, sometimes, or me, to do the shopping.'

This time he looked at her more closely. There still seemed little dismay in him, but there was something which might have been sadness. He shook his head. 'What an ironic way to end.'

She went back to the only thread she could think of that could justify her. 'Madame Lacoste is sorting through the business papers,' she said again. 'His part of the business belongs to Marie-Jeanne now.'

'Of course — his daughter! Naturally.' He nodded, the light flickering on his blunt, powerful face. 'But it is all of the business, not part of it. I ceased to have any share over a year ago.'

Now it was she who was startled. 'Did you? I . . . I didn't know.' Her mind raced. 'Is there someone else I should tell?'

He seemed amused. 'No. No one but a lunatic would take up with Bernave. A madman, but clever. Knew the trade inside out by then.'

'And you . . . don't mind?' It was an impertinent question, but she tried to make it sound like concern, and to keep the bitter disappointment out of her face. She realised how much she had hoped from him, and it seemed none of it could be true. Certainly he could not

289

replace the King for an instant, and it appeared he had broken with Bernave and would not even know anything to help. But why had he said Bernave was a madman? What did he know of him?

Now Renoir was amused. 'Me? Not at all. We were good partners for years — ever since he got out of prison. He had the brains and the imagination, I had the money and the contracts.'

She must have misheard him. 'I thought you said 'prison'!'

He looked at her with a funny, twisted smile. Perhaps there was pity in it. 'You didn't know? Why should you? You are not the cook, what are you? Laundress? Well, it hardly matters now. Someone has been asking. I thought it was all out.' He nodded. 'Yes, when I first met him he had only been free a few days. Had nothing but the clothes he stood up in, and his brains and his nerve. Any amount of nerve.'

Célie swallowed the choking lump in her throat, her heart beating so she felt that he must see her shaking from it.

'What was he in prison for?' She heard the catch in her own voice.

'Rape. Twelve years, roughly. He was out on licence.'

She did not believe it. Not Bernave. It was nothing like the man she knew. She could not even imagine it.

He must have seen the disbelief in her face.

'He was guilty.' He lifted his shoulder in a slight shrug and there was an expression of repugnance in his lips. 'He never denied it. A twelve-year-old girl. Beautiful, so I heard. A rich man's daughter.' His voice dropped as if pity for her still moved him. 'She had a child. It ruined her life. No decent marriage was possible after that. Family were bitterly ashamed, as if she were soiled and it was somehow a mark on all of them. I don't know what they did with her. I think one of the convents took her in.'

Célie could not take her eyes from his face. For a few moments the passage around her ceased to exist. Everything dwindled to what she could see in the light from the torch on the wall, and Renoir telling her of a tragedy and guilt so terrible she could not even think of Bernave's name without fury. Everything she had thought she knew of him was false, a mask behind which there was only horror.

'Bernave went to prison,' he continued. 'Twelve years, roughly. I think he lost count himself. A fearful place. He was about twenty when it happened. It would have broken most men.'

She wanted to say something, but there were no words for the confusion of emotions she felt. And she was vulnerable in front of Renoir. How could Bernave, the subtle, clever, passionate man she had known — and he had been passionate about saving the King, and preventing war and the chaos and hunger it would bring; and about other things, his books, the whole world of thought and beauty — how could such a man have descended to the bestiality, the utter, consuming selfishness of despoiling a twelve-year-old child?

Renoir was staring at her. 'You didn't know, did you?' There was pity for her in his face now. 'I'm sorry. But it doesn't matter any more. Bernave's dead too. It's all history.'

Didn't matter? It mattered hideously. Perhaps everything turned on it. If Bernave would do that, he could surely do anything at all. Betraying those plotting to save the King's life to the Commune would be nothing in comparison. That might conceivably be justified by political belief. Nothing justified raping a child.

And there was another thing. Renoir had said someone else was asking about Bernave. Who? The sudden and awful fear was that it had been St Felix. They had known each other in the past. Was this how?

'Who . . . who else was looking for him about this?' Her voice was a little husky.

Renoir pushed his lip out in a gesture of disdain. 'I don't know. I only heard. People were talking. It's all past, years ago.'

'It doesn't matter to you?' she said immediately.

He smiled, his face crooked, ugly and humorous. 'I accepted the man I knew when I knew him. That was twenty-three years ago, before he married or Marie-Jeanne was born. He had intelligence and wit. I had money and no idea how to use it to make more. We were a good partnership, and — I'll be honest — I liked him. What he had been was none of my business. He was fair with me.'

'But you broke the partnership!' Célie challenged him.

292

'Only when he started taking up political causes. That's no part of trade or making money. A wise man listens and learns everything he can, and says as little as possible.'

'Is that why you're here?' she accused. 'Just to listen?'

'Yes . . . and to say nothing at all, except agree with the right people.' His eyes were mild, laughing at her.

'Then you'd better agree with Citizen Robespierre!' she retaliated.

'Oh, I have, Citizeness,' he said quietly, his voice suddenly bitter. 'And you would be wiser to go home and tend to your laundry, or whatever it is you do, and not ask questions about the dead.'

The heat washed up her face. Now she wanted to escape. The Jacobin Club had become suffocating. Even the wind and rain of the street outside would be better. She must see Georges, tell him what had happened. This threw everything into turmoil again. No one could be trusted.

'Thank you . . . Citizen,' she said hoarsely. 'You have been very kind. I beg your pardon if I was rude.'

He shrugged, dismissing it, and turned away just as a group of earnest young men came around the corner from the stairs, all talking at once.

Outside in the street again the icy air was like a slap across the face, tingling the skin and making her gasp. She pulled her shawl more tightly round her neck and shoulders and started to walk as quickly as she dared, trying not to slip on the wet cobbles in the fitful light from windows and the occasional torch as people passed by. She could smell the smoke in the air, and the tar.

There were shouts. Now and again a musket fired as National Guardsmen faced sporadic violence over in the distance to the east.

She reached the river, a void of impenetrable darkness beneath her as she went over the Pont Neuf. She could hear its freezing waters sucking and swirling around the stone piers, and a hundred yards away to the east the red reflections of more torches dancing like fire on the ripples.

★　★　★

It was three-quarters of an hour later when Célie felt her way in the bitter darkness up the steps to Georges' attic and knocked on the door.

There was no answer. Could he be asleep? It was early for that, but then in the cold and the dark, virtually imprisoned as he was, why not? She should have brought him some candles from the house as well as the food she had bought, but she had not dared. They were too easily counted. Madame Lacoste almost certainly knew how many there were. Apart from that, any search, even half competent, would have found them hidden in Célie's clothes.

She knocked again, more urgently.

There was still no answer.

This could not be right. She beat on the door,

using the flat of her hand to make more noise.

Silence. Nothing moved anywhere.

Her heart was thumping so wildly she could barely control herself. Her thoughts leaped ahead, far too close to panic already. Was Georges ill? Injured? If he had gone away, then why? Where was he?

Without realising it she was banging on the door again. She snatched her hand away. She was making far too much noise. She shrank back against the wall, feeling sick.

Georges! Where was he?

Had Bernave betrayed him after all? Had they come and arrested him? How would she ever know? He could be anywhere! In one of the Commune prisons already . . . facing the guillotine tomorrow. He could be dead, and she would never know, never be able to help!

Where could she go? Who could she ask?

No one.

She felt the hot tears sting her eyes. It was too big a hurt to bear. He could be killed — all that life and courage, the smile, the memories, the belief . . . all destroyed. How could she tell Amandine? On top of her fear for St Felix it would be more than she could bear. She had loved Georges all her life. He was her only link with everything in the past that had been sweet and good.

How could Célie herself bear it? It was as if the darkness and the cold had settled inside her, bone deep. She had never in her life been so alone. Who else could she tell about Bernave? Who else would understand, would be as shattered and wounded as she was? Who else was there for a hundred other things, if Georges was gone?

She did not know how long she sat there crumpled up on the stairs, growing stiffer, losing the sensation in her hands and feet, and not caring. All she could feel was the void inside and the terrible ache of loss. She was afraid for Amandine; she dare not ever imagine her fear for herself.

The sound of steps coming closer, the creak of wood, were almost on her before she was aware of them. Then it was too late to escape. Whoever it was must be on the same flight as she was. The National Guard, or whoever had arrested Georges, were coming back! They were coming to see what else they could find, or who else.

If they took her wherever he was, she might be able to do something!

No, that was idiotic. There was nothing anyone could do, not against the Commune. Georges was a wanted man, because she had made him so.

That was it! She would have to tell them she had lied, and why. It was the only way she could rescue him, and redress the wrong she had done. Then they would execute her instead. Maybe she deserved that.

She stood up cautiously. Her legs were tingling. She had been sitting on her feet and they had become numb in the cold and the cramped position. It was all she could do not to cry out. It was hard to remain upright.

Why was there no light? Why did they not have torches?

The wood was creaking, only a yard or two away. She could sense someone very close to her.

Were they as aware of her?

Then he was there, almost falling over her. He grasped her, holding her hard, drawing his breath in sharply with surprise. She could smell his skin, the warmth of him, the feel of his sleeve against her face, the roughness of his cheek.

'Célie!'

'Georges?' She gasped and found herself choking in relief, joy, tears streaming down her face. 'Georges!' Now it was fury as well. 'Where have you been?' she demanded, swallowing hard and having to sniff.

He was still holding her tightly, as if she might fall over were he to let her go, and she was clinging on to him to hold herself up. Had he noticed the tears on her skin? He must not know how she had felt. That would be mortifying. It could change everything.

'Come inside,' he whispered back, his lips close to her ear.

She regained control of herself with difficulty. Thank goodness it would be dark enough inside and he would not be able to see her expression, or how she was shaking. 'There is something I must tell you!' she gasped, swallowing again.

'What's happened?' He hesitated, his voice sharp with anxiety. He must have heard the tears in her voice. 'Did you find Renoir?' He kept his tone very level, but the rough edge was there, the knowledge of the danger. He pushed the door open and guided her in, then closed it behind them and fumbled his way over to the stub of the candle and lit it. The room was icy.

'What is it?' he repeated, staring at her. 'What happened?'

'I saw Renoir.' She tried to steady her voice but her throat was still thick with tears. The relief of finding Georges, of hearing his voice, knowing he was here so close she could have taken a step and touched him, was almost dizzying. The words poured out with all the pain, the anger and the need to understand. 'He isn't a partner any more. He met Bernave years ago. He had the money and Bernave had the brains. But he broke the agreement when Bernave started getting too involved in politics . . . '

'Just a minute!' A flame flared up, catching the wick and burning more brightly. Georges' face was haggard. There were shadows under his eyes and stubble on his chin. He looked exhausted — beaten. 'You're going too quickly. It doesn't matter about the past, what about Renoir now? Can he help us?'

'Yes it does matter. It could change everything!'

He caught the panic in her. 'Why, Célie? What did Renoir say?' He had put the candle-holder down and come towards her.

She forced her voice to be steady.

'That when he first met him, Bernave was just out of prison . . . for raping a twelve-year-old girl.' It was out; she was no longer alone with the knowledge. She could not steady her voice. 'He got her with child. Her family abandoned her.

298

Her whole life was destroyed.' The tears ran helplessly down her face. 'Georges, how could he . . . how could anybody do that? Bernave wasn't . . . the man I thought I knew! But I don't know anything!' Her fists were clenched, her body aching with the effort of control. 'How could I talk to him every day, listen to what he believed, carry messages for him, and see nothing of what he really was?' She could hear her voice rising, out of control.

She wanted Georges to tell her it was not true, that there was some explanation which would make it all right. She was being a child. She stared at him, seeing the weariness in his face, the lines of strain. All the confidence and the ease had gone. He looked as tired and frightened as everyone else.

'That's not all,' she said wretchedly, hating herself for having to tell him the rest. 'Renoir said someone else had been asking questions about Bernave too. He didn't know who.'

Georges was fighting for reason, for sense in it all. She could see it in his eyes. 'You think it was St Felix?' he asked, struggling for understanding.

She nodded, barely perceptibly, as if the smallness of the movement could make the reality less.

'Don't tell Amandine,' he said quickly. 'Not unless you have to.'

Célie could see how much that would hurt him. He cared for her deeply. Her pain would be his. It was there, naked, in his eyes.

She felt a hot wave of jealousy. No one cared so much for her hurt and loneliness; no one loved her in that way, with such warmth and unquestioning loyalty.

And yet if he had not cared for Amandine, Célie would have thought so much less of him. What would he be worth if he could not love, if it were an emotion he could turn on or off as was convenient to him, if he shared only laughter and good company, never the loss or the wounds?

She stifled her own feelings of loneliness. 'No, of course I won't,' she answered. 'Anyway, it may not have been him: it could be anyone.'

'What do you think?' he asked gravely.

She started to reply as she would have less than a day ago, then stopped. With amazement she realised he needed comfort. He had changed since the last time they had sat here talking. Some hope, some confidence in him had gone. This was a blow which was very nearly too much for him. For the first time since she had known him, Georges was vulnerable — not in physical danger but in confusion, in emotional hurt he could not overcome.

She wanted intensely to give him the right answer, one which was the truth, and yet would restore the core of belief he had lost. It made her newly alone in a different way. He was not there to support her any more, to shore up her courage. She must be the one to help him. Without even being aware of it, she moved closer to him, putting out a hand to touch his arm.

'I would understand if it were him,' she said gently, and with far more certainty in her voice than she felt, and more courage. 'If that girl were part of my family, a sister, I would have killed Bernave.'

'I'm sure you would.' He put his hand over hers. She felt the touch of his fingers, gentle, but as cold as she was. 'I'm sorry . . . I didn't mean — '

'I know you didn't,' she said quickly, answering his grip. 'But it would have been fair enough if you had.' It was the only time he had mentioned her revenge for Jean-Pierre. She had more than deserved it, and yet it had been only a slip of the tongue, not intended. She wanted to cover it quickly, not let the moment lie. It was Amandine and St Felix who mattered — and Georges.

'If that is what happened, we shall have to help . . . protect him if we can.'

Georges said nothing.

'I know it would be hard for Amandine,' she went on, leaning a little forward, studying his face, searching for anything that would give him hope or comfort. 'But if that's what happened, she may find she can understand it. It would not be impossible for her to reconcile with what she believes of him. She'll want to understand.'

'I know . . . I know,' he agreed. 'But how can we protect St Felix?' His face tightened. 'I'm saying 'we', as if I could do anything. I mean, how can you? Do you know what happened to the knife?'

'No,' she admitted. 'But there must be places in the house it could be. The rooms are full of loose floorboards, and cupboards with holes in them. Whoever it was could have put the knife

301

close by at the time, and then moved it later.'

'Or gone over the roof as you did,' he added. 'If they had the nerve!' There was admiration in his voice and in what she could see of his exhausted face in the guttering candlelight. There was no pretence in it, no deliberate flattery or charm. She saw it like a sudden blossoming of warmth inside her.

'Menou searched the roof,' Célie answered. 'And there were men all around the streets. But not finding the knife is only half the answer.' She hated being so miserably practical. 'He isn't going to let it go. I wish I knew of some way of getting him out of the house, giving up on the case — or even thinking he had some other kind of answer . . . ' She trailed off, knowing that there was no other. Menou would only rest when he knew and could prove who had killed Bernave.

Georges did not argue or bother to point that out to her. He knew she already realised it.

'Be careful!' he said softly, searching her eyes. 'He'll be watching you. Don't take food. Madame Lacoste will know what's in the larder. I'll manage some other way.'

'If there was another way, you'd have done it already,' she said drily. She took what she had bought him out of her pocket and passed it across.

He accepted it, half hiding a smile. It was the first time the tension and misery had left his face since he had come back, and she had seen in the candlelight how bad he looked.

'Thank you,' he accepted. 'But don't run any

302

more risks.' He put it on the table near the stove. The room was so small he did not have to stand to reach.

'It's not a risk,' she answered. 'But I'll be careful.' She saw the disbelief in his face. 'It isn't! Amandine gave me the money, but in future she and I can just eat a little less. Madame Lacoste isn't mean, she doesn't run the rations short. I think she's terrified either Fernand or her husband killed Bernave.'

'Why?' Georges asked, his eyes wide. 'If they knew he was trying to save the King they would all have had a motive. They'd disagree with it morally and politically, but if they turned him in, then the house would be confiscated and they'd lose their home. But if they didn't know, then St Felix was the only one with any cause.' His face was pinched again with pain and the bitter hurt of disillusion. All the confidence, the laughter and the ease were stripped from him, leaving him completely unguarded. He was in half-shadow as the candle burned almost to the bottom, the tallow running over.

'What about the King?' he said. 'Can we still try?'

'Because of St Felix?' she said. 'If he killed Bernave, it doesn't mean he would betray us. He's no Communard.'

He frowned. 'I could understand it . . . but why couldn't he have waited just a few days more? It must have been thirty-five years — what would a few days matter?'

'Perhaps he only just found out. Perhaps . . . ' she trailed off. He did not need it spelled out.

He pushed his hand through his hair, dragging it back off his brow. 'If they execute the King it will take a miracle to save us from war.' There was black laughter and anguish in his voice. 'And since there is now no God, that is unlikely! There's only one good thing about the official end of deity. At least Robespierre cannot claim divine approval for what he does, or that he speaks the will of God. There's nothing left now but human reason and human acts. What we don't do ourselves will not be done.'

She closed her eyes. 'What a terrible thought!' She meant it. It was as if an abyss had opened in front of her, bottomless, and there was nothing to safeguard her, or anyone, from being sucked into it.

She felt his hand close over hers, warmer now. He did not say anything. They were simply together on the brink, not each alone. He bent forward and for a moment his lips brushed her cheek.

Then she took a step backward, before the moment could linger too long, or be explained away. She wanted to keep it exactly as it was, to remember that touch as if it were for ever. 'I'll try to get you a candle,' she promised huskily. 'Good night.'

'Good night, Célie,' he whispered.

11

St Felix found it almost beyond bearing to remain imprisoned in the house on the Boulevard St-Germain. He was helpless to do anything either for himself or for the cause. He had not even the comfort of manual work as Fernand or Monsieur Lacoste had. He could not concentrate his mind to his usual solace of reading.

Célie had gone out to see the last two drivers, and of course to shop for the household daily portion of bread and whatever else she could find. She looked exhausted; her thick, pale hair always had a kind of beauty, but her skin was now so pale her eyes were shadowed around and her lips almost colourless. There was an energy, a passion in her that St Felix found uncomfortable. Amandine was gentler, easier to be with. But there was also something in her which reminded him of Laura, and that he could not bear. Even a year after her death she was never far from his mind. She had been the core of his life, the reason for everything — good and bad.

Now she was gone, and all their years together were irretrievable, and that was the true agony of his life which consumed all else, like a darkness that took the light.

He looked out of his bedroom window. Of course the soldiers were still standing around outside and he could see their blue uniforms and the cockades of their hats. Two of them had muskets. They came and went. Sometimes there were more, sometimes fewer, but always at least one. Menou seemed determined to find out who had killed Bernave.

St Felix knew he was Menou's prime suspect. Every time Menou asked questions he made that more and more apparent.

What was the guillotine like? He knew the ritual well enough. The condemned person was taken from the Palais de Justice to the Salle des Mortes — the hall of the dead — until the executioner came, Charles-Henri Sanson. Your hair was cut and, if you wanted it, one of the juring priests still allowed would hear your confession.

Did he want that? He still did not know. Yes . . . and yet it terrified him. Perhaps. Afterwards it was too late.

Then your shirt or bodice was slit at the neck, your wrists were tied behind your back, and you were taken to the courtyard, and then your name was called out and the crowd jeered at you. Half a dozen at a time, you were loaded into the red tumbrels escorted by mounted guardsmen, and set out for the Place de la Révolution, and the scaffold.

Once there you were all lined up in rows, backs to the blade itself, until your name was called again. Then you mounted the steps, your legs were bound together, you were laid on the bascule, the leather strap buckled round your body to hold you down. The bascule was levelled, your head put in the lunette, the two halves closed together — ready for the knife.

Was it really quick, almost no pain at all — no time for it? Or was it, as some people said, that you went on living afterwards, for minutes, in indescribable agony? There were stories of heads that had moved, eyes, tongues . . . It was also the things before death that terrified. The pain, the terror, the humiliation of losing control of bodily function.

Was death annihilation, a black, endless silence, and peace at last? Or was it something else? Was there judgement, a reliving of all the cruel, cowardly, or selfish things one had ever done, condemned to see oneself in ugly and pathetic nakedness? That was the truly awful darkness that he could not look at.

There was a knock on the door. Please heaven it was not Amandine. He had not the strength to be kind, and she did not deserve to be hurt.

The knock sounded again. He was sweating, his stomach sick.

'Come in.'

It was Monsieur Lacoste.

'Yes?' St Felix said abruptly.

Monsieur Lacoste looked anxious, his eyes narrowed, his face tense. He pushed past St Felix into the room and pulled the door closed behind him.

'Menou has been here again, asking more questions.' He spoke very quietly, as if he were afraid of being overheard, even here in the house.

St Felix felt his stomach clench. 'He will — until he knows what happened,' he replied, struggling to keep his voice level. 'He has to have some answer to take back to the Commune.'

'I know that!' Monsieur Lacoste agreed, nodding very slightly. 'He won't give up. His job depends on it. If I were he, I wouldn't want to go back and tell Marat and the Commune that someone had killed a loyal revolutionary, but I couldn't find out who — would you?'

St Felix swallowed hard. His heart felt as if it were choking him, beating too high in his chest. It was difficult to catch his breath. He had seen Menou watching him, heard the direction of his questions. Was that what Monsieur Lacoste meant now?

'It's — it's nothing to do with the Commune!' he protested.

'True,' Monsieur Lacoste said with a harsh laugh, cut off with anger. 'But when did that ever stop Marat?'

'There's nothing we can do about it,' St Felix said, despair engulfing him.

Monsieur Lacoste moved half a step closer to him. 'Yes there is. Bernave treated you abominably, sending you out at all hours, in all weathers. He abused your loyalty to the cause. We all saw that. No one blames you.' He held up his hand to silence St Felix's argument. 'I don't know whether you killed him or not, and to tell you the truth, I don't care. But I know what Menou thinks, and if you are honest so do you.'

Everything he said was true. And no one would bother with a trial now, of all times. It would be prison one day, crammed in with a dozen others, then at dawn the short ride to the

308

guillotine, the great triangular blade with its scarlet edge. The last thing on earth you would hear would be the scream of the knife falling — then what? Oblivion? Or not? Perhaps you did not go instantly, but faded, seeing your own head in Sanson's basket, and your soul, your self, would make a slow journey . . . where? Into darkness — darkness for which there was never again any light.

St Felix felt sick.

Monsieur Lacoste was staring at him. His face seemed very close.

'You all right?' His voice was curiously echoing. 'Look, if you want to make a run, I'll keep the guard distracted. There's only the one right now.'

He did not really need Lacoste to tell him. He had seen it yesterday, and had simply refused to recognise it.

'Yes, yes, I know,' he said softly. 'Thank you.' It crossed his mind that Lacoste was doing this to get rid of Menou as much as for St Felix. Perhaps he was guilty himself, or he was afraid it was Fernand. Maybe one of the Lacostes knew about Bernave's plan for the King. None of that mattered any more. It couldn't succeed anyway. But it was important to take the travel passes with him, so Menou would not find them. He would discover a way of getting them to Célie somehow. 'Yes,' he repeated. 'Just give me a moment. The picture of my wife . . . a few things, not much . . . '

'Hurry!' Lacoste urged. 'When he comes back it may be too late.'

'I know . . . a minute . . . just one.'

Monsieur Lacoste stepped back and went to the far side of the door.

St Felix picked up the painting of Laura, and the passes, and followed after him.

★　★　★

Georges woke cold and stiff, the grey light coming in through the window. This was the last day of the King's life. This time tomorrow he would be dead, the people's decision irrevocable, and everything that would follow from it. They had less than twenty-four hours to do everything that was left.

He turned over, pulling the thin blanket with him, and realised just how cold he was. There was no fuel left, and that had been the last candle. He should get up. At least movement would warm him to some degree.

He thought of Célie. Then he remembered last night, and what she had told him of Bernave and the child he had raped. His body was locked so tight with misery that now he ached all over as if he had been beaten. He could hardly feel his feet. All sorts of fears had filled his mind about Bernave — about who had killed him and why, about his loyalties, or his betrayals — but his wildest thought had never created anything like this.

He remembered when he had first met Bernave. It had been September, hot and suffocatingly still. The Marseillais, the rabble army who had poured out of the dockyards and

310

prisons of Marseille and Genoa, and marched on Paris, were everywhere. Crowds milled around the streets, the smell of fear in the air. Célie had betrayed him to the National Guard . . . and then risked her life to warn him before it was too late.

Something she had seen in Madame de Staël had changed her. But Madame de Staël belonged to the past, gone, like so many of the old values and the old dreams. Gone, like the rich, gentle land of his home. Georges had not realised how much the place was woven into the fabric of his identity until it was lost. He could not bear to remember the spoiling of it, the ignorance and stupidity that had destroyed centuries of nurture.

September, with its horror and madness, was different, an eruption of hell into everyday life, rather than the violation of his home, the heart of what made him.

The arrests had begun on 29 August — all manner of people, mostly ordinary: shopkeepers, traders, artisans, petit-bourgeois, not only to be imprisoned but to be robbed. Many old enmities were satisfied. Men with money were chosen, and, of course, in the rage against the Church — priests, scores of priests.

Then early in the morning of Sunday, 2 September, the news had come that the Duke of Brunswick had broken through the French defending forces at Verdun and was marching on Paris. The Commune had sounded the tocsin, and salvoes of gunfire had added to the general panic. Notices had been posted around the city reading 'The people themselves must execute justice. Before we hasten to the frontiers, let us put bad citizens to death.'

What followed then had drenched Georges' waking thoughts and made nightmares of his dreams. The streets were teeming with people crushed together, sweating in the heat. Georges had been within a quarter of a mile of the prison at the old Abbey of St-Germain-des-Prés. A group of men had been singing that tune which was now more terrible than any words. Even a few bars of it still knotted his stomach.

Then in his mind he was back in the prison of the Carmes again, the smell of dust, closed air, the sweat of terror. Like a tide the rabble had swept in, shouting, bursting open the cells, and gone through and down the fine, curved steps that descended on the other side of the shallow railing into the garden. He saw the marbles above the graves. Even in the stifling heat the white statues were like cold flesh.

It was there, inside the Carmes, that he had seen Bernave for the first time. He must have been caught up by the crowd as well, because he was obviously also a prisoner. He was sitting on the bench opposite, but unlike those to either side of him, he did not betray his fear. He sat upright, hands by his sides, and stared impassively straight ahead, although he appeared to see nothing. His mind was turned totally inward.

Two of the Marseillais had come and hauled away one of the priests. One of those left had crossed himself, his hand shaking.

A moment later another priest had been taken away.

Bernave had turned to Georges, his thick, black hair, unmarked by a tonsure.

'Are you a Catholic?' he had asked.

Georges had been startled. 'No,' he had said honestly. He was born Catholic, of course, but had long since ceased to believe. 'I'm sorry, I can't help you. If you want absolution, or someone to pray with you, ask one of the others.' He had jerked his arm to indicate the dozen or so priests still left.

'It's a little late for that,' Bernave had answered. 'What I want is to get out of here alive, and not be executed for something I didn't do.' There had been a curious bitterness in his voice as he'd said that, as if it had some dreadful double meaning. 'I will swear for you as a loyal supporter of the Commune, if you will do the same for me?' He had made it a question, spoken under his breath — not that the priests with closed eyes and prayers on their lips had been taking any notice of either of them.

Georges had seized the opportunity. He had had no idea who Bernave was, and didn't care.

'Of course. My name is Georges Coigny. What's yours?'

'Victor Bernave.'

They had exchanged more information hastily, whispering so low it was beyond the ears of the others in the room. More priests had been taken out. None had come back.

Eventually it had been Bernave's turn. He'd been led away.

Georges had sat waiting, his mouth dry, his body shaking.

Then the soldiers had come for him. He'd been led into a passageway where a fat man had been sitting behind a table, his belly resting against the edge. His sleeves had been rolled up and his arms stained with blood.

'Who are you?' he had demanded.

'Georges Coigny,' Georges had stammered.

'What do you do?'

'I work for Citizen Bernave, of the Commune,' he had lied instantly. If Bernave was as good as his word, he might be allowed to live; if not, he had nothing to lose anyway.

'And what does Citizen Bernave do?' the man had asked with a sneer.

'Keep the good citizens of the Commune informed on the actions of their enemies, the enemies of the people and of the revolution and the liberty we are all fighting for,' Georges had said boldly.

The man had looked sceptical.

Georges had waited, his heart pounding so violently he'd felt as though his whole body were jerking with it.

The man had relaxed at last. 'So he says. Told me he was a friend of Citizen Marat! Is that true?'

'Of course,' Georges had lied again, despising himself for it. How could anyone willingly claim friendship with Marat?

The man had turned to one of the guards. 'Take him out through the garden . . . and let him go. I mean it! He may be a friend of Citizen

314

Marat. Let him go into the street, you hear me?'
'Yes, Citizen!'

Wordlessly Georges had followed the guard out and down the flight of steps into the garden. The sight that had met his eyes was beyond imagination. Bodies had been lying in heaps, mangled, beaten to death, the dead and the dying together. Some had literally been torn apart. Dismembered limbs had soaked the grass with blood. Entrails had lay on the steps. Already in the heat the flies had begun to gather.

Georges had floundered through it.

He had found Bernave outside in the street, waiting for him. Together they had walked back dazed, in a silent companionship of horror. Near the river they had met a young man, elegantly dressed but his jacket slightly awry, his hair ruffled, his cravat a little to the left. In the strange evening light he had looked like a bedraggled bird. He had regarded them curiously, two men walking side by side, staring ahead, not speaking and yet in some way very much together.

'Have you had an accident?' he had asked. 'There's blood all over you!' Then he had looked beyond them at the sky. 'What's that?'

Bernave had turned towards the glare, his features lit by it for a moment, showing his clear, almost brilliant eyes. 'The light?' he'd asked. 'Bonfires. They have lit them to see what they are doing, I suppose.'

'Doing?' The young man had had an innocent, pleasant face. He'd probably been about twenty-four. 'At this hour? I say, are you sure you

315

are all right? You look terrible!'

'Where in God's name have you been?' Georges had said hoarsely.

The young man had blushed. 'Me? To the theatre, and then a party. Why?'

'To the theatre . . . ' Georges had repeated vacuously, hysteria welling up inside him. He had started to laugh and had felt Bernave's hand like a vice on his arm. He'd stopped suddenly, the pain making him wince.

'Why? What are they doing?' The young man had still seemed undisturbed.

'Do you see that?' Bernave had pointed downwards. 'There, running in the gutter?'

The young man had bent forward, his eyes following Bernave's finger.

'They are killing all the prisoners,' Bernave had said, his voice shaking with anger and pain. 'That is blood you can see. The gutters of Paris are running with human blood.'

From that night had begun the friendship between Georges and Bernave. They had gone back to Bernave's house in the Boulevard St-Germain and drunk wine together in silence until they'd fallen asleep. The following day they had eaten the last decent food Bernave had in the kitchen, and talked of all manner of things that were good and sane and beautiful, it did not matter from where or when. Gradually they had mentioned other things, regret for the loss of loveliness.

Georges had spoken instinctively of his land and his home, always swift to his mind, the loss raw. They had both mourned that ease of

316

friendship was gone — trust in the passing stranger or the turn of good fortune. Bernave had said something of the quiet certainties of faith no longer being there, in the eye or in the heart. Georges had thought from the shadow of laughter in his eyes that he meant faith of others, but from the sorrow in him, perhaps it was for himself also.

Lastly they had spoken of the King: what a fool he was, and what greater fools were those who would destroy him without the least idea of who or what would take his place.

At the kitchen table, with the sunlight streaming in through the long windows, had been born their determination to try to avert the disasters they'd seen ahead for France.

Now Georges was sitting in the grey daylight, shivering and wretched, and all that certainly was shattered, and Bernave himself was dead, whoever, whatever he had been.

He might not be back again. He took the last of his bread and wine and went out into the winter day to check for a last time on the crowd for storming the King's carriage tomorrow. Then he must get the travel passes. Célie had said St Felix had them. If he waited she would almost certainly come out — she always did, to queue for bread. He would see her and ask her. There might be no other chance. He wanted to see her. It mattered with a breathtaking sharpness he was unprepared for. It was worth the risk, even in daylight, even with Menou's men in the streets.

He did not say so in words, even to himself, but since they had not found Briard, for whom the fourth pass was intended, it would be the last time. That hurt more than the knowledge of what the crowd would do to him, which would be violent, terrible, but quick, all over in a minute. But he would never be able to say to Célie all the things he wanted to, needed to. They had shared so much that was hard, but the laughter and the gentleness would be denied them, the time to learn the little things that make pleasure unique, to explore joy and pain together, to grow old.

And that was what he wanted, time with Célie, to share anything and everything.

He must not think of it. It was the one regret which would break him. He forced it out of his mind and walked faster.

When he was in the Rue de Seine almost opposite the Bernave house on the Boulevard St-Germain, he saw a man climb out of the window of the front room on to the street. Very carefully peering both ways as if to make sure he was unobserved, he then hurried east, as fast as he could go without actually running.

For a moment Georges had seen his face in the light: a fine, sensitive, intelligent face, about Bernave's age. Neither his look nor his manner were those of an artisan. There was an innate elegance in him in spite of his very ordinary brown and grey clothes. It must be St Felix. Georges saw instantly why Amandine would be drawn to him.

As St Felix turned into the Rue des Tours, Georges broke into a run himself and went after him. What had happened to panic him into leaving the house? Surely he must realise it would instantly mark him as guilty?

Even as he saw St Felix disappear, Georges heard a voice behind him, sharp with anger. A moment later a shot rang out. However, no bullet past him. The shot was an alarm rather than an intention to hit anyone.

St Felix was going towards the river and the Île de la Cité. He was crazy. He was going right into the open. He must have lost his head completely to do something so utterly stupid. In the Cordeliers at least he would have a chance.

Georges could see him ahead, moving with a swifter pace now. He could not keep that up for long. From what Célie had said, St Felix was unused to much exercise, a scholar rather than a man of action. He was racing down the Rue Dauphine towards the Pont Neuf and the open river.

There was more shouting behind and the clatter of running feet.

Just before the road end, St Felix dashed across between two carts, was yelled at by drivers, and disappeared into a gateway.

Georges slowed down. Following him would only give away his direction. He looked around quickly. There were half a dozen other people on the pavement but all seemed busy with their own affairs.

A National Guardsman in a torn uniform came up to Georges, panting and clasping his side.

'Seen a man in a brown coat running, Citizen?' he asked between gasps.

'Yes,' Georges answered unhesitatingly. 'He went down towards the river, the Île de la Cité.'

The guard raised his hand in thanks and then increased his speed, calling over his shoulder to his men to follow him. Half a dozen others set off at a run, fanning out to cover both sides of the street.

Georges turned back as if going to the Boulevard St-Germain again, still holding his wine and loaf of bread. He cut across the Rue Christine, in the same direction as St Felix had gone. If St Felix had continued moving, he should come out somewhere near the Rue Seguier. If he didn't, then he had gone to ground. Perhaps he knew someone who would hide him. After dark it would be easier. He might get out of the district altogether.

Georges walked quite slowly down towards the river. The street was quiet. An old man lounged in a doorway. A woman sold coffee, her head wrapped up in a shawl which almost hid her face. Two children quarrelled over who had won a game, and a young man with black hair read a copy of *L'Ami du Peuple*.

Georges waited ten minutes and was just about to leave, satisfied that St Felix had found a place to hide, when he saw him step out of an alley entrance, glance up and down the street, and then come towards him, walking too quickly.

The young man with the paper looked up at him curiously. Both children stopped their argument and stared.

Georges stepped forward. 'Oh! There you are!' he said boldly. 'Thought I'd missed you!'

St Felix stopped abruptly, his face white, eyes wide.

Georges pushed the bread into his pocket and strode the last few paces to him and clasped his hand, putting his free arm around his shoulders.

'Good to see you, my friend,' he said loudly, then added under his breath, 'for heaven's sake pretend to recognise me. It's your only chance!'

'Hello!' St Felix gulped. 'Yes . . . sorry. I went the wrong way. How are you?' He looked terrible; his body was shaking and his breath rasped in his throat.

'I've been on the run since September,' Georges said softly. 'I'm a hell of a lot better at this than you are. Come with me.' As he said it he started forward, linking his arm in St Felix's and half pulling him along. 'We've got to get back into the alleys of the Cordeliers. They couldn't find Marat there, even with three thousand soldiers. We might be just as lucky.'

St Felix kept up with him. 'Why?' he demanded. 'You don't know me. Why should you care if they catch me or not?'

'St Felix,' Georges replied. 'They want you for killing Bernave.'

St Felix snatched his arm away, his face ashen, the fine lines around his eyes deep-etched. 'Who the hell are you?'

'Georges Coigny, Amandine's cousin,' Georges replied. 'For heaven's sake don't draw attention to us! Keep your head down.'

St Felix obeyed, but more from alarm than compliance. Together, almost in step, they hurried across the Boulevard St-Germain and into the alley behind the Rue Monsieur le Prince.

'We've got to go west,' Georges said urgently, 'otherwise we'll end up in the Luxembourg Gardens. They won't be looking for two men.'

'Why do you bother?' St Felix asked, but he kept up with him, his head forward, eyes down on the rough stones of the pavement.

A cart rumbled by them, followed swiftly by a high-wheeled single-seated carriage driven at considerable speed. An old woman swore as a spurt of mud sloshed against her. There was a National Guardsman standing at the far corner where Georges and St Felix had passed a few minutes before.

'Hey you! Stop!' he bellowed. 'You in the brown coat!' He turned sideways to someone out of sight. 'Michelet! Up here!'

Georges grasped St Felix again and half-dragged him under the archway into a courtyard.

'We can't get out of here!' St Felix accused him, his eyes wide with fear. 'We'll be trapped!'

'Up the steps,' Georges ordered, waving at the flight of stone stairs that led to a door in the second storey. 'Come on — hurry!'

'Where to?' St Felix demanded desperately, pulling away. 'We can't get in!'

'Yes we can . . . get on with it!' Georges slapped his back hard. 'Run!'

There was nowhere else to go. They lurched forward and all but collided, stumbling up the steps to the door. Georges beat on it with his fist, still clutching the bottle in the other, and then threw his weight against it. The catch burst and they over-balanced inwards just as a large woman in a grey dress came out of the room beyond.

'We mean you no harm, Citizeness,' Georges said, forcing himself to smile at her dazzlingly. 'Some drunken louts abused my friend here, and when he answered back they set on us. Flight is the better part of valour.'

The woman looked at St Felix's pale face with its poet's mouth and terrified eyes. He seemed to be holding his arms over his chest as if he had been hurt. Actually he was a little winded, but she was not to know that.

'Please?' Georges urged, offering her the bottle of wine and the bread.

She closed her eyes and waved an arm in the general direction of the room behind her.

Georges took it for permission, and put the bread and wine on the table. He yanked St Felix forward through the doorway, past a couple of chairs and a table set out in quiet domesticity, into the next room, up a short flight of stairs and threw open the window.

'Out!' he ordered.

St Felix swung around, eyes wide. 'What?'

'Out!' Georges repeated sharply. 'On to the roof. We'll be out of their sight. They won't know where we'll come down. Don't stand there! Do you want to be shot?'

There was shouting in the street below.

St Felix scrambled through the window and slid down the roof slates awkwardly, only regaining his footing when he was almost at the bottom of the valley. He straightened up and started along towards the nearest divide, quite quickly gaining some skill.

Georges went after him, feeling his feet slip on the wet slates and banging his elbow as he tried to get his balance.

St Felix was already disappearing around the corner of the valley into the angle of the next row of houses. There were more shouts from the street below and half a dozen bullets shot into the air.

Georges let go and half rolled down into the guttering. He landed on hands and knees, then went forward as fast as he could, on all fours, keeping as low as possible. At the corner he saw St Felix ahead of him, crouched, undecided which way to go next.

Georges caught up with him. 'Keep going west,' he said quickly. 'Don't let them drive us into the open.'

'We can't help it,' St Felix replied with desperation. 'We can't go round and round these roofs for ever! This is only one block. We'll have to cross a street, and then they'll catch us.' His eyes were wide, his face blotched where wind and exertion had whipped the blood into his cheeks. Georges could almost smell his fear, and he understood it. He had fled just as wildly with the National Guard baying at his heels like dogs, and in less open places than this — places he knew, and where he had friends among other fugitives. He felt a surge of pity for St Felix, a scholar and dreamer caught up in events that were little of his choosing — especially if he were

324

not the one who had killed Bernave.

'Which way?' St Felix repeated. 'They won't take long to work out what we did.' His voice shook. He gulped air.

Georges pointed ahead. 'That way, until we get the chance to go down towards the west. We've got to get closer to St-Sulpice. There are warrens around there where they'd never find us.'

'Why? Why are you doing this?' St Felix demanded with disbelief. 'For all you know I could have killed Bernave. I didn't, but I can't prove it.'

'I don't care whether you did or not,' Georges answered honestly. 'But this is not the place to debate it.' He pushed him, feeling the rigid resistance of his body. 'We'll argue the issues of justice later, if there is a later. Just move!' Now his voice too was rising, panic close beneath the surface.

St Felix obeyed. He seemed to have caught his breath. He clambered along the valley with considerable alacrity, Georges close behind him.

About twenty yards along they found a window Georges was able to lever open. They scrambled in and shut it after them just as there was a clatter on the roofs behind, and more shouting. A shot richocheted against the slates with a sharp whine.

St Felix let out a gasp of terror.

Georges could feel his own heart pounding. He had joined St Felix spontaneously, without weighing what the cost to himself would be if they failed to give the Guards the slip. He was just beginning to realise it now, when it was too late.

He went across the bare floor of the room at the far side, hesitated a moment, wondering what would be beyond it. St Felix was at his back, breathing hard. Whatever was before them, there was no retreating. The roof was impossible now, and any minute the Guard might look through the window and see them.

He opened the door with a creak. There was a small room leading into another slightly larger one. He went in and St Felix came on his heels.

'Close it!' Georges whispered sharply.

St Felix obeyed, his hands fumbling on the door latch.

'Down!' Georges hissed. 'We don't want to hurt anybody, but if we have to give them a swift blow to keep them silent, it's better than the guillotine.'

St Felix swore under his breath.

But no one disturbed them as they tiptoed rapidly down the stairs and out of a first-floor window on to a ledge. Then they dropped rather awkwardly on to the yard below. It was filled with piles of wood, some of it sawn, some not. It afforded excellent concealment as the two men moved towards the entrance to see if the street were clear.

Georges went first, looking around carefully. He felt a cold thread of fear when he saw the white and blue of Guards' uniforms at the far end. He withdrew quickly, turning to St Felix.

St Felix was ashen.

'Change coats!' Georges ordered.

326

'What?'

'Change coats!' he started to take his own off. 'Hurry up!'

St Felix understood. He almost tore his sleeve in his haste. He started to say something, then changed his mind. He did not take his eyes from Georges' face.

Georges took the brown coat and put it on, passing over his own blue one.

'Thank you . . . ' St Felix began.

Georges smiled briefly. 'Hide behind the wood here, then when they've gone after me, cross the street and head towards St-Sulpice,' he commanded. 'You'll be safer there than anywhere else this side of the river. Good luck.' Then before he could lose his nerve, he sidled out into the street and began walking rapidly away from the Guards at the end. He hoped to cross the Rue Mazarine, then the Rue de Seine and disappear into the maze of buildings around the Church of St-Germain-des-Prés. If he threw them off there, he could eventually get to St-Sulpice himself.

He was almost to the end and around the corner into Rue Dauphine when he heard the yell. He started to run. There was a shot fired, and an answering shot somewhere to the north, near the river. Footsteps sounded behind him as if there were a whole detachment of men thundering down the street.

He swung round the corner, almost colliding with a fat woman holding a mug of coffee. It spilled all down his jacket, soaking him through. She screamed and cursed him as she overbalanced against the wall.

He shouted an apology over his shoulder and kept on running. The Rue Dauphine was full of traffic: wagons, coaches, a public diligence so overloaded someone was leaning half out of the door. It was beginning to rain again and everyone was hurrying, their heads down, collars up. The cobbles were slippery.

Georges dodged between a wagonload of firewood and a miller's cart half full of grain. He almost banged into a standing horse at the far side and stumbled up on to the pavement. There was an alley opening ahead. He ran into it, praying it was not a dead end.

There were shouts in the street behind him. Someone let off another shot.

At the far end of the alley was a wall with a gate in it. Georges threw himself against it, and it held fast, locked.

His first intention to help St Felix had been to draw the Guard off. When they caught up with him they would know he was not St Felix.

Now he realised how stupid that idea was. They would be furious with him, and take him in anyway, simply out of revenge. Someone would know who he really was and just as wanted as St Felix, if not more so! He was an idiot!

Now the gate ahead was locked and the Guard were behind him. He could hear their angry shouts on the Rue Dauphine, and people's responses, indignant and sharp with their own fear.

He must find a way out, any way. He looked upward. Was there anything to climb?

328

Nothing.

What about down? Cellars? One might lead to another. The shouting was closer. He had no alternative. He went through the nearest gateway into a kitchen yard, in through the back door and across the stone-flagged floor. There was no one there. It was mid-afternoon; too late for luncheon, too early for dinner. He looked around him frantically. There was the cellar door. He opened it, closed it behind him and fumbled down the steps, feeling the wall for the way. He felt along the ledge and his fingers closed over candle and flint. He struck the light, hand shaking. It was a cellar stocked with wine, root vegetables, a sack of grain and several bales of firewood. There was no other way out. If they found him here he was cornered.

He was shivering. They would be in the kitchen any moment. They might think he had gone up on to the roof again, but one of them would be bound to try the cellar as well. There was nothing for it but to brazen it out. Better to be caught trying, than run down like an animal.

He bent and with an apology to the householder, he set the candle on the ledge and picked up one of the bales of firewood. He went back up the steps, bent double, and pushed open the door. His heart lurched. There was a Guardsman standing in the middle of the kitchen floor. If the firewood had not been on his back he would have dropped it. As it was it slithered precariously and he had to grab at it to prevent it falling.

'Yes, Captain?' he said helpfully, his voice hoarse.

'Have you seen any strangers around here?' the Guard asked. 'We're looking for a fugitive who murdered a good citizen, a good revolutionary. He came this way, then disappeared.'

'What does he look like?' Georges asked, keeping his back bent and his head down. The wood helped, it gave him an excuse not to meet the man's eyes.

'Quite tall, taller than you, I'd say,' the Guard replied. 'On the lean side, about fiftyish, with brown hair.'

'Not lately,' Georges answered thoughtfully. 'I've just been down in the cellar to fetch up wood. Going to sell a bundle to my neighbour.' He hesitated. How far should he take it? Too far and he could raise the man's suspicion, not far enough and he would not escape.

'But when I was down there I heard noises.' He took the plunge. 'Thought it might have been someone at the door, but maybe it wasn't.'

'In the kitchen?' the Guard said quickly.

'Maybe . . . '

The Guard swivelled around and went back to the door. 'In here!' he shouted. 'Went up on to the roof again, by the looks of it. Watch the street! You two, go and watch in the Rue Mazarine! You take the Rue Guenegaud! Quickly!' He looked back at Georges. 'We're going up to your roof.' That was a statement not a request. 'Thank you, Citizen.' And he went over to the further door and into the next room.

'Good luck, Citizen!' Georges called after him,

then with shaking legs, went out of the back door as half a dozen National Guards made their way past him.

He walked as quickly as he could, bent under the wood, then as soon as he was out of sight of the house he dropped it and ran up the Rue de Tours, across the Boulevard St-Germain and into the first of the alleys on the further side. He stopped, leaning against the wall, breathless. His heart was in his throat, beating so violently his whole body shook and his knees would hardly bear him up.

He was still there when he saw St Felix come out of the Rue de Seine a few yards along. He recognised his own blue coat before he knew the face. There were two national Guards on the corner, standing idly, muskets slung casually, and not at the ready. They were not hunting anyone, simply bored.

Georges stiffened, his hands clenched so tight his nails cut into his palms. 'For God's sake, just walk!' he said under his breath as St Felix hesitated. 'Don't stop! Don't give them any reason to notice you!'

One of the Guards had a copy of *L'Ami du Peuple* stuffed in his breeches pocket. His shoes did not match. He looked at St Felix expectantly, a sneer on his face.

St Felix stopped.

'Go on!' Georges said between his teeth.

St Felix seemed rooted to the spot, as if terror had paralysed him.

'You a stranger round here, Citizen?' the other Guard asked him.

'No!' St Felix said quickly. 'No, I live here.'

Georges shut his eyes in anguish. If only he'd said 'yes', it would have explained his behaviour and they would not have suspected him!

'You sure?' The Guard peered forward. 'I don't know you! You look lost to me!'

'Lie!' Georges said desperately. 'Tell them you're ill! Anything to explain dithering!'

'Don't I know you?' the other Guard asked. 'What's your name?'

'St . . . St Just,' St Felix stammered.

As if he could smell fear, the first Guard was suspicious now.

'Oh, yes? Where are your papers, Citizen? Where do you live?'

St Felix swung his arm wildly. 'That way . . . number forty-eight!'

'Where are you going?'

'For . . . for a cup of coffee,' St Felix replied.

Half a dozen National Guards came out of the Rue de Tours.

St Felix spun round, saw them, and started to run.

Georges watched in agony of foreknowledge, as if in his mind he had already seen it happen. The Guards at the Rue de Tours saw the movement and shouted. The Guard who had been talking to St Felix spun around.

'Stop!' he shouted. 'You! Stop!'

St Felix dived into the alley, almost colliding with Georges, stumbled and ran on.

Shots rang out.

St Felix was fleeing in panic, his arms and

legs swinging wildly, foundering, feet sliding on the wet stones.

The Guards filled the entrance. Another one yelled for St Felix to stop.

He kept running, straight ahead, not weaving or breaking his stride.

A volley of shots richocheted all around.

St Felix lurched forward, slipped and fell face down. He moved a little, once, then lay still.

The Guards crowded round him, not even having noticed Georges. One of them bent and turned the body over.

'Dead,' he said with a sigh. 'Is that him?' He looked up at the man nearest him.

The man peered down. 'Yes. Funny though, I could have sworn he was wearing a brown coat. But that's him all right. I know his face.'

'Better take him, then. Citizen Menou'll be pleased. This is the one who murdered Bernave, isn't it?'

'Yes, that's him. Saved the guillotine a job.'

Georges backed further into the shadows and waited until they were gone, carrying St Felix's body with them. Then when the street was silent, shivering with cold and heartsick, Georges went across the Boulevard St-Germain and walked, head down in the rain, towards Bernave's house.

Once he put his hand into his pocket, St Felix' pocket, and pulled out a wad of sodden paper, dark-stained with coffee. Four passes, illegible now, and a picture, only partly damaged, of a beautiful woman with a cloud of dark hair and a gentle mouth. With a murmured word of apology he let them fall into a heap of refuse. They were no use, and too dangerous to keep.

★　★　★

Georges had to wait half an hour in the cold before he saw the last of Menou's men leave, then it was simply a matter of going through the courtyard to the kitchen door.

Except, of course, nothing about it was simple at all. He had to tell Amandine that St Felix was dead. Her grief would be unbearable, except that one had to bear it. Thank God Célie would be there — she would be able to help. She understood grief. That would be no comfort — nothing would be — but at least Amandine would not be alone.

He knocked on the door, then without waiting, pushed it open. At first glance he thought the kitchen was empty, then he saw the light on Célie's hair as she stood in the corner by the stove, a flat iron in her hand. She had her back to him. She was changing one iron for the other, replacing the cold one on the hob.

'Célie . . . ' he said quietly.

She turned round, then saw him. Her eyes widened in horror and she almost threw the iron down, running over to him. 'Get out of here!' she said wildly. 'You'll have to go over the roof! Are you mad?'

He caught her by the arms, holding her hand. 'No! Menou's men have gone.'

She stared at him, then saw the shock and misery in his eyes.

'What's happened?' Her breath caught in her throat. 'St Felix . . . '

'Yes. I'm sorry. They got him . . . '

Her face was white. 'Which prison?' As if it mattered.

'None,' he answered. 'He was running. They shot him. I'm sorry . . . ' There was no need to tell the details, that St Felix had panicked. 'I did what I could, but there were Guards all over the place.' Why tell her even that? She would not blame him. He blamed himself. He should have been able to do better, somehow to keep St Felix out of their hands. He had managed to save himself for over five months!

'He's . . . dead?' She breathed the words painfully, searching his face, longing for him to deny it.

'Yes. It was quick.'

Tears filled her eyes.

He pulled her close to him and held her in his arms, feeling the misery rack her. It was as if he were holding Amandine as well, and all the hurt and fear that was in him also. For a terrible and urgent moment they were as one body, one wound.

They were still clinging to each other when Amandine came in. He saw her immediately, the shock in her face, the fear for him, then the understanding that he brought dreadful news.

She tried to speak but her voice refused to come.

Georges let go of Célie and, feeling him move away, she realised what had happened and turned to Amandine. She went to her without hesitating, holding Amandine as Georges had held her.

'They shot him,' she said simply. 'It's all over. He probably didn't even know it.' She could not know if that was true but she said it with total conviction.

Amandine looked at Georges.

He nodded.

Amandine was so white it was as if she herself were dead. She said nothing. It was a bereavement so complete she could not even weep. There was no anger, no questioning, just despair.

Georges and Célie stood by helplessly, there was no comfort to offer, and no explanation mattered.

12

They were still in the kitchen when they heard the tramp of heavy feet outside in the courtyard. Célie spun round, her heart pounding. It could only be the National Guard again. They must have followed Georges! There was no time to wait or think.

Amandine looked as if she were going to faint any minute, but she was the only one who could help. Célie would like to have hidden Georges herself, but Amandine was too shattered to stop Menou or his men.

'Take Georges!' she commanded. 'Get him upstairs somewhere — anywhere! Hide him!'

Amandine stood still.

Célie pushed her. 'Go on! I'll hold Menou! Hurry!'

As if she were wading through water, Amandine started across the room, Georges beside her. Just as they closed the door into the main house Célie went to the back door and opened it.

Menou was standing outside.

Célie's heart was beating so hard she felt he would see her shaking. She must prevent him from reading anything in her face or her voice. He had spoken to her often enough to notice even a small difference.

'Yes . . . ?' She cleared her throat. 'Citizen Menou?' She tried to meet his gaze and could not quite. All she could think of was Georges somewhere upstairs and St Felix dead in the street. She must do nothing whatever to make him suspect she knew anything. She must think of something intelligent to say — quickly. 'Did you wish to speak to us again? I don't think I know anything more, but please come in.' She forced herself to stand back and allow him to pass. She knew her whole body was shaking.

'Thank you,' he accepted, although he would have entered, even had she refused, and they both knew it. He was wet, his hat dripping, his shoulders and back dark with rain. His boots left wet marks on the stone floor. Beyond him she could see other Guards standing against the walls, trying to get a little shelter, coat collars turned up, but they were still watching!

'Where is Citizeness Destez?' Menou looked around the kitchen for Amandine.

'I don't know,' Célie replied. 'I was just doing a little ironing.' She gestured towards the two irons, one on the table, one on the stove, and the pile of linen half pressed. 'Do you want me to go and look for her?'

'In a minute,' he replied. 'I'd like to ask her a few more questions, just to make sure I know exactly what happened. Tell me again, Citizeness: on the night Bernave was stabbed, where was St Felix standing when the torch from the hall showed up the room, and where was Bernave?' He was watching her, his clear eyes catching the light.

Célie tried to remember. The truth could not hurt St Felix now, and it would get Menou out

338

of the house. She must not look relieved. If he guessed she knew St Felix was dead, he would know someone had told her. The first priority, above all else, was to keep Georges safe.

'As far as I can remember, St Felix was standing a little way from Bernave, nearer to the window,' she replied, keeping her voice almost steady, and wishing she could bring back exactly what she had said the first time he had asked. So much had happened since then, it seemed weeks ago, not two days. And she must not appear to be thinking too hard. Worried but honest, that was how he should see her. But if she said she did not know St Felix had left the house he would not believe that! They all had to know . . . and assume guilt. She must say no more than she was obliged to. She waited for his response.

'And Citizen Bernave?' he asked.

'Just in front of the doorway,' she replied.

'And which way was he facing?' he pursued.

'Towards the crowd.' She had no hesitation in that.

'And he stopped them?'

She forced her mind back to the events, willing herself to live again through the noise, the fear, the crackle of musket-fire, the shattering glass and the sudden cold air and the smell of smoke.

'No. It was Madame Lacoste who stopped them,' she contradicted him. 'I couldn't see because of the smoke, but I heard her voice. Citizen Lacoste was going to help her also.' Her mind was racing, wondering where Georges was, if Amandine had pulled herself together enough to get him hidden.

'And who lit the candle?' Menou went on. He was watching her too closely.

'I did.' She gulped.

'Where was everyone, when you could see again?'

'Marie-Jeanne had gone upstairs to the children. Citizeness Destez was by the far wall, Fernand was by the window, and Citizen St Felix was in the middle of the room.'

His eyes were steady, almost unblinking. 'And Citizen Bernave?'

'On the floor, just where you saw him.'

His eyebrows rose very slightly. 'No one went to his assistance? You all knew he was dead?'

She must be very careful. St Felix's guilt was enough to satisfy his need. He must not think it was a conspiracy.

'No, of course not,' she answered. 'I was the closest. I bent down and touched his neck. There was no pulse. Then we realised he was dead, and Citizen Lacoste went to fetch you.'

'And St Felix? What did he do?'

'I don't know. I can't remember. Does it matter now?'

'We still haven't found the knife.'

She shrugged very slightly. 'I have no idea.'

He was still watching her, as if he would memorise every flicker of her expression. 'There was a rumour that you are hoarding food here, in this house particularly. Did you know that?'

'Yes.'

'Someone started it,' he explained. 'Someone

340

was saying so. It was not an accident they broke in here — it was planned.'

There was a coldness inside her: she felt sick and miserable. She had not thought such deliberation a part of St Felix. Spur-of-the-moment, sudden anger was so much easier to understand.

'I'm sorry,' he said gently, then bit the words off, his face hot. A National Guardsman did not apologise. 'Thank you for your time. Now, perhaps, you would fetch Citizeness Destez.' It was an order.

'Of course.' Before Menou could suggest going with her, Célie went to the door and out into the next room, then across to the stairs and up them at a run. Where could Amandine be? Where would she take Georges? Did she even know anything about pursuit? Might she take him somewhere like the cellar, where if Menou found him he would be cornered?

Stop it! Georges knew more about running than anyone! Funny. She had admired Madame de Staël so much for hiding her lover from the National Guard, even at the risk of her own life. When she saw that, it was what had changed her whole mind and heart about having betrayed Georges. Suddenly she had known the courage and the nobility of it, and that was what she wanted to have, to be. Whether Georges had been guilty of Jean-Pierre's death or not, revenge was no longer of any value. It had become shabby in the witness of a single act.

Now she had the chance to do exactly the same thing, which was what she had wanted all the time, what she would have prayed for, were there a God. And now that she had it, all that mattered was that Georges must be safe — whether she was a heroine, whether she measured up to her dreams or not was of hardly any importance at all.

She hurried up the stairs, her feet slipping in her panic, then up the next flight. Surely Amandine would take him up rather than down? At least that way there was a chance of escape if Menou searched the house.

She met Amandine coming down. Her face was drawn, and her hands gripped the banister as if she were afraid of falling.

'Menou wants to see you,' Célie said breathlessly. 'For God's sake remember, you don't know about St Felix! There's nothing you can do to help him. At all cost we must get Menou out of the house.'

'I know,' Amandine replied, but there was no life in her voice, and nothing in her face but despair.

Célie grasped hold of her arm, hard enough to make her wince at any other time. It seemed bitterly cruel, but she had to say it. 'Try not to look as if you know! He'll be watching you. Georges' life could depend on it. Say you're sick, anything you like, except the truth.'

Amandine did not look at her. 'I know,' she answered, but she still sounded as if she had no heart left.

Célie went down behind her. She must be there to do whatever she could to distract Menou from his observation of Amandine, even

342

if she had to faint or pretend to throw a fit!

Menou was standing in the kitchen waiting for them. He regarded Amandine with interest.

'You look pale, Citizeness. Has something distressed you?'

Amandine hesitated, not sure whether to lie or not, if so what lie to tell. She was too broken in spirit to think.

'We are all distressed, Citizen,' Célie answered for her, pulling out one of the wooden chairs from the kitchen table for Amandine to sit down. 'There has been a murder in our house and we know that one of us must be responsible. Added to that, now Citizen St Felix has gone. It looks as if he has run away. We don't know why, but we can't help fearing the worst. Who wouldn't be distressed?'

Menou smiled bleakly. 'Citizeness Destez especially, it would seem,' he observed pointedly. 'You are very fond of St Felix, aren't you?'

'I admire him . . . very much,' Amandine answered without looking at him, but she was careful to put it in the present.

'Do you? For what, Citizeness?' He sat opposite her.

This time she did look at him and there was a flicker of anger in her. 'For nobility of thought, Citizen Menou. For patience, tolerance and the ability to forgive others even when they trespassed against him appallingly.'

'You are referring to Bernave?' he asked, his eyes unwaveringly on her face, the colour pink in his cheeks.

'I was speaking in general. Fernand was also

343

offensive at times. Citizen St Felix was tolerant of him too.'

Menou looked puzzled. 'Why do you think he was so tolerant of Bernave? Would you not have admired a man more who had stood up for himself, fought back rather than be bullied? Don't you admire courage, Citizeness?'

Her chin hardened and she looked back at him. 'Yes, I admire courage, but I don't equate it with leaping into every quarrel, and placing your own vanity or hurt feelings before the common cause.'

'And is that what St Felix was doing?' he asked with interest.

'Yes.' There was no trace of doubt in her voice or her face. 'Also he was a guest here, and his manners forbade him abusing his host, regardless of how much it might be warranted.'

'And you admire good manners?'

'I do.'

'Something the revolution has not done much to encourage?' He said it almost without expression, as a statement of fact. Looking at him, Célie was not sure if he meant to provoke Amandine into betraying some anti-revolutionary sentiment, but she thought she heard in his tone an echo of regret, as if something in him hungered for the days when grace mattered. Perhaps he would rather have possessed some touch of that past culture than to have destroyed it, but he was caught up in his time and choice was gone.

Amandine did not answer. She had no heart for verbal sparring. The flame of anger had gone

344

as quickly as it had arisen.

Menou changed his line of attack. He leaned across the table a little. 'Did you expect St Felix to run away, Citizeness?' he asked.

Amandine drew in her breath sharply and for a moment she looked so deathly pale Célie was afraid she was going to faint. In her mind Célie accepted that St Felix had killed Bernave, even that he had had just cause to, or believed he had, but she hated Menou for his cruelty to Amandine, whatever he sought to prove now. If she had had a way to, and not been crippled by her own fear for Georges, she would have crushed him for that.

'No . . . ' Amandine whispered.

'You thought he had more courage?' he said quite gently, his voice strained.

Célie was desperate to intercede, and terrified that if she did it would only make it worse; perhaps then Menou would suspect Amandine of complicity, either in St Felix's escape, or even in the murder itself.

Menou waited.

Amandine did not answer.

Célie could bear it no longer. 'We thought he was innocent,' she said abruptly. 'We don't know who killed Bernave.'

'Why did you think he was innocent?' Menou looked across at her. 'More innocent than, say, Citizeness Lacoste? Or Fernand?'

This time she was prepared. 'Because he worked so closely with Bernave,' she answered. 'They must have trusted each other in the battle against those who would undo the revolution.

And also Citizen St Felix was a gentle man, willing to forgive those who were offensive to him. We have all seen it, time and again. He had no ill temper.'

Menou gave up and turned back to Amandine.

'Where were you after Bernave was stabbed, and Citizeness Laurent lit the candle again?' he asked.

'Standing near the window,' Amandine replied.

'Then St Felix was between you and the crowd. You must have been looking directly towards him!'

She glanced up, meeting his eyes. 'Yes, I was. He didn't have a knife.'

He smiled a little sadly. 'I thought that was what you would say. I wish I could believe you were as loyal to the truth as you are to St Felix, Citizeness. It is obvious that you cared for him very much, so I am sorry to tell you that he is dead.' His face was pinched, his eyes surprisingly soft.

Amandine swallowed, her hands gripping in her lap. For several seconds she did not move.

Célie opened her mouth to speak, but Menou held up his hand, palm towards her. It was an unmistakable instruction not to interrupt. If she disobeyed she would be showing her lack of faith in Amandine.

Amandine took a long, steadying breath, then faced Menou.

'How did it happen?' Her voice cracked and she stopped.

For the first time he looked uncomfortable.

There was a flash of real pity in his eyes, and when he spoke there was no satisfaction in him, no sense of achievement.

'We followed him when he left here, but we lost him for quite a while,' he said quietly. 'We watched and waited, then saw him again almost by chance. He panicked and a National Guard in the Boulevard St-Germain challenged him. When he did not stop, he was shot. He was killed immediately.' His voice dropped. 'If it is of any comfort to you, Citizeness, he can have felt little pain.'

She tried to speak, perhaps to thank him, but her eyes filled with tears and she could not.

'So what else do you want with us, Citizen Menou?' Célie intervened, regardless of what he thought. 'What else can you need to know?'

Menou turned to her, almost reluctantly. 'You should be able to work that out, Citizeness. You heard Citizeness Destez say she was looking at St Felix when you lit the candle again, and he did not have a knife. Either she is lying, or someone took the knife from him in the dark.'

'Or it was someone else who stabbed him,' Célie responded before she thought of the consequence of that.

'Then why did he run?' Menou said softly. 'Do the innocent fly before anyone accuses them?'

There was no answer she could give that would not make things worse.

'Precisely,' he agreed with a sigh, leaning back in his chair, and it scraped against the floor. 'Perhaps I should ask the other members of the household once again what they saw, exactly where they were standing. Would you fetch them for me, Citizeness?'

Dare she leave Amandine alone with him? What might he say to her? But if she took Amandine away with her to fetch Madame Lacoste, he would suspect she was afraid of some truth she might let slip. She decided against it. She stood up and went out, obediently.

Menou questioned them all again. They sat in the kitchen around the table, except Fernand, who preferred to remain standing.

'Célie told us you shot St Felix,' Madame said coldly to Menou. 'What else is there for us to say?'

Célie watched her, studying her face with its fierce, level brows and dark eyes. Her lips closed in a tight line. If she felt any sorrow or pity she hid it completely. But she was a proud woman. She would not have shown the National Guard any part of her emotions or allowed them ever to imagine what her feelings might be. Was it actually relief, above all, because now her own family was freed from suspicion? It would be natural enough. Célie could not blame her for it.

Célie glanced across to Monsieur Lacoste. Strangely there was pity in his face, and he looked at Amandine with a gentleness that was rare in him, as if he understood a helpless grief.

Fernand was angry. He resented Menou still being here, and saw no reason to hide it now.

Marie-Jeanne held the baby against her shoulder, rocking it back and forth very slightly, an automatic movement she must be very used to by now. The other two children were upstairs somewhere.

Célie tried to force the thought of Georges from her mind, as if he were miles away, and safe, as if the street were not full of soldiers and he could have escaped over the roof. She must betray nothing, even by a look or a shadow across her eyes, the slightest change in expression.

Menou sat quite casually in his chair, his legs crossed, his fingertips together as he looked from one to the other of them.

'This business seems to have come to a point only just short of a conclusion,' he remarked. 'There are only a few details to satisfy reason, and then all is done. Citizen Bernave may lie in peace.'

'The dead are dead!' Monsieur Lacoste said tartly. 'If you can call dead peaceful, then so be it. It won't affect him one way or the other.'

'True,' Menou conceded. 'Perhaps I should say the spirit of Justice may be satisfied. Would you prefer that?' It was a question and he appeared to wait for an answer.

Monsieur Lacoste shrugged, but there was a flash of satisfaction in his eyes for an instant. 'What are these details, Citizen? Bernave was a bully who abused Citizen St Felix's good nature, used his services, ran him to exhaustion and frequently into danger, until finally St Felix lost his temper and retaliated. You worked this out for yourself.' Sadness was there in his eyes for a moment. 'St Felix knew it, and he bolted. Can't blame him. You shot him. Poor devil is dead.

Assume your justice, if you like. What else is there to know?'

'Not a great deal,' Menou conceded, looking across at him. 'I should like to know precisely how he accomplished the murder.'

'Why? What does it matter now?' Lacoste argued. 'Anyway, nobody here knows!'

'Don't they?' Menou's eyes widened. 'We'll see. At the moment it seems to me as if there might have been someone assisting St Felix, even if it were so small a thing as to have passed him the knife, or perhaps to have hidden it afterwards.'

'Why do you think that?' Marie-Jeanne asked in surprise, an edge in her voice. Fernand was standing behind her now, and he put one hand warningly on her shoulder.

Menou did not answer her directly. 'Let us consider the matter again, a little more carefully.' He looked up at Fernand. 'How long have you lived in this house, Citizen?'

'Six years, about,' Fernand answered. 'All my married life.'

'And where before that?' Menou said curiously.

'In the Faubourg St-Antoine.' Then anticipating the next question he continued. 'I did some work for Citizen Bernave's business office. He liked it, and had me do some here. That is how I met my wife.' His hand tightened on Marie-Jeanne's shoulder.

Marie-Jeanne smiled at the memory, something good to cling on to.

'And your parents?' Menou continued.

350

'They came a year after,' Fernand replied.

'Do you own any part of it?'

Fernand's face tightened defensively, but he could not lie. It would be easy enough for Menou to check if he wanted to. 'No. But we provide for ourselves.' He looked as if he were going to add something else, and then stopped.

Célie wondered if it would have been a remark about property, or equality, and then he had thought better of expressing such a sentiment in connection with his father-in-law. He stood still now, with his mouth closed in a thin line.

'Of course,' Menou agreed. 'You are a carpenter and cabinet-maker. Now you and your family will have to learn how to manage the import and export of fabric as well. It is a very good business.'

Fernand said nothing. Célie could have told him that Menou had no intention of giving up. He would question them all until he heard what he wanted to, and he had the power to hold them here as long as he wished.

Perhaps he would hear what he wanted, and the men outside would go away . . . and Georges would escape over the roofs? Please heaven! If there was a heaven. She wished there were. If there were no God, no divine power, who was there to appeal to when you were far out of your depth and sinking? Was that why Bernave had believed in God: an understanding of need, a hunger for the promise of forgiveness, when the sorrow was great enough and the price had been paid?

But had Amandine taken Georges as far as the

351

attics? What about the Lacoste children upstairs? What about the rest of the men in the street? It was daylight still. At this hour in the afternoon, between luncheon and dinner, there would be people in bedrooms, particularly in attics.

Menou was still asking his endless questions, probing into loves and hates, envy, possible greed. Then without warning he reverted back to the old subject of where people had stood.

'And after the torches disappeared, Citizeness,' he said to Madame, 'did anyone pass near you, or between you and Citizen Bernave?'

'I have no idea,' Madame said coldly.

She was the only one in the kitchen whose composure seemed to be unruffled. If St Felix's guilt or his death distressed her, she possessed sufficient self-mastery not to allow Menou, or anyone else, to see it.

'And it was you who faced the intruders and spoke to them so they were ashamed, and turned away,' he observed. 'You are as slight as a girl, and you had no weapon. You have great courage, Madame.'

A brief smile lit her face, of black amusement as much as any knowledge of the compliment.

'How gallant, Citizen Menou. Under your blue and white I think there beats the heart of a gentleman. Please do not take that as an insult. I mean it by nature, not by birth.'

He was flattered. Célie could see it in the flush on his cheeks, even though he strove to hide it. He was annoyed with himself for his own vulnerability, but he could not bring himself to rebuff her. Célie realised with a sudden jolt of surprise that he admired Madame Lacoste. There was an innate dignity in her, a grace of the old gentry that he could not let go. It was sweet to him, awakening a memory or a hunger.

Monsieur Lacoste lost his patience.

'It seems plain enough to me,' he said acidly. 'St Felix had had all the abuse he could take, and he had a knife in the front room. He was out often enough. He may well have known of the riot in advance, or at least that it was likely. We have enough of them these days, over food or soap or candles, or any other damned thing!' His face was tight and hard. 'Maybe he took the knife earlier, in case he should have the chance. Then when the rioters broke in, he went forward naturally, and in the confusion — there it was. He took it. He had provocation enough!'

'And what did he do with the knife afterwards?' Menou asked.

'I don't know.' Monsieur Lacoste avoided looking at Amandine. 'Perhaps someone helped him. We all saw how Bernave used him. Our sympathies were with him.' His tone grew more belligerent. 'Either way, you'll not prove it. You've got St Felix, poor devil. Let that satisfy your justice and leave us alone.'

Menou sighed. 'And where is the knife now? St Felix didn't have it on him.'

Célie drew in her breath to say he could have got rid of it over the roofs, then just as she started the first word, realised her mistake, and changed it into a cough.

Menou looked at her, eyes questioning. 'You had a suggestion, Citizeness?'

She had to say something. He knew she had been about to speak.

'Didn't he have it when he ran from here?' she suggested. 'Perhaps he threw it away when you were chasing him?'

'Why would he take it?' he asked. 'It was little use in defence, awkward to run with. If he tripped or fell he could have injured himself. And it would only be incriminating if we caught him with it.' He shook his head. 'No. I think it is still here, somewhere. And I would like to find it — just to tidy up the last details. It would satisfy my mind. Close the case, as it were.' He stood up. 'I'll search one more time.'

The moment was come. Cold inside, her legs wobbling, Célie stood also. 'I'll conduct you, Citizen,' she offered. 'You will need help, and I'm sure you would wish to leave the cupboards as you found them. You are a soldier, not a vandal.' Without waiting for his assent she went to the door, her fingers so stiff she fumbled with the latch. She opened it and went out, listening for his footsteps as he followed her, and hearing nothing. She stopped, her heart pounding, her throat tight. Where was Georges? Where had Amandine put him?

Perhaps she should have let Amandine take Menou? She would know where to steer him away from! Célie, in ignorance, might lead him right to where Georges was!

But on the other hand her innocence might be his best protection! Menou was clever. He would read any deliberate attempt to guide him, and do the opposite, thinking it was the knife they were hiding.

Where was he? Why had he not come with her?

She turned around. The kitchen door was still open. She was gulping air, trying to keep control of herself, steady her voice, her hands.

Menou came at last, smiling very slightly. 'I am sure you understand, Citizeness, but I had to post a couple of my men in the kitchen, just in case anyone felt disposed to leave the room, and move something. There is little point in my searching the house if the knife is being constantly taken one step ahead of me.'

'Of course,' she agreed, trying to smile back, but afraid it was more of a grimace.

They began with the front room in which the stabbing had taken place. She stood silently watching while he opened the cupboard again where he had found the bloodstains. There was nothing in it but candles. He felt behind them, then in the drawers, tapping the wood to make sure there was no false panel or bottom. He turned up the chairs and poked his hands down both sides. He examined every part of Madame Lacoste's sewing table, then gently rapped his knuckles along all the walls as if hoping to find a loose panel. Finally he kneeled and examined each board of the floor, even under the rug. He found several loose, but the spaces yielded nothing but dust. He was quick and deft, as if searching were something he was used to. She watched his hands with a kind of fascination as they moved delicately over every surface — fine hands, with clean fingernails. It took him just over half an hour to finish that room and the one immediately beyond, which was little more than a hallway to the front entrance.

'Let us try Citizeness Destez's room,' he suggested. 'That is just up the stairs, is it not?'

'Yes.' Célie found her chest tight, her breath catching in her throat. Surely Amandine would not have put Georges there? Would she? Was it a sort of double bluff? Was she thinking clearly enough even to imagine such a thing? Georges did not know the house. He had been in hiding since before she and Amandine had come here.

He followed Célie up and pushed the door open.

She held her breath.

It also was empty.

Menou was equally diligent here. She watched his face as he searched the bed, leaning on the blanket and mattress, lifting the pillow. Then he bent and went through Amandine's chest, taking out her clothes a piece at a time, running his fingers over the linen. She saw his expression change very slightly as the fine embroidery touched his skin. It was feminine, delicate, a total extravagance left over from the days when she had been a lady of the minor nobility — when such a thing still existed. It was extraordinary to think that had been less than five years ago. So short a time, and their whole world had changed, as had that of half of France, if not more. Only the poorest, whom it had all been meant to benefit, were still the same; still cold, hungry and dispossessed, such as Marat's hordes in the

Faubourg St-Antoine, and places like it. It was an irony that there were so many more of them now.

She watched Menou as he replaced everything. She could not read in his face whether he was disappointed not to find the knife among the linen. It would have closed the case and at the same time satisfied his suspicions of Amandine's loyalties.

And yet if she had tried to conceal murder, something in him would also have been disillusioned, and it would have hurt him; Célie was sure of that. Whether he loved it or hated it, if he even knew which, a dream in him would have died.

He stood up. His eyes met hers very briefly, then he looked away. For the first time it was she who was the emotional intruder, not he.

'Now St Felix's room,' he directed her, walking to the door without looking back, his shoulders stiff, self-conscious.

She passed him and led the way. She did not hesitate, although her mind was racing ahead, full of imagination. Would Amandine have put Georges there? It would have been a nice irony. Would she even have made a connection without realising, automatically — she had loved St Felix, she loved Georges? It was the sort of step one could take when the brain was numbed with grief.

Menou was behind her. He would watch everything. He was not satisfied. There was a puzzle in this house he had not solved yet, and it gnawed at his mind.

357

Célie opened the door with pounding heart. The room was empty.

It was very tidy, as if St Felix had half prepared himself to leave it. The few possessions were placed neatly on a single shelf: mainly books, and a small clock. She realised with a jolt the one thing that was missing from the time she had sat here telling him about Jean-Pierre: a miniature portrait of a woman with wide eyes and a soft mouth, her dark hair fallen loose around a slender neck, as if she had been caught unaware, not expecting the artist to immortalise the moment.

Célie felt a sudden ache, a mixture of loss and resentment. It must have been his wife, the woman whose death had left him so alone, and whom Amandine could not replace. Whether he would ever have loved her she would not know now, only dream. And that woman whose face was so individual, so full of emotion, was dead too.

She looked down at the books. Menou stood in front of the shelf looking also, reading the titles. There was a copy of Dante's *Divine Comedy*, several volumes of poetry, some Voltaire, Cervantes' *Don Quixote*, a translation of Shakespeare. No Rousseau.

Menou said nothing. He turned away from the shelf and started to search the room: bed, clothes chest, chair.

At first glance Célie had thought the room was impersonal; there was so little in it that belonged to St Felix. But as she stood watching Menou she began to feel differently. The emptiness, the lack of material possessions, the clear spaces, were part of St Felix also, part of the elusive quality about his nature. It said something about his dreams that all he had brought with him apart from clothes were books, one picture and a clock.

In the chest his clothes were neat, all very clean, nothing frayed or unkempt. There was little enough, but it was of high quality. Menou knew that as he looked through it for the knife, shaking out and folding up again, his fingers on the fine fabric, the wools and clean cottons, though of faded colours. They would be taken at a glance for artisan's clothes, except for the grace of the cut — better than Menou's own uniform, and probably also warmer and more comfortable.

Menou did not find the knife, or anything else of relevance to Bernave's death, or the work he had done for the Commune. All he learned was a little more of the grace and abstemiousness of St Felix's character, and possibly he also guessed at the inner grief that filled him. It was the room of a man whose life had no hunger or passion left, only memory.

Would she be like that if he found Georges, and took him away to be executed? Would she become someone whose heart lived only in the past?

Menou said nothing as they left. He did not justify the search, or regret having found nothing useful. He simply went to the next door along.

'Whose is this?' he asked.

'Fernand and Marie-Jeanne,' Célie answered.

'Their bedroom and their sitting room. They have a small kitchen up here too. And of course the children's rooms as well.'

'Citizen Bernave was good to them!' he said quickly.

'Yes,' she agreed. 'Yes, he was.' She wondered if they had appreciated it.

Menou searched these rooms carefully as well, talking to the children as he did so. He was watched with curiosity by three-year-old Antoine, but guarded resentment by six-year-old Virginie, who was old enough to recognise an intrusion.

'We haven't got anything here,' she said with a frown. 'You looked before.'

Menou did not stop searching. 'Were you fond of your grandfather?' he asked casually.

She was puzzled. 'Of course.'

'And Citizen St Felix?'

'Yes. He talked to me sometimes. He never got cross if someone cried.' She did not look at Antoine, who was watching Menou gravely. 'Or left toys around. But we didn't see him very often. He went out a lot. So did Grandpapa,' she added. 'He was always working.'

'What sort of work?'

'I don't know.' She glanced at Célie.

'Were you here the night your grandfather was killed?' Menou asked curiously. His tone of voice suggested it was of no importance.

'Yes.'

He looked up at her from where he was stooping over a chest of linens. 'Were you awake?'

360

'Yes,' she nodded. 'There was a lot of shouting and banging in the street. Men fighting — again. I think they came into the house.'

'Were you frightened?' he asked.

Again she nodded, watching him all the time. 'Yes.'

'And your Mama came up to look after you?'

'Yes.'

'Did anyone else come up here? Anyone at all?'

'No.'

'Are you sure?'

'Yes.'

Menou smiled bleakly. Perhaps he believed her, but he still went through every cupboard and chest and stripped the beds.

Afterwards he and Célie went upstairs to the next floor to Monsieur and Madame Lacoste's rooms. Menou did not seem surprised not to have found anything.

Célie was terrified. They were near the top of the house. There were no rooms above but her own. If Amandine had taken Georges up towards the roof, then it could only be a matter of minutes before they found him. She must do something, anything to divert Menou. But what? He already suspected something was being hidden, to protect Amandine.

What would Madame de Staël have done? Been charming, eloquent, or flirted a little.

But Madame de Staël had been sophisticated, the most brilliant conversationalist in France, perhaps in Europe! She had studied literature, politics and philosophy, held discussions with the

361

best minds of the age! Célie knew how to talk, her parents were Girondins! But that was all empty posturing, the last people on earth to have wit! If they had known how to laugh, they would have seen their own absurdity, and they never did.

And she was useless at flirting! How could she be light-hearted, amusing, when everything that mattered most in the world hung in the balance?

Georges might be just the other side of the door. His life depended on what she did, or failed to do! Or was he in her own room? Or downstairs in Bernave's rooms? If only she could read Amandine's mind and know what she had done!

'What is the matter, Citizeness?' Menou asked, watching her with his eyes puckered.

She smiled at him as sweetly as she could, as frankly, and felt her heart almost choke her and her muscles lock as if they were cramped. 'I suppose I am afraid you will find the knife,' she lied. 'And that then you will suspect one of us of having put it there — to help St Felix.' She took a deep breath. 'But if you don't, then you will keep on looking, and we shall never know. I'm not sure whether I want to, or not.'

He regarded her steadily, almost unblinking. For a moment it was as if they understood each other completely.

'Of course,' he agreed, then turned and opened the door into Madame Lacoste's room.

Célie stood behind him, her mouth dry, her stomach knotted.

There was no one inside. She was almost sick

362

with relief. It came over her like a wave and she was giddy with it. But where was he? Surely Amandine could not have been so absent-minded, or so daring, as to have put him in Célie's own room?

Or had she expected him to go over the roofs — with Menou's men in the streets? With all the shouting and gunfire there had been, no one would let him in their house. It was more than their life was worth, and everyone knew that!

What would Madame de Staël have done now?

Then suddenly an idea came to her — be bold. Maybe it was madness. On the other hand, perhaps it was the only chance.

'Citizen Menou . . . '

'Yes?'

'Will you excuse me. Nature requires I leave for a few moments . . . '

'Of course,' he agreed without looking around from his search through the cupboard of household linens.

'Thank you.' She went out as quickly as she could in case he should change his mind and follow her. Of course she could move the knife, and he must realise it.

Then she heard him stand up. He was coming with her! She froze inside. Her knees were weak. She had one chance to guess rightly. Where had Amandine put Georges? There were only two places left — her own room, or Bernave's. Which? Her room was small. There was no place to hide. There was none in Bernave's rooms either. Which? She must decide now! She was at the stairs — up or down.

There was no facility for the requirements of nature upstairs.

Down. If Georges was in her room she would have to try to convince Menou he was a lover she had hidden there. He might believe it — maybe? There was a bitter laughter in that — a joke on her!

She was going down the stairs. Menou was behind her. She could not stop; she was committed now. She found she could hardly breathe. She was leading Menou straight to Georges.

At least there was a private cupboard for the use of nature in Bernave's rooms. It would not make a liar of her. She crossed the hall and stopped at the door. She turned to face Menou.

'If you would give me a few moment's privacy, Citizen. You may search me when I come out. I shall not be carrying a knife, I promise you. I have no more idea where it is than you do.'

He nodded. 'I hope that is true, Citizeness. It would give me no pleasure to catch you protecting Citizen St Felix . . . or Citizeness Destez.'

She forced herself to smile at him, then turned and opened Bernave's door.

She went in and closed it behind her before she even looked up. She did not see Georges at first. He was standing in the shadows near the bookcase. He was looking towards her, his face set, white, eyes wide and almost black.

She went across to him immediately.

'Menou is outside the door,' she whispered. 'I

have come to answer nature. When he searches the room here there is nowhere to hide. Our only chance is to be bold.' She ignored his horror, the rigidity of his body. 'Bernave mended his own books when they were old and torn,' she hurried on, softly, standing only a few inches from him. 'Break the spines of a few, damage them — quickly. You will find his tools for repairing them in the second drawer of the desk.'

Instinctively she gestured towards it. 'It's not locked. When we come, you are the book repairer. I sent for you so we can sell his books for the best price. Keep working. If you can find his magnifying spectacles, wear them. They will at least cover your eyes a bit.' She searched his face to see if he understood. It was too late to matter whether he agreed or not.

He nodded, staring back at her, then suddenly realised that Menou could open the door any instant, and he moved to the desk and pulled out the drawer.

Célie went to the cupboard and relieved herself, then came out again. Georges had the tools out on the desktop and the spectacles on his nose.

'Break a few of these books,' she whispered. 'Not too many!' Then she went to the door again.

Menou was outside.

'Thank you,' she said graciously.

'I'm sorry, Citizeness,' he apologised, and made a careful and deliberate search of her person. He seemed pleased when he found nothing.

She looked him directly in the eye. 'Do you wish to search my room now?'

'When I have completed the Lacostes', yes, I do.'

He followed her back upstairs, finished the Lacostes' rooms, and then hers, and discovered no knife. At last they came to Bernave's door again.

'It must be here,' he said with a frown. 'Our man has nerve, I'll say that for him! Or woman? Kill Bernave, then hide the blade in his own rooms!' He opened the door and stopped abruptly.

Georges looked up from the desk. The spectacles reflected the light from the lamp he had lit and made him look different. The books were spread around him and the knife, glue, paper and fabric were at his elbow.

'Who are you?' Menou demanded, startled.

'Good day, Citizen,' Georges replied. 'I am Citizen Abbas, bookbinder and repairer. The Citizeness asked me to mend the last of these books so they could be sold for a fair price. I understand the owner is recently deceased and his heirs have no wish to keep them.'

'How long have you been here?' Menou looked puzzled. 'I didn't see you come in!'

'Nor I you,' Georges answered. 'You must have been here when I arrived. I charge by the book, not by the hour, but I came about twenty minutes ago, I should imagine.'

'I see. Are there many books damaged?' Menou was still dubious. 'I'm surprised Bernave allowed them to be. My impression of him was he was a careful man who loved his books.'

'Indeed,' Georges agreed. 'But when one is a collector one purchases books in all conditions, and then has them repaired.'

Books were something Menou had never possessed.

'Yes . . . I suppose so,' he conceded. 'Well, I am sorry to disturb you, Citizen, but I require to search this room.'

'Of course.' Georges lowered his head.

'Including that desk!'

Georges stood up obediently, moving away. Menou began opening the drawers and going through them methodically, but there was a frown on his face, and he was obviously considering something profoundly.

Célie did not look at Georges. The silence permeated the air. Her heart was pounding and the sweat covered her body even though she was shivering.

'Where do you live, Citizen Abbas?' Menou asked without looking round. 'Do you have a shop?'

Georges barely hesitated. 'Rue des Augustins. I used to have a shop, but I cannot afford it these days. I work for other people.'

Menou finished searching the desk and went over to the bookshelves.

The invention was dangerous. If Menou were to question any of his men he would know Georges had not come twenty minutes ago. If he had been here before Menou arrived, Célie would have mentioned it. If Menou were to speak to anyone in the household, even

367

Amandine, they would not know to substantiate Célie's story. She must divert his attention, before he had time to become more suspicious. What would do that? What would Menou care about more than who Georges was and why he was there?

The knife. But she had no idea where it was — if it was here at all.

She must say something — now!

'Citizen Menou — I have been thinking a great deal about what has happened.'

'Naturally.' He did not look up.

'About the messages Citizen Bernave asked me to carry for him.'

He kept taking books out of the shelf and piling them on the floor, so he could search behind them. Did he imagine she had hidden the knife there just now?

'Yes,' she said a little too loudly. 'Yes.' She must be decisive, not frightened. 'If Citizen St Felix killed him he must have had a very compelling reason. He was not a fool, and he never appeared to any of us to be even the least bit violent. He was provoked often enough, but he never lost his temper.'

This time Menou did turn. 'What are you saying, Citizeness?'

She had to go on now, and the idea was forming in her mind. It was a high risk, but above anything, more important than St Felix's reputation or Bernave's, was her awareness of Georges sitting a few feet from her, his head bent over the books again, trying to look as if he were busy mending them. His fingers were unused to such work.

She breathed in deeply. 'I am saying that the only thing I can imagine moving Citizen St Felix to such an act would be if he discovered that Bernave were not the revolutionary he claimed to be, working for the Commune, but a double spy — actually working for the royalists.'

This time she certainly had Menou's attention. His body had stiffened and his breathing changed.

'Why would you think that?' he asked, frowning at her.

'He always sent St Felix to Marat and the Commune, but he went to the royalists himself,' she replied, inventing frantically as she went, desperately conscious of Georges listening to her with amazement, his hands frozen on the paper. 'He didn't trust anyone else with their names,' she went on. 'He didn't even write them down.' He had, but she was sure she had destroyed any that were not matters of public knowledge. 'Find out if any good came of the information he gave the Commune, Citizen Menou!' she urged him. 'Were any plots ever foiled, anyone arrested? Perhaps Citizen St Felix realised he was being used? He was an ardent republican. He loved the principles of the revolution.' Her voice was gathering conviction. 'He loved liberty and brotherhood. He would have killed anyone rather than allow some royalist plot to reinstate the King, or the Comte d'Artois.' She made her expression keener, more alight. There was nothing to lose now; everything was in this desperate throw. She dared not look towards

369

Georges. He was moving his hands again, stretching fabric, smoothing paper, gently placing the glue.

Menou was watching her intently, his search for the knife forgotten.

'If the King were restored to the throne,' she went on, 'we would lose all we have gained. We could never trust him. He has proved that in the past — over and over again. He listens to whoever spoke to him last.'

Menou said nothing for several seconds.

Georges continued mending the book, his head bent, his fingers slow and careful. Perhaps unintentionally doing nothing that would make a sound.

Very deliberately Célie walked to the desk and opened the drawers with the money. She was so close to Georges her sleeve touched his shoulder. She could sense the warmth of him, the smell of his skin. The money was still where she had seen it before. She took a Louis and a handful of sous and turned to him. 'Thank you, Citizen Abbas, for what you have done. I think it would be more suitable if you were to come back another time. Perhaps when we have a buyer in mind we shall have the rest repaired. Good day to you.'

Georges glanced at the money.

'That was the amount we agreed, wasn't it?' she asked, swallowing awkwardly.

'Yes, and thank you.' He folded the glue, knives and papers away in Bernave's case and rose to his feet. 'You know where to reach me.'

'Of course. Good day, Citizen.' She must not be too urgent. Menou must not hear anything

370

different in her voice.

'Good day.' He hesitated.

She did not say anything. Please God he thought to take the case with him!

He looked at her for a second longer, then picked up the case and went to the door and out, closing it gently behind him.

She must not listen as if she dreaded hearing the Guard stopping him, asking him who he was. She must assume he would just walk out and be free. Anything else was beyond bearing. She must concentrate on Menou as if that were all that mattered.

'It would explain a great deal,' she said with only the slightest tremor. Perhaps Menou would not hear it, as it was very slight.

'It would not explain why he did not merely tell someone, instead of murdering him,' Menou said sharply.

'Yes, it would,' she rejoined. 'If Bernave went to the guillotine as a traitor, this house would be forfeit, and we should all be out on the street. St Felix would not have done that to us, particularly to Marie-Jeanne and the children. He was not that sort of man. That would be a crime to him.'

He regarded her steadily, his eyes thoughtful.

She waited.

'You know, Citizeness, I think you are possibly right,' he said at length. 'That would explain much. But I wish St Felix had not run. Perhaps if he had told us his reasons . . . ' His voice trailed off, realising the impossibility of such mercy. 'No, I suppose not. The house would still have been forfeit. And one cannot rely on

371

verdicts of justice these days.' He flushed slightly, as if he knew he should not have committed himself to such an opinion, not aloud.

'I can understand being afraid,' she agreed softly. 'I think we all are, if we are honest. These are very uncertain times.'

'I haven't found the knife,' he pointed out.

'I know. But if Amandine helped him, is that so great a sin?'

'Perhaps not.' He sighed. 'Perhaps it doesn't really matter so much. Life is not always tidy, and I should not let my vanity assume I can find everything. Thank you for your help, Citizeness Laurent.'

'You are welcome, Citizen Menou.'

She opened the door and held it for him while he went out, then with trembling legs and dry mouth, dizzy with relief, she went after him.

13

Célie followed Menou into the kitchen where the rest of the family were about to begin a late meal. Each one stared at Menou as he came in, the question in their eyes.

'No,' he said abruptly. 'I did not find the knife. I don't know what he did with it.'

'Does it matter now?' Monsieur Lacoste asked, breaking his bread on to his plate. There was only that for the meal, together with a couple of onions and a little cheese. Amandine was too shattered by grief and dismay to have cooked anything, and even Marie-Jeanne could not collect her emotions sufficiently to care about it. She sat at the table now with her two elder children on either side of her, and the baby asleep in what had once been the wood-basket and now, lined with a blanket, served as an excellent crib.

Menou's answer was prevented by a knock on the back door. He strode over and yanked it open. A middle-aged man stood on the step. He was not very tall, a little heavy-set. His white hair was ragged about his face and his skin was very pale. He had a long nose and faded blue eyes. His clothes were well cut, and had once been good, but time and constant wear had reduced them to a threadbare state.

Everyone turned to stare at him, especially Virginie, her eyes growing wider and wider.

'Excuse me,' the man said politely to Menou. 'Is Citizeness Laurent at home?'

'Who are you?' Menou demanded a trifle abruptly.

A ghost of humour passed across the man's face and vanished. 'Citizen Lejeune, but she may not know my name. Is it permitted to speak with her?'

Menou hesitated. He had no reason to deny it, and perhaps not any authority, now that St Felix was dead, but he was suspicious.

Célie had no idea who the man was or what he could want of her, but she did not wish to leave him standing in the rain. He looked tired and there were lines of strain in his face, as if he were ill. She moved forward, beside Menou.

'Come in, Citizen,' she invited him. 'At least stand inside in the warm while Citizen Menou considers.'

'Thank you, Citizeness,' he accepted, stepping past Menou with a determination that surprised Célie. He had seemed so diffident, so willing to be denied. He was dressed as if he had once been a merchant or lawyer, but had fallen on hard times and was reduced to begging. However, there was a dignity about him which marked him out from most men, even here in the kitchen waiting for a National Guardsman to grant, or refuse, him permission to speak to a laundress. He must surely have been a gentleman once, perhaps even an aristocrat. Maybe he had been a friend of Bernave's, but the name Lejeune meant nothing to her. She could not recall having heard it before.

'I am Citizeness Laurent,' she said to him. 'You look cold. May we offer you something? We have only bread and onion and a little hot coffee.'

'Thank you, Citizeness.' He inclined his head and she noticed again how pale he was. 'I offer you all my condolences on the death of Citizen Bernave,' he went on. 'I was most sorry to hear of it by chance in the street.'

Virginie was still staring at him, her eyes wide, her lips parted.

'What is it you want with Citizeness Laurent?' Menou asked sharply. 'There has been another death in this household and this is not the time to trouble them over unimportant things.'

'Another death?' Lejeune said softly, his voice lifting with surprise. 'I am sorry to hear it. I grieve for you.'

Virginie leaned a little closer to her mother.

Fernand glanced at her, then at Lejeune.

Célie went to the stove to pour a cup of coffee for Lejeune. It was weak, with little flavour or colour, but at least it was hot. She brought it back and gave it to him.

He took it with a smile, warming his hands on it. She noticed they were blue with cold. He turned back to Menou.

'Citizen Bernave requested the services of a tailor to alter a coat for a gentleman who is to leave Paris shortly . . . to change his style of life . . . '

'You asked to speak with Citizeness Laurent,' Menou pointed out.

'And you said you knew Bernave was dead!' Fernand added.

'Citizeness Laurent is the laundress, is she not?' Lejeune asked mildly. 'I imagined she would be in charge of such things.'

'I suppose so,' Menou conceded. 'But you said it was Bernave who asked for it, and he cannot need it now.'

Fernand was also staring at the man, his eyes narrow, puzzled.

'It was not for himself,' Lejeune said steadily, obviously uncomfortable, but refusing to back away. 'I wished to know if the gentleman was still requiring the alteration.' His face was very white and he looked exhausted, as if he might have walked for miles in the cold, and eaten little.

Perhaps he needed the work. Célie felt a rush of pity for him. If Bernave had offered him the job, she should see that wish honoured. The poor soul looked as if he were close to desperation. But how could she accept on Bernave's behalf? She had no idea what he was talking about, or who the man was who wished a coat altered. She tried to remember if there had been any note of it among Bernave's papers. But why should there be if it were merely a service for a friend?

'What was the gentleman's name?' she asked.

Menou looked at her, then at Lejeune, waiting.

Lejeune hesitated. He seemed curiously undecided.

'What was his name?' Fernand repeated more sharply. 'There may be something in Citizen Bernave's papers, if we look.'

376

Lejeune's hands clasped the cup so tightly his knuckles shone white.

'I have looked through the papers,' Madame Lacoste interrupted, moving a step forward. 'It must have been a private arrangement, a kindness for a friend. There is no note of having a coat altered, or who it might be for. But I dare say the gentleman will turn up and ask.' She looked at Lejeune. 'Perhaps in view of Citizen Bernave's death he is leaving a decent space of time before coming.'

'I . . . I thought the matter was of some . . . urgency,' Lejeune said haltingly. 'Possibly I misunderstood.' He looked at Célie as if imploring her to help, but she had no idea how to. She had no money even to offer him any other task. She sewed her own clothes; it was part of her job. And no one else in the house could afford a tailor, or had need for one.

'I'm . . . sorry, Citizen . . . '

'Of course.' He bowed his head very slightly. It was a gracious, old-fashioned gesture. 'I understand. People die unexpectedly, and plans have to be changed.' He put the coffee cup down on the table and turned to leave, his shoulders stooped in defeat.

His words rang in her head: 'plans have to be changed'. He was middle-aged, thick-set, not very tall. She had looked at his eyes rather than his nose or mouth, the heavy jaw. Could it be . . .

'Citizen Lejeune!'

He turned back slowly.

How much dare she risk? Georges had said he had found someone else, not excellent, but

377

better than no one. She was staring at the perfect man now. Everything might depend on it. She gulped, her heart beating wildly. She recalled the name on the passes she had found in Bernave's desk.

'Citizen Bernave mentioned something to me. Could it be . . . ' she could hardly get her breath, 'for a Citizen Briard?'

They were all watching her, even Menou, but she saw no start of recognition, no flash of understanding.

Lejeune looked at her very steadily, his blue eyes clear and bright again. 'Yes, Citizeness. I do believe that was the name. Does Citizen Briard still plan to leave the city, do you know?'

'Yes,' she said, more firmly than she had intended. 'I . . . believe so.' She prayed he would understand why she was now equivocating. She dared not appear to know more about it than she could explain. They were all looking at her. She could feel them listening, weighing what she said and thinking what she meant.

'You know who this Briard is?' Fernand asked, frowning at her.

She was caught. If she said 'no', she would appear to be lying, because she had just said she remembered. If she said 'yes', one of them would ask her, and she knew nothing at all. If she invented it Madame, at least, would know, and be suspicious.

They were waiting, watching.

Menou was frowning now also.

'I . . . I heard Citizen Bernave speak of him,' she said awkwardly. 'I don't know what it was about, except it seemed important to him.'

'But you just said he still plans to leave the city,' Fernand pointed out. The suspicion was bright in his eyes.

Célie wished someone would rescue her, say something — anything! But Amandine was ashen-faced, too absorbed by grief even to think, let alone help. And St Felix was dead.

She must look to her own resources now. At least she had managed to effect Georges' escape. Perhaps, when it no longer mattered at all, when her own fulfilment meant nothing, she had at last become as charming, as quick-witted and as brave as Madame de Staël.

She turned and smiled directly at Fernand. 'Why would he change his plans, if he had somewhere to go? I only know that it mattered to Citizen Bernave, and he was a loyal man to all that the revolution stands for, for equality between people, for the freedom for all to pursue their talents and improve their lives, and for equal justice for everyone. He wanted to end hunger and fear and all unnecessary pain. Isn't that right, Citizen Menou?'

'Yes, it is,' Menou agreed, the anxiety smoothing out his face. 'He was a great man. If this Citizen Briard is a friend of his, and he wishes to help him, then we should honour his intention. You have acted well, Citizeness.' There was a trace of admiration in Menou's voice.

But then he could not possibly imagine the irony of the situation. 'Thank you,' she said demurely, not meeting his eyes. She turned to Lejeune. 'I shall find out more about the coat, and . . . and Citizen Briard, and I shall let you know exactly what is needed. Where may I leave a message for you?'

'I come and go,' he replied. 'I do not have a shop any more. There is a woman who sells coffee on the corner of the rue Mazarine and the Rue Dauphine. If you leave word with her, she will tell me.'

'I'll do that.'

He smiled and turned again to leave.

'Citizen!' she said quickly.

He turned. 'Yes?'

'Thank you . . . for coming.' How absurd. He was going to give his life for his people, not even at the guillotine, but to be torn apart by an enraged mob, and she said 'thank you for coming' as if he had performed no more than a courtesy. But what else could she say, in front of them all?

'It was nothing,' he said softly, and opened the door to the courtyard, and the rain. Menou followed a few moments after.

When he was gone they resumed their meal. Fernand was very quiet; he barely spoke to anyone. Monsieur Lacoste mentioned odd items of news he had heard, and what a relief it would be now that they were free to come and go as they pleased.

'I'm sorry about St Felix,' he added, and there was a sincerity in his voice Célie could not disbelieve.

No one answered.

Célie was aching to go to St Felix's room and look for the passes. He had had them, and without them, even finding Briard, or Lejeune, whatever his name really was, did not help. She had watched Menou search for the knife through the entire house, and not find it. Most particularly she had followed every move in St Felix's chest, under the bed, the shelf with the books. But Menou had not looked through the leaves of the books, where a pass could be hidden, but not a knife.

She glanced across the table at Amandine. She looked like a ghost, almost as if the spirit had gone from the body and there was nothing left but a shell animated by will, but without heart or hope. Célie longed to be able to comfort her, but what was there to say? Perhaps later, after tomorrow, when there was no more need for care or courage, she could tell her what Renoir had said of Bernave? Then she would understand why St Felix might have thrust the knife into Bernave's back, in spite of the King, and all there was to lose. It was not noble, or wise, or brave . . . but it was understandable. Amandine, of all people, was compassionate. She would be quick to understand, and to forgive.

Célie could not sit still any longer. She stood up, excused herself, and went upstairs to St Felix's room. She closed the door and stood, trying to think, in which book he would have hidden the passes. He must have known how close Menou was to arresting him. That was why he had run. Had he had time to think about the passes? Had there been anything but terror in his mind? But Menou had been likely to search any time before that. He would have kept the passes somewhere safe right from the beginning.

She looked around at the bare room. It had held so little of the essence of the man. She remembered thinking that when Menou was here. Nothing personal except books.

There were only a dozen. She was on the second to last one and growing desperate when she heard a sound in the doorway and froze.

It was Amandine, her eyes accusing.

'I'm looking for the passes!' Célie whispered fiercely. 'None of it's any good without them!'

'Oh . . . ' Amandine's shoulders relaxed. 'I see. Have you found them?'

'No!' She shook the book she was holding. Nothing fell out. She put it back and took the last one, the translation of Dante, and fingered through it, then held it by the ends of the spine and shook it. Nothing. Despair welled up inside her. He must have taken them with him! He could not know he was going to be shot.

Reluctantly, tears stung in her eyes.

'They aren't here.' She swallowed and put the book back, hiding her face for a moment. She wiped her hand across her cheeks. It would do Amandine no good to see her weep. 'I'll have to go and tell Georges. He might be able to do something. I don't know what.'

'I'll tell Madame you've gone for something,' Amandine said flatly. 'Cheese . . . I don't know . . . '

'Thank you.' Célie turned back to face Amandine, and tried to force herself to smile for a moment. 'Thank you. I'll even see if I can find some . . . or soap . . . or onions . . . or anything!'

It had stopped raining. The sky was full of patches of blue, and shafts of sunlight lit the pavement and danced in the puddles. But there was still a hard edge to the wind, and there was every excuse to hurry along the street, looking to neither right nor left. There was not enough of her face showing for anyone to have recognised Célie as she turned into an alley, unless they caught sight of her pale hair. It was far too cold to stand around, and in a short while the light would fade. Tomorrow morning the King would die. Tonight everyone had something to think about, to fear or to celebrate. The cafés were full. People talked, drank, made wild gestures and predictions, promises and threats. The smell of fear was in the air.

The sun was gold on the rooftops and the shadows black when Célie reached the alley. She went up the stairs, feeling her way in the gloom, and at the top she knocked sharply.

Georges opened the door, a candle burning so low on the table behind him she knew him only by the outline of his head.

'Célie?' his voice lifted in surprise, and both pleasure and alarm. 'What is it?' He stepped back for her to come into the room.

She closed the door behind her. 'Briard came to the house this afternoon!'

He stopped, then turned slowly, eyes wide.

She watched him intently, the slightest change in expression or inclination of his body.

'Just after you left,' she went on. 'He was very

383

discreet, and it was ages before I realised who he was. But he really looked like the King. He would be perfect.' She hesitated.

'What?' he demanded, his voice cracking with an emotion she could not read, but so intense it shook his body. She could not see his features in the dim light.

'I liked him,' she answered quietly. 'It was stupid. I spoke with him for just a few moments, but it hurts to think what will happen to him. And of course he knows.' She needed Georges to understand.

He said nothing. There was no possible answer.

'But we don't have the passes,' she hurried on, before he could hope, crushed by having to tell him. 'I searched St Felix's room everywhere, even after Menou went, but they're not there. He must have taken them with him in case they were found. We've got to have papers to get the King out of Paris, past the section leaders, if there are any still on duty. They'll send men out in every direction after him.'

'I know about the passes. St Felix took them when he ran. They were destroyed.' Now his voice was different. There was excitement, even a rush of joy in it he could not conceal. 'We might get by in the panic, but I doubt it,' he went on, gathering emphasis. 'Somebody's head will have to fill the basket, and it will take a lot of them to replace the King's. Everyone leaving Paris will be suspect, especially fat, elderly gentlemen who look ill and terrified.'

It seemed hopeless. Célie was cold in this grim

room with the last of the winter daylight fading over the rooftops, and now barely reaching the windows. There was no sound up here but the creaking of the wood settling and a faint thread of the wind. They seemed removed from the bustle and the anger of the streets, but not from the desperation, and certainly not from the hunger.

'Who can we get new papers from?' she asked quietly. 'Dare we forge them ourselves? Will they look that closely?'

His answer was immediate, and touched with a glint of humour. 'Yes, they will. It's the first thing they'd think of. They need to be real, and with a signature no one will argue with.'

'Well, we can't ask Robespierre!' she said drily. 'He's suspicious of everyone. He'd want to know all the details, ask endless questions, and then refuse.' She remembered the venomous little face and the consuming passion in it. 'He's obsessed with purifying everything. He'll go on until there's nobody left, unless someone stops him. He's always talking about the 'Virtue of the People', but I sometimes wonder if he sees real people at all, if he knows they have feelings and can be hurt or deceived, and it matters!' She felt a sudden anger so sharp it twisted inside her as she saw Monsieur Lacoste's face in her mind's eye, and his blind belief, all the hope he had invested in a man who did not see him, or anyone like him, as real, with flesh to bleed and dreams to be betrayed.

'And don't even think of asking Marat!' she added. 'All he can think of is blood — rivers of it

— seas of it. The only people he cares about are the Communards — and all they can think of are their empty plates.'

'Who can blame them, poor devils,' Georges answered with sudden gentleness. 'It has to be Danton. He is still the sanest, the most like an ordinary man. He's reachable, and that makes the difference. And he's a patriot, not in love with dreams, but with reality. That's what's wrong with all the rest of them.' He gestured to the chair and she sat down on it. He folded up on the mattress opposite her. A sharp twist of humour touched his lips. 'Have you read any of Jean-Jacques Rousseau, Célie?'

She hesitated. Should she be honest? Her parents had quoted him as if he were a prophet of the new light, and she had turned from him in disgust, holding his endless ideas responsible for their obsessions. Even though Madame de Staël and her friends had spoken of him often, with respect, it had not softened her resolve never to read him herself.

She knew they all praised the breadth, sensitivity and originality of his ideas. Even those who did not agree were thoroughly familiar with his work. Half the dreams of the revolution had been fired by idealism such as his, the belief in a better world founded on the innately noble nature of man, if educated rightly and freed from oppression and injustice. She had heard that Robespierre admired him passionately, as had so many of the leading revolutionaries, except Danton.

Georges would not admire her childish

386

stubbornness, and his disapproval would wrench inside her like a sprain. She had proved her courage, loyalty, imagination, quickness of thought. But it did not free her from the pain of caring, to which she could see no end. The pain would only become deeper if he found her ignorant or silly, or knew that she was trying too hard.

'You haven't.' His voice cut across her thoughts.

The colour burned up her face. She should have been honest. She was furious with herself. How stupid!

'No,' she said quickly. 'I was just thinking of what I had heard people say of him. I suppose it is something I should read, in order to understand what is happening, but I always thought I would dislike it.'

'I'm sure you would!' he said with a sudden grin, laughter flaring up in his eyes in desperate relief for an instant of triviality far from the real.

'You have far too much knowledge of life to be taken in by people who wander around falling in love with each other's spirits,' he went on, his voice edged with derision. 'Weeping and arguing and sympathising together, but never reaching anything so natural as touching one another.'

That was not what she thought of as falling in love. Love was a joy that welled up uncontrollably, making your heart almost choke you, the thought of it unreturned was another name for hell. It was what gave you courage to do the impossible, lit the most pedestrian things with magic, and made another person so precious the thought of them in danger made you weak with terror. Above all it was touching, even if only in dreams.

But she did not want him to know that!

He was watching her face. 'Everyone in his works is discontented, without knowing why,' he continued, his voice charged with amazement and derision. 'They are all starving in the soul, but no one has the wit or the physical instinct to know that love, with its power and laughter, its pain and sweetness — and absurdity — is the answer.'

It was the first time she had heard him speak of love. She was afraid of what he might say, but she could not let go. She needed to know — whatever it was. The impression she had of Rousseau was of an emotion she did not understand, and certainly could not share.

'I thought they were all in love?' she questioned, trying to keep her voice level, the urgency and the emotion out of her eyes.

He dismissed it with a jerk of his hand, contemptuously. 'Not real love, not love that can give and take, and find any fulfilment, only anguish that is always travelling but never arrives.' He was still watching her just as intently. 'Anyway, every time they are on the brink of actually doing anything, they stop and philosophise for pages!'

'Isn't that because he's a philosopher?' she asked, feeling a warmth begin to open up inside her. She recalled an ardent admirer in Madame's salon talking about the purity of Rousseau's characters, their nobility and chastity. Did

Georges see that in them? Was that what he admired?

'In treatises, yes,' he answered, meeting her eyes. 'Not in life. What is the use of knowing everything, if you never actually practise it? They are forever cooking and never eating.'

'Oh . . . I see.'

'Do you?' He touched her lightly, so lightly she barely felt more than the brush of his hand on her arm. 'You would if you read Rousseau.' His voice was soft. 'But please don't waste your time.'

Her mind raced away with thoughts she dared not entertain, imagination not of Rousseau's dreamers' love, but of Georges', urgent, intimate and real.

There was no time for it. It would be too precious, too consuming. She forced it away.

'Can we really ask Danton?' She brought them back to the immediacy of the present. They had barely twelve hours, and Georges was right: without passes they could not succeed. Briard would have sacrificed himself for nothing. 'I suppose there's no way without telling him the truth?' she asked.

He looked at her steadily, weighing his answer.

'None at all,' he said at last. 'There's no one else. And he'll guess anyway. Wiser not to look as if we are trying to deceive him. I'll go . . . now.' He straightened up.

'No!' she said sharply, instinctively reaching out and grasping his wrist. 'Better I go. Danton'll know who you are. You could even be stopped before you've had a chance to tell him the whole story . . . the reasons . . . the truth.'

'Do you know where he lives?'

She was standing beside him now.

'Of course I do! Everyone knows where Danton lives!'

He winced, his lips tightening. He hated sending her on a dangerous errand yet again. In getting him out of the house on the Boulevard St-Germain she had proved her nerve, shown that she could be as clever and as brave as she wished to be, but it had undone nothing as far as his freedom was concerned.

She turned to the door. She must give him no time to argue the issue, or herself to weaken.

'If I get them, I'll come back.'

'Be careful!' he urged her, fear sharp in him.

She knew from his voice, the quick intake of breath, what he was going to say now. She did not want to hear it. It would make it harder. She opened the door. 'I'm always careful.' She smiled at him quickly and went out.

★ ★ ★

It was a little after nine o'clock by the time Célie reached the Cour du Commerce towards Danton's house. The night was crisp, thin moonlight on the rime of frost, freezing roofs gleaming in its pallor, black shadows below. Her heart was beating so hard her breath caught in her throat, and her stomach was churning around, making her feel slightly sick. She was frightened of Danton, the immense power of him. It was like facing a violent force of nature,

390

unpredictable, capable of destroying everything. If she misjudged it, she could be seized and go to the guillotine the same morning as the King!

And if she told Danton too much he might forestall the plan, and all of them would be taken: Briard, the crowd who mobbed the King's carriage . . . Georges.

She was at Danton's doorway. She was shaking so badly her own breathing all but choked her. This was the moment of decision. Once she had knocked, it was too late. Forward — to see Danton to ask him to sign a pass for the King to escape, to risk her own life if it went wrong. It would be immediate, right here in Danton's house. No one would be able to help her. No one would even know, until it was too late.

She would not see them again — not Amandine, nor Madame Lacoste. She was surprised to think how much she liked Madame. And she would not see Georges again. It was not enough to have proved she could be as brave as Madame de Staël. She had thought it would be, but it was barely a beginning. She wanted so much more than that! She wanted to love with all her heart and mind and passion, to feel everything there was, all the joy, even all the pain.

Even if Georges never saw her that way — never as more than a friend, an ally in the cause — to try, and fail, would have been better than not to have tried at all — far better!

She thought of the tumbrels and the guillotine. Would it be quick? Would she be able to face it with courage, as other people had? Or would she humiliate herself by having to be carried?

She stood shivering on the step.

Did she believe in God? Was there anything after the blinding pain, except oblivion? Would she cease to exist? Was all the passion and the hope and the love nothingness in the end? Had all humanity down the ages been deluded by dreams? Or was there some heaven where she and Georges might meet again, and even Jean-Pierre . . . and all this great, impossible plan would have been worth it?

Bernave had believed. She remembered his saying that he wanted the King back because one day he wanted the Church as well — the return of the sacraments, the mercy and the hope that the belief in holiness could give.

But then so much of what he said might have been lies! What about the girl in Vincennes?

If she turned and ran away now, what was there worth having? Nothing. Cowardice was a kind of betrayal of herself, which she would have to live with for the rest of her life, every day, every night.

She knocked on the door, and then instantly wished she had not.

It was too late to run. The door was opened almost immediately by a woman roughly her own age, with a gentle, pretty face shadowed as if some deep tragedy threatened her. She looked at Célie enquiringly.

There was still time to escape, invent a lie. However, Célie said a little hoarsely, 'I have a

392

favour to ask of Citizen Danton. It is terribly important to me, and it is urgent, or I would not interrupt you at home.' She tried to smile, but it felt stiff in her face.

Gabrielle Danton smiled at her. 'You're lucky, Citizeness. He is at home. Please come in.' She held the door wide.

Célie stepped inside and was immediately aware of the warmth of the house, the kind of brightness that is created by a woman who loves her home and her family and whose joy it is to care for them. There were ornaments, simple but pleasing to the eye, embroidered cushions, a painted jug. The aroma of herbs and vegetables filled the air and she could hear the sound of children laughing in the next room. It was as Georges had said, an island of startling sanity in a world of madness.

She followed Gabrielle into the next room where there was a fire blazing in the hearth. Danton sprawled at ease in the largest chair, his knees apart, a smile on his huge, grotesque face. She had never been this close to him before. He was younger than she had thought, little over thirty. He had a shock of hair, his skin was pock-marked and had the scars of all manner of farmyard encounters from his childhood. He was so large he seemed about to burst out of his clothes, and yet there was nothing threatening about him. He was at home here, and his happiness in it pervaded the air.

'The Citizeness wishes to ask a favour of you,' Gabrielle said to him. 'She says it is urgent, and matters to her very much.'

'Come in, Citizeness,' Danton said expansively, rising and gesturing to the other chair for her to sit. He thanked his wife, smiling at her with a softness in his expression sweeter than words.

Gabrielle flashed him an answering smile, then excused herself and went back to the kitchen, humming softly, tucking a loose lock of hair back into its pins.

Célie sat down near the fire. The thought of war, of foreign soldiers tramping through here, stealing and destroying, was obscene. Any price at all would be cheap to preserve this decency of life.

Danton was waiting, looking at her curiously. She must begin. This was the moment of risk, to win or lose it all. She had gone over and over it in her mind, imagining the scene — what she would say, what he would answer, all the arguments she would use. None of it seemed adequate. But she must speak.

'I have been listening much to what people have been saying lately.' Her voice was hoarse, squeaking at points, she was so afraid. She knotted her hands together in her lap to stop them shaking, digging her nails into her palms. 'In the Convention, and the Jacobin Club, and in the streets.'

He was staring at her, waiting for her to get to the point.

She swallowed, looking up to meet his eyes. In that instant she knew she must be honest. Otherwise she would lose him completely.

'I am afraid of war, Citizen Danton. If we are

invaded by the monarchist countries around us, we shall lose all that we have gained in the revolution. Everything will be swept away and the old opinions will be back, perhaps even worse — and foreign as well! Not even French.'

He leaned forward. 'I know that, Citizeness. I am aware of the dangers, believe me! I love France as much as anyone.' There was a passion in his face as he said it, a gentleness and an urgency which made doubt impossible. 'We will fight to defend her . . . and die if we need to. There is no more anyone can do.'

'Yes, there is!' she plunged in. Surprisingly, she did not even want to hesitate. 'If we wait until we are stronger before we execute the King — then . . . '

A shadow of sadness crossed his face. 'I cannot change that, Citizeness. If there had been any chance of reversing the decision, I would have tried. You said you had listened to people in the Convention; surely you know that for yourself?'

'It couldn't be reversed by persuasion,' she agreed.

His eyes widened, but he did not interrupt, waiting for her to complete the thought.

Now was the moment. It was too late to retreat. She drew in her breath.

'If the King did not reach the scaffold . . . if he disappeared from the carriage between prison and the Place de la Révolution . . . ' She saw the amazement in his face, the dawning incredulity. Was he going to arrest her now? She spoke a little more clearly and more forcefully. 'It could be done! Then England and Spain would have no provocation to go to war against us.' She leaned towards him, speaking softly. 'It would give us time to establish peace and show the world that we can govern ourselves without a king or a Church, and that we can do it better! We can administer justice, keep order, feed the people just as well as any other land. But they won't believe it until they see it!' She stopped abruptly, her heart pounding, watching Danton's face for rage — or understanding.

'You have courage, Citizeness — I'll say that for you.' His voice was low, full of surprise. 'What makes you think such a thing is possible?'

It was the question she dreaded. And yet she would have thought him a fool if he had not asked.

'Many people see the dangers just as I do,' she replied. 'They will risk their lives, some though they know there is no chance of their survival, even if they succeed.' She thought of Briard and went on with a sudden catch in her throat. 'They love France. They love our people — and they want all the gains of the revolution preserved, everything so many have already died to achieve. They don't want our homes invaded by Austrian soldiers, or English; our land, our fields and streets trodden by other countries' armies who have no love for them and no care.'

Danton winced, and she knew she had struck a nerve in him. She did not add anything further. Let him answer what she had said. She saw in his eyes the struggle of emotion in him.

'You risk a great deal in telling me this,

396

Citizeness,' he said quietly. 'You must want something of me you cannot do without. What is it?'

'A pass for Citizen Briard to leave Paris and travel in whatever direction he wishes.'

'Briard?' he repeated, watching her face. 'That's all? Just a pass for Citizen Briard?'

'Yes. Joseph Briard.'

'Is he wanted by the Commune?'

'No. He is just an ordinary man, who is ill, and wishes to leave Paris and travel.'

He breathed out very slowly. 'I see. And you think this Joseph Briard might be stopped, and my name on the pass would prevent that?'

'Yes. No one would question a genuine signature of Citizen Danton.' She said it with certainty. She was daring to hope. It almost suffocated her, as if she were poised between life and death, darkness and light.

Now it was time for him to make the great decision. He looked at her with a slight smile. 'I suppose Citizen Briard is an ordinary sort of merchant, a middle-aged man who trades between the city and the country in something or other?' His eyes were very steady. 'The sort of thing the King should have done — if fortune had put him in the right place, instead of on the throne of France.'

She swallowed, and nodded.

There was silence in the room except for the flickering of the fire. In the kitchen Gabrielle replaced a pot lid, and the heavy chink of it carried through the motionless air.

'If Citizen Briard is unable to leave,' Célie said

397

in a voice barely above a whisper, 'then the pass will be destroyed — in case it should fall into the wrong hands.' She watched his face.

'I have as much courage as you do, Citizeness,' he answered softly, 'and I love France as much. I'll sign your pass.'

She felt the heat rise through her as if she had turned to the fire. The relief was like a tide, engulfing everything.

'Thank you, Citizen Danton,' she answered. 'Few people will ever know what we owe you.'

Although his smile was dazzling, it made his face look like a gargoyle. 'God — I hope not! There's nowhere to go but forward, Citizeness! Let's do it with heart! To hell with our enemies.'

'To hell with them!' she agreed, in spite of herself, tears spilling down her cheeks.

* * *

She took the pass and put it down her bodice. Then she went immediately to the Rue Mazarine to find the woman who sold coffee, and she asked for Citizen Briard. Ten minutes later she was standing in a tiny room off a courtyard and Briard, looking even paler than before, was accepting the pass with profound respect.

'You are very brave, Citizeness,' he said gravely. 'Citizen Bernave spoke well of you, but your courage would have surprised even him, I believe. May God be with you.'

She found the wish surprisingly sweet. A day ago, even an hour ago she would have dismissed the idea. Now it was exactly the right thing to have said. They were on a wild venture, desperate. She needed to believe in a power greater than her own, one with a higher justice, and a kinder mercy.

'And you, Citizen,' she replied, and meant it passionately.

★ ★ ★

Jean-Paul Marat left his house on the Rue de l'École-de-Médecine, crossed the courtyard past the wall and went under the archway into the street. He was joined almost immediately by two men clothed in rags as torn and filthy as those he wore himself. They accompanied him to watch his back, safeguard him against attack. They had the hollow-eyed, copper-skinned faces of the workers in the tanneries of the Faubourg St-Antoine. Years of harsh acids and alkali had burned them; hunger and disease had made them wolfish of heart as well as of feature.

They fell into step beside Marat in silence. There was no need to exchange greetings as if they did not understand each other and share a common purpose in all things. Appearance was nothing. Perhaps the red bandannas all three wore mattered. Presumably that alone had meaning, as a sign of loyalty to the Commune, but the rest was irrelevant. They did not notice the smell of dirt — it was part of their lives, like daylight and darkness. The sour odour of decay that was peculiar to Marat, the rotting of his flesh with his terrible disease, they were either too tactful to appear to notice, or too frightened.

Or perhaps they were too accustomed to the raw stench of the tanneries to notice any other smells.

Tomorrow morning Louis Capet would go to his death, and it would be the beginning of a new age. Of course the Girondins would have to be got rid of afterwards. They were nothing but a nuisance, a bunch of posturing idiots who got in the way. Marat himself was the brain and the core of the Commune. Whatever happened that was of importance would centre on him. Soon he would be able to do anything he liked.

The street was windy and cold. It had stopped raining. A few stars glittered thinly above and there was a skin of ice forming on the cobbles, making it even more difficult to walk. He was obliged to move in an extraordinary, sideways gait, half shuffling, half hopping, like some gigantic frog, because the suppurating tetters that covered his body also ran agonisingly between his legs. Sometimes it was all he could do not to scream with the pain. Vinegar baths eased it a little, but only temporarily.

He thought perhaps someone was following him. He was aware of footsteps, the same rhythm as his own all the time, always a dozen yards behind him. He was not afraid, only interested. No one could harm him. And if they tried, the men beside him would dispatch them rapidly enough.

He was heading across the river towards the Rue St-Honoré and the Convention. There was plenty of light in the street from windows of houses and shops, the occasional torch flare and groups of soldiers, or now and then a carriage with lamps. If he turned he could see who it was following, but he refused to do that. Probably it was just somebody going the same way. Lots of people were out tonight. There was an excitement in the air, a nervy sort of edge, a prickling, as if everyone were counting the hours to daylight, and the last great act to end tyranny.

They were crossing the river. The water ran dark and noisy under the spans of the bridge. He could hear it sucking at the stone, folding in and burying under the ice cold, shiny currents, reflecting together torchlight from the further bank, red fire dancing on molten lead.

The dead black mass of the Louvre shut out the paler night sky. Marat and his companions turned left. Half a dozen National Guardsmen carrying torches passed by.

'Good evening, Citizen Marat!' the leader called, tipping his hat.

Marat waved in answer, acknowledging them almost casually, and continued on.

They passed a group of well-dressed men, prosperous and plump. They too recognised him. Even if they had not seen his face in the torch flame, his agonised, crab-like gait was unmistakable.

One of them kept talking, as if he had not noticed, averting his eyes.

Marat stiffened. He had been insulted so often in his years in the wilderness of rejection, he was quick to see it. He knew it far too well to misunderstand.

The men drew a little closer together. In his

401

anxiety to avoid Marat, one of them almost scraped the wall of the house they were passing, careless of bruising himself. Another laughed nervously, ending with a cough.

The man who had been talking changed his mind. He forced himself to smile, too widely, showing all his teeth in the gloom.

'Good evening, Citizen Marat!' he said loudly, his voice jerking up at the end.

Marat did not reply but he stood still.

'A cold night,' the man went on.

Marat stared at him.

The man's nostrils flared at the smell. Marat could see the fear. He was breathing rapidly and he all but choked on his own saliva. 'Long live . . . the Republic!' He swivelled away and ran along the street, swinging round the corner into an alley and disappearing. Marat knew it was not the way he had intended to go. It led nowhere. His companions fled after him.

Marat resumed his way with as much of a swagger as he could manage, but there was contempt in it. He knew their words were driven by fear, not honesty, and he despised them for it.

He had seen that kind of tension in people's faces before: the artificial praise, the hollow agreement, the eyes that were loath to meet his, and at the same time dare not look away. There were times when he wondered if anything anyone said to him was true. It was exhausting, living amongst so much terror and lies, evasions, a constant state of near-hysteria.

That was why he loved his mistress, Simone Evrard. She had no political ambitions or

402

opinions. She saw the human and precious in him, not the doctor, the writer, the avenger of the oppressed, the political demagogue or the terror of the Girondins, but a man of passions and frailties like any other.

They were close to the Convention now and there was more noise in the street. Smoke was blowing in the wind from half a dozen torches, and there was a sharp, tarry smell that caught in the throat, but was not unpleasant.

Marat turned and went in through the doorway of the Convention. His two companions stayed close behind, although he was safe now. It was almost deputies in here, arguing, drunk with the sound of their own voices, as usual, and absorbed in the struggle for power within their individual factions.

The man from the street had entered behind him, tentatively, uncertain if he should be here or not. That meant he was following Marat!

Why should he? But there was no reason to suspect anything amiss. He was probably just another citizen eager to hear the debate, and share in the moment of history.

A plump man with thinning hair approached Marat earnestly, his eyes glittering in the reflected torchlight.

'Citizen Marat,' he said earnestly, 'I beg you, just a moment or two of your time, if you would be so gracious.' The words were preposterous. Marat had never been gracious in his life. The rage inside him burned like lava, scorching everything it touched.

'What do you want?' he asked. His voice was

hoarse, rasping, and held a peculiar mixture of accents. One remembered that his father was Sardinian and his mother Swiss. He could read and write in English, Italian, Dutch and German, as well, of course, as French.

'Citizen Aulard,' the man introduced himself.

Marat was impatient. He gestured sharply with his hands, fingers jabbing at the air, his weight shifting from foot to foot.

'What do you want?' he repeated.

'Your advice, Citizen,' Aulard replied. There was a certain ring of confidence in him. If he was frightened he hid it well. 'So many of our more educated men have fled from Paris, as if they were guilty of something and had cause to fear.' He shrugged. 'And who knows, perhaps they have.' He saw Marat's temper rising. 'But it has left us without men of certain skills, men who are widely read and have inventive and subtle minds in the sciences.'

Against his will Marat was caught.

Aulard must have seen it. He knew his flattery worked. Marat did not hunger any more for power — that was satisfied — but nothing would ever assuage his need for glory, for the recognition he felt he had been denied all his life. He had published volumes of work on all manner of subjects as varied as optics, electricity and the nature of the human soul. The Académie Française had steadfastly ignored them all. But he would be revenged. After tomorrow he could do anything.

'What can I help you with?' he asked Aulard, standing still at last.

404

The flicker of a smile touched Aulard's mouth.

'I have a plan to set up treatment for our soldiers who have suffered amputations in battle,' he replied. 'But I cannot persuade the doctors at the School of Medicine to listen to me. Their minds are closed . . . '

Marat nodded.

Aulard knew he had his attention, even his sympathy. It was so easy. It was like offering sweets to a starved child. With all Marat's power and his rage, he was still so vulnerable, the pain in him so naked.

Marat vulnerable?

He ruled the Commune by terror, and the Commune were the real rulers of Paris, and thus of France. Marat could raise his hand, and send anyone he wanted to the guillotine.

'They haven't learned anything or thought of anything new in twenty years,' Aulard went on, knowing exactly what to say. He had probably studied Marat's career. He knew of the endless works written, Marat labouring crouched over his desk by candlelight, eighteen and twenty hours a day, living on next to nothing, driven to exhaustion by the hunger for recognition, exploring every avenue of thought he could aspire to, and always being passed over. Volume after volume had poured from his pen, every one to be derided and turned away.

He had scraped a living as a doctor in places as diverse as the household of the Comte d'Artois, of all people, and the village of Pimlico on the edge of London. Always the passion for acknowledgement of his genius had impelled

405

him on. Failure had embittered him, caused quarrels, dismissals, and in the end persecution, as he had allied himself with the desperate, the starving and the dispossessed. His towering, blazing anger for their misery was the pain of his own rejection.

But that was all over now. Nobody would ever reject him again.

Out of the corner of his vision Marat saw the man who had followed him in the street: he looked to be in his mid-thirties, a very ordinary man, with brown hair and well-worn, workman's clothes.

'Your medical opinion would carry more weight with them than mine,' Aulard went on. 'If you were to consider my plans, Citizen, and find yourself able to recommend them, then everyone else would take them seriously also.'

'Let me see them,' Marat agreed. 'Bring them to my house tomorrow.'

'Thank you, Citizen,' Aulard said enthusiastically. 'Your help will mean everything to me . . . and to the poor men who have suffered in the cause of patriotism.' His face was already gleaming with the prospect of victory. His smile widened; his shoulders relaxed.

The man with brown hair moved forward, almost to Marat's elbow.

'Will this be free to the good citizens who had offered their services in Paris as well?' he asked.

Aulard stared at him. 'And who are you?' he demanded angrily. 'I am speaking with Citizen Marat! How dare you interfere? Citizen Marat does not need your opinion.'

'Fernand Lacoste. Why does it matter who I am?'

Aulard moved towards him.

'Wait!' Marat snapped, holding his hand up. He turned to Aulard. 'Will it be free? Or will you make money from this, and fame?'

'I seek only the wellbeing of my fellow citizens who have been injured in the cause of freedom,' Aulard answered sententiously.

Marat was not fooled twice.

'Good! Then take it to the Army. If they recommend it, then you don't need me. Go and see Citizen Pache.' He was not sure how it had happened, but he was aware that he had been used.

Aulard was fortunate to escape so lightly.

He swung round to Fernand. 'I'll not forget your interference, Citizen!' he spat.

'You'd be wise to forget you were ever here,' Marat retorted. 'I do not like to be used, Citizen Aulard.'

Aulard paled, stood his ground for a moment, then spun round and strode off, leaving Marat alone in the corridor with Fernand Lacoste.

The man seemed nervous, excited. He stared at Marat as if transfixed.

'What is it, Citizen?' Marat asked softly, his voice little more than a hiss. 'You followed me all the way from the Cordeliers. What do you want?'

Lacoste paled, but he did not back away. He licked his lips. 'There is something wrong,' he said with a little shake of his head. He was frowning. 'I don't know what it is, but I believe it has to do with the King.'

'Citizen Capet,' Marat corrected him, but he was not listening. He knew one should never ignore whispers, gossip. People like this were the eyes and ears of the revolution.

'Citizen Capet,' Lacoste repeated obediently. 'I live on the Boulevard St-Germain, in a big house. It used to belong to Citizen Victor Bernave.' He was speaking too quickly, almost gabbling. He needed to say everything, but he was afraid of losing Marat's attention.

Marat knew it, and waited. It was possibly nothing, but it might matter.

'But he was murdered,' Lacoste went on. 'Now it belongs to my wife.' He looked acutely uncomfortable. He had said something he did not mean to. Marat could see it in his eyes.

'What has that to do with Citizen Capet?' he asked.

In spite of his nervousness, Lacoste did not flinch or lower his gaze.

'Something was going on in that house since long before Bernave was murdered. I thought it was all to do with money. His trade was in cloth and he did well. People were coming and going on errands at all hours. Then today a man came to the back door with a story about being a tailor who had been asked by Bernave to do a job altering a coat for someone, but he still expected to do it even though Bernave is dead.'

Marat was losing patience. This was tedious and of no possible importance.

'My daughter stared at him as if she could barely believe her eyes,' Lacoste went on. 'She is six years old. Afterwards I asked her why. Then I realised it!'

'What? So far you have said nothing!' Marat snapped.

'The King! Citizen Capet!' Lacoste replied urgently. 'The man looked exactly like him! And he was offering to alter a coat for a man who intended to leave Paris within the next few days. I don't know what it means, Citizen Marat, but I thought you should know.'

Ideas whirled in Marat's head. So the man was not a fool after all. A middle-aged man who looked like Louis Capet, people making plots and plans, coming and going at all hours. Victor Bernave had been a clever, slippery man, not to be trusted. Good thing he was dead.

'You have done well to bring this to me, Citizen,' Marat said gently. 'Who else have you told?'

'No one!' Lacoste said with feeling. 'Who else could I know would do the right thing for the people?'

'Nobody,' Marat agreed. Excellent. If no one else knew, then if this was indeed some kind of plot, he would foil it himself. He could use men from the Commune, men he could trust. The Girondins were useless. They would argue with one another and end up achieving nothing, as always. They would be too busy trying to make personal gain out of it to reach a decision . . . like a roomful of frightened old women running around tripping over each other when someone yells 'Fire!'

Danton was no good. He was greedy and

409

indecisive. He had actually wanted to save the King's life in October! He was an oaf — a buffoon! He had revolution on his lips, but not in his heart.

And Robespierre had no heart, the frozen little worm. All he would do was get his own glory out of it, use it to climb one step higher up the ladder of power.

Marat would deal with this plot himself. Trust none of them.

'What else have you seen?' he asked Lacoste. 'Who comes to the house? Who goes out? What have you overheard?'

Lacoste's eyes widened. 'You think it is real?' There was awe in his voice.

'Maybe!' Marat was abrupt. He didn't want Lacoste to think too much of himself. He could get exaggerated ideas of his importance. Marat fixed him with a sullen, smouldering look.

Lacoste told him everything he could think of or recall, reciting it obediently like a schoolboy repeating his lessons.

'Thank you,' Marat nodded when he was finished. 'Say nothing to anyone! You have done the right thing. Now go home and keep silent.'

'Yes, Citizen Marat,' Fernand promised. Seeing that Marat had given him leave to go, he turned on his heel and escaped.

Marat went to the hall of the Convention, his mind whirling. He did not go to the seats of the deputies but to the front of the balcony above, where spectators crowded together to watch and listen to the proceedings.

Who would have the courage or the

intelligence to plan a rescue of the King right from the jaws of the guillotine? Not the royalists. None of them had the nerve. They were all too busy taking care of their own skins — and fortunes, feathering their nests in England, in Austria, or wherever they thought they had the best chance of living out an exile in comfort.

Marat stared down at the circle of seats stretching wide in tiers, and the rostrum with its short wooden stairs up one side and down the other.

The people nudged each other and moved a little away from him, out of respect, or because of the smell.

So who was it then? His mind roved over all the possibilities, thinking of the ambitious, the dissatisfied, all those of whose loyalties he was uncertain.

It had to be more than one person. Only a group could accomplish such a thing. But there would be one leader, there always was, a sly, ruthless man with the audacity to think of rescuing the King almost from the scaffold's edge.

A man like that conniving devil, Bernave! Never knew what he really thought, or meant.

Except that he was dead ... murdered, apparently. Now there was an interesting thought! He should learn more about that.

The deputies were divided not according to the region they represented, but from left to right depending upon the extremity of their political opinions. Those of the most conservative sat to the right, those of the most wild and revolutionary to the left. The large mass who were undecided dominated the centre, known as the Mountain.

Marat looked around for faces he might recognise, and saw Barbaroux. His handsome profile was unmistakable. He had once been told by someone that it was noble and very Roman. Now he was forever leaning back to display it the better. Fool! If he had spoken as well as he looked, he might have achieved something.

Brissot appeared harassed and uncertain, like a man who has been set on a horse he knew perfectly well he had not the strength to ride, and that he would eventually have no choice but to cling on to for dear life and be carried wherever it chose to take him. Marat despised him, as he despised them all. Idiots, poseurs, the whole lot of them.

He would show them, tomorrow, if there was a plan to rescue the King. He, Marat, would be the one to expose it.

He looked for Danton but did not see him. He would have been noticeable instantly, even in this crowd. It took him a moment to find Robespierre. The light caught the white of his powdered hair and the flickering movement of his little hands. He was whispering to someone. Effete little swine. He claimed to love the people, and yet his neat little nose wrinkled in disgust if one of them came anywhere near him! Hypocrite!

And there was Saint-Just, sitting like stone. He could have been a monument on a grave. Better he were! That was where he belonged.

The debate seemed desultory, and without emotion. Then suddenly there was a rustle of movement. People sat further upright. Some craned forward. They were staring up. They had seen him. He smiled. He did not know how grotesque the gesture was with his wide, sagging mouth.

This time tomorrow he would drop the bombshell that there had been a plot to rescue the King — which he had brilliantly foiled. That would make them all take notice — not just here but all over Paris — all over France! It would be the end of the Girondins. Smug little Robespierre could not be the hero of that! He would be ignored, and he would hate it! Marat's smile widened.

Next to him a man moved a few feet further away. Another wrinkled his nose then instantly covered his face with a handkerchief.

A busy little deputy shot to his feet and scurried round to climb the rostrum. Almost before he was there he began to speak of a glorious new age born of blood. His eyes kept glancing towards Marat.

Marat nodded.

The deputy spoke of the imminent death of the King, and what a glorious day it would be: the birth of the Republic, of liberty and justice for everyone.

Marat watched the Girondins to see if any of them had the courage to argue what he knew they believed.

They looked wretched, embarrassed, fidgeting with their hands, but not one rose to speak.

Cowards! Exactly what he expected.

Another deputy asked a question about the war with Prussia, and if there were any way to prevent it escalating. He showed a spark of courage, but no one responded.

Brissot turned to Vergniaud, the spokesman for the Girondins, beside him, and for an instant Marat wondered if he were going to rise, but he did not.

Marat stared down at the sea of faces; at the Girondins in whom so many hopes had been placed: their gravitas, their virtue, their noble ideals! They sat in little huddles. One could tell just by looking at them who had quarrelled with whom, who felt insulted or cheated of some honour. It would be amusing, if the fate of France did not hang on it! They aspired to the dignity of the senators of ancient Rome. They talked endlessly and wrote terrible treatises. Roland was the worst: a sour, unhappy man with literary pretensions infinitely beyond his ability to realise. It was said his memoranda were the most complete ever written. He took it as a compliment. It was not. They were dry enough to choke a horse.

They all had dreams of literary immortality, and their works were almost unreadable. They had exasperated Bernave. Marat remembered that now. He had been funny about them at times, and yet there was irony and tragedy beneath the laughter. He had cared too much.

Marat cared too. He knew what it was to be tired and poor, to be sneered at and excluded, to be hungry, cold and frightened and have no

414

weapon with which to fight back. He remembered when the Marquis de Lafayette had sent three thousand soldiers into the Cordeliers to hunt him like a rat! And failed.

And where was Lafayette now? Gone over to the Austrians!

Tomorrow Marat would put the final seal on his glory and make irrevocable the steps forward into the new age. But it must be done his way: through the men of the Commune, not these ineffectual talkers in the Convention. He had no more patience with them. Whatever had been planned, by Victor Bernave or whoever else it was, it would happen between the prison of the Temple and the steps of the guillotine.

So that was why Bernave had told him of the royalists' plan in the Temple! It made exquisite sense! It could not succeed. He did it to protect his own plan!

He turned and pushed his way through the crowds back to the corridor. He must hurry. The pain of his sores was crucifying, but there was no time to give in to it. He had borne everything in the past: hunger, cold, illness, persecution. Only a little longer and the fruits of it would be his. All the glory in the world.

He did not even see the men he passed who stepped back too hastily, making way for him, faces tight with fear, hands to their noses.

14

Célie woke early. Last night after leaving Briard she had gone back to tell Georges. She had found him in the alley outside the house where he had lived, standing shivering in the dense shadow of the wall.

The National Guard were moving too close and it was time for him to go. He had waited only to tell her. Even as they'd stood under the eaves they had heard the sound of heavy feet and caught the red reflection of torch glare against a window above them.

He had stayed almost too long.

'Run!' she'd hissed in agony of fear for him. 'I'll stop them a moment. They don't want me.'

He had hesitated.

'Run!' She had put up her hands to push him physically.

He'd caught her arms, holding her close to him. She could remember with a piercing sweetness the smell of his skin and hair, the touch of his lips on hers. Then he was gone, and the next minute the torches, burning red and yellow, and half a dozen Guards had come into the alley, mist swirling around them.

Célie had stepped forward, head high, eyes and voice steady. She must have a good lie ready.

'What are you doing out at this time,

Citizeness?' the leader demanded suspiciously. 'You should be at home in your own bed!'

'I know I should, Citizen,' she'd said demurely. Then she'd looked up at him with a smile. 'But there is someone else's which is warmer, and much more fun.'

The man had wanted to disapprove, but in spite of himself he'd had to smile back at her.

One of the others had laughed.

'Go on home, you baggage!' the leader had said smartly, waving his arm. 'It's dangerous to be out here. There are wanted men around, enemies of the revolution.'

She had wanted to answer him, but it was wiser not to. You could never be entirely certain of anybody's real loyalties.

'I will,' she'd promised. 'Good night, Citizens.'

She did not know how far Georges had gone, or even for certain that he had escaped. She had slept only from exhaustion, and then it was broken fitfully with dreams of fear in which she was pressed in on all sides, watching helplessly as someone was executed. At first she was sure it was the King, then when she looked again she saw with heart-stopping horror that it was Georges.

Then it was time to get up. January 21 at last. It had come. No more waiting, no chance to change anything. She must be there with the others to crowd the carriage, to shout and press forward, making the exchange.

This was the day she did not ask anyone's permission to leave the house. She simply went out, and walked alone in the thick, silent fog, down to the river, across the Pont St-Michel, past the Palais de Justice, and over the river again. She turned east until she came to the Hôtel de Ville, then up the long sweep of the Rue de Temple towards the prison at the end, where they had kept the King and his family. It towered in the distance, its four sharp pinnacles outlined against a grey sky.

Célie put her head down and walked into the slight wind. There was ice on the edge of it. It seemed right with the terror and anticipation that knotted her stomach.

The moment had come. It was too late for any further planning or changes of decision now. It was all to play for: win or lose. In an hour or so it would be over. The King would either be on his way out of the city, or they would all be on the steps of the guillotine, a moment from whatever lay in eternity: oblivion — or God.

The streets were not full. Maybe most people would be along the route the King would take in his last ride through his city, or in the Place de la Révolution beside the scaffold, finding their positions from which to witness the ultimate act.

She looked at the faces of the few there were, pinched with cold and hunger, but excited. There was a nervous energy in the air as if they were on the brink of something new and full of promise. Had they any real knowledge of what they were about to see? This would not be just one more execution: an ordinary, fat little man being sent from life to death in a matter of minutes. It would be the passing of an age, and everything good in it as well as all that was stupid and ugly and corrupt.

Had they any idea what would happen tomorrow, and in the days and weeks after? Did they know what war would be like, really like: the constant fear, night and day, and the hunger and the marching of enemy soldiers in the streets, the loss of those they loved, too often never learning what had happened to them, whether death had been easy or hard?

Célie was almost at the Temple now. It loomed over her, massive and dark in the drifting fog. There was an old man in front of her, standing bare-headed, his white hair plastered down. He squared his shoulders and stared at the gateway into the prison. His skin was whipped pink by the cold but his faded eyes did not waver. She did not need anyone to tell her he was a monarchist, and probably a Catholic; it was there in the quiet despair in his craggy features and the unbending pride. He had come alone to watch the end of the world which he had known destroyed piece by precious piece — all the old ideas he had lived by and loved — mocked, denied and at last torn apart. He probably still believed God had placed Louis XVI on the throne of France to rule it by divine appointment, and this was not only regicide but blasphemy as well.

She hoped he would not show it. That would be a public offence, and very probably end with him being jeered at, even arrested himself. Or perhaps he would not mind that, even count it a privilege to be accused of such loyalty?

She admired him for that — if it were true. It was stupid, of course. If he were noticed it would be another pointless death; but the ability to care for anything with such integrity was a purpose in itself.

The streets towards the Place de la Révolution were lined with National Guardsmen in their blue and white, with their tricolour cockades, but the scene was all peculiarly lifeless. All windows and shutters on the houses were closed, by order of the Commune, and the fog seemed to shroud everything.

Célie wondered if Menou were here, and what he felt: no doubt something more complex than simple jubilation at a republican victory, the ultimate triumph of the common man over all kings. Maybe it would be the last thing they could celebrate for a while. If she and Georges and Briard failed, then in a few weeks the Convention would have their hands full with war. This was the time of great promises, but soon, when they had the ultimate power, they would have to deliver all the peace and justice and prosperity they had been talking about all this time.

There were lots of armed citizens around as well, standing to attention holding pikes or muskets. Would they have to stay here? Or would they all be allowed to troop down to the guillotine, that most mercifully intended invention of Deputy Joseph Ignace Guillotin, who had sought to make death as quick and as painless as possible, to avoid for evermore the bungling and torture of the wheel or rope. Once beheading

420

had been available only to the aristocracy. Now it was freely available to any — and everybody.

There was a movement in front of her, a rustle of sudden attention. The gates of the Temple prison had swung open. A man appeared, ashen-faced, paunchy, barely of average height. He walked slowly towards the large, green carriage which was waiting on the cobbles. God in heaven — he looked like Briard! Célie's stomach clenched at the sight of him. She almost expected to see Briard's blue eyes, but she was too far away.

In front of her the old man's breath caught in his throat with a sob.

Célie stared ahead. She had never seen the King before. He walked slowly, as if he needed all his concentration simply to place one foot in front of the other without stumbling.

Twice he turned and looked back at the tower of the prison, and his grief was unmistakable in every line of his body.

'That woman and her children are up there,' someone said behind Célie. 'But we'll have them too.' He hawked and spat his contempt.

A sudden, unaccountable rage boiled up inside Célie. She had no love for the King. He had no more right to life or happiness than anyone else, and he had certainly behaved like a fool. He had largely brought this upon himself. But at this moment, beaten finally, he was merely a fat, pale little man taking leave of his family for the last time on earth. All she could feel for him was pity, and the passionate need within herself for some knowledge of dignity.

She turned and glared at the man who had spoken, but he was not looking at her, and she could think of nothing to say which would reach any humanity in him.

The air was full of swirling moisture, and bitterly cold. Célie's whole body was shivering and her feet were numb. It would not be long now till she would have to force her way right up to the carriage, even perhaps be the one to yank the door open. She must watch all the time for Georges, and Briard.

The King climbed into the green carriage, accompanied by his 'citizen minister of religion', as priests were known these days. Célie had heard that this one was an Irishman called Henry Essex Edgeworth.

Two gendarmes got in opposite and closed the doors with a thud. The carriage began to move forward, preceded by a number of drummers who seemed determined to make so much noise that even if there had been anyone brave enough to shout 'Long live the King!', it would have been drowned out.

The old man with the white hair started to walk, keeping pace with his monarch, pushing through the crowd.

Célie followed after him, jostled and elbowed as others tried to press in the same direction. The cobbles were wet and slippery. There was more noise now: marching feet, horses' hoofs, drums, the occasional shouting and baying of the crowd.

More than once Célie was close enough to look into the carriage window and see the King and the priest passing a small breviary back and forth, each reciting something from it in turn. She knew the old man saw it too, because she was aware of him making the sign of the cross, almost invisibly, so no one in the crowd would identify his act. A sudden thought came to her of Bernave and his volume of Thomas à Kempis. Had he clung to that in his worst moments?

She wondered if Marat was somewhere in the throng. Had he come to witness the culminating moment of his power? Had he the faintest idea what it would bring in its wake? Did he imagine an age of peace to follow this, a time of prosperity and justice built on this terrible act of public humiliation and revenge, not for anything Louis himself had done, but for the whole rotten system which had finally collapsed upon itself? Surely this fat, solemn, little man reciting his prayers was as much a victim as anyone?

And what about Robespierre? Was his lust for blood part of the 'purity of the people' he longed for so much? Was he also here to see it? Rumour had it he never came to executions. He found the physical reality of blood and terror and bodies repulsive. What kind of man has the will to command death, but not the courage to see it?

The carriage was moving at a steady, even pace. Where was Georges? It must be soon! Every second ate up more of the time they had left.

Célie did not know by sight any of the others who were going to crowd the carriage. She had searched the faces around her but she had not seen Briard. Fear prickled over her skin. Had something gone wrong? Had Bernave betrayed them after all, and they were all arrested, apart from her?

She swung around wildly. Where was everyone? Why were they not acting, now, quickly, before it was too late and they were in the Place de la Révolution?

She was carried along by the crowd, bumped and buffeted. She could not have stopped even if she had wanted to. There was a force here driving people, like something in the air. She was helpless. They were pushing, shouting, men and women, their faces distorted with anger, fists raised. She was being dragged towards the middle of the street and the carriage.

Someone took her by the arm, impelling her forward. She tried to free herself, yanking away with all her strength.

'Forward!' The word came clear and sharp — Georges' voice!

With wild, blazing relief, an upsurging of joy that he was alive and here, she pressed forward. They were only yards from the carriage. Someone reached out and grasped the lead horse's rein, slowing them up. The shouting grew louder. She saw Briard's white head in front of her.

A hand lunged forward and caught hold of the carriage door.

'Death to the king!' Someone yelled, and the cry was taken up.

On the far side the door was open; people were pulling the two gendarmes out.

The door in front of Célie flew open. There was a glimpse of terrified faces inside. The priest cried out in desperation.

'In the name of God, can you not wait till we reach the scaffold?'

The King seemed frozen. She was close enough to see his pale, almost bloodless skin.

The far door slammed to.

Briard, whose plain dark clothes were like the King's, but covered now with a rough brown tunic, mounted the carriage steps and reached inside. He took the King by the arm.

Behind Célie the mob was waving pikes and staves, threatening the Guards who were shouting at them to move on.

Briard leaned forward and said something to the King. The priest turned one way then the other, his face masked with terror.

There was shouting and turmoil all around. The carriage lurched forward a step, then came to a halt again. Further up the street someone fired a shot and one of the horses squealed and reared up.

Inside the coach Briard was struggling to take off his outer jerkin. He spoke again to the King.

Hurry! Hurry! Célie was in an agony of impatience.

The moment seemed frozen.

Then the King shook his head.

Célie was knocked sideways and lost her balance, falling against a fat woman and sending them both stumbling.

The carriage door was gaping wide, then slammed shut. Someone slithered down the step

— a small, stocky man with white hair and a pallid face.

Célie regained her balance and stood upright, swinging around desperately. The carriage had not moved. Georges was a couple of yards away. He had lost his hat and his black head was instantly recognisable.

Then she saw another face that sent her heart into her throat: a face with slack, gaping mouth and black eyes staring into hers. The greasy, red bandanna around only half his straggling hair. He smiled, and raised his hand in signal.

The edges of the crowd began to press inward, violently, purposefully. There was shouting further ahead. A volley of shots rang out. The carriage jolted another step forward, and again stopped.

Marat yelled something which was lost in the uproar.

The man with the white hair was being half-supported, as if he were too weak to stand alone. He was surrounded by men and women in browns and greys, ordinary people, workmen and artisans, and they closed in and then tried to move away, but the men on the edge, armed with pistols, were crushing inwards.

Célie hurled herself forward at the carriage door. 'We'll get you out!' she screamed, willing Marat to hear her over the din. 'We'll get you out!' She grasped at the carriage door and yanked it. A pain shot through her wrist as claw-sharp fingers dug into it, holding her almost helpless.

She turned to look up, and saw the leering

426

face of Marat a foot away.

Her throat closed so tight her voice was strangled. She could smell the sour stench of him, even out here in the street in the fog-laden air, with the wood and leather odours of the carriage and the sweat of frightened horses.

The moment hung in eternity.

Then she felt a weight behind her, dragging, and a voice in her ears.

'Come back! You can't do anything. Citizen Marat's right . . . leave the King to the guillotine. The people have a right!' A woman's voice, insistent, hands pulling at her strongly. Madame Lacoste!

Marat looked from Célie to Madame.

Where was the King . . . or Briard? Above everything, where was Georges?

Marat's iron grip eased.

'Come on!' Madame urged. 'It is the law of the people. Let it be!' She looked up at Marat. 'Thank you, Citizen, for stopping her from doing something stupid. The King's death belongs to all of us.'

Marat let go. 'Of course it does,' he agreed. He turned to Célie. 'Go and watch it with everyone else, Citizeness.'

Célie fell back.

The crowd ahead parted and the green carriage went on down towards the Place de la Révolution and the guillotine. Who was in it? Briard or the King? If they had succeeded it would be Briard. They needed it to be Briard. Otherwise the country would be at war within months, perhaps weeks.

But she found tears stinging her eyes and spilling down into the damp on her cheeks. She wished it were the King, and Briard safe.

Why was Marat there? Bernave had betrayed them after all! He had always intended that they should be caught, but in the act, not before. Coldness filled her. Tears stung her eyes.

She turned to Madame. The crowds were surging past, leaving them.

'Come,' Madame said firmly. 'There's nothing more you can do here.'

Célie stared at her. How had she known? Surely not by chance! It couldn't be. How long? All the time? She wanted to laugh . . . and cry.

'Come!' Madame repeated. 'We mustn't seem to be different. They are going to create history. It is the end of the old world.' Her voice dropped. 'You can't save it.'

Where was Georges? Had he got away? Had Célie delayed Marat's attention just long enough?

She was beginning to walk after the crowds and the green carriage, Madame beside her.

She could not help the tears running down her face. Why did it matter that Bernave had betrayed them? She should have stopped hoping anything about him ages ago, when she heard about the girl he had raped. What good could be in the heart of anyone who could do that?

They were being left behind by the crowd. The green carriage was getting further away. Madame was urging Célie along, half dragging her over the slippery cobbles. In spite of herself

Célie hurried, her feet hurting and her hands numb.

They finally arrived in front of the Palace of the Tuileries and Célie saw the stark machine of execution, its two great prongs high above the wooden platform, the triangular blade suspended between them.

It was half-past nine. There were thousands of people here, as if everyone in Paris had come.

The swirl of the crowd had carried them almost to the front.

Suddenly there was a hush. The carriage stopped a few yards from the scaffold, the horses stepping nervously and shifting their weight, stamping. One of them threw its head high, rolling its eyes as it caught the smell of blood and fear in the air.

The carriage door opened and a man climbed down, his legs steady, his face forward. It was not Briard. Célie knew it the moment she saw him move. This was the King. He had been offered freedom, even if only to run, but at the cost of another man's life. And he must have declined it, whether from nobility, or only weariness, or the lack of belief that it could work, they would never know.

Sanson and two assistants approached him, their feet unheard on the sandy gravel. They attempted to begin removing his clothes, but he shook them off with a gesture, and undid the buttons of his coat himself. Louis unfastened his collar and opened his shirt, fixing it so that his neck was exposed. He had barely finished when they pinioned his arms.

He drew his hands back. 'What are you doing?' he exclaimed, his voice clear and close in the damp air.

'Binding your hands,' one of them answered.

'Binding me?' The King turned to his priest, indignation in his voice.

Edgeworth shook his head. 'Sire,' he said gently, 'I see in this last outrage only one more resemblance between Your Majesty and our Saviour who is about to be your recompense.'

Célie glanced at Madame Lacoste and saw the pity in her eyes, and the knowledge of the end of things good and bad which could never be recovered.

The King's arms were tied behind his back, after which Sanson cut his hair, leaving his neck bare and pale.

There was a murmur from the throng. Someone yelled.

The King went forward, and climbed the steps of the scaffold, awkwardly, leaning on the priest for balance, but when he was up he walked across it with a steady step.

There was a vast, whispering, breathing silence, every face turned towards him.

He spoke in a loud voice, very clearly.

'I die innocent of all the crimes of which I have been charged. I pardon those who have brought about my death and I pray that the blood you are about to shed may never be required of France.'

Whatever he would have said next was drowned as an officer on horseback shouted a command, and fifteen drummers immediately

430

resumed a frantic beating.

Sanson and one of his assistants guided the King to the bascule of the guillotine where so many others had been bound and lowered before, and obediently Louis XVI of France laid his neck in the lunette.

Sanson pulled the rope. The blade hissed down between the posts. It slammed into the King's neck, and stopped, the flesh too thick for it to do its work in one blow. It was unbelievably hideous. The King screamed.

Célie was drowned with horror.

The executioner's assistants rushed forward and threw their combined weight on the blade, forcing it downwards.

Célie gagged and looked away.

The man to the other side of her wore the rust-coloured leather jerkin of an artisan, and his face was seamed with lines, but there were tears on his cheeks and his eyes were blind. His back was ramrod-stiff and his chin high.

For a moment Célie felt a surge of grief, a pride, a wild emotion something like victory that the King had met his death with a courage no one could take from him, and an overwhelming relief that it was over and there was no more pain for him. Shorn of his crown and his power to do good or ill any more, parted from his family, even from his clothes and his hair, he was simply a human being whose neck was too fat for the mercy Dr Guillotin had intended. Her pity for him twisted inside like a knife.

Then the silence erupted into noise. All

around the square the cry went up, echoing and re-echoing 'Long live the Republic! Long live the Nation!' Hats were tossed in the air. The cavalry waved their helmets on the points of their sabres, and people began to shove and push forward to dip handkerchiefs, pieces of paper and their hands into the blood that spilled on to the scaffold.

In front of Célie a large man in a brown coat put his blood-wet finger to his lips. He turned to his friend. 'It is well salted!' he said in a cheerful voice. They both laughed.

Célie and Madame had seen all that was history. The rest was barbarism. They together turned and pushed through the crowds, trying to make their way towards the river.

Célie's legs ached and her feet were sore. The fog was still thick, clinging and wet. She had enough money for two cups of coffee, if they could find someone selling any. Actually they passed the first coffee seller without either of them noticing her. Physical discomfort was so small a part of the confusion and misery which descended over her. They had risked their lives to prevent the future that would now come, and they had failed.

There had been no sense of a great new birth in the King's execution, nothing ennobling, no sense of shackles falling and a people glorying in a new freedom. The only heroic thing at all had been the King's own courage, the great dignity with which he had faced a baying mob. Reduced to a solitary little man, paunchy, pale-faced, standing in the mist with shorn hair, he had still managed to embody what was best in humanity. Those who had taken his place were less in spirit. They had destroyed false gods, and now seemed to have left no gods at all.

15

The wind off the river was raw but Célie was glad of every step that took her and Madame Lacoste closer to the Boulevard St-Germain, and found herself increasing her pace. Behind them she could hear shouting, howls of jubilation as the news spread. The King was dead. Long live the Republic! Long live freedom and brotherhood!

What was freedom worth without safety from injustice, violence and hunger? Freedom to do what? The last restraint had been taken away. People could do anything that entered their imaginations. There was no King to govern the country, no aristocracy. The laws changed every day. And above all there was no God to reward those whom the world neglected, nor to punish those who were so powerful or so secret they escaped society. In their ignorance they had pitched all France into an unknown future.

The Boulevard St-Germain was all but empty as Célie and Madame Lacoste turned into it. For once there were no National Guards hanging around and they were able to enter the courtyard without any explanations.

Madame led the way into the kitchen. There was no one else there. Whether they too had gone to watch the execution or not Célie did not know, and Madame did not say.

Madame closed the back door and went over to the stove, her wet boots squelching very slightly on the stone. She put another piece of wood on and fanned the embers, then poured water from the ewer into the pot and set it to boil.

Suddenly Célie found her throat thick with tears again and she had to blink to stop them from spilling over. 'I never saw the King before today,' she said, 'except in pictures. He was . . . so small . . . so terribly ordinary.' She remembered it with fierce, painful clarity. 'But he went up the steps with little help, even though they tied his hands and he couldn't keep his balance. He didn't shake or stumble.'

'I know,' Madame said softly. 'He was a fool, but no one ever said he was a coward. He didn't know how to rule . . . ' There was a catch in her voice also, 'but he knew how to die — better than they knew how to kill him.'

Célie looked away. 'We've done something to ourselves, something petty and vicious, and it frightens me.'

'It should,' Madame agreed. 'Go and take your wet clothes off or you'll catch your death.'

Célie hesitated. She may not have another opportunity to speak alone with Madame. How much did she understand?

'Thank you,' she said awkwardly. All the way home they had not spoken. Célie's mind had raced with desperate fears over Georges. Marat had gone after him, and after Briard. She had no way of knowing if he had caught them, or what he would do if he had. They had done nothing illegal, but did that matter? Did it even make any difference?

Madame shrugged, still with her back to Célie. It was both an acknowledgement and a dismissal of the subject.

Should Célie ask why Madame had been there? She wanted to, and was afraid.

'Go and take off your wet clothes,' Madame repeated.

Reluctantly Célie turned to obey. She was cold and tired now it was all over. It was strange to have it in the past. Now there was a kind of emptiness with nothing to work for, nor to fear, any more. The plan had filled her life. Everything else had revolved around that. Until it was accomplished nothing else mattered. Now it was over, and had failed, she found there was nothing else anyway.

She was standing in her room in her petticoat, looking for a dry blouse and shawl, when there was a knock on the door.

She waited a moment. 'Yes?'

Amandine came in and closed it behind her. Her face was white, her eyes hollow.

'Is Georges all right?' she asked hoarsely.

'I don't know,' Célie answered. 'The King is dead. He wouldn't come. Marat was there.'

Amandine gave the shadow of a smile, as if she had expected him to be.

'No, I don't mean in the crowd,' Célie corrected her. 'I mean right at the carriage. He actually touched me!' She did not explain her attempt to distract him long enough for Georges and Briard to escape. 'Then he went after

Georges, but he was only a moment or two behind him. The crowd closed in, trying to press forward and see what was happening. He had to fight his way.'

'And Georges?'

'I don't know,' Célie said again.

Amandine looked down. 'I'm sorry,' she whispered. Her voice was thick with tears also.

Célie went to her quickly, putting her arms around her and holding her tightly. She shared the fear, the loss, the disillusion, and through it all the overwhelming tiredness.

Amandine wept at last, her body shaking with sobs that racked through her with total heartbreak.

Célie did not try to stop her. She stood in the cold, aware only of Amandine's pain and her own fear that Georges too could be dead! And even if he were still alive, she might never see him again.

Then finally she pulled away and reached for her dry blouse and shawl.

Amandine straightened up and blew her nose. 'I'm sorry,' she apologised. 'I can't bear to think St Felix killed Bernave, but if he did, he must have had a reason, one that overwhelmed everything else, or he wouldn't have done it. He was a good man . . . really good!'

Célie was not going to argue, although she was less sure. Even if he had loved the girl in Vincennes, if she had been his sister, he could have waited until after the King's execution to take his revenge on Bernave. But there was no need to say so now. Instead she told Amandine

437

in a few sentences what Renoir had told her.

'Twelve years old!' Amandine was horrified, her face filled with grief. 'Who was it? His sister?'

'I don't know. I don't know if it had anything to do with St Felix at all! It's just a possibility. Renoir didn't know anything about the other person who had been asking.'

Amandine's lips tightened. 'It must be St Felix. If he killed Bernave it was either that, or because he knew he'd betrayed the plan. Either one could have been a reason, never mind both!'

Célie did not argue. None of it mattered now. She was shaking with cold.

Amandine looked at her. 'Come down and have some hot chocolate,' she said gently. 'I've got a little left. There's probably nobody in the kitchen now. I'll make it. Come on.' And she turned and opened the door.

Célie followed willingly. Anything hot would be good, chocolate best of all.

Amandine was right, the kitchen was empty, but Célie was only partway through drinking the chocolate when there was a knock on the back door. When Amandine went to answer it, Menou came in. His cheeks were pink with the cold, and also perhaps with the excitement of the day, and his hair was plastered to his head.

Célie's heart lurched. Could he be here about something to do with Georges? She and Amandine were the only people he would leave any message for!

'What is it?' she demanded, her voice strangled and high-pitched.

He frowned, looking slightly embarrassed, but

438

there was apology in his face rather than tragedy. But then why would he care about Georges?

She started to speak again but her voice would not come.

'I still don't understand,' Menou said awkwardly. He stood stiffly, looking at Amandine, then at Célie. The colour stayed in his cheeks. 'I'm sorry, but I am not satisfied about Citizen Bernave's death.'

Amandine's face was hard, anger blazing up in her eyes.

'What does it matter now?' she said furiously. 'You shot Citizen St Felix. You can't do anything more to him. He's dead. What do you need to prove?'

Menou looked profoundly unhappy, and Célie wondered for a wild moment if it were caused by the problem which troubled him, or by Amandine's pain. She remembered his fingers touching the lace on her linens when he had been searching for the knife.

'I need to prove that it was really St Felix who killed Bernave,' he replied. 'Even if only to myself.'

Amandine's eyes widened. Hope and fury fought within her.

But it was Célie who spoke. 'You mean you think maybe it wasn't?' She turned on him. 'But you shot him anyway!'

'I didn't shoot him,' Menou corrected her quietly. 'One of the patrol in the street shot him because he ran. If he had stopped they wouldn't have.' His face was dark with awareness of tragedy and misgiving. 'But I am wondering now if he may have run because he was afraid rather than because he was necessarily guilty. Perhaps he had no faith in our skill, or our justice, and thought we would blame him anyway.'

Neither Amandine nor Célie answered. Nothing they could say was free from the danger of implying they were less than wholehearted revolutionaries.

'I never found the knife,' Menou went on. 'I went up on to the roof. I took men with me and searched everywhere. And I asked all the neighbours, in case it was put in through someone else's window. If they'd found it they would have told me. No one would dare hide it, not when they knew it had been used to murder a friend of Marat's!'

No one argued with him.

'But I didn't look under the slate Monsieur Lacoste repaired,' Menou went on. 'I'm going to do that now. It has to be somewhere, and I'd swear no one carried it out of the house.' He looked at Amandine. 'Have you got something I can prise the slate off with? Monsieur Lacoste is still out, and his shed is locked. I don't want to break in, but I'd prefer to go up before he returns.'

Amandine looked through the kitchen drawer. 'I've got one of his old chisels,' she offered. 'It's broken, but it might do.' She held it out.

'Thank you.' Menou took it from her gently.

'Bring it back,' she said. 'I use it to lift the stove lid.'

'Of course.' He nodded.

'I'm coming with you,' Célie told him. 'You'll

need help anyway, even if it's only with the window. It sticks.'

He drew in his breath to argue, then changed his mind and allowed her to lead the way upstairs.

He held the attic window open while she climbed very carefully out on to the wet and slippery roof, clinging on with cold fingers. She crawled up precariously towards the ridge, her feet sliding beneath her weight. She had worked out where the slate should be corresponding to where the leak had been on the inside.

Menou came behind her. She realised that if she slipped and fell she would almost certainly carry him down with her too. Had he thought of that?

Foot by foot, she got as far as the ridge. The fog had lifted a little and it was beginning to rain again, turning to sleet. The sharp spire of the finial on the end of the dormer roof was like a black dagger against the grey sky. That was where the leak was, in the bedroom.

'Here!' she said aloud, searching for the repaired slate. 'Somewhere near here.'

Menou was beside her now, his face streaked with rain, his hair stuck to his head and across his brow.

'I see it,' he answered. 'That one, paler than the others. But I don't know how I can get it off without cracking it — and we haven't got another to replace it with.'

She was shaking with cold. 'It has to be somewhere!' she said stubbornly. 'Somebody murdered Bernave — and I'm not sure it was St

Felix either. Anyway, whoever did it, they still had to hide the knife somewhere! It was thick-bladed — almost square at the handle. I saw the wound.'

'Like a sword bayonet,' he agreed.

She half swivelled around. 'Yes!' She was holding the broken chisel in her hand.

'Or like that?' he said softly, looking at it.

She stared down, then up at him. 'Yes . . . only this one is broken! And you looked all through Monsieur Lacoste's tool box . . . and paints, and varnishes and everything else.'

He did not answer, consumed in thought.

It was growing colder by the second. Pellets of ice were rattling on the slates around them. Soon she would be too frozen to cling on. The wind was stronger and the clouds were scudding past the black point of the finial. It was a sheer drop to the alley below.

Then she understood.

'There!' she said between chattering teeth, inclining her head.

'What?'

'The finial!' she answered. 'It's different from the others! Take the paint off — and it's a chisel blade! Look at it! The knife was never under the slate — it was right there in plain view!'

Menou remained frozen only for a moment, then very carefully he inched forward towards the dormer. She held her breath, body shuddering, while he worked his way to within a yard of the finial, then back again to where she was.

She knew from his face before he spoke.

'You're right!' he said, his teeth chattering with cold. 'Now get down, before we both fall off!'

He climbed in the attic window and helped her through. He looked at her steadily.

She stared back. St Felix was dead: nothing could alter that, or make it hurt less. But surely Amandine had the right to know that he had been innocent? These thoughts passed wordlessly between them.

'For Amandine's sake?' she suggested. 'It's a terrible way to lose someone you care for so deeply. This way she would at least keep her dreams.'

Menou nodded. 'Dreams are precious. They last all life long, and there are times when they're all we have.'

★   ★   ★

Amandine was still in the kitchen. She turned from the stove as they came in.

Célie spoke before Menou could.

'Amandine, we found the proof it was not St Felix. He only ran because he knew they were after him, and he had no defence.'

Amandine raised her head and turned slowly to Menou, her eyes wide, red-rimmed. She looked from one to the other of them. When she spoke her voice was husky. 'What?'

'A chisel,' he answered. 'It had been put on the old finial where it had been broken. When it was painted it looked pretty much like the rest.'

Amandine looked from one to the other of them, emotion welling up inside her with such

443

power and confusion she could find no words big enough to express it.

The silence was broken by a tap on the back door. Menou walked over and opened it. A middle-aged man in brown clothes stood on the step, his white hair plastered to his head, his blue eyes mild.

Célie's heart leaped.

It was a moment before Menou recognised him.

'Citizen Lejeune? What can we do for you now?'

Briard looked beyond him to Célie. 'I just wanted to thank you for your kindness, and say that I spoke to the gentleman myself. He decided to remain in Paris after all. I believe he felt going now would cause trouble for too many other people.'

'That's . . . that's all right,' Célie stammered. 'Thank you for coming to tell me. And . . . ' How could she ask about Georges?

Briard smiled. 'Your kindness enabled me to find another client, in a rather insalubrious area of St-Antoine, but a nice enough gentleman. I thank you for giving me his acquaintance.'

St-Antoine! Now she knew where he was, and that he was alive. She found herself smiling idiotically. She wanted to throw her arms around Briard, but it would be ridiculous — and probably offensive to him.

'Thank you! I — I mean . . . you are welcome, Citizen.'

He was about to reply when Fernand came in through the other doorway. His clothes were dry

444

but his hair was wet and dripped down his forehead. Monsieur and Madame Lacoste were immediately behind him. Perhaps they had heard the voices in the kitchen, but more probably they were hoping for hot coffee or chocolate. Monsieur and Madame stared at Menou.

'What are you doing here?' Monsieur Lacoste demanded. 'It's all over. Go back to keeping order in the streets.'

Madame looked beyond him to Fernand, whose mouth was open as he gaped at Briard.

'I thought . . . ' he started, then whirled to Célie. He started to say something else, but bit off the words.

'You thought he had the misfortune to look like the late Citizen Capet,' Célie said for him, pushing the words between her teeth. 'So he does. But now that Citizen Capet is dead, it doesn't really matter, does it?' She met his eyes unflinchingly, and saw reflected in them that it was he, not Bernave, who had told Marat of the plan.

Perhaps he recognised that in her face, because he paled, and looked away.

Célie turned to Briard again. 'Thank you, Citizen Lejeune. We will not detain you any longer. Good day.'

He understood. He bowed very slightly. 'Good day, Citizeness.'

Madame glanced at Célie, but her eyes betrayed nothing.

'Well, why are you here?' Monsieur Lacoste said, turning back to Menou.

But it was Amandine who answered him, her

445

voice thick with uncontrolled fury. 'He wants justice, Citizen Lacoste! We all do.'

'Of course we do,' Lacoste sighed, frowning. 'Isn't the King dead and a new republic enough for you in one day?'

'No. I want justice for Citizen St Felix.' Her body was shaking. 'I want his name cleared of murdering Bernave. And I want you to answer for his death!'

This time everyone froze, staring at her with incomprehension.

Monsieur Lacoste's face was immobile. 'Me? I had nothing to do with St Felix's death.' He jerked his hand at Menou. 'This man shot him — I presume because he ran away.'

Amandine was breathing so deeply she seemed to gasp. 'He ran away because Menou thought he'd killed Bernave, and he couldn't prove his innocence! But you could have!'

Fernand turned to his father.

Marie-Jeanne stood in the doorway, drowned by the shouting.

Madame did not move her eyes from Amandine.

'What do you mean?' Fernand asked. He looked at Menou. 'Did you start all this?'

'Perhaps,' Menou agreed. 'You see I know what happened, and I know why. I just wanted to find the knife. I'd looked so many times, but it had to be here.'

Monsieur Lacoste was white-faced, but he did not back away.

'Are you accusing my father?' Fernand moved a step closer to him. 'That's ridiculous! Why would he harm Bernave?'

'Because he discovered Bernave was spying for the royalists, not for the Commune!' Amandine answered, swinging round on him. Her lips were dry, and two frantic spots of colour marked her cheeks. 'None of you could report him, or you'd all lose the house.'

Menou shook his head a little, his brows furrowed. His voice, when he spoke, was remarkably gentle. 'It was very clever, and quite deliberate. First Citizen Lacoste spread the rumour that you were hoarding food in this house, so the mob would riot and force their way in here.' He held up his hand to stop Fernand interrupting him. 'It all worked perfectly, and would have looked just like another incident of looting gone too far, but Bernave was braver than Citizen Lacoste foresaw, and the intruders backed away from him.'

Amandine was shaking, her hands clenched into fists by her sides.

Menou glanced at her once, then away again.

'You struck too soon,' he said to Monsieur Lacoste. 'Perhaps you were afraid someone would come back with torches. There were none of the rioters behind Bernave when you stabbed him. It did not take me long to see that, and that he couldn't have been shot by the soldiers in the street. But I thought it was a knife. I never imagined a chisel . . . until I found it tonight.'

There was total silence in the kitchen. The noise of the rain outside was clear and soft, deadening all other sounds.

'On the roof,' Menou said quietly, a certain

447

admiration in his voice. 'Not under the slate. I thought of that. That was clever, loosening a slate to give yourself an excuse to go up. It was nothing to do with the slate — it was the finial. Painted black — where everyone saw it — and yet no one.'

Fernand swallowed. 'Well, if Bernave was plotting against the Commune, he deserved to die! My father is a hero, not a criminal. You should be grateful, not coming here to persecute him.'

'I'm not persecuting him,' Menou answered. 'I have no intention of arresting him.' He lifted his hand slightly in a small gesture. 'You see I came alone. But Citizen Lacoste did not kill Bernave for betraying the Commune!' He looked very levelly at Monsieur Lacoste. 'You asked about Bernave, from many people. I don't know where you first caught a thread of the story, and it hardly matters now. But I heard about it. I wanted to learn who was enquiring, and why.'

Monsieur Lacoste glared at him.

'I went to Vincennes too,' Menou continued. 'I saw the records and read them. If I had been in your place I think I might have done the same things. But you should not have let St Felix perish for it.' His voice dropped. 'I hope I would not have done that.'

'Why?' Amandine shouted, her voice choking. 'Why did you kill Bernave? What could there ever have been that was worth letting St Felix be killed for?'

They all turned to stare at Monsieur Lacoste. He gazed at Amandine, his shoulders hunched, his head forward. When he answered her, his voice was hoarse with a passion of loathing so bitter it filled his face and his whole body trembled. 'He was evil!' He spat the words between his teeth. 'Irredeemably evil, and he deserved to die. I'm sorry I could only kill him once. If I could, I would have killed him a dozen times, a hundred, and relished watching him die. I would like to have seen his face when he saw me, and understood!'

'What are you talking about?' Marie-Jeanne asked desperately. 'You're talking rubbish!'

'I'm sorry,' Monsieur Lacoste said to her, and for a moment his face softened as if he really were. 'But you didn't know him as I did. You couldn't. I wish you would never have to — but blame Amandine for that and Menou, with his enquiries!'

'What?' Marie-Jeanne was still completely confused. 'What do you know that we don't? How could you?'

Lacoste shook his head, his eyes filled with pain. 'Before you were born, before Fernand was born, Bernave raped a twelve-year-old girl.' He stared at her ashen face. 'I'm sorry — but it's true. He served twelve years in prison for it, where they tortured him almost to death, but he could never undo the wrong for me.' His voice was choked thick with tears. 'Because that girl was my wife! And he made her with child — you, Fernand! Her family threw her out of their lives, out of their world, the whole society she was born to! I found her and married her when she was fifteen, alone and all but starving.' He looked forward, his lips snarling. 'And more than that, Marie-Jeanne — you are his daughter, and Fernand is his son! Think of that! He allowed you to marry — that's obscene, a crime against nature — and he stood by and let it happen rather than admit it to you!'

Marie-Jeanne waved her hands, as if she would push him away, and the whole, hideous truth with him. 'No! No — it isn't possible! How could you know?' She shook her head. 'You're wrong! You have to be!'

'I'm not wrong!' There was no doubt in his eyes, or his voice. The passion of hate burned uncontrollably in him. 'I grew suspicious of him with the royalists and the Commune, and always sending St Felix out, and why he used him so horribly, with all the worst and the dirtiest jobs, and St Felix accepted it. I found other people from Vincennes. They told me. There's no doubt — don't torture yourself seeking for it. He was a man evil to the heart and soul.' He slashed his arm violently through the air. 'Disown him and forget him!'

Marie-Jeanne was numbed and confused, cowering away from what she'd heard.

Fernand took a step towards her, then changed his mind. He too was shattered. With one fact his entire life had been stripped apart and broken. He seemed limp inside, as if his whole being were bruised. 'You did the right thing, Papa,' he said awkwardly. 'I would have done it myself, if I'd known.' He turned to his mother, regarding her with amazement and pity. He started to say something, but the idea died before it reached his tongue. What could he offer his mother who had borne him as the result of rape, and then been forced to live in the house of her attacker? The tears spilled down his cheeks. 'God! I wish I had killed him myself!' The words choked in his throat. 'It wouldn't have been one quick stab to the heart!'

Amandine put her hands over her face, then looked up slowly at Lacoste.

'I understand why you killed him,' she said slowly. 'I can't blame you for it. Nobody could. He was as evil as you say — monstrous! But I can't forgive you for letting St Felix be blamed in your place.'

Madame raised her head, her face like a mask, only her eyes blazing. When she spoke her voice held a lifetime's passion and pain.

'Except that you killed the wrong man, François. It was not Bernave who raped me.' There was paralysed silence in the room. 'It was dark,' she went on. 'I was terrified and I was hurt. My family would have nothing to do with me. The Church took me in, for a while. But I couldn't stay there — and help my baby. It was only later, when I met the man again, that I recognised him. By then Bernave had been tried and convicted. I went to the Mother Abbess, but she wouldn't listen to me. No one wanted to know — '

'He confessed!' Lacoste cut across her, shaking his head, his voice loud. 'You don't know what you're saying! You were only a child! You didn't know any more.'

She looked at him with anguish. 'I know he

confessed!' Now she spoke softly, the words torn out of her. 'They both loved the same woman — but she preferred the other man — the one who raped me! And Bernave loved her enough to take the blame for him, so he could go free — and marry her!'

'Oh, Mother of God!' Fernand breathed out in agony.

'That's not true!' Lacoste cried hoarsely, but even as he said it he knew from her face that it was. He saw the horror in her, the anguish beyond his power to understand or to touch. 'Then who?' he shouted. 'Who was it? Who did that to you?'

They all stared at her.

Célie felt cold, and sick inside. From Madame Lacoste's eyes she knew the answer was terrible — beyond bearing.

'Jacques St Felix,' Madame replied with a rage of loathing so intense it seemed to scorch the air.

Lacoste was speechless.

Amandine tried to cry out, and it died inside her.

It was Célie who splintered the silence. 'Then why did St Felix come here, of all places, to Bernave's house?' she asked softly. 'And why in God's name did Bernave let him in? St Felix must have known that of all men on earth, Bernave could never forgive him!'

'You are wrong.' Madame met her eyes unblinkingly, her voice a whisper. 'That is exactly why he came here. Laura was dead, and he realised then, when it was too late, what his sin had done to him. He longed to be with her in some kind of heaven, but he had mortgaged his soul. He wanted to earn some shred of forgiveness. He was desperate.'

'And Bernave . . . ?' Célie said huskily.

All the fury dissolved from Madame's face and it became suffused with a strange, passionate radiance. 'Bernave forgave him,' she answered so softly they barely heard her. 'He allowed St Felix to work out his redemption by doing all the worst jobs, the most difficult, the most sordid or dangerous. If it had killed him, St Felix would not have cared — in fact I think he half sought it — except that in the end his courage failed him, as it had in the past. When it came to the moment, he ran.' She looked at Amandine with a terrible pity. 'I'm sorry. He had intelligence and wit and great dreams, but he was not the man you believed. Victor Bernave was. He was the noblest man I ever knew.'

She turned slowly to Fernand. 'I wish he had been your father, but he was not, except in so far as it was his money that fed and dressed you when I was cast out by my own people, and then by the Church — before I met François. He gave me everything he had before he went to trial. The law saw fit to leave it that way. They thought it recompense; they never knew it was compassion.'

Fernand stared at her, the truth dawning on him. 'You loved him, didn't you?'

To have denied it would have been pointless. The answer shone in her face, transfiguring it so the years fell away and they saw the woman she

453

had been long ago: beautiful, passionate and alone.

Célie turned to Monsieur Lacoste.

He tried to speak but the torrent of emotion inside him was too great and too terrible for words to convey it. A darkness had engulfed him, a wound which devoured all of him.

Amandine was also faced with a disillusion so fierce it destroyed everything else she could think or say. She stood perfectly still, but she seemed to sway a little, as if only her body were truly present, and the will to be, to survive, had left her.

Menou looked at her with a naked and fearful gentleness, but he knew enough not to speak.

Monsieur Lacoste stumbled towards the door and went out, and a minute later they heard the outer door slam and the echo of his footsteps across the courtyard.

'He'll be back,' Marie-Jeanne said hesitantly.

Madame Lacoste raised her head. 'No, he won't,' she answered. 'Not yet, perhaps not ever.'

Fernand stood helplessly, turning from Amandine to his mother, then to Célie. 'What can we do?' he begged.

'Nothing,' Madame answered him, rising to her feet slowly, as if lifting a mighty weight. She went to Amandine and very gently put her arms round her. 'I have lost the man I loved — to death; and the man I married to an abyss of guilt he will probably never climb out of. You have lost the man you loved to reality. He never existed. I'm truly sorry.' She touched Amandine's dark hair with her hand, in an intensely compassionate gesture, as she would have touched a wounded child.

Then she looked beyond Amandine to Célie.

'You have courage, enough to risk everything for your beliefs. I've watched you. You love Coigny. Don't deny it to yourself any longer, and lose the one thing you truly want. Don't live in the past, or hope too much of the future. You've lived up to the best in yourself at last. Hold that precious. Don't waste it.' She glanced at Menou, then back to Célie again. 'Leave while you can — safely. I don't know what François will do. He has nothing left to lose, and no God to hope in. I'll care for Amandine, I promise you.'

Célie hesitated.

'Go,' Madame Lacoste commanded. 'No one can say what tomorrow will bring. The King is dead and we are on the edge of chaos. I think we will fall headlong into it. There will be war, hunger, more violence. Cling to what you love. Never let go. Take some food, and the money Bernave left in his desk. He liked you. He would be glad for you to have it.'

Célie glanced at Marie-Jeanne.

Marie-Jeanne nodded, her eyes brimming with tears.

'Thank you,' Célie whispered.

In no time she had collected her things and the money. She went to Amandine, kissed her once on the cheek, and turned and walked away, then took a great gasp and ran, her feet flying.

★　★　★

They had failed to rescue the King, and now France would slide into civil war, probably even war with England and Spain as well. But all through the wet streets only one thought beat in Célie's mind. The guilt, the contempt for herself was gone. It had slipped away like a forgotten thing, leaving her a shining freedom to love, and to be loved.

She clattered up the steps of the house in the Faubourg St-Antoine and flung the door open. Georges was there, bending over the stove. He turned and stood up. Then he recognised her and his face filled with joy.

She dropped her bag on the floor and went straight into his arms, holding him as tightly as she could, clinging to him with all her strength.

His arms closed around her. He bent and kissed her cheek, then her eyes, then her mouth. She answered with absolute certainty, knowing exactly what Madame Lacoste had meant, and she would do it, with all the passion of her being. She had no idea where they were going or what would happen to them, but to be with him, with a clean heart, was everything that she needed. Happiness sang inside her, soaring upward above and beyond all else.

We do hope that you have enjoyed reading this large print book.

Did you know that all of our titles are available for purchase?

We publish a wide range of high quality large print books including:
Romances, Mysteries, Classics
General Fiction
Non Fiction and Westerns

Special interest titles available in large print are:
The Little Oxford Dictionary
Music Book
Song Book
Hymn Book
Service Book

Also available from us courtesy of Oxford University Press:
Young Readers' Dictionary
(large print edition)
Young Readers' Thesaurus
(large print edition)

For further information or a free brochure, please contact us at:
Ulverscroft Large Print Books Ltd.,
The Green, Bradgate Road, Anstey,
Leicester, LE7 7FU, England.
Tel: (00 44) 0116 236 4325
Fax: (00 44) 0116 234 0205

Beatrice and Miriam are sisters, loving but not entirely uncritical; each secretly deplores the other's aspirations. Their lives fall short of what they would have wished for themselves: love, intimacy, exclusivity, acknowledgement in the eyes of the world, even a measure of respect. Each discovers to her cost that love can be a self-seeking business and that lovers have their own exclusive desires. In search of reciprocity, the sisters are forced back into each other's company, and rediscover their original closeness.

THE LADY ON MY LEFT

Catherine Cookson

Alison Read, orphaned when she was two years old, had for some years lived and worked with Paul Aylmer, her appointed guardian. Paul, an experienced antique dealer whose business thrived in the south-coast town of Sealock, had come to rely on Alison, who had quickly learned the trade. But when he had asked her to value the contents of Beacon Ride, a chain of events was set off that led to the exposure of a secret he had for years managed to conceal. As a result, Alison's relationship with Paul came under threat and she knew that only by confronting the situation head-on would her ambitions be realised.

FLIGHT OF EAGLES

Jack Higgins

In 1997 a wealthy novelist, his wife and their pilot are forced to ditch in the English Channel. Saved by a lifeboat crew, they are returned to land at Cold Harbour. But it is the rediscovery of a fighter pilot's lucky mascot — unseen for half a century — that excites the greatest interest at the disused airbase. The mascot's owners, twin brothers Max and Harry Kelso, were separated as boys and found themselves fighting on opposite sides when the Second World War broke out. They were to meet again under amazing circumstances — and upon their actions hung the fate of the war itself . . .

ON BEULAH HEIGHT

Reginald Hill

They needed a new reservoir so they'd moved everyone out of Dendale that long hot summer fifteen years ago. They even dug up the dead and moved them too. But four inhabitants of the dale they couldn't move, for nobody knew where they were — three little girls, and the prime suspect in their disappearance, Benny Lightfoot. This was Andy Dalziel's worst case and now fifteen years on he looks set to re-live it. It's another long hot summer. A child goes missing, and as the Dendale reservoir waters shrink and the old village re-emerges, old fears and suspicions arise too . . .

ME AND MY SHADOWS

Lorna Luft

This is the autobiography of Lorna Luft, a
remarkable woman and singularly talented
performer. Often highly amusing, sometimes
harrowing — but always candid — it is the
inside story of one of the world's most
famous showbusiness families. Lorna Luft,
the daughter of Judy Garland and producer
Sid Luft, and half-sister of Liza Minnelli,
grew up in the hothouse of Hollywood screen
royalty. It is the story only she could tell, not
only as first-hand witness to events others
have only speculated about, but also of
coming to terms with her mother's, her own
and her family's patterns of addiction.

21